The
FURY
of
KINGS

The FURY of KINGS

R.S. MOULE

SECOND SKY

Published by Second Sky in 2023

An imprint of Storyfire Ltd.
Carmelite House
50 Victoria Embankment
London EC4Y 0DZ

www.secondskybooks.com

ISBN: 978-1-83790-054-1
eBook ISBN: 978-1-83790-053-4

For Eloise, who made me finish it.

PROLOGUE

The morning air was thick with cold, so sharp Gelick could almost taste the frost on his tongue. It was the one part of him not yet numb. He had been up to his knees in snow for three days now, and each morning had woken with his furs coated by a fresh white blanket. He doubted any Lutum had been this high up the Mountain in generations. Most of his tribe crossed into the White just twice in their lifetimes: once to come of age, and once to die. It was the paradox of his people. Young men would face the Mountain alone to prove themselves, never to return until all strength had fled from them.

Lutum tradition dictated that at the end of his fifteenth year, a boy would brave the White, bathe in the blood of the first animal he slew, and return wearing its hide, as a man, honed and hardened by the beast's spirit. Most came home with the skins of rabbits or goats draped across their shoulders. Those who returned wearing the pelt of a stag and dragging its skinned corpse were heralded; those who clutched the remains of a rodent were mocked. For six years Gelick had planned this journey, and resolved that when the time came, he would settle for no less than a stag or a bear, or a lion if the Norhai favoured him. His was the blood of kings, and if he one day hoped to lead the quarrelsome collection of tribes living under his father's rule he would need to be equal to his lineage. He had seen his uncle Carhag watching him, counting the years and wondering whether Gelick would grow to be a warrior or a weakling. Carhag had been the last man to return to Redfort dragging a stag, meat and bone and all, ten years ago. They had feasted on venison for a month.

Gelick pressed on, upwards, buffeted by the whistling winds that hurtled down the Mountain, stinging his eyes and obscuring the sun to a grey halo of shadow behind a sheet of twisting snow. Flakes melted against his skin, dripping down into his auburn beard and freezing again.

The winds came so strong and the snow so thick that together they blotted out the sky. Gelick had no idea how high he was – did altitude mean anything when there was no summit? – nor which side of the Mountain he was on. He had begun walking straight up the eastern slope, but after days levering himself through snow with the butt of his spear and barely able to see three feet in front of him, he could easily have ended up on the wrong side. The western mountainside was home to the Adrari, backward fisherfolk who married their sisters or bartered them for fish with the mermen of Eryispool, not that Gelick actually believed in mermen. The Adrari were the Lutums' sworn enemy, going back centuries, before the two tribes had been conquered and brought to heel under the Kingdom of Erland. Gelick did not think they lived this high, but if he encountered a group of Adrari his spear would offer little protection.

By evening, the storm had died, and the early rising moon painted the snow silver, mottled black and grey by the clouds as they glided across the sky. Despite the stillness, Gelick felt the cold's bite more than ever. When had he last eaten? The muscles in his legs trembled with exhaustion. Every breath of bitter air sent cutting tendrils of ice through his lungs. All across the white wastes, nothing stirred.

Distracted by tiredness, Gelick stumbled forward as his foot caught a hidden tree root. His spear stuck in the ground and spun from his hand, and he collapsed clumsily into the snow.

He rolled onto his back, taking deep breaths. The cold stung like a bed of nettles. *There are reasons nobody climbs this high*, he reflected bitterly.

The hopelessness of his position struck him like a thunderbolt. This frigid cold was as good as a death sentence. *I am going to die on this Mountain*. He had climbed too far, deluded by foolish visions of greatness, and they had come to nothing. Would it truly have been so shameful to walk into the White for a day and return with a rabbit skin slung over his shoulders? He lay in the snow with his eyes closed, letting the cold seep into his bones.

He did not know how long he lay there, but when he woke the moon was high and bright, and his limbs felt as heavy as iron. He opened his eyes and recoiled. Barely twenty yards up the slope stood a monstrous bear, sniffing the air and eyeing him hungrily.

Fear pushed Gelick to his feet, clutching his spear, staring wide-eyed. The muddy-brown bear appraised him hungrily, ready to spring.

The Mountain had given him deliverance. No Lutum in living memory had returned with a bearskin about their shoulders. Gelick gripped his spear in both hands and took a tentative step towards it.

The bear just stared at him, steam emanating from its nostrils, its haunches rippling with thick muscle. Gelick steadied, and took a few more slow steps. He was well within range to throw the spear. He would have put it straight through the bear's mouth, but if he missed he would be defenceless. Doubt gnawed at him. Even with a spear in its shoulder, the bear could strip the meat from his ribs and pick its teeth with his bones. He took another step.

The bear snorted, and suddenly leapt off its back feet and bounded towards him, its boulder-sized front paws churning the snow in a maelstrom of white horror.

Gelick's stiff limbs and frozen senses gave him no time to react. The bear cannoned into him, and they fell together down the Mountain, Gelick pinioned to the bear by its bulk and their collective momentum. With one hand he clung to his spear, his only hope of survival, while desperately clutching the bear's fur with the other.

It might have been seconds or hours, but finally they landed on a plateau, their impact cushioned by a snowdrift. To his surprise, Gelick had somehow rolled backwards away from the bear, still holding the spear. He could have been crushed. The bear was just yards away, panting and looking around confusedly.

Gelick would get no better chance than this. He did not hesitate. At a run, he drove his spear up into the bear's chest.

The beast roared with anger, rearing on its back legs so Gelick had to release the spear to avoid being lifted into the air. It swung a paw into his face, cleaving flesh from bone with its claws and lifting him off his feet, sending him flying over the edge of the plateau, and once more he was tumbling through snow, grasping for purchase and finding only air. His spine crashed heavily into a tree some thirty yards below, driving the breath from his body. He screamed as he felt something crack inside him.

He sat there, groaning with the pain in his back and ribs, trying to will the air back into his lungs. Every breath stabbed at his chest like a spear. At least the cold no longer bothered him. He laughed darkly, and his laughter became a scream as a broken rib scraped against his lung.

It was several minutes before he felt he could breathe. He

pressed a steadying hand to his torso and tried to come to his feet, grimacing.

Gelick had been fortunate to escape the bear with his life, but it would not live long with his spear buried in its chest. If he could follow the path his rolling body had made back up to the plateau, he could track the bear from there. He looked hopefully up the Mountain.

'Do not concern yourself with the bear. Look behind you.'

The voice echoed inside Gelick's head, a discordant melody that brought him stumbling to his feet. He whirled around, looking for its source. There was nothing there. Nothing except a white doe, calmly lapping at a small pool behind him.

'Yes, the doe. Kill it. Bathe in her blood.'

Gelick looked at the doe. He did not trust the voice. Perhaps the cold had driven him mad. He shivered. The doe shimmered silver under the moonlight against the black water. Gelick had never seen anything so beautiful.

'Quite a prize, and you'll never get that bear back to your home. Kill the doe, or you will die on this mountain.'

The voice rang against the insides of Gelick's skull, echoing what he had already known. He drew his knife, and edged towards it. The doe had stopped drinking from the pool, and was looking at him with eyes of sharpest blue. Old eyes. Human eyes. They beckoned him onward, and never moved from his face, not even as Gelick drew the blade across the doe's neck and let its warm red blood wash over him.

CHAPTER 1

The sky was a cloudless eggshell-blue, as idyllic as only a summer sky can be. All around the well-tended sandstone walls of Violet Hall, the purple flowers for which the castle was named shone in bright yellow sunlight. High above, a lone hawk glided in lazy spirals, while in the long grass crickets chirruped to one another.

It was Pherri's idea of a perfect day. She sat in the orchard, under the shade of an apple tree with her back against its trunk. Her tutor Da'ri was seated on the other side, and she was reading to him aloud, from the histories of the Imperium. '... *reformed the Imperium's ruling council as a Senate of two hundred and fifty, only half of whom were permitted to be magi. At the head of the Senate would stand the kzar...*'

'Will you never tire of this?' remarked Da'ri. His voice was warm, tinged with well-meaning mockery.

'Not as long as there is breath in my body,' said Pherri, indignant at the interruption.

Da'ri chuckled. 'I don't doubt it; you would be content to read all night if your mother would allow you a candle.'

That she was not permitted a candle was something of a

sore point with Pherri. She was eleven now, and perfectly capable of using one responsibly without setting her bedchamber on fire. Sadly her mother disagreed, and Pherri kept a guilty trove of them hidden under a floorboard. She had needed one the night prior, woken by a shadowy nightmare of beasts and blood and swirling snows, and had read long into the night until exhaustion claimed her.

'The Imperium sounds very different to Erland,' said Pherri. 'I could be a senator there, or even the kzar.' Women in Erland were not usually permitted to rule, unless on the explicit authority of their husband. Pherri's father was the second most powerful man in the kingdom, but her mother's power ended at the bounds of their lands, though she ruled Violet Hall like her own personal fiefdom.

'Or you could be a slave. Or one of the magi, who were driven out of Ulvatia just a few hundred years later.'

Pherri bit her lip. 'Sorry.' She had spoken without thinking. Da'ri was from Thrumb, a small country in the hills to Erland's west, where they lived high in the trees and worshipped nameless forest gods. She might be a girl, but her lofty position as the king's niece was a foolish thing to complain about while the king's son was invading Da'ri's home. Prince Jarhick was her cousin, she supposed, though she scarcely thought of him as such.

'Have you ever met a magus?' she asked, changing the subject.

Da'ri chuckled. 'Fewer than you, I expect. The king's advisor Theodric is a magus.'

'I've not met him.' Pherri was not allowed to leave Violet Hall without an escort. The furthest she had been from home was the town of Lordsferry, half a day's ride away, at the edge of her father's lands.

'Are you done reading?' asked Da'ri. 'We could move on to mathematics, or horticulture.'

Pherri thought for a moment. The practice yard was not far, and her second brother, Orsian, would be there. She could hear the harsh song of blunted swords, and the high-spirited shouts of men-at-arms. Orsian was fourteen now, old enough to be trusted with live steel. 'Could we walk the walls?' she asked hopefully. 'It seems too nice a day to waste it reading.' She had gone off the idea of the Imperium.

'Is the allure of your brother hitting people with sticks so great that you would rather do that than read? Your brother's too clever for all that really.'

'It's because he's clever that he's a good swordsman,' said Pherri defensively. Her eldest brother Errian had always ignored her, but she loved Orsian fiercely, and he was clever, in his own quiet way. Her mother said that when Pherri was a baby, he was the only one who could make her laugh and his name was the first word she had ever spoken. They had been close ever since. Tucking her book under her arm, she got to her feet, and Da'ri joined her.

She noted the dark looks Da'ri got from her father's guards as they walked the walls, admiring the rich farmland that stretched to the horizon. The dashing Prince Jarhick's invasion of Thrumb in response to their raiding of the land on Erland's western border was the talk of the kingdom, and she knew many regarded Da'ri's presence here as an affront. Da'ri took no trouble to disguise himself. He still wore his greying hair in six plaits, in the style of his countrymen, and unlike the men of Erland trimmed his beard until only a moustache remained. As her tutor he was under the protection of her father, and no man crossed Lord Andrick Barrelbreaker.

They came up to above the practice yard, and Pherri instantly recognised Orsian, clashing swords with a taller and likely older opponent. Pherri knew that she and Orsian did not look the least bit like siblings. He was dark and stocky, with dark hair like their father's in a wild mop of curls, while she was small and skinny as a rake, with fine hair the colour of straw.

His opponent's reach was longer, but Orsian moved like a dancer. The other man was defending bravely, but Orsian's every step and stroke seemed designed to unbalance him. Pherri watched, so transfixed that she almost stopped breathing. Finally, the taller man stumbled to the ground under the weight of Orsian's blows, and yielded. She wanted to clap, but knew that it would embarrass her brother.

To Pherri's surprise, their father was not there. As the king's *balhymeri*, his closest military advisor, his duties were many, but if he had reports to look at he would have brought them to the yard with him.

Naeem, her father's second-in-command, was nodding appreciatively. 'Not bad, Orsian.' Naeem had the unremarkable look of a soldier, save the two holes where his nose ought to have been, barely disguised by his wiry brown beard. 'You though.' He turned to the other combatant and barked a laugh. 'Are you sure you're my son? Always thought your mother looked at the baker funny.' This earnt strong laughs from the assembled warriors, while Orsian pulled his opponent to his feet. Naeem pointed to another man, who could have been the other's twin. 'You next, Derik. See if you can restore some family pride. I almost beat his father once, you know.'

Orsian looked up at the ramparts and caught Pherri's eye. 'Could I have a few minutes, Naeem?'

Naeem barked gruffly again. 'Barely says a word in the yard but demands a break to speak with his sister. Some warrior we've got on our hands, lads.' This earnt another loud laugh from the men, and Orsian blushed. 'Take your time, young lord. Sword practice isn't going anywhere.'

Pherri met Orsian halfway down the stairs, while Da'ri stayed on the wall. She expected he would prefer to keep out of the way of so many armed Erlanders. When they were younger,

Orsian might have greeted her by lifting and spinning her above his head, but her once playful brother had grown into a serious young man, at least in public. She did not mind; just as there were expectations on her, there were expectations upon Orsian. Playing with his little sister was not behaviour befitting an Erlish warrior. The tension in his jaw made him appear even more serious than usual. Something was troubling him, Pherri could tell.

'Well fought,' she said.

'Thank you.' Orsian wiped a sheen of sweat from his forehead. 'I've only been able to beat Burik for a few months, and his brother Derik still beats me more often than not.'

Pherri might have questioned the wisdom of practising with steel against your own people, but it seemed to please Orsian. 'Where is Father?'

Orsian frowned, indicating to Pherri it was their father's absence that troubled him. 'He left before first light. The beacon fire at Lordsferry went up in the night. He woke me but wouldn't let me go with him.'

Pherri had not been woken, nor had anyone even thought to mention it to her. She knew it was not a slight – she was only eleven, and a girl – but nonetheless, it bothered her. 'Could it be news of Errian?' Errian was away, warring against the quarrelsome Lutum tribe on the eastern side of Eryispek Mountain. He had been meant to go to Thrumb with Prince Jarhick, until the Lutums began causing trouble. It was odd, Pherri thought, that the Lutums had risen in rebellion at the same time as the Thrumb had begun raiding Erland. She would ask Da'ri about that later.

Orsian scowled, as he usually did when Errian was mentioned. Pherri's brothers were alike in many ways: they both lived for the sword, they were both proud, and they both hated one another. 'Wrong direction. It's probably something over the river. We might still be able to see the beacon from the walls if it's still burning.'

With Orsian, Pherri returned to the ramparts. Lordsferry was many miles away, but Violet Hall had been built on a high hill, giving it a wide view of the lands within its dominion, and a natural defensive position so it did not require an outer wall. The snowbound shadow of Eryispek dominated the horizon to the east, but instead they looked west.

There were three horsemen, galloping east towards them. They were too distant to make out their features, but there was no mistaking their muddy-green banner. 'That's Father,' said Pherri, pointing.

'He's riding hard.' Orsian frowned. 'He must have news from the west.'

Pherri bit her lip, her gaze following the riders. West Erland and East Erland had been one country for over a century and a half, but remained divided by the vast and sweeping Pale River.

'We should go to the yard to meet him,' said Orsian. 'Come on.'

They were not the only ones to have noticed. As they made their descent to the main yard, the great horn over the gate groaned like a dying giant, scattering the castle's nesting birds into the sky. Grooms rushed from the stable, and the gate creaked as four guards worked to open it.

Pherri felt a hand in her hair, and turned around to see her mother tucking loose strands of mousy hair back into Pherri's band. 'You could try taking more care,' she said reprovingly. 'You've got grass stains on your dress as well.'

Pherri tried her best to look contrite. She wanted to please her mother, but the distance between who Pherri was and who her mother seemed to think she ought to be was insurmountable. It was fine for her; she had been born to be the lady of a castle, to organise her household and dispense justice in her lord husband's name, with never a hair nor a thread out of place. All Pherri wanted was to be left alone with her books. Her mother looked radiant as ever, in a pale blue dress hemmed with gold thread and with her thick blonde hair flowing unbound past her shoulders. 'Sorry, Mother.'

Her mother smiled, and leant down to kiss the top of her head. 'I know you aren't, but you are getting better at lying.'

They heard the clattering beat of horseshoes, and her father flew through the gate, his great black stallion Valour foaming at the mouth with effort. Servants cringed back as the horse skidded to a stop, throwing up sparks as metal horseshoes shrieked against stone.

Pherri lived in awe of her father, though she usually had very little to do with him. He was often away from Violet Hall, and when he returned he would find a hundred matters to occupy himself. Sometimes in the evening he would tell her stories, but his attention was usually taken up with the king's business, and her brothers' violent squabbling.

His armour of leather and iron fit like he had been born in it. His face was stern, his black brows hooded over his dark eyes. He barely looked at the groom who came forward to take the reins from him, and unusually did not spare a moment to thank him. Behind him, his enormous wolfhound Numa dogged his steps.

'Orsian, Viratia, Naeem, follow me,' he growled, with not even a glance at Pherri. He strode purposefully in the direction of the keep, while the three he had summoned hurried after him.

Pherri ran after them on her skinny legs. Something important was happening, and she did not intend to be left out.

They went inside her parents' rooms, but when Pherri tried to follow she found her way barred. Her black-bearded father smiled down at her. 'And where do you think you're going?' He scooped her up with one arm as if she weighed no more than a doll.

'I want to hear the news from the west,' she told him. They had to let her. Orsian was not so much older than her, and Naeem was not even family.

Her father laughed heartily, a little too loudly she thought, as if to hide his unease. 'It's not news for the ears of little girls, I'm afraid.' At that moment, Da'ri rounded the corner. 'And here's your tutor. Back to your lessons, I think.' He kissed her on the forehead and handed her to Da'ri.

'Try to take better care of my daughter,' said her father to Da'ri, scowling. He looked as if he were about to say something else, then seemed to think better of it. He stepped into his chambers, and slammed the door behind him.

'That was odd,' said Da'ri, setting Pherri back on the ground with a wince. 'Your father's usually unfailingly courteous.'

'He's worried about something,' said Pherri. She quickly pressed her ear against the door, but the wood was thick oak, and all she could hear was her own heartbeat. She had to know what was going on. Orsian would tell her later, but what if their father swore him to secrecy? She thought quickly. There was a window high in that room, leading out onto the roof of a storage outhouse. She ran before Da'ri could stop her.

'Pherri!' Da'ri called after her, but Pherri was already gone, sprinting in the direction of the outhouse.

She raced outside, narrowly missing two servants bearing trays of food. There was a stack of barrels against the outhouse, and Pherri clambered up nimbly onto the roof. Da'ri would be able to follow her, but he would not give her away for fear of angering her father. She was pleased to see the window was ajar, and positioned herself against the wall to listen.

Inside, Orsian took a seat at the table next to Naeem. His parents' antechamber was furnished simply, with wall hangings sewn by his mother and hard wood furniture. The only sign of their wealth was the gilded sword with rubies embedded in the hilt that hung above their bedroom door. He could never recall seeing his father wield it; the hilt protruding from his scabbard was black leather, worn and faded. Orsian's own sword had also once been his father's. Lord Andrick Barrelbreaker did not believe in wasting good steel.

His father sat at the head of the table, waiting for the servants to set down their food and leave. Orsian was anxious to learn what news had drawn his father away before dawn and left him in such a foul temper. If it was to be war, he was ready. He had proven himself time and time again in the practice yard; nobody could doubt his skill at arms. If he fought well he might even be permitted to join the *Hymeriker*, the king's elite guard.

He knew he would need every ounce of his skill if he was to make a life for himself in the years to come. As the first son, his brother Errian would inherit all the family's land, from Violet Hall down to the meanest bog. Orsian's only hope was to find favour with King Hessian and his heir Prince Jarhick. He could not rely on Errian to treat him fairly once their parents were gone.

Orsian glanced at his father, and immediately felt foolish. Andrick Barrelbreaker could have decades left to live. Even his enemies would acknowledge him as the finest warrior in the kingdom. He looked as if he had been hewn from oak. His black beard was flecked with grey, but there was no doubting his strength, of will and of arm. He had put down a rebellion aged just sixteen, and when West Erland had risen again, sixteen years ago, he had quelled that too. No man in Erland commanded the respect his father did, not even the king. If ever there was a man who would live to see old age, it was him.

'Leave us,' ordered his father, once the servants had finally set down all the food and drink. Naeem immediately moved to pour the ale, and the servants fled.

His father did not mince his words. 'Prince Jarhick is dead.'

Orsian's mother gasped, and Naeem's jaw fell open with his drink halfway to his mouth.

Orsian was as shocked as them. Prince Jarhick was just eighteen, and a skilled warrior. He tried to keep his expression stony and impassive. His father would want to see him as a man, not an emotional child.

'How?' demanded Naeem.

'The prince accepted a peace envoy from the garrison at Thrumbalto. He expected their surrender, but an assassin in masquerade was among them. It seems our prince took a wound from a weapon coated with poison. He died ten days ago.'

The table fell into silence. Orsian eyed his father carefully. He had not known Jarhick well – he was close with Errian – but the prince had not seemed the sort to allow himself to be taken unaware at a peace negotiation.

But what did it mean for the succession? King Hessian had two daughters, but the crown of Erland could pass only by a male line. It was a law going back to the Meridival tribe, who had wandered the southern wastes before crowning themselves kings of Erland.

'May Eryi take him from the Earth and to Eryispek above the clouds,' mumbled Naeem, speaking the traditional words. The others echoed him, and they all drank.

'Is Princess Tarvana's boy the heir now?' asked Naeem, hopefully, though Orsian was sure he knew their laws as well as he himself did.

'No.' Andrick's voice was grave. 'The crown will pass to the king's cousin, Lord Rymond Prindian.'

Naeem exhaled through his teeth. 'No. We can't allow it.'

'That is the law.' Andrick gave Naeem a hard stare. 'Regardless of his family's past crimes, Lord Rymond is now the heir. We took oaths to serve the crown, Naeem, not to serve the king of our choice as a passing fancy.'

'And what will Hessian do?' asked Orsian's mother Viratia, speaking for the first time. That was just like his mother, to contemplate in silence and then speak straight to the heart of the matter. 'Will he marry again? A king must have an heir.'

Hessian's wife had died giving birth to Princess Helana, before Orsian was born. The thought of Helana made Orsian's heart beat a little faster. The king's second daughter was wild and beautiful, and though they had played together as children he now often found himself nervous and tongue-tied around her. He worried his thoughts might show on his face and hid momentarily behind his tankard, under the guise of taking a long draught of ale.

'He must,' said Andrick. 'He's grieved for sixteen years. Elyana would not have wanted him to die alone and allow Erland to fall to the Prindians. And Hessian knows his duty. He will wed. It shames me that I have never persuaded him to before.

'But we must also prepare for war. We are already fighting on two fronts, and who knows what this will do to Prindian's ambition? When his mother hears she will be pushing him to assert his claim at the point of a sword. They could make common cause with the Thrumb, or the Imperium.'

Naeem snorted. 'He can make common cause with whoever he damn well pleases. We'll kick him back across the Pale River, and the Imperium too if they decide to stir themselves.'

Orsian was not so sure. The Imperium was far across the mountains, but it was far wealthier and more populous than Erland. There were tales of how Erland had once defeated them, but Orsian barely believed those; they usually involved seven-foot-tall kings killing five thousand men single-handed.

'But the *Hymeriker* must be ready,' admitted Naeem. 'Do we ride for the capital?'

Andrick nodded. 'In the morning. Ready the men, and tell them of Jarhick's death. And if any of them demand we ride for

Thrumb you can tell them I forbid it. The Thrumb can wait. We ride at first light. You as well, Orsian.'

As Orsian left with Naeem, he found his heart swelling, beating like a marching drum. His father meant to take him to war! He felt ready, fighting back the butterflies that had settled in his stomach. This was what Orsian had trained for, and for a moment he even forgot that the prince was dead and he ought to be grieving.

'Dark news, boy,' said Naeem as they walked together towards the barracks, bringing Orsian back to the present. 'Always knew the Thrumb were savages, was one of them that took my nose.' He tapped twice at the scar where his nose had once been. 'I taught the prince to fight, and he was one of the best.' He spat on the ground. 'The Thrumb would never have got close to him in battle, the cowardly faithless bastards.'

Jarhick's death grieved Orsian – he would have been Orsian's king one day, and he felt a natural loyalty – but he could not forget that Jarhick and Errian had been inseparable. Errian was brash and vain; any man who counted him among his friends was diminished in Orsian's eyes. 'Do you think it will be war?' he asked. Naeem was easier to talk to than his father; a hard master to please in the practice yard, but quick to laugh outside of it, and an accomplished storyteller.

'Yes.' Naeem was direct, clearly in no mood for tales. 'West Erland will rise again, just as they did under Ranulf Prindian. Norhai strike me down if I'm wrong.'

Orsian had heard about Ranulf, Lord Rymond's elder brother. He had kidnapped and killed Queen Elyana's family to provoke Hessian to battle, and started a war to reclaim West Erland. After Andrick defeated him, the king had thrown him in an oubliette in the lowest dungeon of Piperskeep. It made Orsian shiver to think of it. It was said there were levels to the dungeons so deep and forgotten that only ghosts patrolled them.

'All I've heard of Rymond Prindian is that he is lazy and unambitious.'

Naeem snorted. 'Blood will tell. I know he's meant to be a lazy sod, but his mother isn't. Breta Prindian's never forgotten the Old Line, even for a day. She knew Ranulf was too stupid to rule, so she tricked him into an unwinnable rebellion so the lordship would pass to Rymond. And every day of these past sixteen years she'll have been filling his head with crap about his birthright and their kingdom that your father's fathers stole. It will be war if she gets her way, mark my words.'

Pherri had heard every word of their meeting. Da'ri had given her a severe telling-off afterwards, but he had been happy enough to listen once he had struggled up onto the storeroom roof. 'It means war,' he had told her grimly when Pherri asked what the news meant. 'Civil war for Erland, destruction for the Thrumb, and for me...' – he shook his head morosely – 'who knows? Violet Hall may no longer be safe for me, if it ever was.'

It was late, and Pherri was abed, but she could not sleep with worry about Da'ri. That he was a Thrumb had caused enough hostility already, and now the prince's death would make it worse tenfold. She hoped he had locked his doors tonight; by now the news would have spread to the soldiers and guards, and after an evening of drinking in the barracks their thoughts might turn to vengeance.

Perhaps her father would send Da'ri away, to keep him safe. But then who would teach her? She had already read every volume in their small library twice over. Piperskeep's library was said to contain over a thousand books, but her mother would never let her go there. And what of Orsian? Perhaps they could persuade their father to let him stay here, to protect

Pherri and their mother. She could not imagine him going to war, to kill other men, or be killed himself.

As she could not sleep, she read by lanternlight under her bedsheet. This lasted until there was a knock at the door, which shocked her almost into knocking it over.

'It's me,' came Orsian's muffled voice. Pherri set her lantern on her table and stood to unlatch the door.

'You've heard, then?' he asked as he sat down, noticing the book of the Erland nobility's ancestries on her table, with which Pherri had been tracing Rymond Prindian's ancestry to see why he was the heir. 'Of course you searched for answers in a book first.'

'Everyone knows now.' She would not tell Orsian she had spied on their meeting. 'I heard you're leaving.'

Orsian nodded sombrely. 'It could be war if the Prindians stir themselves. We'll have to fight.'

The thought of Orsian going to war made Pherri's chest tight. She leapt up and threw her arms around her brother, startling him. 'Please don't go.' Tears sprang to her eyes. Orsian was leaving, and Da'ri might have to go as well. She would be left here alone, with nobody to protect her from her mother's disappointment. 'Tell Father you should stay here and protect me and Mother.'

Orsian laughed and embraced her, but when he pulled away his face was grave. He seemed older now than he had only hours earlier. 'I need to do this, for Father. For all of us. This is what I was born for. Do you think we will be safe if Rymond Prindian takes the crown? Father is half a Sangreal; we would be seen as a threat.'

Pherri tried to quell her tears and bury the knot of fear in her gut. Orsian had never thought to question the rightness of war or his place in the Kingdom of Erland. His straightforwardness was one of the things she loved about him. 'Where will you go?'

'To Merivale first, to speak with the king. Father is going to try and persuade him to marry again. The difficult part may be finding him a bride. Every noble girl in Erland had their heart set on Prince Jarhick.'

Pherri thought for a moment. She went to her table, and turned the book she had been reading to a page towards the back. She scanned the text, flicking the pages back and forth.

'There,' she said, triumphantly pointing a finger to the page. 'Lady Ciera Istlewick, sixteen and betrothed to Lord Rymond Prindian. Her father is one of the richest lords in East Erland. The king should marry her.'

Orsian leant over the page. 'So ask Lord Istlewick to annul the betrothal? And have her marry the king instead?'

Pherri nodded. 'Take an ally from the Prindians and gain one for us. Lord Istlewick is the king's vassal; he would have to say yes.'

A smile spread across Orsian's face. 'Eryi's teeth, Pherri, that's brilliant!' He lifted and spun her around, making Pherri laugh giddily. 'I'll tell Father. You should be a lord with thinking like that.'

Pherri grinned. She was glad to help Orsian. And maybe if the king made an advantageous marriage, war would be averted. Then Orsian could come home and Da'ri could stay, and nobody would have to die.

'I need to go,' said Orsian, embracing his sister again. 'I came to say goodbye. We ride at dawn.'

Pherri hugged him back fiercely, and kissed his cheek, which was coarse with black fuzz that she did not recall being there before. 'Stay safe, Orsian. And come home, as soon as you can.'

CHAPTER 2

They left as the sun was rising, the twin banners of Sangreal and Barrelbreaker flickering in the summer wind, their shadows long and lazy in the dawnlight.

Andrick set a hard pace, too fast for any man to ride along-side and speak with him, with only his two wolfhounds for company, wiry ink-black beasts bounding along at Valour's tail. He needed to think, alone, and there were few better places to think than astride a horse, with only the steady beat of horse-shoes to trouble his concentration.

This was his forty-seventh summer, thirty years since his first war; more than half his life spent in service to Erland. Longer in truth; he had been Hessian's man now for over forty years, since his half-brother had found him playing on the floor of Piperskeep's great hall, an unwanted royal bastard born to a dead foreigner.

Forty years of loyalty, for the gift of a wolfhound pup and a toy wooden horse. Hessian said he had never made a better bargain, but Andrick felt much the same. A fine keep with fertile land, a loving, beautiful wife, and three children. None of it would have been possible without the king's favour. If not for Hessian, Andrick would likely have been long dead, smothered in his sleep by some servant of Hessian's mother, or banished from the keep and stabbed in a Merivale alley over a heel of bread.

He had said as much to Viratia, when she had urged him not to go, to wait for Hessian to send for him, to let him fight his own battles for once. 'I will never understand,' she had told him after he refused her. 'The man is beyond reason, Andrick. What more could you possibly owe him than what you have given him already a hundred times over?'

'Everything,' had been his simple reply. 'I swore an oath to him when I was a boy, and in time I came to love him as a brother. He is still that man, Viratia, and he will always have my loyalty.'

It made the death of Prince Jarhick all the harder to bear. Andrick had advised Hessian sixteen years ago to marry again, but the king would not hear of it. The loss of Elyana had diminished him. He had hidden himself away, content to let others run the kingdom while he stewed in paranoia and bitterness. It could last no longer.

The truth that Andrick would never speak was that Jarhick had been a fool. He had never learnt caution, and anybody who spoke against his whims was swiftly expelled from the coterie of young lords who surrounded him. But Andrick also blamed himself. He should have gone to Thrumb in the prince's stead, but Jarhick had been desperate for his first command, and Hessian had indulged him.

There was no time to dwell on that now though. They needed to act, and Andrick could not do it alone. He was a warrior, and that was all he had ever wanted to be. He needed Hessian's guile. For all his frailty, the king's wits were still sharp. Perhaps the death of his heir would shake him from his slumber. If not, they were lost.

The sound of advancing hooves broke his contemplation,

and he turned to see Orsian, riding hard and calling to him. Andrick slowed slightly to allow his son to catch up. He had hoped once that his sons might grow to fight for Jarhick, as he had fought for Hessian. Now Andrick wondered if he might still be warring alongside them in fifteen years' time, to secure the crown for some unborn boy king. Andrick would be in his sixties then, far past the age that most men hung up their swords.

Looking at Orsian, with his curly hair and dark features, was like seeing a ghost of the boy he had been, though he had been just as brash and foolish as Jarhick. That was not a charge anyone would ever level against Orsian. His second son was serious and studious, in everything. It would serve him well. Errian's temperament was more like Andrick's had once been, though they looked nothing alike: too proud, and too ready to take offence at any slight, but unflinching in both words and deeds. His sons would have complemented one another well if only they had the sense to get along.

'What is it, Orsian?'

'Have you given any thought to the king's bride?' he asked, panting slightly from spurring his horse to catch Andrick.

His son had got straight to the point, which Andrick appreciated. 'I confess I have not.'

'Lady Ciera Istlewick, of Cliffark. She's promised to Lord Prindian.'

Andrick recalled that betrothal being announced, years ago. The Prindian boy ought to have claimed her as his bride by now; it spoke to his idleness that he had not.

'Lord Istlewick rules in Cliffark,' said Orsian eagerly when Andrick did not reply. 'It's a thriving port; he's a wealthy man.'

'And you propose that we claim her for Hessian instead.' The girl was young, too young perhaps, but that was not uncommon. And Andrick knew Lord Istlewick: if he was half as timid as he had been in their younger days he would not refuse them.

'It's a good plan, but it isn't yours.' Andrick smiled. Orsian was clever, but too guileless to come to such an idea himself.

Orsian's face fell. 'It was Pherri's,' he admitted. 'She had this big book of Erland families.'

'My clever daughter.' Perhaps he should have included Pherri in their council the day before. It was the sort of idea Viratia might have had, though she would have been loath to suggest such a young bride for Hessian. Finding Pherri a husband one day would be difficult; many men did not want clever, curious wives. 'Thank you for bringing this to me.'

It was a three-day ride to Merivale, and though Andrick did not wish to delay, he allowed that they stop and make camp each night. There might come a time soon when he would require his men to ride through the night, and he needed them not to become weary of such a demand.

There was also a part of Andrick that did not wish to hurry, so that the news would reach Hessian days, and not hours, ahead of him. If Hessian gave an order in the midst of his grief, Andrick would be honour-bound to obey it, no matter his request. A day or two could make all the difference. The messengers would have ridden through the night, switching to fresh mounts at waypoints. They should have almost reached Merivale by now.

The second day was uncommonly warm, leaving both riders and horses thirsty and bad-tempered. The heat lingered into the evening, and they did not bother with a fire when they stopped for sleep. Nobody was particularly in the mood for drinking, nor telling stories, and Naeem's best efforts fell on deaf ears.

Andrick stayed awake long into the night, as the ground turned cold beneath him and the fire faded to embers. The night sky was cloudless, and a tapestry of twinkling stars spread across it to every horizon and beyond.

Between the Thrumb incursions and the Lutums' rebellion,

it had already felt as though Erland was coming apart at the seams. And now they might have to fight the Prindians too. They were the true threat, the one that had given every Sangreal king since the Accord sleepless nights.

Strange and unfortunate enough that we had to deal with two threats, half a country apart. Now a third. And the Norhai saved the worst till last.

If there were to be a war, unity would be key. Every lord swore fealty to Hessian, and each who kept his oath would be one less for the Prindians.

Andrick did not even have unity within his own house. He had sent Errian to fight, partly to exact vengeance for the Lutum attack on the town of Basseton and partly to separate him and Orsian. His sons had been at odds since they could first hold a sword. It had been easier for him and Hessian; they had been born more than a decade apart, and each had recognised what the other could offer them. Errian and Orsian were too close in age, too different, and both too fond of fighting.

It was a bridge he would have to mend. There was still time. Errian had been close with the prince; it would grieve him deeply when he learnt of his death. Perhaps if Orsian were with him, the two of them might find some accord.

It was the evening of the third day when the city of Merivale came into view, like some great dark blemish across land and sky. Piperskeep's high towers loomed over it, stretching upward like grasping fingers. The city sat upon a hill's gentle incline, with three gates around its stout walls, and a forest to the north. The buildings closest to the keep were forged in stone, but there were also some of timber, and the homes nearest the walls were simple structures of mud and straw. He had not caught it on the wind yet, but Andrick knew how much the city would smell in the heat of summer. All the city's waste ran down the hill into the moat, and the stench of it would be putrid.

'Orsian.' Andrick called back to his son, a few yards behind him.

Orsian trotted his horse forward. 'Yes, Father?'

Andrick pointed north-east, past Merivale, towards Eryis-pek. It was impossibly large. The sheer scale of it made Merivale look tiny by comparison. He did not himself believe the Mountain could be endless, but he would never scorn those who did. 'You'll ride towards the eastern slope of Eryispek, to your brother. I need word of the Lutums' rebellion.'

Orsian's jaw fell open. 'But—'

Andrick raised a hand to silence him. 'You will return to Piperskeep once you have spoken with Errian.' He had resolved to do this, in the hope that his sons could reconcile. Also, Hessian was not well at the best of times, and grief would diminish him further. It would be easier if Orsian were not too close to him; it might lessen his thirst for battle if he saw for whom they fought. 'You will tell him Jarhick is dead, and you will grieve together. You don't have to love your brother... by Eryi, you don't even have to like him, but you will respect one another and fight together, not against. Do I make myself clear?'

Orsian mulled it over before he answered, his mouth set in petulance. 'Yes.'

'Good. And you'll need someone to go with you, an old hand.'

'An old hand like our father, Lord?' called one of Naeem's sons, grinning. Burik, Andrick thought, but he struggled to tell him apart from Derik at the best of times. 'He's not the sharpest, but a face like that is a better defence than any shield.' The two twins roared with laughter.

Naeem laughed along with them, grotesquely stretching the hole where his nose had been. 'Aye, why not? It's been years since you let me out of your sight, Lord. Always thought my wife had you keeping an eye on me.'

Andrick gave a grunt of amusement. 'You'll do. But let Orsian do the talking; you'll only scare them.'

Orsian and Naeem split off, while Andrick led his escort towards Merivale. The blood-red flag over Piperskeep was at half-mast, and a soft shadow of crimson smoke hung over the city, billowing from the chimney of the Church of Eryi, where the priests burnt coloured candles to mark the passing of one of the Blood. Word of the prince's death must have reached them.

They entered by the quieter Ram's Gate rather than the King's Gate. Andrick did not have the patience for an honour guard up the Castle Road while thronging citizenry called out for him to go and fight the Thrumb. The war had been a fool's quest from the start, a response wholly disproportionate to a few Thrumb bandits troubling the bleakest reaches of West Erland, and if Hessian did try and send him there, he would tell him so. The true threat was within Erland.

Despite their unheralded arrival, when they reached the castle yard Theodric was waiting. The king's magus had an irritating habit of knowing things before they happened.

'He's waiting for you in his tower solar,' said Theodric as Andrick dismounted. Andrick nodded to him and walked straight past.

He strode to the top floor of the keep and began the long climb to the king's tower, his heavy boots echoing on the cold stone floor. As a child, he had avoided this part of the castle, for the guards then had hit him with the reverse of their spear if he was found wandering where he ought not to. His domain had been the great hall, and the kitchens, where his youth and desperation often won him a slice of pie from a sympathetic serving girl.

I wonder if anyone alive remembers how I lived then, apart from Hessian.

The two sentries at the top of the staircase were known to him. They raised their fists in salute as he rounded the top stair, and stepped aside to allow him entry to the solar. Andrick stopped to speak with them for a moment, to praise their skill and enquire after their families. They might be at war soon, and a warrior ought to know for whom he fought. He clapped them each on the shoulder in farewell and advanced into the solar.

King Hessian Sangreal turned from surveying Eryispek at an open window. He had never been a well man, but now he looked more corpse than king. His face was gaunt with grief, his sharp features marked by deep shadows, and his rheumy eyes bloodshot and hooded. He did cut an impressive figure though, with his uncommon height and long grey hair, garbed in a deep red sable gown edged with black trim.

'Tell me, Brother.' Hessian's voice was heavy with exhaustion. 'Does it please you to praise your men like a cheap whore looking for a tip?'

'It pleases me to please my men, my King. Men fight better for a commander they like.'

Hessian gave a small, sad smile and collapsed into a chair at his table, cut in the dimensions of Erland, with a cone-shaped flagon set in place of Eryispek. 'In truth, Brother, I envy your easy way with the common soldier.' He looked down at the table. 'Though not as much as I envy you your two sons.'

Andrick sat down opposite and moved to pour the wine. 'I would not grieve a son any less for having another, nor my daughter any less for having two sons. For a parent to lose a child is the most grievous tragedy imaginable. I am sorry, Hessian.'

Hessian wiped his bloodshot eyes. 'You are not wrong of course, but I have not only lost a son and heir. I have lost a dynasty, a kingdom, and my life's work.'

'It is not too late, Hessian. You must wed again.' Andrick spoke firmly, hoping to cut through his brother's despair. He had spoken of a dynasty, with something of his old fire.

'I have two other sons, you know.' Hessian swigged at his

wine. 'By peasant girls. They would be in their middle age by now. I wonder what became of them sometimes.' Andrick jumped as he suddenly slammed a palm on the table. 'Oh, the hand that Eryi has dealt me!' Flecks of red wine sprayed from his mouth. 'For sixteen years I have loved the memory of a dead woman, and though it breaks my heart, I must now marry again, and with this ailing body sire an heir. Tell me Andrick, which lucky young maid did you have in mind for such disappointment?'

'Brother, I do not believe you will be a disappointment. Older men and young women often make the best match; was not your father decades your mother's senior? We have identified a potential bride. However, there is one alternative you may not have considered.' Andrick swallowed. He had not spoken of this plan to anyone. Hessian had sent men to the dungeons for less. 'Marry Helana to Rymond Prindian. Their son, your grandson, will one day rule.'

Hessian went very still, and though the breeze from the open window had suddenly died, the room's temperature seemed to drop. His red eyes found Andrick's, piercing him like arrows.

'Never.' Hessian lurched to his feet and sent his chair crashing to the stone floor. 'You! You would have me marry my daughter into that nest of vipers? Have you lost your wits, Brother?' Hessian was wild, clutching the edge of the table with bright white knuckles, and the wind rose again as if in tune with him, scattering his long greying hair. 'What a fine reward for killing my wife's family: my daughter, and the crown of Erland! Perhaps I should give him my first daughter to fuck as well!'

Hessian's rages were as brief as they were manic. He slumped back into his seat and drank long from his cup. 'No... I think not.'

'Forgive me, Brother.' Andrick spoke carefully, keeping his eyes down. 'I should never have suggested it.' He had known the risk. Hessian's hatred of the Prindians was a madness in him, ever since they had rebelled in the wake of Queen Elyana's death. Hatred was good though; he would fight to the end to pass the crown to his own dynasty.

'Oh, little Brother!' Hessian chuckled. 'If only folk could see this. The fierce warrior Andrick Barrelbreaker scorned to silence by the feeble King Hessian.' Hessian's mood was as swift to move to mirth as it had been to anger. 'I would have my scribes record this, but I fear that future scholars would never believe it. And who is your proposed bride?'

'Lady Ciera Istlewick,' said Andrick. 'Lord Istlewick's sixteen-year-old daughter.'

'The Lord of Cliffark. Since you rid him of the pirate Portes Stormcaller he has increased his revenues tenfold. But is the daughter not betrothed?'

'To Rymond Prindian. But he is yet to claim his bride.'

Hessian smiled. 'So, I weaken the Prindian brat while strengthening my own position. It is fortunate that he never thought to claim her, or we might have enemies to the east and the west. An inspired choice. Did you think of it yourself?'

'I did,' said Andrick. He did not want Hessian to know he had discussed this with his family.

'Well I am sure Lord Istlewick can see the advantages of an alliance with his king over one with a mewling pup who my spies report never rises before noon. The Istlewick girl it is.'

'Very good, Majesty.' Andrick let out a breath of relief. 'Should I send an envoy?'

'Oh no, Brother. I have no envoy more suited to the task than you, returning to the site of yet another famous victory.' Hessian stood and began pacing the room, invigorated by the intrigue of stealing another man's bride-to-be. 'You will convince her father to set aside the betrothal, and stand in for me at a proxy wedding, then bring the girl to me without delay. Each day we lose is a day less in which for me to sire an heir!

And sire an heir I will. Rymond Prindian will never wear my crown. The Sangreal dynasty must endure.'

Andrick looked up at him, his brow furrowed. 'But what of the Thrumb?' He had been sure that Hessian would command him to march west immediately with the *Hymeriker*.

'Strovac Sigac will ride to Thrumb with three hundred men. I mean to keep the *Hymeriker* close to me; you will only need a small escort to Cliffark.'

Andrick knew Strovac Sigac only too well. He had a grudging respect for his skill at arms, but Strovac was as unscrupulous as he was cruel. Though not a lord, by Hessian's favour he was the master of Fenhold, a keep deep in Erland's bleak eastern marshes, and surrounded himself with warriors just as black-hearted as himself, the so-called Wild Brigade. That Hessian made use of such a man was a dark blot upon his kingship. 'Strovac is fierce, but he has not learnt a soldier's discipline.'

Hessian snorted. 'It is you who would not take him as a *hymerika*, so whose fault is that? I know about Sigac, and it is not up for discussion. He has less honour than a rutting dog, but he is a fearsome fighter, and better a tame dog than a wild one. I intend for him to extinguish the Thrumb, root and branch. This is no longer a matter of dealing with their raiding, Brother; it is a war of eradication. But you must go to Cliffark. Leave as soon as you are ready.'

Andrick nodded. 'Yes, Majesty, I will not fail you. I will begin my preparations tonight.' He had known Hessian would order the Thrumb's destruction, but at least it would not fall to him to do it. And the Thrumb knew their lands better than any warrior of Erland; they would hide away in the deep forest and never be found. Strovac Sigac could no more eradicate the Thrumb than he could jump over the walls of Piperskeep. Understanding the king's instruction as a dismissal, Andrick stood and strode purposefully towards the door.

'Andrick,' said Hessian from behind him as he reached for the handle. Andrick turned. Hessian was looking at him softly, as if seeing him for the first time. 'I know you won't. You have never erred, have you? Never been tempted to tie your fate to somebody else's, or betray me and steal the crown. For all your victories, you have stayed true to me. You humble me, Brother. In my younger days, men said I had a honeyed tongue, for I could convince them in an hour to yield what they had sworn I could never have. Yet for all that, I believe the best deal I ever struck was forty years ago, when I bought a little boy's loyalty for a dog and a wooden toy.'

'You would always have my loyalty,' said Andrick. 'It is the loyalty that every subject owes his liege. What you bought that day was a brother's love.'

Hessian smiled a slow smile, melting the years from his ailing face. 'Go then, Brother, and bring me back my bride. The fate of a kingdom and a dynasty ride with you.'

Outside, Andrick bade farewell to the two guards and began his descent. A careless servant had allowed the row of sconces that lined the spiral stairs to burn low, and as he made his way down Andrick could see little more than the steps in front of him, until the warm orange firelight from the corridor below came slowly into view.

There was something about his meetings with Hessian that always left him feeling like the boy he had once been. For all his victories, he was still the little brother. Perhaps he ought to have been more understanding of Orsian; Errian would always see him as a child, not an ally.

'You should be careful walking around in the dark like that.'

The voice was low and guttural, and came from behind Andrick. He whirled around, searching for the source, and started as a looming shadow emerged from a dark alcove, high and menacing.

After an instant of dread, the huge frame of Strovac Sigac

came into the light. He towered over Andrick even more than usual, filling the stairwell with his bulk. The first thing a man noticed about Strovac was his size.

His face wore a broad and satisfied grin, savouring the triumph of having shocked his target. Over a decade ago, Strovac had been just one of many boys sent to Piperskeep for Andrick Barrelbreaker to make a soldier of. He had been strong and skilful beyond his years, but deceitful and cruel, and in Andrick's eyes not worthy to join the *Hymeriker*. But Strovac was now a man, and every inch a warrior. Except his eyes. The second thing a man noticed was his eyes: small and beady, ever darting like insects about his otherwise handsome face. They were the eyes of an assassin, cold and calculating and devious.

'Did I scare you, Lord?' asked Strovac, smirking. 'I am sorry, I was on my way to see the king. I am told he has need of me.'

Andrick's face gave nothing away, but his eyes were flint. 'You are being sent to Thrumbalto to take command following the prince's murder, may Eryi take him.'

Strovac's mocking smile could not hide his surprise. 'But I would have thought that a job for you, the storied hero Andrick the Barrelbreaker. Unless you have finally decided to hang up your sword? It would be a shame if so; I had hoped we might cross blades before you retired.'

'Enjoy your jokes, Strovac. I assure you the Thrumb will find them as amusing as I do. Does it please you to be back in the capital? You must miss the city, but the kingdom relies on you to guard the western marshes. The toads and egrets will not hunt themselves.'

For half a moment, anger flashed in Strovac's eyes. The man was at least easy to rile, ever conscious of the relative meagreness of his position. 'The kingdom relies on me to perform the deeds that would stain your vaunted honour. Now as much as I would like to stand in the stairs and bandy words with you, the king requires me. Enjoy your retirement, old man.'

Andrick watched him leave, warily. Strovac Sigac was not someone to turn your back on. Dark rumours swirled around the man like phantoms – of Fenhold servants who mysteriously vanished, of strange screams in the night that echoed across the wetlands – and Andrick believed them. The one tale he did not believe was that Strovac was an illegitimate son of Hessian. Even after Elyana's death, Hessian had never taken anyone else to bed since their wedding, Andrick was sure of it. He could only imagine it a story spread by Strovac himself.

Relying on that man is folly. Would that he had died at Thrumbalto, and that Prince Jarhick still lived.

CHAPTER 3

Rymond Prindian reclined on his cushioned chair, nursing his headache with a smokestick and a carafe of blackcurrant wine. His antechamber was awash with bright silks and artwork from before the Accord, but today the tapestries were not pleasing to him. He would still be in bed, had his mother not sent a serving boy to tell him to be prepared to receive her before noon. Rymond's head was pounding, and his robe was drenched in sweat. If it were not the height of summer and the sun not so bright he would have caught the breeze on his balcony, but instead he had closed the curtains. The room's only light came from his smokestick, and a small, luminous-green crystal from the Imperium that he had won in a game of chess against a ship's captain.

He had been out drinking in Irith's New Quarter last night. Formerly a shanty town of vagabonds built amidst the ruins of an old castle, the area was undergoing something of a renewal thanks to a few enterprising tavern-owners specialising in unusual liquors. Of course, having the custom of the second-in-line to the throne of Erland had not done any harm to their business ventures; every citizen in Irith now knew that Lord

Prindian was a patron of the Smoking Sow. Rymond could not recall precisely what he had been playing last night, nor with whom, but there had been a healthy weight of gold in his pockets this morning, and he had shown the good sense not to bring a woman back to his bed.

He was mid-reverie when there was a knock at the door. Rymond sat upright, rushing to cover himself with his robe and almost spilling his wine.

Lady Breta Prindian waltzed in without waiting for an answer, enveloping the room in a cloud of fragrant perfume, resplendent in a flowing midnight-blue dress, her thick burnt-copper hair tied up in an elaborate knot. She was nearing sixty, but that never seemed to stop tavern girls gushing to Rymond about his beautiful mother, with her slender waist and an unblemished, angular face dominated by dazzling green eyes. It was a topic Rymond could not abide; he went to taverns to forget about his family, not be reminded of them.

'Did you consider getting dressed for me? At least there are no tavern sluts here this time, though it does smell like an inn in here.' Breta moved busily around the room, lighting candles, and then looked at the carafe of wine on the table. 'What are we celebrating? Your father was one for wine before lunch.'

Rymond bristled. 'I feel unwell. I would not usually.' When Rymond was a boy, his father had drunkenly bet that he could jump his horse from a balcony on the second floor of the keep onto the stable roof. After coaxing the poor beast up the stairs he made the jump successfully, but the terrified horse had bucked violently on landing and thrown the old Lord Prindian to the ground thirty feet below, cracking open his head and killing him on impact.

'No more.' She picked up the carafe and poured herself a generous measure. 'We have much to discuss, and I want you to remember it when we are finished.'

'So is it one rule for you and another for me?' asked Rymond indignantly. The wine had been expensive.

'I know my limits,' replied his mother, with a wave of her ringed fingers. 'And I am not a fool. Your father was a fool, your brother was a fool, and when you are drunk you, too, are a fool. I had hoped I'd raised you to have slightly more ambition than to be another drunken noble gambling away his birthright and spreading his seed among any woman greedy enough to spend a night with you, but we are where we are. I have news, and I need you to have your wits about you.'

Rymond came to his feet, careful to keep his robe around him. He lit another smokestick and walked to fetch the jug of water that stood on his dresser. 'I actually won money last night—'

'I am not speaking of money. Do you think I care how much you win or lose in the tavern? It would take you several lifetimes to empty this family's vault. It is not money you lose, but your right to respect from the common people. Do you expect them to obey your rule when half the town has seen you passed out in your chair or in an alley with your hands up a whore's skirt?'

Rymond inhaled deeply on his smokestick, resisting the urge to pour himself another glass of wine. This was not fair; she always managed to make his life sound so seedy. 'I am generous with my coin, and I am loved by the people for it. What can I gain from respect that I cannot buy with money?'

His mother stared at him in disbelief for a moment. 'You are truly and utterly hopeless,' she said, with a shake of her head, 'but you are my only living son, and so I will make do. Prince Jarhick is dead. You are the heir to the crown of Erland.'

Rymond started, and choked on his smokestick, forcing him to place a steadying hand on the dresser. He had met Jarhick a few times. The prince had been a fine gambling companion. Rymond had liked the man, and though his mother had sowed poisonous tales in his ear from an early age with stories of stolen crowns and barbarians from the south, he had been prepared to accept their respective places in the succession.

And now Jarhick was suddenly dead. Rymond supposed his mother expected him to celebrate, but his immediate emotion was dismay. If he became king, he would be expected to move to Merivale, and the capital was not to his tastes. The food and drink were foul, the citizens were ugly, and it stank like a privy. There was no sense in being king if you had to live somewhere like that. He would have to move the capital to Irith.

'May Eryi take him from the Earth and to Eryispek above the clouds.' He returned to his seat and reached for the carafe to pour himself another wine in Jarhick's honour, but his mother pulled it away from him.

'May Eryi take him,' she replied with a tight smile. She leant forward and looked at him devilishly. 'But what do you really think?'

Rymond thought for a moment, covering his pause with a sip of water. His mother had seen fit to burst into his room and ruin his morning, so he felt it within his rights to tweak her nose a bit. 'I should ride to Merivale immediately,' he said, leaving his face impassive. 'If the king and the people are to accept me as his heir I must go.' He had no intention of doing anything of the sort, but he wanted to see how his mother would react.

Her face turned to thunder. 'No. Do you think playing a good game of chess makes you clever? You really are a bloody fool. What if Jarhick had been murdered on my orders? Would you still believe you were safe to ride to Merivale?'

Rymond started with surprise. 'Mother... Did you have him murdered?'

'It's something I thought on.' She took a nonchalant sip of her wine. 'But no. As it turns out, boys with swords do not need any help getting themselves killed.'

'I am relieved.' He took a long drag on his smokestick. 'We should not make enemies of the Sangreals.' He would admit to knowing little of politics, but he was aware enough to know that East Erland had the finer warriors.

'We are their enemy, whether you like it or not. You may be the heir by law, but you are a threat to Hessian's dynasty. He has two nephews, two daughters, two grandchildren, and two bastards that I know of, and I assure you that he would have any one of them rule before you. Hessian will not risk the return of the Old Line, and nor will his followers.'

Rymond shrugged. 'Law is law. I am the heir.'

'Only while you live. And Hessian will not suffer you to live for long. However, he is not a well man. If fortune favours us, you could be crowned within two years, but it will not happen if we sit and wring our hands about what is lawful. I assure you that Hessian will not.'

Rymond sighed. It seemed to him the last thing they ought to do was anything that might draw Hessian's attention to them. 'Very well. You've clearly thought on this already. What do you advise we do?' He had earnt another glass of wine, but when he grasped for the carafe his mother moved it again.

She stood and carried the carafe to Rymond's dresser, away from him. 'Finally you ask the right question. Ride to White-water and take a ship to Cliffark. It is time you claimed your bride.'

Rymond stared at her in confusion. *Bride?* He choked back a laugh when he finally remembered. 'The Istlewick girl! I did not realise I was still betrothed.'

'Well, you're not married, so of course you're... Eryi's bones, you're not married, are you? I'd assumed you just fucked them, but fool that you are, nothing would surprise me.'

Rymond rolled his eyes. 'No, Mother, I am unwed, and shall remain so. Marriage can wait.' He was not yet twenty-two, too young for the demands of marriage.

'I'll be the judge of what can wait.' His mother was staring at him pointedly, her hands set firmly on her hips. 'Hessian may grieve, but he does not wait. Even now, he will be planning a marriage to consolidate his position and sire an heir. You will need support in East Erland, and Lord Istlewick is the richest of them. Marry the girl.'

'I will wed when I am ready. What else would you have me do? Besides marriage.'

'Prepare for war. You will not restore our family to the throne unless you press your claim, and I do not intend to watch you drink, whore, and gamble your life away while that claim withers on the vine.'

Rymond swallowed anxiously. 'We could never hope to win. They have the men, and they have Barrelbreaker.' Rymond had not seen Lord Andrick since the day he had crushed his brother's rebellion. He had been a child, and terrified, but he had stood on the highest balcony to watch the fighting. When the gate to Fallback Lodge had broken, Barrelbreaker had been the first man through. Rymond had seen him cut down half-a-dozen men before he could blink, every swing of his sword finding flesh. The fear had stayed with him to this day.

'You fear him. Good, shows you've got some sense. It's not just his sword you should fear though. You know the stories. The man knows more about war than you could ever hope to learn. And he's loved! Those proud men of East Erland love their bastard son of a foreign whore. Make no mistake that he is the more dangerous of the brothers. Hessian inspires fear, but Andrick inspires devotion.'

As his mother talked, Rymond stood and walked to the dresser, where he finally reached the carafe ahead of her grasping fingers. He triumphantly poured himself a glass, savouring its sweet smell. 'We cannot hope to defeat Barrelbreaker in the field,' he said. 'He brings too many men, and too much knowledge.'

His mother nodded. 'You see the truth of it. Which means you also see the truth that this must eventually come to pass.

Whether you are heir or not, there are many East Erlanders who will not suffer you on the throne unless you take it for yourself. We cannot assassinate half a country.'

Rymond relit his smokestick with a candle and took a long drag. Could he truly be so disliked that men would ignore the line of succession to pass him over for the crown? It was likely. He knew the memory of his brother Ranulf was still hated. And though they had nominally been one people for almost two centuries, there would be those on the other side of the Pale River who would baulk at the idea of being ruled by a West Erlander.

But reclaiming the crown and restoring the Old Line was his mother's dream, not his. A bloody war of succession followed by a lifetime dealing with the troubles of a realm weighed up against his current life was no contest at all, and that was if he won. Dying on Andrick Barrelbreaker's sword would be even worse.

'If Hessian were to die tomorrow, do you suppose they would crown somebody else?' he asked.

'Yes, but not before they killed you. It would not be Lord Andrick – he values his honour too highly – but he would not send a single sword to protect you.'

Rymond furrowed his brow, and took a deep swig from his glass. Regardless of whether Hessian lived for a year or a score of years, he would need to win in the field to claim the crown. To do that, he would have to remove Lord Andrick, and he had a better chance of jumping his horse over the walls of Irith. He did not want a war. He did not even particularly want to be king. He would have to find a way to put his mother off.

'Thank you for bringing this situation to my attention, Mother.' He kissed her dutifully on the cheek. 'I will think on what you have said, but for now I mean to wait and see where Hessian's dice fall.' He could delay for months by saying he was 'waiting', and by then the issue might have resolved itself.

'You can't put me off like that.' She fixed him with a sharp gaze. 'At the very least, you can call your men to arms and have your lords do the same. You do not need to call them to your banner yet, but we cannot allow Hessian to think West Erland is ripe for the taking. Write to your lords near the river and have them send out men to watch the eastern bank.'

Rymond sighed, cursing his mother for having so easily seen through his ruse. 'Very well.' Those were steps that did not commit him to any particular course. And it would allow him to see where the loyalties of his lords lay.

'There is something you ought to do yourself as well. Resume your lessons with Adfric and learn to swing a sword like a man. You cannot hope to press your claim or protect yourself from those who would set you aside without that.'

Rymond's face fell. It had been years since he had held a sword. He had abandoned his lessons in warfare with his humourless master-at-arms, Adfric, as soon as he had come of age. To his dismay, he realised his mother had trapped him; he could not very well expect other men to prepare for war if he did not do the same himself. 'Fine.' He slumped back into his chair. 'If it will please you.'

His mother smiled, triumphant. 'It will, and you best learn quick. Your dear old mother won't be here to protect you forever.'

CHAPTER 4

It was a warm summer night, though fleeting whispers of wind from Eryispek still pricked at their skin. They made camp under the starless sky, the clouds hanging over them like a blanket. Somewhere an owl hooted, and a lone wolf howled, too fearful of the scent of men to approach their fire.

Orsian stared into the crackling flames, quietly seething. Errian had been away for months, and his life had been all the better for it. He had been expecting to go to the king with his father, but instead had been sent away to fetch his elder brother. Did his father still think him too young to speak with Hessian? He had not even been able to spend a night in Piperskeep, where he might have seen his cousin Helana.

Naeem had trained him for years, and to Orsian's annoyance saw straight through his black mood. 'Your father's just doing what he thinks is best, lad,' he said, whittling away with a knife at something in his lap. 'He obviously trusts you. He'd never have sent Errian riding off alone when he was fourteen.'

Orsian had not thought of that, and felt a little foolish. This was not a punishment; his father was putting trust in him. He ought to be grateful, and honoured. Their father had usually taken a firm hand against Errian's wild ways, and would never have trusted him to ride off alone. Orsian knew he was the cleverer brother; Errian still moved his lips to read. He might be bigger and stronger, but Orsian was hopeful that would change soon; he had grown several inches since last winter.

'The best thing you can do,' said Naeem, jabbing his knife at Orsian to emphasise the point, 'is prove yourself worthy of that trust. That means no scrapping with Errian. We've enemies enough without you two fighting; especially now the prince is dead.'

'I won't if he doesn't,' said Orsian defensively. It was likely hopeless though, no matter the wishes of their father. His brother's pride would be ten times worse now, since joining the *Hymeriker* and seeing battle. Orsian would never be more than an annoyance to Errian, and to him Errian would always be the bully who had stolen his food and jabbed him with a wooden sword when nobody was looking. But to prove to their father he was right to trust him, Orsian supposed he would have to put that aside.

Naeem grunted. 'Suppose that'll have to do.' He lay down on the ground and pulled his cloak around him. 'Now let's get to sleep. We've a week's hard riding to get to the eastern face, and I want to be away early.'

They made good time the next day. The sun was warm, and they stopped regularly to allow their horses to graze upon the long grass. To their north, Eryispek loomed over them like a vast icy sentinel, blocking out the sky. Its landscape would change as they circled it, Orsian knew, the sheer rock and snow giving way to the arid red clay of the eastern side. The fog that shrouded its upper reaches was unusually thick for the time of year, and as they had the night before, the winds blowing off it raised light gooseflesh where his skin was bare.

Orsian wondered what awaited them. Perhaps Errian had won a great victory against the Lutum tribesmen. It would make him more insufferable than ever. Or what if he were dead? War was never without risk. He did not wish his brother dead, no matter how much he disliked him.

'Don't think too much,' said Naeem, faced with Orsian's pensive silence. 'It's a hard road, and there'll be plenty of time for that. What you need, lad, is a woman, some strong-thighed shepherdess to make a man of you and stop you being so damn serious all the time.' He laughed, pointing south towards a flock of sheep.

Orsian turned away to cover the blush rising on his cheeks. 'What are the Lutums like?'

Naeem spat. 'Vicious bastards. Rock-worshipping savages. When they're not fighting the Adrari they fight each other. They'll be no trouble for your brother and our lads though.' He patted his scabbarded sword as if to reassure himself. 'They've no steel for one thing.'

'Why do you think they rebelled so suddenly? They've barely stirred in the last century.' It was peculiar, especially for it to occur at the same time as events in Thrumb.

Naeem shrugged. 'Boredom? Ancestral resentment? Maybe the Mountain told them to. That's what they pray to, you know: Eryispek, though they won't call it that, only the Mountain.'

Orsian had known that. The Lutums worshipped the Mountain as the pillar that supported the heavens, the earthly representative of the Norhai through which the ancient gods made their will known. They were generally considered to be a little backwards, but to him it made no less sense than worshipping the god Eryi who held court at the summit above the clouds. His father had never been particularly devout, so had not forced either religion on him. Many in Erland prayed to Eryi and to the Norhai, just to be safe.

Orsian wondered what was happening at Merivale. Suppose the king immediately sent his father west to fight the Thrumb? He and Naeem might be weeks behind him when they returned. His father did seem intent on finding the king a bride though; perhaps Hessian would turn his eyes to vengeance against the Thrumb only once he was wed. Or would the Prindians declare war and split Erland in two? Orsian's heart leapt at the thought of it; he wanted to fight for Erland, to make his father and the king proud.

'Do you truly think the Prindians will risk war now the prince is dead?'

Naeem shrugged. 'I'm less sure than I was. Depends on Lord Prindian and his mother's influence. Might be the odds are in his favour without a war. The king will marry, but who's to say the bride will prove fertile, or that she'll birth a boy? I know the women say certain food and scents help, but my wife and I had five boys before we got a daughter, and then she had three girls in a row, so who knows? It's too complicated for the likes of me.'

Hours later, a few miles from where the grass began to slope upwards, they found the mountain road that would lead them around the base of Eryispek to the eastern slope. It was a sorry and unfinished thing, wide and muddy, bordered by pitiable rows of patchy hedge.

They met few travellers, and those they did moved to the side of the road to let them pass. Orsian and Naeem carried no banners, and travellers were always wary of banditry. Orsian tried waving to a few, but received little by way of a response.

At mid-afternoon, they saw a billowing cloud of dust on the horizon, and the rumbling of horse hooves shook the ground beneath them. Orsian squinted into the distance, but saw no riders. *There must be hundreds of them.* Orsian felt a swell of excitement in his gut. The Prindians would come from the west, so who could be riding with such a force from the east?

His mood sank as a swarm of horsemen came into focus, and Orsian recognised the twin standards they carried: the deep red of Sangreal and the green and brown of his father. That meant Errian, and judging by their numbers he had won a great victory, sooner than anybody had anticipated. Orsian had expected to have weeks to prepare to face his brother, and now it was being thrust upon him barely a day's ride from Merivale.

As the horde came closer, Orsian's mouth fell open slightly in fascination. He had never seen so many soldiers riding together at once. Every man was ahorse, hundreds of hooves beating out a staccato rhythm, stretched along the road like some great many-legged beetle.

At the head of the march, Errian rode high in the saddle. He had inherited the famed Sangreal height, and wore his dark blond hair fashionably long. In his months away he had grown a coarse auburn beard over his proud jaw. His shoulders were broad, though his lean body lacked his father's barrel-chested brawn. His nose was aquiline, his lips pale and thin, his eyes bright blue. He and Orsian could barely have looked less alike. Nobody would have thought them brothers to look at them, and perhaps that was part of the problem. Orsian noticed that Errian's once-pristine riding gear was stained and shabby from his time at war, and felt a pang of jealousy.

Naeem called out to him. 'Well met, Lord Errian!' He raised a hand in greeting, and in response two bowmen notched an arrow and aimed towards them. Orsian frowned. His brother's men were on edge for some reason. 'Your father sent us to speak with you,' called Naeem, studiously ignoring the archers. 'We've been riding for hours, the sun sits high in the sky, and I have a thirst. Shall we find some shade and retire for a mug of ale?'

Errian gestured for his men to lower their weapons. He raised his hand in a fist, and behind him hundreds of riders reined their mounts to a stop. 'I think not, Naeem. I've been trapped under this Norhai-cursed sun for over a month. There's a bath in Merivale with my name on it, and no doubt a couple of pretty girls eager to wash me.' His jest was met by a gale of sycophantic laughter from the men behind him. 'Why are you here?'

It was just the sort of arrogant reply Orsian would have expected of his brother. 'We have news,' he said, ignoring his brother's brusqueness.

Errian looked around in mock confusion, scanning back and forth above Orsian's head as if he did not know from where his voice had come. 'Little Brother!' he greeted him when he eventually let his gaze fall on him, his smile glinting with malice. 'Forgive me; I did not see you.'

'You're returning sooner than expected,' Orsian continued, as if he had not heard his brother's weak jest. 'Can we assume that you won a great victory over the Lutums?' Appealing to Errian's pride was usually the quickest way to get him to speak civilly.

Errian's mirth gave way to a scowl. 'Never mind the Lutums, I'll tell Father of them when I return. What is your news?'

Orsian gritted his teeth against his desire to enquire further. If Errian had won a great victory, he would have crowed about it at the first opportunity, so why was he returning with his full strength if that was not the case? 'If we could ride a short way together I will tell you.' He did not want to share the death of Jarhick with hundreds of men. He had thought to have this conversation with Errian in the privacy of a command tent, not while he marched his army home.

Errian looked at him a moment. He blinked slowly, then laughed. 'It cannot be that important if Father sent you. Let me guess: he's come to his senses, given up trying to train you as a warrior, and you're travelling east to become a merchant.'

Errian's jibe drew laughter from his men, and blood rushed to Orsian's ears. He felt shamed before so many warriors, who had fought for Erland while he practised swordplay behind the stout walls of Violet Hall. 'It is important, Errian.' He tried to avoid the humiliation of pleading with him. 'It's best shared in private.'

'Orsian's right, Errian,' said Naeem. 'Your father sent us to speak with you.'

Errian looked on the verge of agreeing. He squinted suspiciously at them both, and Orsian knew he was weighing up whether his curiosity was greater than his wish to embarrass his younger brother. 'I know what your news is,' he said, a broad grin spreading across his face. Orsian's heart sank. 'You're a foundling! I knew such a stout, dark fellow could not be my natural brother.'

Errian's joke drew more laughter from his men. Orsian bit down his temper. He looked like their father, but Erlanders were usually blond, and Errian looked the archetypal Erland warrior, like one of the old kings memorialised in stained glass at Piperskeep. The laughter of so many soldiers hurt worse than any injury earnt in the practice yard.

'This won't do, Errian,' said Naeem sharply. 'We're here—'

'Prince Jarhick is dead,' said Orsian, speaking over Naeem. He had tried to break the news gently to his brother and honour his father's orders, and Errian had thrown it back in his face. 'A Thrumb assassin killed him.'

Errian's features went slack, losing every trace of his previous mirth. He searched Orsian's face for some sign of mischief. 'A poor jest, Orsian,' he said eventually, unconvincingly. 'Has Jarhick returned to Merivale then?'

'It's true, Lord,' said Naeem. 'I heard it from your father's own lips.'

Errian opened and closed his mouth stupidly. His horse

snorted nervously as his grip tightened on the reins. Orsian was suddenly reminded of Errian aged eight, when Orsian had thrown his toy sword on the fire as revenge for a particularly vicious beating. Anguish played across his face, contorting his features and misting over the whites of his eyes.

'I am sorry, Brother.'

'What for? You never knew him.' Errian swallowed, and Orsian thought he saw a trace of tears in his eyes. 'How did he die?'

'Poison,' said Naeem.

Errian went very still, his jaw tight, his knuckles simmering white. His horse snorted and tossed its head restlessly. For a moment Orsian thought Errian might be about to attack them. When he finally spoke, it was to the man who rode at his side. 'Keddick,' he said, in a cracked voice, 'pass word down the line. We ride for Thrumbalto, to avenge Prince Jarhick.'

Orsian opened his mouth to speak, but Naeem cut across him. 'Lord Errian, do not act rashly. Your father would—'

'The Norhai take my father, and you as well.' Errian's eyes blazed. 'I will take the head of every living soul in Thrumbalto. I will burn it to the ground and sow their lands with salt.' His eyes flicked to Orsian. 'Jarhick was my brother. Not you. Now get off the road, or I'll kill you where you stand.'

Naeem and Orsian exchanged a glance. Orsian had grown up with Errian, and Naeem had taught him at arms. Both of them knew he meant it. Reluctantly, they steered their horses off the road, and watched grim-faced as Errian raised a palm to signal his men. He led them westwards, kicking up dust and dirt in their haste.

Naeem's face was grim. 'You tried, Orsian. But not nearly enough.'

'I did my best!' Orsian knew as soon as he spoke that it was a lie. He could have ignored Errian's jibes; he could have done more to reconcile with his brother. But why did Errian have to make it so hard? He shook his head. His father would not want excuses.

Naeem tugged at his reins to pull his horse around. 'Come on. We need to get back to Merivale. If we ride through the night perhaps your father can stop Errian doing something stupid.'

CHAPTER 5

The thickets grew wild and dark, untamed and untouched by the scythes of men. The sun had barely completed its slow creep above the horizon, leaving the forest cloaked in bleak semi-darkness.

In the brambles, Helana crouched, thorns prickling at her exposed skin. She and Creya had set out before dawn with spears and bows, but as the forest had become thicker they had been forced to abandon them. Only their long hunting knives remained, tied to their lower legs.

The huntswoman was ten yards to Helana's left, barely visible through the gorse, camouflaged, and silent as an icy pond. From all around them came the sounds of the forest: rustling branches, twittering songbirds, and the gentle trickle of a brook.

But there was only one creature Helana and Creya were interested in that morning.

They could see it through the undergrowth ahead of them, where the thicket ended in a muddy clearing. A great boar, with rusty-brown fur and tusks the length of a man's forearm, wallowing contentedly in the mud. A male, undoubtedly.

Helana gritted her teeth and touched the knife at her ankle. The beast was probably twice her weight, and those tusks were sharp enough to tear her guts to shreds. What she would not have given to be holding her spear.

She glanced at Creya, who looked back at her. The huntswoman raised a stiff palm, signalling that Helana was to wait.

Creya had spent over half her life in the forest north of Merivale, and Helana trusted her like nobody else, but spear or no spear, she was in no mood to wait. She had come out here to kill something, not to cower while the prey was right in front of her. The boar was so close she could hear its breath, heavy and hot like a blacksmith's bellows, and so absorbed in its wallowing that Helana fancied she could slit its throat before it even knew she was there.

Helana raised her own palm in response, spreading her fingers and thumb. *Five seconds.* Creya's eyes widened, and she shook her head furiously, but Helana ignored her. She counted to five, drew her knife and crept forward through the bushes into the clearing.

She stepped softly towards the wallowing boar, until sooner than expected it seemed to notice her, and its beady yellow eyes met hers. The beast squinted up at her, coming to its feet steadily, its tusks and snout dripping with wet mud. It growled, deep and throaty and threatening.

Helana stopped in her tracks, still some ten yards away. The blade in her hand felt of little more use than an eating knife, faced with something twice her weight and with twice the weaponry. The beast growled again, and stamped a front hoof through the mud.

Helana took a deep breath, and spread her stance wide, willing herself not to run. If she dived back into the forest the boar would come after her, and in the dense woodland it would

have the advantage. Perhaps she could scare it? She waved the
knife back and forth between her hands.

If it was scared, the boar did not show it. It stamped on the
ground again and grunted. Helana felt a singular moment of
dread, and the boar put its head down and charged towards her.

Others might have run, but not Helana. She was not Creya,
but she was a princess of Erland, and she had stared down
beasts and men far worse than this. She roared a challenge, and
stood on her toes, ready to dive out of the way and drag her
blade across its snout.

It was five yards away from her when Creya leapt from the
bushes. Lightning-fast, she vaulted onto the boar's back and
drew her knife across its throat, spraying crimson blood like
warm rain.

The boar squealed violently, Helana forgotten, bucking its
legs as it tried to shake its assailant. Creya held firm, gripping it
between her powerful thighs and pulling back its enormous
head as the blood and fight drained out of it.

Helana stood back, gaping, her knife hanging uselessly at
her side. The boar slowed, staggering under Creya's weight and
its lost blood, until its legs collapsed and it dropped into
the mud.

Creya stood, her handsome, weather-beaten face dripping
with the beast's blood, her hair plastered with it. 'By the Norhai,
girl, what the bleeding hell were you thinking?' She pulled out a
wineskin and took a long draught. 'You could have been killed!'

'I was fine! I was about to kill it myself until you got in the
way.'

'Were you bollocks, he would have gored you from cunt to
chin! You can't be taking risks like that!'

'You do!'

'I bloody don't.' Creya sank to sit upon the boar's corpse. It
somehow looked even bigger in death, like a monster dredged

up from the sea. She threw the wineskin to Helana. 'Sit down so I can explain to you the facts of life.'

Helana drank deeply, until the sweet wine dripped down her chin. She felt a little shaky, but she was not going to show Creya that. The huntswoman had dozens of scars; Helana refused to believe she had got them without taking more than a few risks. She sat down next to Creya and handed her back the skin.

'I don't take risks like that,' Creya said, 'because I can't afford to make mistakes. Worst outcome is I die; best outcome is I'm injured. Either way, my family relies on me; if I can't hunt, there's no food on the table.

'You don't think about dying – the young always think they'll live forever – and if you get injured, you can just rest up in your fancy castle for a few months while servants run around making sure you're comfortable.

'Risks are a luxury, Princess, and few people can afford luxuries. And your risks aren't just your own – they're mine. You think your father would have let me live if this boar had so much as broken your nail?' She took another pull on the wineskin and passed it to Helana.

Helana snorted. 'He wouldn't care. And don't call me Princess.' She came hunting to forget about her title, but Creya's lecture had only served to remind her of her rarely privileged position. She would not admit it to her, but the clear truth of it had stung a little.

Creya shrugged. 'It's what you are, Princess.' She indicated to the horn at Helana's belt. 'Give that a toot and the boys will come running. We can't get this beast back by ourselves.'

Helana had to bite her tongue to hold back an ill-tempered response. Arguing with Creya was like arguing with a wall, a particularly stubborn one. She had got better at that recently, holding her tongue. Better to save her wrath for those who truly deserved it. She blew long on her horn, sending alarmed birds flying for the sky.

'War then, by the sounds of it,' said Creya, as she cleaned her knife. 'You reckon?'

Helana sighed. That was the worry that had kept her awake the night before: the war that everyone thought was sure to come. There were rumours that the West Erland lords were already calling together their levies, and sending out men to patrol the Pale River.

And all because her brother Jarhick was dead. She had loved Jarhick, and days after she had learnt of his death it was still like a hole had been torn out of her. She had come hunting to forget about that too. Why would Creya mention it? They might have been the first words Helana had ever heard from her that were not to do with hunting.

There was a loud rustling, and Creya's husband Yarl emerged from the bushes, followed by his three sons. Helana smiled at the eldest of them, Yarl the Younger, and he blushed like a maid. She had kissed him, months ago, back in Yarl and Creya's hut when they found themselves alone, and he had stepped away from her stammering, even though he was eighteen, two years older than her, and ought to have known what he was doing. A shame, Helana thought. He had broad shoulders, and big hands from cutting meat. His loss though, even if she was slightly offended to be turned down by a huntsman's son. Probably scared that her father would cut his balls off, or get Theodric to turn him into a toad. She was reminded of Creya's words – kissing Helana was a risk to him, but not to Helana.

'Took your time.' Creya stood, and pointed to the boar's corpse. 'Get that meat back to the hut. Seeing as we did the hard part we'll meet you there.'

Helana felt slightly frustrated. Going hunting and not sticking something with a spear or an arrow was like being served a meal without wine. But she followed Creya out of the clearing, and the two of them picked their way through the undergrowth back the way they had come.

'If there's war, will my sons have to fight?'

'Probably,' said Helana. The king had the *Hymeriker*, his best warriors, and a separate standing force of paid soldiers, but every able-bodied young man of Erland trained one day a week with sword and bow, and would be expected to come forward if East Erland went to war with West. 'Why?'

Creya sighed slightly, her brow creased. 'It would be a shame, Princess. A damn shame.'

'Please just call me Helana, I hate it when you pretend we aren't friends.' Creya had taught her to hunt – to master bow, spear, and knife – and never asked for anything in return. She was a truer friend than any of Helana's peers, despite their difference in station and age.

Creya nodded. 'I love my boys, Helana. I want them here with me, not dead on some Eryi-forsaken field in West Erland.'

Helana gave a small, sad smile. Women like Creya should not lose their loved ones as she had lost her brother. Helana had felt the cruel sting of death ever since the day of her birth. Her mother had died labouring to bring her into the world, as had hundreds more in the short-lived rebellion that followed. How many more sons and brothers would die if the two halves of Erland went to war again? How many more families would weep?

But there was nothing she could do. She was the king's daughter, and yet powerless to stop a war that would tear her country apart. Her father could have reached out to the Prindians, but instead he hid in his tower solar, scheming with her uncle.

'I can't protect them,' she said.

'But there must be something? You could speak with the

king?' asked Creya. She sounded desperate, far from the woman who had wrestled a boar to the ground.

Helana had to stop herself laughing at the idea she would have any influence with her stubborn, distant father. That Creya had even mentioned him was a measure of how shaken she was. She found it unnerving; the huntswoman was steadfast, utterly unwavering.

Helana took her friend's hand. It would be too hard to explain her lack of influence with Hessian. 'I will see if there's anything I can do.'

Creya nodded. 'Thank you, Princess. And sorry for your brother. He was a good hunter.'

Helana traipsed back towards Piperskeep, shaking her head at the foolishness of the idea. Nothing would quench her father's fiery hatred of the Prindians, least of all his estranged daughter. She could try though, for Creya, and for all the others like her who loved their sons. Perhaps Jarhick's death might mend the schism between her and her father; her brother had loved them both.

She returned to her rooms, and undressed. She usually would have changed into riding garb, but instead chose a flowing black mourning dress that had once been her mother's. She had inherited the uncommon Sangreal height from her father, but it fitted her well.

One of the few things she knew of Lord Prindian was that he was unmarried. He was young, but still of an age when most lords were wed. Helana could understand his reluctance. She had refused every suitor to come to her door, and once lashed by her sharp tongue few returned to try again. One of the advantages of an absent father was her relative freedom for a noblewoman, and she would not give that up for any man.

She stepped from her bedroom into her antechamber. Her furnishings were simple: the wood chairs at her dining table were without cushions, and aside from a sheepskin rug by the fire the stone floor was uncovered. A small portrait of her mother hung above the fireplace. It was the only image Helana had of her. She had long straight dark hair, like Helana, big dark eyes and concave cheekbones. It was said by some that Helana looked just like her, but she barely saw it herself. Her mother had been beautiful, and after a sleepless night and hours tramping through the undergrowth Helana felt even less so than usual.

She was just preparing to ring the bell to summon her breakfast when there was a polite double knock at her door. Helana frowned. Nobody ever called on her this early.

She opened the door warily, and was met by Theodric's unassuming face looking up at her. Helana suppressed a sigh. Her father's close advisor was the last person she wanted to speak to. Theodric was a magus, one of the few who had survived the Imperium's purges, and had an uncanny ability of appearing right where he was, or was not, wanted. Helana had heard half-a-dozen stories of his origins, probably all put about by Theodric himself – 'Theodric was born in a barn a stone's throw from Piperskeep'; 'Theodric was born too soon after lightning struck a slave-ship'; 'Theodric came to Erland in shame after he sold out his fellows to the Imperium' – but these were never heard outside the keep. Most Erlanders were too afraid even to say his name, lest they accidentally summon him. 'Obey your father, or the king's wizard will get you,' the peasants told their children. In the flesh though, he was just a short man with more hair in his ears than on his scalp, wearing midnight-blue robes that were too big for him.

'Princess,' he said, keeping his hands hidden in the folds of his robes. 'I had the sudden urge to call on you this morning, and to my good fortune you are already awake.' He smiled, crinkling the crow's feet around his eyes. He looked around sixty or seventy years old, but it was rumoured the magi could live for hundreds of years and conceal their age with a glamour. 'I was so sorry to hear about your brother. He would have been a great king one day.'

Helana looked down at him. 'I was just about to have breakfast. Can it wait?' Theodric was her father's creature; was he here to report on her to him?

'I had hoped we might have breakfast together, and it seems I've timed it right. Don't worry; I brought my own.' He gestured behind him to three servants bearing trays overflowing with bread, cheese, bacon, and much more. Despite his small stature, Theodric ate like a horse.

Helana sighed. She could hardly refuse him now. 'If you must.' She held the door open to him.

The two of them sat down together. Theodric ate his enormous breakfast in the time it took Helana to eat her small one, and then immediately rang for more food. Finally, when he had sated his hunger and was leaning back contentedly in his chair with crumbs down the front of his robe, he spoke. 'What do you know about Rymond Prindian?'

Helana scoffed. 'You barge into my room with enough food for a small army, and it's to ask me about Rymond Prindian of all people?'

Theodric dabbed at his chin with a napkin. 'Our new heir,' he continued, as if he had not heard her. 'They say he is more at home in a tavern than dealing with matters of governance. If he were ever to inherit, it would be ill news for Erland. Your father may not be the force he was, but he cares for his people at least.'

Helana stared at him incredulously. Had Theodric seen the poverty in the city? Her father didn't care a damn about his people. 'What is it you want, Theodric?' she asked, losing patience. 'If it was to cover my table in crumbs and ask oblique questions you've undoubtedly succeeded.'

Theodric sighed. 'Very well. I had hoped we might build up to it, but I know you value directness. I want you to marry Rymond Prindian.'

Helana blinked at him, then threw back her head and laughed, as much to cover her shock as with genuine amusement. 'You'll be wanting a long time. I don't intend to marry anybody.'

'That rather depends on your father.'

'My father has never taken the slightest bit of interest in my marriage prospects, not that I'm complaining.'

'That was before Jarhick died.' Theodric took a sip of weak beer. 'Your father needs allies, and you stand as the most eligible maid in the kingdom. Sooner or later, his eye will fall on you, and he will marry you to the man of his choice, perhaps even to somebody outside of Erland.

'War is coming, Princess. When you've been around as long as I have you recognise the signs. War is in Erland's bones. I am offering you the chance to do your duty. If you marry Lord Prindian, it will bring the two families into an alliance. If your father cannot sire an heir, blessing this match would ensure his grandson takes the crown after Lord Prindian. You can solve the succession crisis at a stroke.'

'Have you even spoken to him about this?' Her father hated the Prindians with a passion close to madness. 'I am surprised you are still among the living.'

Theodric chuckled. 'Of course not; he would hate the idea.'

'One thing we have in common.'

'I had hoped we might persuade him together.'

Helana had to laugh at that. 'You know the influence I have with my father. If I suggested it was time for dinner he would starve himself. And that's if I wanted to marry Rymond Prindian, which I don't.'

'Not even for peace? Jarhick will not be the last man of Erland to die if we fight the Prindians. Think of the lives you would be saving. And if he becomes king, Prindian will need a strong wife. You could rule Erland.'

An image of Creya and her sons shimmered in Helana's

mind. But by Eryi, no. When Helana had told her she would do what she could, she had not had marriage in mind, and certainly not to Rymond Prindian. If only her sister Tarvana were still unmarried. 'The answer's no, Theodric. Leave me out of your scheming.'

Theodric's face fell. 'Very well,' he said, rising from his chair, covering a slight burp with his fist. 'Thank you for breakfast, in any case.'

He made to leave, but as he reached for the door he turned back to face her. 'I trust you understand what this means? If your father suggests a husband for you, which he will, I will not speak up for you. You will be wed, Helana, whether you like it or not, and likely to somebody far worse than Rymond Prindian.'

Helana resisted the urge to throw her plate at him. 'Just get out, Theodric.'

He left, and Helana slumped in her chair. She suddenly felt very tired. Her sleepless night was beginning to catch up with her. Had she done the right thing? Or was she very selfish, not to help Theodric avert war?

There was another knock at her door, slightly timid.

'Go away, Theodric.'

He knocked again. Helana got to her feet and marched to the door, angry now, ready to give the magus the tongue-lashing she ought to have given him earlier. She flung her door open, and was startled to see her cousin Orsian standing there, his fist raised to the door and ready to knock again.

'Orsian! Why are you sneaking around outside my door barely after dawn?'

A blush rose on Orsian's cheeks. He opened his mouth to say something, then closed it again, seemingly tongue-tied.

'Did some nymph steal your tongue? What is it, Orsian? Don't make me stand here all day.' They had played together as children, but since Orsian had entered the strange years between boyhood and manhood, moments like this had become all too frequent. She knew that he had developed something of a fancy for her, which would have been awkward even without him holding onto his childlike stockiness; until a year ago she had been as much as half a foot taller than him.

That had changed now though. Helana looked at him again. Orsian was fourteen, and finally growing into his body. He was still stocky, but his once chubby cheeks had receded to a handsome jawline, his torso was now thick with muscle, and he was of a height with her. There was a silhouette of a beard on his face, and it was Helana's turn to blush as she realised she was staring. Her cousin was dressed for riding, and wore a sword at his hip which she did not recall being there the last time she had seen him.

Orsian finally seemed to come to his senses. 'I'm riding to Cliffark, with my father,' he said with a grin. 'Thought I'd come and say goodbye.' His smile fell as he noticed Helana's black dress. 'I am sorry, Helana. I did not know Prince Jarhick, but my father's men always spoke well of him. They all grieve his passing, as do I.'

It might have been the first sincere condolences Helana had heard. Even Theodric's words had been tinged with empty courtesy, but there was something reassuring about Orsian's earnestness. On a whim, she leant forward and kissed him on the cheek. There was a pleasant scratch of black stubble where once there had been only fuzz. 'Thank you. I pray that my brother is with Eryi now.' His face turned to fire where she kissed him. 'How long will you be gone?'

'Some weeks, I expect. It's a hard ride, and Lord Istlewick may prove a tough negotiator.'

Helana doubted that Lord Istlewick was brave enough to refuse her father anything, even his daughter. 'I'll come out to the yard and see you off,' she decided. Anything to take her mind off Theodric.

They spoke in quiet voices as they walked, linking their arms and leaning in conspiratorially, like they had as children, all awkwardness between them seemingly forgotten. 'You've grown since I last saw you,' said Helana. 'You'll be as tall as Errian soon.'

Orsian scowled. 'I am nothing like my brother. I take after Father.' He spoke a little too forcefully, momentarily reminding Helana of a sulky child. He winced. 'Sorry, I saw him a few days ago. We quarrelled.'

Helana patted his arm forgivingly. The distance between her and her sister ran deep – Tarvana was five years her senior, with two children, married to the odious Lord Balyard, and never shy to berate Helana for spurning every suitor – but she knew that differences between sisters did not run as deep as the rivalry of brothers growing up in the shadow of a famous father.

The main yard was a hive of activity. Grooms ran to and fro, as Lord Andrick's men packed their belongings into saddlebags, while their mounted fellows shouted coarse insults at them for their perceived slowness. They looked to be almost ready to leave.

Helana searched the yard, and eventually saw her uncle standing a few paces apart from the towering figure of Strovac Sigac. The two men were staring at one another, set in stances that suggested a disagreement. They were speaking, but she could not hear them over the noise of the yard.

Seeing them too, Orsian frowned. 'I should see to my father.' He hurried towards them, and Helana followed.

Strovac Sigac wore a broad grin. 'So, while I ride off to war, you are sent to fetch the new royal broodmare. Does the king no longer trust you with men's work, or have you turned coward?' He towered over Lord Andrick, and every other man in the yard. He lowered his voice, but Helana caught every word. 'Perhaps he is worried about your loyalty. Your mother was a Thrumb, wasn't she?'

Helana stared at him. He might be a giant, but the man was not right in the head to speak to her uncle like that. Andrick never spoke of his mother.

Andrick looked up at him levelly. 'Your talent for savagery requires sterner tests than the servants of Fenhold. Or perhaps the king has tired of the absurd tales you spread of your own parentage. Do you honestly think anyone believes that Hessian could be your father?'

It was a rumour Helana had heard before, though only in whispers. Strovac's reaction was immediate. His sword was half out of his scabbard when Andrick's knife reached his neck. Helana gasped. Even when they were on the same side, men could not resist quarrelling, but this was taking it too far. A tight anger rose in her chest; fighting in the yard was a poor tribute to her brother's memory.

'I dare you, boy.' Andrick held his knife hand steady against Strovac's throat. 'Nothing would please me more.'

Strovac's eyes bulged with rage. Helana suddenly saw one of Strovac's men rushing towards Andrick's back with his sword drawn. Orsian shouted a warning, and Andrick twisted backwards, slashing his knife across the man's neck. The attacker fell, spraying blood, and Strovac Sigac whirled away from Andrick, drawing his sword.

'Stop!' Helana threw herself between them, her face hot with fury. 'I am of the Blood, and I command you to stop!'

Andrick pulled up short, just feet away from Helana, and dropped to one knee. 'Forgive me, Princess.' His eyes remained fixed on Strovac Sigac.

Strovac did not kneel. His blade rested menacingly in his right hand and he smiled and bowed elaborately. 'Yes, forgive me also, Princess.'

Helana marched up to him, and though the warrior over-topped her by nearly a foot she was furious enough to ignore the naked steel in his hand. 'Is this how you honour my brother's memory?' she demanded, her voice rising. It flowed out of her in a torrent: her pent-up grief for Jarhick, her frustration that she had not killed the boar herself, her anger at Theodric and her father. 'By trying to kill his family in my father's house?' She turned on Andrick. 'And you, Uncle! Have you forgotten whom you serve?'

Andrick stood. 'I never forget, Princess.' He looked at the other man contemptuously. 'If only Strovac Sigac had your spirit.'

A groom leading a horse approached them nervously, and Andrick sheathed his sword and pulled himself up into the saddle. He turned his horse around and rode for the gate, while Orsian and two dozen other men spurred their mounts to give chase. Orsian looked back longingly towards Helana, raising a hand in apology and farewell.

Helana stared after him. If men who were supposedly on the same side could not stop themselves crossing swords within the grounds of Piperskeep then there was no hope of peace. She strode back inside, fighting the urge to weep.

CHAPTER 6

Pherri sat in her parents' antechamber, on a chair that was still slightly too high for her, kicking her legs while her mother busied herself with their tea, content to prepare it herself rather than trouble a servant. To distract herself, Pherri studied the ornate sword mounted on the wall which had been a gift from King Hessian. When she was younger, Pherri had been fascinated by it, though she had never dared to ask her father about it. She had interrogated Da'ri about it instead, who when pressed on its value told her, 'Enough to feed a small country for a year, or ransom your father.'

Pherri had corrected Da'ri on this. Her father was the world's greatest fighter; he could never be imprisoned. If he were, he would just fight his way out again. One of her brothers maybe, but they were not worth as much, so they might need to make a smaller sword. Da'ri had laughed long and hard at this, as had her family when he had recounted the story to them.

She would usually have been taking lessons with him, but her mother had summoned her, and Da'ri had been excused. He had seemed troubled ever since the news of the prince's murder by the Thrumb; he said the dark looks that the guards and

servants gave him made him fear for his life. Despite her own
concerns, Pherri had tried to assure him that no harm would
come to him; they were her father's men, and her father bore no
ill will towards Da'ri.

'Why am I here?' asked Pherri when her mother had finally
served the tea. She was impatient to return to her studies, and
her mother seemed to have summoned her just to sit in silence
and drink tea.

'It is time to talk about your future,' said her mother, sipping
carefully at her hot tea. 'Da'ri is a good man, and we have
indulged your interest in topics that would not ordinarily be
taught to girls. However, you cannot stay a child forever. We are
nearing a time when you must learn other things, like sewing,
and household management. I would do you no favours by
neglecting these.'

'I don't want to learn any of that. Da'ri is teaching me horticulture, and navigation.' Both topics fascinated her, especially
the methods that sailors used to find their way by the stars.

Her mother pursed her lips, and Pherri realised she had
said the wrong thing. 'I have no patience for needlework
either, as these graceless tapestries demonstrate.' Her mother
gestured towards a simple pattern that hung behind her.
'However, one day you may have your own household to
manage, and while I lean heavily on the servants to repair
your father and brothers' clothes, sewing and darning are
essential skills for any woman. I wish to prepare you for the
life you will have, not the life of a gardener or a smuggler.
Those skills would not be useful to me in running this
household.'

'I don't care about any of that,' said Pherri with a dismissive
flap of her hand, narrowly missing knocking over her tea. 'If you
want me to learn other things, maybe you could get somebody
to assist Da'ri? Like somebody from the Imperium.' Da'ri had
extensive knowledge of the Imperium, but he had never been

there. 'I'd like to learn about another people, one that isn't us or the Thrumb.'

Her mother pursed her lips again and furrowed her brow, like she was holding back from saying something. Pherri could tell her mother was displeased, but did not understand why. Why couldn't she just speak straightforwardly?

But when she spoke, her mother's tone was gentle. 'Pherri, if you could spend all of your days reading and learning, nothing would make me happier.' She paused for a moment, as if searching for the words that would make Pherri understand. 'But that's not a life anybody gets. You have duties to your family, to me and your father. Someday, you will be married, and your life will not be dissimilar to mine. As your mother, that is the life I must prepare you for.'

'Cousin Helana isn't married. She hunts and hawks and goes to bed when she wants.'

'Helana is not my daughter, and she did not have the benefit of a mother when she was growing up, to the sadness of us all. Next time you see Helana, tell me if you think she's happy.'

Pherri sipped her tea thoughtfully. 'Maybe cousin Helana would know how to be happy if she'd had her mother there to teach her. Maybe mothers are there to teach their children to be happy, not how to live as they are supposed to.'

'Maybe those are the same thing.'

Pherri opened her mouth to disagree, but her mother shushed her with a finger to her lips. She sighed, and reached out to stroke Pherri's straw-coloured hair. 'My clever daughter,' she murmured. 'I can let you stay a child for a little longer, but war is coming, and war has a way of making children grow up.'

Pherri was still pondering this when the antechamber's door suddenly sprang open. Pherri and Viratia looked up, and there in the doorway stood Errian.

He had grown a beard, Pherri noticed. Errian was nearly a decade older than her, and the two of them had never been close. He always looked at her like he might look at a tapestry; something that was simply *there*, but devoid of any actual purpose.

'Errian!' Viratia stood to embrace him, and Errian bent down to kiss her on the cheek. 'It is so good to see you well. We heard terrible things coming down from Eryispek.'

'Never mind that,' he said fiercely. There were deep bags under his eyes, and tired lines around his cheeks. 'Jarhick is dead. The Thrumb killed him.'

'I know.' Their mother embraced him again. 'I'm so glad you're safe. Come and sit down.'

Pherri was sure she would not be allowed to stay now Errian was here. She was not supposed to know about what had gone on on Eryispek.

'I can't stay long,' he said. 'We only came here to resupply before we ride west.'

Viratia looked at him carefully. 'West? You don't mean to—'

'Father has commanded it. He's sending me to Thrumb, where I should have been all along.'

Pherri knew that Errian was lying almost before the words left his mouth, but her mother did not appear to have noticed. 'Will you at least stay the night?' she asked. 'We are going to Lordsferry tomorrow, for the fair. You and your men can buy supplies there.'

Errian thought on it. 'My men are tired,' he said slowly. 'It might do them well to spend a night here.'

Viratia beamed. 'Good. Now join me for tea.' She gestured for him to sit down. 'Pherri, you can run off and play for a bit. We will discuss this again another time.'

'But—'

'Now.'

How had her mother accepted Errian's obvious lie so easily? Pherri had never been able to get anything past her. She left reluctantly, partly glad to be excused from her mother's views on Pherri's education and partly irritated to have been usurped by Errian. Her brother had not even bothered to acknowledge her.

She thought about going to find Da'ri, but she was curious about Errian's adventure on Eryispek, and the rebel Gelick Whitedoe. The Mountain was not so far, but the tribes who lived there were isolated, and hostile to outsiders. Pherri rushed back to the open window above the storage outhouse where she had listened before, startling several servants as she hurtled past.

She positioned herself against the wall and listened.

'I don't care,' Errian was saying. 'They must die. For Jarhick.'

Errian's voice sounded strange. Pherri risked a peek, and was shocked to realise tears were rolling down her brother's cheeks. Errian did not cry; he only raged, and argued with Orsian. It was like seeing a dog walking on its front legs.

Their mother was holding his hand, trying to comfort him. 'We all grieve for the prince. Perhaps you should wait here for a few days, though? Your father would not want you to do anything rash.'

'It can't wait.' Pherri realised he was speaking of avenging the prince. She was struck by her mother's patience towards him, as though Errian were still a child and seeking forgiveness for breaking something of Orsian's. 'Jarhick was my cousin, my brother, and he died hundreds of miles away, surrounded by his enemies. I was meant to be there with him! Even if they burn him in Merivale, how will his soul ever find its way to Eryispek above the clouds?'

'Avenging Jarhick will not bring him back. Is one death in our family at their hands not enough? If your father has commanded you to go I will have to accept it, but I forbid you to take any stupid risks. Now, what of Eryispek and the Lutums? Did you go to Basseton?'

'We did. The whole town was burnt to ashes.' His face took on a distant expression, as if recalling something troubling. 'I will spare you the details.'

'And the Lutums?'

'Gone,' Errian said simply. 'We rode all the way to Redfort, and saw neither hair nor hide of them. Was as if they'd disappeared into thin air. We went no further after that; we weren't equipped to follow them up into snow, if it's up Eryispek they've gone.'

That did not sound right to Pherri; she swore she had read somewhere that the Lutums barely went up into Eryispek's higher reaches, only for ceremonies and rituals. She heard no lie in Errian's tale though, so he must have believed it. Why had they attacked Basseton only to flee up Eryispek afterwards?

'Basseton will need to be repaired and resettled with a proper garrison,' said her mother, 'but I'm sure your father will see to that. Were there any survivors?'

'We found one cowering in the ruins of the keep. She's old and ugly and a bit odd, but I was hoping you could make use of her. Delara, her name is. Says she was a senior servant to the lord there.' His voice dropped to a growl, so Pherri had to strain her ears to hear it. 'She scares my men half to death, always mumbling to herself. They think she's a witch.'

Viratia barked a laugh. 'Why is it that when you put an ugly old woman in front of men they swear blind she's a witch? Where are all the young and beautiful witches? That poor woman, of course she will stay here. Our steward Tammas is not as young as he was, and with your father having taken most of the garrison with him we could do with the help. She might be a good tutor for Pherri.'

Pherri almost shouted out in protest, before remembering she was hiding at a window. Her mother was speaking as if she meant to replace Da'ri immediately! Not worrying whether they heard her, Pherri raced down from her hiding place and towards Da'ri's room, running all the way there as fast as her little legs would carry her. She knocked once but then pushed her way in without waiting for a response.

Pherri stared around the room. It was almost bare. All his decorations and curiosities were gone. Pherri was about to burst into tears when Da'ri stood up from behind his bed.

'Pherri! What are you doing here?'

Tears welled in her eyes. Orsian had gone, and now Da'ri was leaving too. Everything was changing. 'Where are all your things? Are you leaving?'

His glum expression confirmed her worst fears. This was why her mother had taken her for the day, so Da'ri could pack. He sat down on his bed, looking every inch his age. He gestured for her to join him, and Pherri leapt up and threw her arms around his neck.

'You can't go. I'll get my mother to order you to stay.'

'I must, Pherri. Every day I stay puts me, and you, in more danger. The servants look at me as if they are readying to stab me in my sleep, and while your father's men are sworn to protect me, the looks they give me say otherwise. I discussed it with your mother, and we both agreed it would be best if I left.'

'But why?' Pherri's lip trembled. 'You didn't kill the prince.'

'To them it is as if I did. I am guilty by my existence. I have the nerve to live and work among them, when I should be in Thrumbalto, waiting to be conquered and slaughtered. I can die here, or I can die there, among my countrymen. And I am ready to go home, Pherri. I do not know what has driven my people to trouble Erland after all this time, but I know it has been too long since I sat on a high walkway drinking sweet cider with my feet hanging over the edge, or watched the sunset over the forest from atop the Irmintree. There is a word in our language, without a direct translation: *ealagny* – a longing so deep that the pain in your heart wakes you in the night. I never thought to know it myself, and yet...' With his thumb, Da'ri wiped a tear from Pherri's cheek. 'If this is the end for my people, I wish to see it with my own eyes.'

Pherri was silent for a moment. Since Orsian had left, Da'ri was her only friend, not counting her mother. Without him there would be nobody left to teach her, and she was already eleven, with endless things still to learn. There was so much she ought to have asked him about the Thrumb. 'You'll be killed. Stay here and live.'

Da'ri laughed. 'I will be sixty-five next summer. A good age. I cannot know how many more years I have, but I would live every one of them in guilt if I stayed here protected by your father while my brothers died.' He stood awkwardly, wincing at the pain in his old knees. 'Pherri, teaching you has been one of the great privileges of my life. I do not think your parents truly understood what you are when they invited me here. You are the most gifted child I have ever met, without a doubt. Erland is a country driven by bloodlust, and divided by revenge. I pray that, in time, gentler, wiser souls might prevail. Souls like yours. Give yourself to Erland. It is the greatest gift you have to offer them. Perhaps more than they deserve.'

Pherri felt fresh tears welling in her eyes. Nobody else she knew spoke like that. 'Will you at least come to Lordsferry tomorrow? You could buy supplies for your journey there.'

Da'ri smiled. 'I suppose I can.' He looked down at Pherri's dress, now coated in a layer of dirt from crawling around outside her mother's window. 'Were you spying on your brother? I heard he'd returned.'

Pherri swallowed, knowing she was about to confirm what Da'ri feared. 'He means to ride for Thrumb tomorrow, to avenge Prince Jarhick.'

Da'ri shut his eyes, and flashed a brief, sad smile. 'All the more reason I must go. And what of your brother's offensive against the Lutums?'

'He said they'd gone,' Pherri told him. 'Up into the snows of

Eryispek. Odd, isn't it? You told me that they always keep to the lower parts.'

To Pherri's surprise, Da'ri appeared more troubled by this than by the news that Errian was riding west. His face seemed to turn to ash, his brows pinched in calculation, and Pherri noted that one of his hands trembled slightly. 'Most odd.' He turned away from her suddenly, towards his desk. 'I have to write a letter. I will see you tomorrow. No more spying.'

'But—'

'Please, Pherri!' He was already hunched over a blank piece of parchment.

Shocked and a little scared by his tone, she retreated quickly, and exited his room as quietly as she could, closing the door behind her with the care of a thief leaving the scene of a crime.

He had never raised his voice to her before, and it left Pherri even more confused. Just what was going on with the Lutums, and what about it had scared Da'ri so?

<hr>

The next day, what seemed like half the household journeyed to Lordsferry. It was the river town's summer fair, and nobody wanted to miss it. Sleep the night before had been a challenge for Pherri, beset again by the same dark dreams, but she had risen early and eager. The dreams were becoming clearer now; she remembered a great bear bellowing at a spear in its chest, and a doe with sharp blue eyes that seemed to look straight through her, and a scared boy with a shadow riding upon his shoulder. For a moment she shivered at the vague memory of it.

Her mother rode at the head of the column, but Pherri kept further back with Da'ri. He had worn a wide-brimmed hat to protect himself from the sun, and to hide the tell-tale plaits that marked him as a Thumb. He gave no sign of the previous day's temper, laughing and joking with Pherri good-spiritedly as they rode towards Lordsferry.

There was a queue of people at the gate to Lordsferry, but recognising Viratia the gate guards bowed and allowed them straight through. Pherri's parents maintained a house in the town with a few servants, and it was to there they rode and tied up their horses.

'I need to run some errands of my own,' Pherri's mother told her, as she handed her reins to a stableboy. 'Can you explore the fair by yourself for a few hours with Da'ri? You'll have guards.'

Pherri agreed eagerly. She had never been allowed to enjoy the fair without someone from her family there. The guards would stay at a safe distance, and she would be able to enjoy her last few hours with Da'ri. After sleeping on it, Pherri thought she understood his reasons for leaving, though it was still all she could do not to beg and plead with him to stay.

Lordsferry was a riot of noise and colour. Tightly packed stalls sold all the goods Pherri could have imagined: wool coats dyed all the colours of a rainbow; plump piglets squealing their way around a pen; wooden chessmen with features so finely carved they seemed to look at you from their miniature eyes; tiny bowls of sweet-smelling spices; smouldering meat with smoke that made Pherri's eyes water. Da'ri bought them each a pie, so rich and tasty that Pherri could not wait for it to cool down, and did not care when it burnt her mouth.

The inns were doing a roaring trade as well, Pherri noticed, with men and women spreading out into the street for lack of space inside. She was too young to go in, but she thought she saw Errian dipping into one with some of his men. She frowned; she had thought he would have wanted to be on his way as soon as possible, but obviously a day at the fair had been too tempting for him.

There was a noisy crowd outside one of the inns, packed in a circle around something Pherri could not see. She ran over to it, too thrilled by the atmosphere of the fair to heed Da'ri's calls to wait.

Peeking between the people in front of her, Pherri glimpsed two angry clouds of feathers squawking wildly as they flew at each other. The crowd cheered. Pherri felt a little sick.

She felt Da'ri's hand on her shoulder. 'Cockfighting,' he said with distaste. 'Come on, before your mother sees you, and don't run off like that.'

They turned away, but a group had formed behind them, crowding in to watch the fight. As they tried to pass, Da'ri clipped the shoulder of one of the men, sending him stumbling backwards.

'Fucking watch it!' said the man, staggering, barely keeping his feet. His eyes were bloodshot, and he smelt sour.

'Apologies, friend,' said Da'ri, stepping aside to walk past the man.

The man moved to block their path. 'You will be,' he said with a hiccough. He pointed to his mud-stained breeches. 'You'll have to pay for these.'

Looking at the state of his breeches, Pherri had to assume they had already been that way. She realised the man was drunk. One of his companions held an open liquor bottle in his fist. She looked around anxiously for the two guards who had been shadowing them, but could not see past the press of people. The crowd towered over her, a wall of stomachs and chests blocking their escape.

'Here.' Da'ri reached for his purse. Pherri knew he would do anything to avoid conflict, but as he reached down the man flicked Da'ri's hat off, revealing his six plaits.

One of the man's companions gasped. 'He's one of them Thrumb! One of them who killed the prince!'

Da'ri held up his hands placatingly. 'I don't want any trouble.' Several more people had turned to look, and Pherri realised they were penned in on all sides, with at least a dozen men all looking murderously at Da'ri. He took a step back, and walked straight into a man behind him, who pushed him forward again.

'Leave him alone!' said Pherri, finding her voice, despite her terror. 'I am Lord Andrick's daughter, and I command you to leave us alone!'

The first man squinted down at her, then looked back at Da'ri. Pherri's words had barely seemed to register with him. 'What're you doing with a girl, Thrumb?'

There were shouts of assent from the crowd. 'Go home, Thrumb!' 'Murdering savage bastard!'

'They sacrifice them to their gods and drink their blood,' said the man who had pushed Da'ri from behind. 'Get away from her, Thrumb.' He pushed Da'ri again, hard. Da'ri sprawled into another man, who punched him hard in the gut with a sickening thump. He groaned, doubling over and collapsing to his knees. Another man followed up with a vicious kick that cracked against Da'ri's ribs. He fell to the ground with a cry, breathing heavily, the colour draining from his face.

Pherri screamed. Where had the guards gone? She looked around frantically, but the crowd was so tight now she could barely see through them. Most people had turned away from the cockfight now, and were instead eyeing Da'ri with interest. None of them moved to help him up.

To Pherri's relief, she saw Errian, several inches taller than most of the crowd. 'Errian,' she called, waving to him. 'Help!'

Errian looked at her indifferently. He said something to a companion, then used his bulk to force his way through the crowd towards her. Several men glared at him, but seeing his size and the sword at his waist they did not block his path.

The crowd was baying for blood now, the two cocks completely forgotten. Another man ran towards Da'ri with a knife, but Errian pushed him back. The man ran in again, and Errian punched him hard in the mouth, spraying blood and teeth everywhere.

On the ground, Da'ri groaned and rolled onto his back. Errian looked down at him, blinked, and drew his sword, raising a hand for silence. Pherri had never been so relieved to see him. He was acting just as their father would have.

'Men of Erland.' He scooped Pherri up one-handed, and put her over his shoulder. 'I knew Prince Jarhick as well as any man alive. The grief I have for him is like a wound that will never heal. I, Errian Andrickson, ride now to avenge him, and I swear that I will not leave a single Thrumb alive.'

There were cheers from the crowd. Pherri's blood ran cold with dread. She struggled helplessly against Errian's firm grip.

Errian looked down at Da'ri, his handsome face frozen in hate. Da'ri was curled up on the ground, gasping and clutching his ribs. 'This Thrumb was in my family's service. Until this morning. Now he is just a Thrumb, and his presence in Erland is a stain upon our country. Do what you will with him.'

The crowd closed in. Some of the men carried knives and broken bottles. Pherri screamed again, and Errian clapped a hand over her mouth. He carried her away, ignoring the awful shrieks as the town of Lordsferry tore Da'ri apart.

CHAPTER 7

Orsian had predicted they would reach their destination within a fortnight, but dense rain and biting wind slowed them across East Erland's moors and marshes. It was not until weeks after their departure that they reached Lord Istlewick's seat overlooking the shoreside city of Cliffark.

A few hours after they rose out of the grim lowland marshes, in the late evening, they climbed the final hill before the sea. The city came into view in the coastal vale below, spreading out before them like a birthmark over the tranquil water. Tired as he was, and though driven to ride on only by the dream of a feather bed and a well-tended fire, the view was enough to make Orsian stop and stare. In the bay, the lamps of at least a hundred ships blazed, their reflections dancing in the black water, and in the town itself a thousand more lights flickered in the twilight. A faint but firm sea wind swept up the hill, and with it Orsian caught the scent of salt and aroma of ale, and the imagined calls and clamours of sailors squeezing all the life they could from a single night of shore leave. Merivale was barely a village next to this.

'You can discover Cliffark another time,' growled his father, as if reading his mind. 'Maybe tomorrow, if I do not require you.'

Orsian grimaced. He had told him of his encounter with Errian, and while Naeem had agreed it was not wholly Orsian's fault, his father had made no secret of his disappointment. He had sent two men back west to intercept Errian before he did anything rash, but they had received no word in response. Being kept close at hand rather than being allowed to explore the city was evidently his punishment.

Andrick gestured to the bluff overlooking the city and a towering keep at the end of a precipitous causeway. 'Let's see what sort of welcome Lord Istlewick has for us. Word of our coming should have reached him by now.'

They rode on towards the lonely light of Cliffark Tower.

Cliffark's playhouse was high and flat-roofed, with a single large window overhead opening it to the daylight, and two circular galleries overlooking the yard in front of the stage. It was the final performance of the month's play – *The kzar's Folly*, a farce detailing some long-dead ruler of the Imperium's attempt to restore magi supremacy – and the pit was nearly full: bowlegged sailors and swaggering apprentice boys, washerwomen with the afternoon off and loud-laughing barrow-girls unable to get the fish smell out of their clothes. It was the interval, and a discordant babble of chatter bounced off every wall, completing the sense of eager anticipation, as serving boys bearing foaming mugs of ale buzzed like flies from patron to patron.

Among the crowd, Tansa prowled soft-footed as a cat, keeping herself to the shadows and casting curious glances up to the two galleries. Across the yard, her brother Tam was doing the same, while their companion Cag lounged against a pillar, a head taller than anyone else.

'What do you think?' Tansa asked them both, once she and Tam had completed their round and reconvened around the back of Cag's pillar, hidden from view but close enough that he could hear them.

Tam gave a broad, gap-toothed smile. 'Only two in the upper circle,' he said eagerly, 'some woman and a girl who might be her daughter.'

It was a disappointing turnout, Tansa reflected, glancing up again to the lower circle. The day before there had been a whole cadre of richly garbed merchants with fingers dripping in golden rings; the pickings on the soldiers there now would be scant in comparison. As for the upper circle, the woman looked to have barely a bauble on her. 'I can't even see a purse,' she said. 'We'd do better robbing those soldiers in the lower circle.'

Tam shook his head vigorously. 'Didn't you see the red mark on their armour? That's the *Hymeriker*. They're worse than the Imperial guards.'

'I know they're *hymerikai*,' Tansa replied, trying to keep the annoyance out of her voice. The king's warriors were hardly ever seen in Cliffark, but she recognised them well enough. It was not like Tam to act as the voice of reason; usually it was her talking him out of taking risks. 'I know even you're not mad enough to rob from the Imperials, but the *Hymeriker* don't know the city, and all that mail will slow them down. I can see their purses hanging from their belts bold as brass. They must be heavy if they're planning to keep drinking like they are.'

Cag spoke from the other side of the pillar, a little too loudly, as ever. 'Think of how famous we'll be if we rob from the king's own soldiers; we'd never go thirsty in Pauper's again!'

'They might have swords though,' Tam added doubtfully.

'No weapons in the playhouse. You know that.' Tansa

touched at the slender knife hidden inside her shirt to check it was still there.

'Still, I don't know, seems risky.'

'What has got into you?' Tansa asked, letting her frustration show a little. 'I once saw you try and steal from the reeve himself with half his men around, and now you're pissing yourself because of a few inlanders with red paint on their armour.' Tansa looked up again at the girl in the upper circle, and realised her mistake. Her face broke into a knowing smile. 'Oh, I see. Pretty thing, isn't she? You just want to get a closer look.'

At sixteen, Tam was a year younger than Tansa, and there was nobody she would rather have thieved with. He had the quickest hands of anyone she had ever seen, and cleverness to spare, when he was not being distracted by pretty, rich strangers. They had lived their whole lives in Cliffark, scraping out survival on little more than their wits, always on the lookout for a mark with a heavy purse in their pocket, or perhaps a hefty chest of valuables back in their boarding room.

Cag had joined them two years ago. The younger boy had come in on a travelling circus ship, as an improbably large twelve-year-old who fought a bear cub with his bare hands and had the cuts and bruises to prove it. Tam had freed him, and since then the two of them had been inseparable. When the circus had returned to Cliffark earlier in the summer, the ringmaster had no trouble spotting Cag, now well over six foot. He had received a broken arm and some missing teeth for his attempt to recapture him. The close friendship between her brother and Cag sometimes made Tansa feel the odd one out, but she was under no illusions about her role in the trio: without her picking their marks and poking holes in Tam's schemes the other two would have caught the hangman's noose long ago.

'So what if she's pretty?' asked Tam. 'She's not in the upper circle because she's pretty, she's there because she's rich.'

'We never even discussed robbing the upper! You want to

change the plan at the last moment for the sake of a pretty face. It's bloody typical of you.'

'Couldn't we just rob them both?' asked Cag. 'You can take the girl, Tam, and Tansa can take the soldiers.'

'Yes!' exclaimed Tam, reaching around the pillar to slap his friend on the shoulder. 'It's brilliant! It's that sort of thinking that makes us the best thieves in the city.'

Tansa rolled her eyes violently. 'If we're the best thieves in the city, why do we sleep on a rooftop and go to bed hungry? A good thief wouldn't waste all his money on tavern girls.' She ran her hand through her cropped brown hair. 'Fine. But don't think I'm breaking you out of jail if you get caught.' She looked up at the stage. 'We need to move; they'll be starting the third act soon.'

Tansa waved Tam off as he headed towards the servants' stairs at the rear that would lead him to the upper circle, gave Cag a pat on the shoulder, and made her way towards the very back of the yard where the crowd was thinner, to another pillar shrouded in the shadow of the lower circle.

It had taken several visits to the playhouse for them to be sure of the timings, but when the play reached its climax, where the kzar and his followers went forth into the night to attempt their coup and found their enemies from the Senate waiting for them, the whole playhouse would be plunged into darkness by a vast cloth shroud being pulled across its one great window. Once Cag had incapacitated the boy on the roof whose job it was to pull the cloth back again, while the audience were focused upon the shadowy events on the stage, Tam and Tansa would have ample opportunity to relieve some of the wealthier audience members of their purses without being seen.

Simple, in Tansa's head. That there were several soldiers added a layer of complexity – and in truth she was a little old to be cutting purses – but at least she would likely be able to rely on the citizens of Cliffark to help her escape. The city had hated the *Hymeriker* since Tansa was a babe, since they had quashed Portes Stormcaller's uprising.

Tansa looked up at the wooden pillar supporting the lower circle. It was straight and smooth, barely thicker than a man's torso. There was a slight gap at the top between the wall and the gallery, just large enough for her to squeeze through. Most folk would never have thought of scaling it and slipping through the gap, but Tansa was rail-thin and had been climbing across the rooves of Cliffark ever since she was small. She was not so strong a climber as Tam – she swore sometimes her brother was half spider – but strong enough.

When the kzar began a rousing speech to his followers, Tansa began to climb. She moved hand over hand, gripping the pillar either side while walking up it on the balls of her feet. It creaked slightly, but nobody turned to look; the whole audience was engrossed in Kzar Mizstel's final speech before his doom, delivered by a portly trouper with a booming voice and a black moustache so long and oiled that it shone like polished steel.

'*My dear friends... In all the history of our divine empire, has there ever been a nobler assembly of men? At the dawn of our millennium, let this be the night we prove ourselves the heirs to our ancient brethren, those brave seers who...*'

Tansa rolled her eyes. The same lines delivered the same way, with every syllable accented just as it had been the day before. She could have been an actor, she thought, but somehow her trade seemed more honest than turning out the same tired story every day and charging people for the privilege of attending. Though to credit the man, the whole audience was watching with bated breath, and when he took his long, dramatic pauses you could have heard the drop of a pin.

Tansa squeezed between the stone wall and wooden gallery, and dragged herself up over the rail, landing soft-footed in a crouch behind the crowd. It was not so busy up here, and among the colourful citizens of Cliffark she could see a clear path to the six soldiers in mail and leather, leaning against the rail with mugs of ale in their hands, the coin pouches attached to their belts beckoning to her enticingly.

'*And so to arms, to arms! Let courage be your shield, and magic be your sword! Today the Senate, and tomorrow the Imperium!*'

That was the cue for the shroud to be pulled across the window, and as darkness was dragged across the playhouse the whole audience looked up in surprise, before their eyes were drawn back to the stage by a shout from a trouper as Mizstel's men stepped from their meeting and straight into the waiting mob.

Tansa was already moving. As the curtain fell into place, and the senators' knives began to rise and fall, glinting silver in the half-light of a candle hidden behind the stage curtain, Tansa drew her own slim blade across a soldier's purse string and let the satisfying weight of the man's pouch drop into her hand. The actors screamed in terror, while the crowd whooped and hollered to see the avaricious Mizstel receive his comeuppance.

The warriors never even realised she was there. Her other hand was already moving, slicing through the next string as she shoved the first purse into the deepest pocket of her jerkin, keeping her hand on it just long enough to muffle the clinking of coins.

She was on the fourth of the six purses when the great cloak was whipped off the window, casting Mizstel's corpse and the rapt audience in warm daylight, and revealing to the soldiers a skinny girl in threadbare clothes relieving them of their coin.

With a cry that was equal parts surprise and fury, the fourth warrior grasped for her, and caught nothing but air. Tansa let the man's purse fall through her fingers, and it landed with a clatter, sending coins rolling across the gallery and plummeting into the yard below. She dodged two more of the men and vaulted onto the rail, leaping for the upper circle as a warrior's fingertips brushed against the hem of her trousers.

Tansa landed with her arms over the upper rail and pulled herself up, silently praising Eryi for blessing her with fast feet and quick wits. Below, she could hear the soldiers shouting, and the Cliffarkers' indignant cries as they were shoved out of the way by them barrelling towards the stairs leading to the upper circle.

Damn you, Cag. What could have gone wrong? She looked around, and found Tam, for some reason heaving the woman into a chair while the pretty girl watched with wide eyes. She had taken them for mother and daughter at a distance, but by the quality of their clothes the woman was the girl's maid, a square-shouldered homely woman who her brother was having difficulty holding up.

'What did you do to her?' Tansa demanded, rushing towards them. She could hear heavy boots on the stairs.

'She fainted!' cried Tam, easing her down.

'Does the door lock? There must be a key!' Any moment the men she had stolen from would burst through that door and beat her and Tam bloody.

'Move out of the way.' The girl pushed her aside, and reached up to a shelf by the door to grasp a long brass key which she shoved into the lock. It clicked, and barely a moment later the door shook on its hinges as the first of Tansa's pursuers cannoned shoulder-first into the heavy wood. Somehow it held.

'What in Eryi's name did you do?' the girl demanded, turning on them, her face filled with fury. 'Give me one good reason why I shouldn't unlock that door and turn you over to them.' Her heart-shaped face was porcelain pale, with plump lips pouting in noble indignation, and her chestnut hair rested upon slender shoulders in a clumsy mass of curls. 'Don't just stare, say something!' From behind her came the pounding of heavy fists upon the door and angry demands for admission.

Tansa could see why Tam had been desperate to come up to the upper circle; the girl was pretty beyond words, a fairytale come to life. Tam gaped at her hopelessly, before he finally managed to get his mouth working. 'Er,' he began. He ran a hand through his hair. 'Well, my sister sort of robbed them. And I was sort of trying to rob you.' He smiled sheepishly.

She stared at them in disbelief. 'You stole from the king's warriors? Are you mad?'

The hammering of fists on the door was like rolling thunder. The wooden frame around the lock was beginning to split. 'Not our best idea, admittedly,' said Tansa.

'That's putting it lightly. You know they're *hymerikai*? The king's brother is in Cliffark to see my father.'

It was Tansa's turn to gape. 'You're Lady Ciera Istlewick.' Of course. Tansa cursed herself for not realising before; if she had known Lord Istlewick's daughter was up here she would have been robbing her, not trying to steal from the *Hymeriker*. Her cream gown was edged with lace at the cuffs and decorated with tiny, sparkling white gems, each probably worth more than any of the king's soldiers earnt in a year, and there were bright blue stones dangling from her ears and hanging from a chain around her neck as well, and gold bands on her wrists. Tam bowed awkwardly, and Tansa followed his lead, unsure of what else to do; she had never met a noblewoman before.

Ciera scowled at them, crossing her arms across her chest. 'You can spare the formalities. I give that door another minute at most. You want to live, I imagine?'

She was right. Splinters exploded from the door as a heavy boot crashed through it. Tansa chanced a look over the balcony at the chaos below. There were shouts and screams as the audience spotted her, the play long forgotten. Even if they could climb back the way Tansa had come, they would never escape through so many. She cursed.

'Is there another way out?' asked Tam.

The girl took a moment's pause, as if deciding what she meant to do with them. Tansa's heart was in her mouth; if they broke through, would Lord Istlewick's daughter make a good hostage? Probably, but it would cost them their only ally, and she might be fierce enough to fight them off if she had a mind to, and the way Tam was looking at the girl he would probably fight the *hymerikai* himself before he let Tansa threaten her.

'This way.' Ciera seized Tam by the hand and hurriedly led him round the circle away from the door, towards a wooden shutter with moveable slats that opened to the outside, while Tansa followed behind. 'Can you climb?' she asked, pushing it open as far as it would go, just wide enough for them to squeeze through.

'You first!' said Tam, stepping out of the way for Tansa.

Behind them, there was a crack like a ship's mast being ripped in two as the door's lock finally gave way, and with a cry the first of the warriors burst in. Tansa vaulted through the shutter, the blood pounding in her ears drowning out the man's fury.

She heard Tam delaying. 'My name's Tam, by the way,' he was telling Ciera.

'Not the time, Tam, by the Norhai!' Tansa cried. She shimmied up the outside wall, her fingers seeking the hidden gaps as her feet found purchase where the bricks protruded from the mortar, praying that her brother was following. From inside, she heard Ciera Istlewick's outraged cries of 'Thief! thief!' *The girl could have been on stage*, Tansa reflected bitterly. The *hymerikai* would likely have no idea she had helped them.

Even several storeys up, Tansa could hear the confusion on the ground as the audience fled the playhouse out into the street. She could not help feeling a moment of pride at her own foresight to insist they agree a meeting place if their plan went to ruin, not that she had expected to reach it by scaling the playhouse's exterior. She climbed up and clockwise towards the place they had agreed: a flat roof that touched the playhouse wall, with a hidden stairway accessible via a usually deserted courtyard.

Mercifully, Cag was on the roof waiting for her.

'You're alive!' The younger boy embraced Tansa so fiercely that he almost sent her flying, and she had to struggle to extricate herself from his bear-like grip. 'I couldn't get up, they had guards on the stairs to the roof, four of them, armed with spears!'

Tansa looked back, and was relieved to see Tam following the way she had come.

For reasons she could not fathom, her brother was beaming. Her face felt so tight with tension she doubted she was capable of smiling. 'Look what I got off her wrist!' he declared, dangling a golden bracelet between his fingers. 'And she kissed me! They almost got me because of it, but it was worth it!'

'You can't go round just kissing girls, Tam.' Tansa was not sure whether to hug him or cuff him round the head. They had been seconds from death and all he could think about was girls. 'If anyone did that to me I'd stick them in the gut.'

'But she kissed me back, I swear!'

Tansa took a mental note to remind her brother later of the likely consequences of stealing kisses from nobly born girls – they would be much more serious than those of stealing bracelets. Angry shouts floated up from below. The king's warriors had made it down to the street, and were pointing upward, gesticulating wildly to a pair of blue-clad watchmen. 'Come on!' Without waiting for a reply, Tansa ran, and with a daredevil cry vaulted across to the next building. Tam and Cag followed, and they set out across the maze of Cliffark's rooftops, leaving the cries of their would-be pursuers in their wake.

CHAPTER 8

Ciera was surprised when her mother came to help her dress in the morning, rather than one of the maids. People said they looked alike, but her mother's interest in her had never been more than cursory. It had taken Ciera years to realise this was because her mother had not been able to give her father a male heir, and rather than cherishing her only child resented her for it.

'Because your father wishes to speak to you,' she answered brusquely when Ciera asked why she was attending her. She had brought her a new dress, tighter at the waist than she was used to. 'And you are to wear this. It is time you started dressing like a woman.'

It was not like her mother to take an interest, but Ciera could hardly argue with her; it was only because of her father's insistence that she still dressed like a girl rather than a woman ready to be wed. It was a relief; after the events at the playhouse she had half-expected her father never to let her leave her chamber again. Fortunately he did not know about the kiss that young rogue had stolen from her, nor the gold band he had somehow sneaked from her wrist.

Thieves they might have been, but Tam and his sister embodied the virtues Ciera associated with Cliffark and its citizens. Ingenuity, daring, and a fierce independence that meant they saw no issue at all with stealing from the king's soldiers. In twenty years' time they might be fat, successful merchants, if the hangman did not get them first.

She touched a finger to her lip where Tam had kissed her, smiling at the memory of his broad, honest face and the gap between his front teeth. An infuriating pink blush spread across her skin. *One common boy kisses you and you start simpering like a child*, she silently scolded herself. *And he stole your bracelet.*

For a horrified moment, as Ciera walked to her father's solar, she wondered if her mysterious betrothed, Lord Prindian, had finally come to claim her. She had never met him and rarely thought of their long betrothal, but that would explain her mother's sudden interest in her garb. It was better than spending the rest of her life hidden behind lock and key in Cliffark Tower, but even so the idea of marrying a stranger left her fearful. Though why then would the king's brother be here?

The new dress pinched uncomfortably around her abdomen, but she did her best to smile when her mother led her to her father's study. As ever, he was sitting at his table, bent over a ledger. His head was entirely bald, save a few wispy strands around his ears. His walking stick leant against the table. Lord Istlewick was not yet fifty, but the years had not been kind to him.

He beamed when he saw Ciera, melting the years from his face. 'My daughter.' He rose awkwardly and kissed her forehead. 'You look beautiful.'

Ciera embraced him. He had always been occupied with work, happy to let others attend to his daughter, but she knew he cared, in his own way. When he had first inherited the lordship, he had almost lost Cliffark to a rebellion over his new taxes. He had spent the years since attending obsessively to his domain, determined that would never happen again. Cliffark now stood as one of the most prosperous places in Erland.

Her father's eyes were bloodshot, with heavy bags underneath. This was not unusual; he often stayed up all night reading, but he looked paler than usual, and one of his hands tremored slightly. He collapsed back into his seat. 'You should sit.' He gestured to one of the chairs, which Ciera took.

'You know Prince Jarhick is dead?' he asked.

'Of course.' The whole of Erland knew that by now. 'But why is the king's brother here?'

'Lord Andrick.' Her father gave a tired sigh. 'I stayed up all night with him. It took many hours, but I think we have reached an agreement. I am sorry, Ciera.'

'Stop coddling her, Per; she's too old for it.' The scorn in her mother's voice cut Ciera to the bone. She glared at her daughter. 'You are to marry King Hessian.'

Her words broke upon Ciera like a wave of icy water. King Hessian was an old man! Older than her father! She tried to take a breath, but her throat seemed to have contracted to the width of a reed. This could not be happening. They said Hessian was half a corpse, a heartless recluse who meted out cruelty from the safety of his tower solar.

'No,' she said, horrified. 'No!'

Her father looked up at her with his tired eyes. 'I will not make you marry against your will. It is your decision. If I must refuse him, I will.'

'You won't,' said her mother. 'You know what happens to those who defy the Sangreals. All of Erland learnt that three hundred years ago, and when the Prindians needed a reminder they received one, more than once. If we refuse, once they are done with the Prindians their eyes will turn upon Cliffark, and within a year all our heads will be on spikes. Lord Andrick is already ill-disposed to us after that business with his men being robbed at the playhouse, which his men insist Ciera was partly to blame for. That's before we even touch on the freedom you have granted the Imperials in the city; Hessian would never have allowed it. If word reaches him, which surely it will—'

'I know, Irena, I know.' Her father covered his face with his hands.

Ciera found her voice. 'I won't do it,' she said, almost choking on her words. She imagined sharing the king's bed, his old, withered hands crawling over her in the night. Bearing his babies. If she had eaten that morning she was sure she would have been sick. 'You can't make me.'

Her mother's face hardened. 'We can and we will. I've just told you we can't refuse them. You will marry Hessian.'

Ciera ran to her father. She buried her face in his shoulder, and the tears came like a rainstorm. Surely he would not make her?

'That's enough, Ciera.' Her father came to his feet, holding his daughter but with one arm gripping the table as if to steady his will. 'I had hoped to delay Lord Andrick, but what happened at the playhouse has weakened our hand. And if the king commanded him to tear this tower down to the founda-tions, he would do it. And Hessian would command it. Your mother is right. This is how it must be. This is how it *will* be.'

Ciera raised her tear-streaked face to look at him. 'And when will this wedding be? Do you mean to drag me to Merivale in irons?'

He blinked at her. 'Tomorrow,' he said, unable to meet her eye. 'I asked for longer, but Lord Andrick insisted. He will stand in for the king. The day after he will escort you to Merivale.'

Tomorrow. And then she would leave Cliffark, perhaps forever. Ciera pulled free of her father's embrace, threw the door open and fled, ignoring the angry shouts of her mother. She broke into a run, dashing through the keep, barely seeing the shocked servants who dived out of her way.

She raced outside, hardly knowing where she was going. Her path led her to the north wall, right at the edge of the cliff. She leant against a tree, panting, and slumped to the ground. The grass would ruin her dress, but she did not care.

What else could I have done? Ciera covered her face with her hands. She had not been prepared to watch two of her people be torn to shreds over a few coins; she would have gladly repaid the men from her own jewels given the chance.

And what could she do now? She had always known that her father would choose her husband, but it had been far easier to accept it was the young, handsome Lord Prindian.

Ciera wiped away the sheen of tears from her cheek. She wished she could have spoken to Tam longer, without blood-crazed warriors pursuing him. By the state of his clothes, patched and slightly too small, he might not even have a home to call his own, and maybe had to sleep outside, stealing to feed his family. She might have given him the bracelet willingly if he had asked. Next to his life, what right did she have to be unhappy? And what right to disobey her father? She would be queen, and mother to the future king if Eryi favoured her. And she might outlive Hessian by half a century. Her life was not over. She would survive this.

And if she refused, they would force her, or the Sangreals would raze her home to the ground. She could not do that to her father. Ciera wiped away her tears, smoothed out her dress, and stood. She began walking back towards the keep.

When she reached the solar, her mother had left. Her father hugged her tightly. 'Men who refuse Hessian Sangreal seldom live to see old age. But I swear I will not accept without your agreement. Some say an old man and a young woman are a good match, but they also say that the young Lord Prindian is a hand-some and courteous youth with his mother's beauty. Say the word, and I will tell them you are promised to Lord Prindian. I will go to war with them if I must.'

He was trembling. Ciera kissed him, and it struck her how feeble her father was, with his stick, and his bowlegs, and the white threads of hair around his ears. She swore to herself that she would give him a grandson before he died, and the legacy he deserved. 'I will not make you defy the crown. It is a good match for our family.'

Her father gave a sad smile. 'There are other reasons for this match, Ciera. Good reasons beyond the survival of our family, which your mother is right to be concerned by.' He dropped heavily into his chair and patted the thick ledger in front of him. 'Do you know what Cliffark's tax income per head is compared to Merivale's?'

Ciera closed her eyes in concentration. Not content to simply count his own revenues, her father liked to estimate revenues elsewhere also, and make sure Ciera appreciated the figures too. 'Per head, around double. We have fewer residents, but our total revenues are similar.' She had thought Tam poor, but no doubt there were many worse off in Merivale.

Her father was nodding. 'Near enough.'

Clutching his walking stick and with his other hand encouraging Ciera to follow him, Lord Istlewick hobbled towards the window. It overlooked Cliffark, giving a broad view of the whole bay. The tranquil water sparkled under the morning sun, and the whole city seemed to glow, so bright it was as if it had risen newly formed with the sun.

'My life's work,' said Lord Istlewick, fondly. 'When I was a boy, a man could set out from one end at dawn and, by the time he reached the other, everything on his person would have been stolen. My father's treasury was down to rats and cobwebs. When I inherited, I swore that Cliffark would rise with me.

'I was not prepared for how hard the pirates would fight me. It took Lord Andrick and a thousand men from Merivale to quell the Stormcaller Rebellion. He called me a fool afterwards, said that the only way I would have my reforms was at the point of a blade, that I was too weak, and it would be better for me to be satisfied with my and Cliffark's lot.

'And now look at it!' Her father laughed joyously and cast an arm over the city from west to east. 'A thriving merchants' guild, an Imperial enclave bringing wealth the likes of which I've never seen, thousands and thousands of ships coming to trade every year.' He pointed north-east, to where Ciera could see a high, yellow-brick building under construction. 'It is my hope that will become a school when it is finished, for any child of Cliffark who wishes to attend, and perhaps one day a seat of great learning, where men of intellect from the world over might congregate.

'Being on the coast is an advantage of course, but one I have made the most of.' Ciera could hear the pride in her father's voice. His achievement would earn little respect from other lords, but in her view its worth was beyond measure. 'I have set taxes that encourage trade, and my treasury and the citizenry flourish together.

'In Merivale it is a different matter.' His smile fell away. 'Hessian sucks wealth from his people like an insatiable babe at the teat. The rich still prosper, but the poor barely endure, and Merivale and the kingdom suffer for it.

'For three hundred years, the Sangreals have been kings, and what have they given Erland with their crown? Only war and ruin. Erland would have been better off if they had remained wandering the southern wastes. Their ways will work no longer. A poor crown is a weak crown, and unless they change, Erland is doomed. We will be another territory of the Imperium within a generation.

'You have seen my ideas, Ciera, how Cliffark has thrived under my rule. I desire the same for all of Erland. As queen, you will have Hessian's ear. You can change what I cannot.'

Ciera thought on it, as her father returned to his seat and slumped into it, breathing heavily. She could do it; she knew she could. She was proud of what her father had achieved, and proud to be from Cliffark, where worth was measured in gold and not by the strength of a man's sword arm. If here, then why not Merivale?

'I will do it,' she said. *I will make Hessian love me, and in time all of Erland will prosper.*

CHAPTER 9

Riding down to Irith's New Quarter, Rymond felt as if a great weight was being lifted from his shoulders. He meant to enjoy himself this evening and, by Eryi, he had earnt it. In the weeks since Prince Jarhick's death he had barely had a moment to himself. Part of each day was spent with Adfric, his humourless master-at-arms, practising swordplay or poring over maps and ledgers. He had collapsed into bed each night without a drop of wine, and his already lean body was becoming hard and wiry.

So when his friends Dominac and Willam had arrived at Irith Castle demanding an audience with him after not seeing him for several weeks, he had decided to allow himself a moment of freedom. When he met them in the hall they were drinking wine straight from the bottle, and Dom had a giggling maid in his lap and his hand halfway up her skirt.

'Stop harassing my servants, you ill-mannered peasant,' Rymond had greeted him.

'Only if you come out to play, Majesty,' Will replied, mocking him with a deep bow, 'or is Erland's new heir too well-born for the likes of us?'

He was in truth, but Rymond valued their company. Let his

mother worry about the merits of their birth. Even taking his
mother's view, Dom was practically kin, the legitimate son of a
bastard daughter of Rymond's grandfather. Dom often joked of
a familial resemblance, but Dom was crew on his father's
trading galley *Eight Winds*, and so had calloused hands and skin
burnt brown from months spent at sea, a remarkable contrast to
Rymond's pallor.

Will had been born even lowlier than Dominac. Twenty
years ago, Will's father had owned a tavern called the Blushing
Bride, where it was said you could find whatever you were
seeking for three bits of silver. It had been one of the few
taverns in Irith that allowed all-night gambling, and Rymond's
father had been a regular patron. One night, so the story went,
he had bet Will's father he could balance atop a toppled barrel
of beer while being pleasured by a serving girl and not spill a
drop of his drink. Needless to say, it ended in disaster, and the
lord had laughed uproariously before handing over what for
him was a trifle but for the barman was several years' profit.
Will's father now owned a chain of inns, a brewery, and shares
in several ships, not all of which operated entirely within
Erland's laws.

The three friends went straight to the Smoking Sow, their
inn of choice, where Willam insisted on a drinking game that
involved Rymond buying a drink for anyone who would bow to
him and call him 'Majesty', at which point Rymond would also
have to drink.

Many hours and many drinks later, Rymond was slouched
in a chair with a pair of girls on his lap, while from his own chair
Dom serenaded him tunelessly with an oud:

> 'Oh courageous King Rymond was such a fear-
>   some sight,
> His queenly bride was shaking on their
>   wedding night.

She said, "I've never seen such a mighty sword
    as that,
I'm afraid that'll never fit in my twat."'

Will laughed uproariously from the bar, where he was persuading more patrons to confer a bow upon Rymond to earn their drink. Rymond smiled while the girls on his lap giggled. 'Thank you, Dom, for that stirring melody, but now this courageous king has to go and empty his mighty sword.'

As Rymond staggered to the alley to relieve himself, Will yelled from the bar to his companions. 'Make way for the king! Bow, you useless bastards!' and bowed so low himself that his feet went from under him and he turned it into a clumsy one-handed spring, somehow coming to his feet without spilling a drop of his beer. He turned to his companions hooting with laughter, barely believing his good fortune.

Still laughing, Rymond leant one-handed up against the wall of the alley and relieved himself. It felt good to be out with his friends again. No crown was worth giving that up for. Did they even have proper inns in Merivale? If he became king he would have to raise Will and Dom to lordship.

He had just relaced himself when he felt a cold blade against his throat, and a small, soft voice in his ear that sobered him quicker than a swim in an icy river.

'Easy does it, lad. Don't make a sound. Just nod your head if you're not going to try anything stupid.'

Rymond chanced it, and as the man finished speaking aimed a vicious stamp towards his shin. But Rymond's foot found nothing but air, and his face collided with brick as the man strong-armed him against the wall.

'I said nothing stupid, yeah?' the man whispered, his voice sharp as his blade. 'Do you think if a pup like you were going to give me trouble I'd have waited till you finished pissing? Now I've been polite, so you just be thankful you're not standing there with your cock in your hand, yeah? I'll ask again, nod your head if you're not going to try anything stupid.'

Rymond nodded. The man knew his business. A bubble of fear rose in his stomach.

'Good lad.'

The man shifted the point of his knife to the base of Rymond's spine. Rymond heard a cord tighten, and suddenly his hands were bound tightly together behind his back.

The man walked him towards the far end of the alley, to a quiet street where a horse was waiting. He had not shown even a glimpse of his face, and before Rymond knew what was happening he had been thrown over the horse's back and strapped to it with a rope around its underside.

'Where are you taking me?' It was difficult to get the words out, with his arms behind his back and all his weight resting on the horse.

'Hush, lad.' The man shoved a mass of cloth into his mouth. A heavy woollen blanket was thrown over him, and Rymond felt the horse begin to move over the cobbles.

The whole thing had taken barely a minute. How long would it be before somebody from the inn thought to check on him? He could be long gone by then. At least his life was unlikely to be in danger, or the man would have just killed him in the alley. Then Rymond remembered his brother's end, trapped in the depths of Hessian's dungeon, with only the rats and his own fear for company. Icy sweat prickled on his skin.

His kidnapper seemed to be leading the horse through Irith's quieter streets off the main drag, but Rymond soon lost his bearings, until he felt the New Quarter's muddied paths turn to cobbles. He guessed they were nearing one of the town's exits, most likely the quieter eastern gate. He tried to shout out, but his voice was muffled by the rag in his mouth and easily drowned out by the horse's hooves on the cobbles. There was a jingle of coins as the man tossed a small bag of silver to one of the guards.

Soon enough, they were outside the walls, and Rymond heard the low panting of a second horse. He was momentarily relieved when the man removed the blanket, cut Rymond's bonds, and assisted him to the ground, until a knife was pressed up against his cheek. 'Get on,' the man growled.

Reluctantly, Rymond mounted, and in an instant the man rebound his hands and tied them to the saddle's pommel, then ran a loop of rope under the horse and tied Rymond's feet together.

The man threw a hood over Rymond's head, leaving him blind, then mounted his own horse and led Rymond off at a gallop.

Eryi's blood, where is he taking me? He felt the horse race into the fertile plains that spread from here all the way to the Pale River and on to Eryispek. The answer could only be to King Hessian. If the man had not allowed Rymond to relieve himself before ambushing him, he might have wet himself with terror. It was said that his brother had gone mad before he finally starved to death in his oubliette.

Resting against the horse's mane, Rymond might have slept. The night was dark, and no sliver of starlight penetrated the coarse hood that covered him. In his drunken state, the steady rhythm of the horse's hooves was almost a lullaby.

A few hours later, his body aching with the horse's constant motion and his mouth dry with an oncoming hangover, Rymond felt their pace quicken, and the thud of the hooves became a thunder that even with the rope binding him bounced him against the horse's back. The hood covering his face fluttered, and Rymond found that if he tossed his head he could move it slightly, catching a glimpse of dark ground as his mount galloped on.

It took a few attempts, but he eventually caught it right. The hood flew off him, and he could feel the cool air on his face as they hurtled on into the night. He turned to look back, and by moonlight glimpsed six shadowy horsemen a few hundred yards back. His heart leapt. Somebody had sounded the alarm. It was hard to tell, but he thought the pursuers might be gaining on them.

The man seemed to sense Rymond's thoughts, and shouted back to him from his own mount. 'Don't get your hopes up, lad. Those might be the best horses in your stable, but this is the finest I've ever sat on, and yours could be its sister. There's a wood up ahead we can lose them in.'

An arrow whistled past about five feet to their left.

'Buggering bastards!' The man dug his heels in, urging his horse on towards the woods. More arrows flew past, mere feet away from them, but at this range in the dark Rymond thought they had no chance of hitting anything, or, worse, might hit Rymond himself.

They plunged into the wood. The man slowed their pace as they weaved between trees, Rymond looking back all the while in search of his would-be rescuers, hoping for one of them to come crashing through the trees and free him.

To Rymond's disappointment, the man appeared to have judged rightly. When they emerged from the wood a few miles later, dawn was breaking, and there was no sign nor sound of pursuit.

Just as Rymond was ready to lose hope, an arrow whistled from their left, passing just feet above his captor's head. Rymond tried to look back. The bow thrummed a second time, and this time its whistle was cut short by the sound of the arrowhead piercing flesh, and the man's scream.

The man urged the horses on, but Rymond could feel them slowing. He looked up and saw his kidnapper clutching his side, an arrow protruding just below his armpit. The hooves were getting closer.

Their horses slowed to a stop as the man vainly tried to stem the flow of blood. To Rymond's relief, two men wearing surcoats of Prindian green pulled up ahead of them.

'Nasty wound you've got there,' said the first of them. It was Adfric, the grizzled master-at-arms who had been putting Rymond through his paces with a sword the past weeks. 'Don't reckon you'll be taking my lord any further with that arrow sticking out of you.'

'Fuck you,' spat the man. Adfric responded with a vicious backhand slap that sent him tumbling from the horse. The man screamed as his wounded side hit the ground.

'You can thank young Derry here for that arrow, even if it took him a dozen goes before he got near you.'

'Nobody else within fifty miles could have made that shot,' said the younger man, a youth in his late teens, fingering his bow absent-mindedly.

'So you say. Release Lord Prindian while I see to our friend here.'

Rymond felt overcome with gratitude, resolving never to take his guards for granted again. His bindings were cut with a knife, his gag removed, and Derry helped him to the ground. He winced as he rubbed his rope-burnt wrists, and stretched his aching back, feeling fortunate to be alive.

On dead legs, Rymond stumbled to where his kidnapper lay. He had not had a chance to get a good look at him before. He was of middling age, middling height, and middling looks, entirely unremarkable save for some nasty scarring on his cheeks, which were rapidly losing colour as blood continued to leak from below his arm.

'Who sent you?' Rymond demanded. He resisted the urge to strike the man.

'Piss off,' groaned the stranger, for which he received a brutal kick from Adfric. The man rolled over, howling.

'Let's start with something easier, shall we?' Adfric drew an ugly-looking knife. 'What's your name?'

The man opened his mouth to say something, and as he did Adfric knelt, and stuck the point of it where the arrow met the man's flesh. Adfric twisted, and the man's answer turned into a howl of pain.

'Was that going to be another "Piss off", or were you about to answer my question?'

'Jory, my name is Jory!'

'That's better. And who sent you?'

'Never caught his name,' the man gasped, 'only met him yesterday evening. Just gave me them horses and a pouch of gold and told me what to do.'

'Let's just pretend I believe you. Where were you taking Lord Prindian?'

Blood was spreading across the ground, and blossoming on the man's tunic. His voice was weakening. 'The mill...' he gasped. 'Just over the Pale River. Said someone would meet me.'

'What did the man who hired you look like?' asked Adfric.

Jory did not reply. His eyes were glazed, staring up at the sky. He was dead.

Adfric frowned. 'Thought he had a few more hours in him at least. Hadn't lost that much blood.' He slapped the dead man's face, sending it lolling to the other side.

Derry was staring down with wide eyes. 'They say the king's wizard can kill people with his mind, from hundreds of miles away.'

'Don't be daft, Derry. You just caught something important with that arrow. Stubborn bastard.' Adfric aimed a heavy kick at the corpse, making it fold over like a rag doll.

Rymond's mouth was dry, his ribs were bruised, and he could feel a terrible headache coming on. Nonetheless, he felt giddy with relief. Giddy, and a bit sick. The horse that had carried him had wandered over to nibble the grass at his feet.

He leant against her, trying not to throw up. 'Do you have any wine?'

Adfric handed him a filthy, half-full skin. 'Would have thought you'd had enough of it last night, Lord.'

Rymond drank from it with abandon, ignoring the cheap wine's acidic sting. It tasted glorious. 'How did you find me?'

'Probably I'm not best placed to say, Lord. You can ask your lady mother.' Adfric pointed behind Rymond, and he turned to see a group of riders rallying towards them, his mother's unmistakable figure at the head. Rymond's heart sank, and he took another swig of wine. She was the last person he wanted to see.

They pulled up, and his mother dismounted. 'I will speak to my son. Leave us.'

'Begging your pardon, Lady, but the man might have accomplices,' said one of her guards.

'Then you may keep an eye on us. Adfric, you may stay.' The others departed to a respectable distance, leaving Rymond alone with Adfric and his mother.

'How did you find me?' Rymond asked. 'Did Dom and Will rouse you?'

His mother laughed throatily, and Adfric gave a wry smile. 'That pair of sots? They were passed out in their chairs. They are presently enjoying a stay at our pleasure in the cells.' She paused meaningfully. 'I knew, Rymond. I know Hessian's mind. His wizard has spies everywhere. I have my own, and no sooner did you not return to the tavern, arrangements were made. It is only because those gate guards are such useless fools that he was able to leave the town. They will be dealt with.'

'You had me followed?' Tired and aching, Rymond could not keep the irritation out of his voice.

'Of course, and I would hope you might thank me for it, given you are clearly too much of a fool to take an escort, or to consider the motivations of your two so-called friends.'

'Dom and Will wouldn't have! They have nothing to do with this.'

'They have everything to do with this. Your association with them is a distraction. You should be making use of men like that, not gallivanting about with them as if they're your equals. Future kings do not get drunk in taverns with sailors and innkeepers.'

'Lady Breta is right, Lord,' said Adfric, wiping his knife on the grass. 'I can teach you swordplay and warfare, but it's no help if you go out of your way to put yourself in danger.'

Rymond could see their point, but he was not going to admit that. Muscles protesting, he pulled himself up onto the horse, and did his best to look noble. 'We will discuss this at home,' he said, with as much dignity as he could muster.

When they returned, Rymond immediately had Dom and Will released from the cells, unharmed, but did not grant them an audience. The next day, when he felt well again, he sent for Adfric and his mother, and received them in his rarely used study, with a map of Erland on the table.

'While I have been playing at swords,' he began once they were seated, 'which has not been a wasteful endeavour, Hessian has moved against us and sought to have me abducted. I would welcome your counsel.'

Adfric and Breta exchanged a glance. Clearly they had already discussed this. 'There is more than you know,' said Rymond's mother. 'Ciera Istlewick has married Hessian, or rather Lord Andrick has married her as a proxy at Cliffark Tower. Her slippery father has betrayed us.'

Rymond manipulated his features into an approximation of woe. He was relieved in a way. He had never met the girl, and his pledge to marry her had been less than enthusiastic.

'Don't try to pretend you care,' scolded his mother. 'This will unite East Erland under Hessian, and he'll soon be free to start trying to get a child on her. This could all have been avoided if you had just married the girl, but as ever you knew best.'

Rymond opened his mouth to reply, but his mother spoke over him.

'You will ride tomorrow, to gather men for war. Adfric will accompany you; I have told him where you are going. I shall ride to Merivale.'

'Have you gone mad?' said Rymond. 'The man tried to kidnap me. He'll put you in a cell, or worse, take your head off.'

'You should pray that he does. Nothing would so well turn people against him as murdering an old and still beautiful woman who shares a bloodline with him.' She smiled, as if recalling something distant. 'I have not been to Merivale in an age. I have a sudden urge to renew my acquaintance.'

CHAPTER 10

Pherri had never slept much, but since Da'ri's murder she slept even less. When she tried, she could only lie there with her eyes squeezed shut, her mind tumbling with useless rage.

Her mother had found her weeping over Da'ri's butchered corpse. By then Errian had been long gone, riding away from Lordsferry, and away from justice. The ringleaders of the murder had been caught, and were currently in Lordsferry's jail, awaiting trial. Pherri did not care about them. The only person she held responsible for Da'ri's death was Errian, who hated the Thrumb more than he loved his own sister. Nobody had ridden after him, despite her pleas, and that her mother had finally listened to her that Errian had lied about having orders to go to Thrumb was no balm to her broken heart. Everyone except Pherri seemed to consider that one dead Thrumb was not worth troubling a lord's son over. The injustice of it was like a barb in her chest.

This night though, it felt unusually cold, especially for late summer, and with her shivering hands Pherri could not light her lantern. Disappointed she could not finish the book of Thrumb legends Da'ri had given her, Pherri curled up under the sheets, clutching her knees, trying to stop shivering and not to think about Da'ri's ruined body.

She dreamt a new dream that night, more vivid than those that had troubled her before. A vast host of ragged beggars, armed with ancient weapons dripping blood, dragged themselves across a snow-covered wasteland, buffeted by an icy wind and strafed with hail.

Pherri blinked, and suddenly she was one of them.

She raised her hands to protect her face against the fierce snow, but instead of hands, she had great bear paws, as large as dinner plates, with curved black claws that shone under the moonlight. Large as they were, they did nothing against the wind, which rustled her fur and blinded her in a shower of ice.

Lowering her head to the gale, she saw, where her feet should have been, the legs and hooves of a deer. She tried to scream, horrified, but all that came out was the plaintive moan of a pained beast.

When she looked up again, the snow had ceased, and the ground was as soft and untouched as a blanket of cloud. The ragged band were gone, and she faced a white doe, a spectre by a frozen lake, staring through her with icy-blue eyes, searching for the girl who cowered inside the deer. She blinked, and the doe's eyes spread like pale, sinister moons.

She turned to run, but her hooves slipped in the snow, and suddenly she was tumbling, endlessly, into the sweet embrace of cold, with darkness and stars all around and boundless nothing beneath. As she fell, she heard the voice of the doe, a clashing melody that made her ears ring. '*I see you.*'

Invisible hands grasped for her, and Pherri screamed.

She woke, in her bed, breathing hard and drenched with sweat.

She did not sleep for a long time.

Pherri yawned, and rubbed her tired eyes with her fists. After Lordsferry, she had wept until her eyes ran dry, but now Violet Hall was returning to normal, as if nobody called Da'ri had ever lived here. She had resumed her lessons, with the new servant-woman Delara.

Pherri had been dreading the prospect of learning from this woman. All the servants of Violet Hall thought with one mind, pulling faces over Pherri's desire for a tutor, and chiding her for the smallest indiscretions, like running in the corridor and dirtying her clothes. Of course Delara was not a witch as Errian claimed – witches were not servants, and Errian was not to be trusted; the lessons would be endless hours of sewing and balancing ledgers.

That had changed as soon as Pherri met her. Delara's face was weather-beaten with age, she wore her hair in a long white ponytail, and she stood proud as a gargoyle, her gnarled fingers gripping a wooden staff, in clothes that were unusually scruffy for a lord's servant. She looked nothing like the other servants of Violet Hall. Her mother had put her appearance down to the relative rusticity of Basseton, situated as it was at the foot of Eryispek.

Nor were the lessons as Pherri had expected. There was needlework, and ledgers, but Delara seemed to tire of these as quickly as Pherri. More often, she taught her the history of Erland, and expressed dismay at what she evidently regarded as a severe inadequacy in Pherri's breadth of knowledge. Sangreal history began three hundred years ago with the settling of East Erland, but the tales Delara told her went back centuries beyond that, of displaced tribes that had fallen out of memory, and back even further to how the Prindian ancestors and their people had come from the sea and formed Erland while the Sangreals were still nomads of the vast wildness beyond the Sorrowlands. Pherri doubted that her parents would have been in favour of her learning such things, but she was not fool enough to report it to her mother.

Today though, Pherri could not concentrate. In a pocket of her dress, she touched the only thing she had left of Da'ri, a peculiar letter she had found on his corpse. It had taken many painstaking hours for her to deduce its meaning – it was written in the Thrumb language, and disguised – but Da'ri had taught her the basics of ciphering a letter, and armed with the notes of translating between Thrumb and Erlish from Da'ri's room, last night Pherri had finally solved it, with *ealagny* as the keyword, the deep longing for home he had spoken of. Had he meant for her to find it? She had read it so many times since it felt as though Da'ri's strange, unsent missive was seared onto the insides of her eyelids.

Dear Cousin,

I no longer plan to return to Thrumb.

The Lutums have left their lands. Storms swirl the higher reaches, and the winds that roll down to the plains chill my old bones. The tales that reach me from our homeland are no less odd – I know it was not you who began raiding or killed the Prince.

They are waking, and they may have found a way to affect events outside their prisons. Such strangeness does not occur by accident.

I will ride to the western slope, to our ancient brethren. If they remember as we do, perhaps all is not lost.

Stay safe, Cousin. May the trees ever guide your way, and the sunlight ever warm your back.

Yours,

Da'ri

Pherri understood little of it. Da'ri's cousin was presumably another Thrumb, and Da'ri had evidently been driven to write it by the strange news of the Lutums, but the final few lines raised almost endless questions. What linked Jarhick's death and the Lutums? Who was waking? And why were they imprisoned? Who were the Thrumb's ancient brethren?

'Pherri!'

Pherri sat bolt upright, aware that in her daydreaming her eyes had been drooping and she had not heard a word Delara had said for the last several minutes. 'I wasn't falling asleep. Just rubbing my eyes.'

Delara looked at her shrewdly. 'Why are you tired, Pherri? A girl your age needs sleep. Should I search your room for candles?'

She could not let them take away her candles. Night was the only time she would be able to safely read Da'ri's secret letter. 'I'm not tired, I swear. I was only thinking about Erland, and what you're teaching me.'

Delara raised a sceptical eyebrow. 'Do you have a question?'

'I do actually!' Pherri could see an opportunity here. 'You've told me lots about all the tribes who had their lands taken, but you've not taught me anything about Eryispek, or the tribes who still live on the Mountain: the Lutums, the Adrari. I was just wondering what was going on on Eryispek while this was happening. Has there ever been a prison on it?'

Delara had listened patiently and without expression, up until Pherri's last few words. The look of black thunder that passed across her face told Pherri that the question had been a mistake. 'Where did you learn that?' she demanded. She hobbled towards Pherri, her gnarled staff clicking rapidly against the floor. 'Did your old tutor tell you that?'

'N-no!' Pherri said, pushing her chair back from Delara's advance. She could not reveal the letter. 'It was in a dream I had. There was snow, and blood, and a doe that looks at me! And a voice—'

'There is no meaning in dreams,' interrupted Delara. 'Just the ramblings of the unconscious mind. Whatever you may have dreamt, I assure you, there is nothing up there.'

'What about Eryi?'

Delara's staff twitched in her hand. For a moment, Pherri thought she was about to strike her with it. Instead, Delara walked to the window and pointed forcefully towards Eryispek. It was shrouded in unusually thick cloud today, as it had been for many weeks, but Pherri could make out the Mountain's shape. 'Do you see any damn man up there? There is no man-god! It's false, a backward, superstitious nonsense, and yet somehow the Adrari talked you all into following it.'

'You don't believe in Eryi?' Pherri was not sure she did either – as she understood it, the reason the old Meridival tribe had taken Eryi as their god on their arrival in Erland was in exchange for Adrari submission – but that was not commonly talked about. Both the ideas of worshipping the man who lived at the top of Eryispek and worshipping the Mountain as the messenger of the Norhai seemed similarly absurd to her.

'We will speak no more of this.' Delara loudly slapped a hand against the windowsill. 'I will brew you something to give you dreamless sleep, and then if you doze in my lessons again, I assure you I will have your room searched for candles.' She turned, and sighed heavily. 'For the rest of today, I want you practising your stitching.'

Though Pherri's heart sank, she was not prepared to argue. She had kept Da'ri's letter safe, and that was the important thing, no matter how strange Delara was being. Meekly, she reached into her desk and retrieved her needlework, thinking only of when she could finally return to her room and study the deciphered letter again.

———

Delara knocked at Pherri's door that night, and she had to hastily blow out her lantern and hide it with Da'ri's letter under her pillow. Swatting at the whisps of smoke that hung in the air, she rose and opened the door.

The old woman sniffed at the air as she stepped in. 'I know you've been reading with candles. I can smell it. But this will help you sleep, and without any troubling dreams.'

She held out a small flask. The liquid inside was the shade of mushrooms, and when Delara pulled the stopper off Pherri almost gagged at the foul smell, like wet earth and wood rot. 'What's in that?' she asked, trying not to choke. She did not want to have another nightmare. The voice that had spoken to her had left her fearful of her dreams, and if not for Delara's intervention she might have read long into the night until she could run from sleep no longer. However, trying to drink the contents of the flask might be a worse fate.

'No more than what you need. Herbs for sleep, and tranquillity, and something to help you grow as well. You are unfortunately small for your age.'

Pherri bristled. She did not see what her size had to do with Delara, nor why she needed to drink something for it. 'Does my mother know you're here?'

'Your mother charged me to educate you. This is part of it.' Delara cupped Pherri's face with her hand. Her palm felt like shrivelled parchment, and was strangely warm. 'I want to help you, Pherri.'

A feeling of calm came over Pherri. Delara was only trying to help, and the strange dream had been troubling her all day.

She took the flask carefully from Delara's hand and swallowed it in one, holding her nose and resisting the urge to gag. It slipped down her throat like warm, sweet wine.

The effects were almost immediate. Pherri felt the potion warming her from inside to out. Her eyelids were like anvils, and Delara's face swam in and out of focus. She swayed on the spot. The liquid had been nothing to fear. She felt happy, and carefree, and ready to sleep forever.

Pherri stumbled, and Delara was there at her side, bearing her weight and easing her back towards the bed. She laid her down on the mattress, and tucked her in tenderly. 'Sleep well, my dear.'

By the time Delara closed the door behind her, Pherri was deeply asleep. She did not dream.

CHAPTER 11

Contrary to Theodric's prediction, Hessian did not summon Helana in the weeks that followed their discussion of her marriage prospects. He barely emerged from his tower; the only time Helana saw her father was to burn Jarhick's body, and he did not say a word to her. Helana fell back into her usual routine. She hawked, hunted, and sneaked into the barracks to play cards with the guardsmen, anything to distract herself from Jarhick being dead and the country teetering on the brink of war.

So she was surprised when a servant appeared at her door one morning, summoning her to Hessian. To prepare, she donned the same black mourning dress of her mother's she had worn since Jarhick's death. Helana hoped it would remind her father that he was not the only one who grieved.

She climbed the long stairs to Hessian's solar. What did he want? Nothing good, she suspected. Certainly not to reminisce of Jarhick. She had learnt long ago not to expect anything of her father.

What if Theodric's prediction had come true, and he had promised her hand to some lord? A lump of anxiety settled in her gut. She would not go through with it without a fight, that was for sure. She could go and live with Creya in the woods – her father would never find her there – or seek sanctuary with the Brides of Eryi.

Hessian had doubled his door guard since Jarhick's death, so four men met her at the top rather than the usual two. She gave them a stiff nod, and one of them knocked at the king's door before opening it.

Her father stood inside, speaking conspiratorially with Theodric. Theodric smiled welcomingly, but Hessian looked at her as if she were a stranger. A shadow of recognition passed over his face, and his brow furrowed hawkishly, his eyes fixing her with hatred.

'Where did you get that dress?'

He did not look well, Helana thought. His eyes were bloodshot, and his skin hung off his bones like old parchment. 'It was my mother's.'

'I know whose it is!' Hessian's voice cracked like a whip. 'You will not wear it again; I forbid it. Go and change.'

Helana stared at him. She ought to have known he would not take kindly to her wearing her mother's old clothes. He did not even like other people to even talk about her, as if to keep her memory all to himself. Had he known of the portrait in Helana's room he would surely have seized it.

But she would not be forced to leave purely on account of her garb. Her father had ordered her here. If he wanted her to change, he could have the guards drag her back to her room and make her. She smiled sweetly at him. 'I can just take it off here, Father. I'm sure one of your guards would be willing to fetch a replacement from my chambers.'

Hessian scowled, biting back another vicious rebuke. 'If you would rather shame me than obey me then I suppose I am compelled to receive you. You were a wilful child, and you have not changed. I should have had it flogged out of you.'

'Thank you, Father, I am grateful.' She flashed a satisfied smirk, stepped past the guards, and closed the door behind her.

Hessian lowered himself into his chair, still looking at her malevolently. 'This display of yours just proves what I was telling Theodric. You are a disobedient wretch in need of a firm hand, but I will not be the one to give it to you. It is past time you were married.'

Helana looked at him squarely, standing her ground. 'I will marry whom and when I please.' She spoke boldly, but inside she was shaking. She knew people thought her stubborn, but Hessian's will was like iron. She looked to Theodric for support, but the magus stood apart from them, silent.

Hessian laughed at her. 'You will marry whom *I* please, if I have to drag you before a priest in chains. War is coming, if you had deigned to notice this while running about the forest with peasants and gambling with my guardsmen. I need allies, and what use are you if I don't use you to secure one? Do you mean to be some peculiar old maid, living in my home, making me pay for your upkeep? I won't have it. The realm will not have it. By Eryi, you will do your duty.'

There was no point arguing while he was like this. Helana would need to distract him. She took a deep breath. 'Very well.'

Hessian looked at her in surprise. 'What do you mean, "Very well"?'

'I mean I will marry. Theodric mentioned a potential husband, actually.' She paused, with her father's eyes fixed on her, and slowly poured herself a cup of wine from the flagon next to him. Theodric was looking at her in alarm. She took a long sip and plunged forward. 'I should marry Rymond Prindian. Then if you cannot have an heir of your own, one of your grandchildren will take the crown.'

The king went very still. His rheumy eyes glistened red, bright like molten iron. His eyes flashed to Theodric. 'You cowardly wizard. Andrick put you up to this, didn't he?'

'Majesty,' said Theodric, raising his hands placatingly. 'If we are to have peace—'

'Peace!' Hessian lurched to his feet, waving his cup like a weapon, sloshing wine over the floor. 'There will be no peace!' He turned suddenly and raised a withered finger towards Helana. 'You're all in on it, aren't you? You're all conspiring against me! You want to kill me and steal my crown!' Flecks of spittle flew from his mouth.

Helana could not help recoiling in fear. 'I—'

'Get out!' He grasped a tankard of ale from the table and threw it towards her. She narrowly ducked out of the way, but the contents soaked her even so. The pewter tankard clanged against the wall behind her. 'You will not take my crown! None of you! Get out! Get out!'

Helana turned on her heel and fled, with cold ale dripping down her face and stinging her eyes. She ran down the stairs, willing the tears not to fall until she was back in her rooms.

They came when she was halfway down the tower, great wracking sobs that made her abdomen hurt. She leant on the wall, trying to compose herself against the cold stone. She had held her grief for Jarhick in for weeks, believing herself to be strong, and now it cascaded out of her, unleashed by her father's anger. Jarhick had been the only one in the family who gave a damn about her. Without him, what use was any of it? *Let it fall*, she resolved. *All of it. Let it crumble around my father's ears.*

She did not notice Theodric until he was right beside her, offering her a handkerchief. Helana grasped at the wall in shock, as if his very presence might send her tumbling down the stairs. 'Thank you,' she sniffed once she had recovered, taking the handkerchief from him and wiping her cheeks. 'Sorry, I think I dropped you in it there as well.'

'He calms as quickly as he angers,' said Theodric solemnly.

'It is partly my fault. I had just given him some disappointing news.'

'Why does he hate me? I never knew my mother, and he's been making me pay for her death my entire fucking life. My brother is dead, and he still despises me.'

'He loves you too, I think. You are your mother's daughter.' There was pity in Theodric's eyes, and for a moment Helana loathed him for it. 'But yes, he hates you. Not just because of how she died, but because you remind him of her. Seeing you in that dress... I suspect it was like seeing her ghost. I would request you stay away from your father for the time being. You bring out the worst in him.'

Helana fought back her tears. 'Am I pathetic, to be grateful for even that small measure of attention?'

Theodric gave a sad smile. 'That I cannot say, but you probably don't have to worry about him marrying you to anybody for the time being. You may keep the handkerchief.' He patted Helana on the shoulder and turned back up the stairs.

Helana wiped her face and returned to her rooms, ignoring the servants' stares. The guards would have heard almost every word, and by evening the story would be all over the castle. She hated them, all of them.

She went to her bed, ready to collapse into it. She almost missed the note on her pillow. It was thick, yellowish paper, creased down the middle.

Frowning, Helana opened it.

The Witch's Abyss. After sunset. Come alone. Tell no one.

She stared at it. The writing was in a looping, elegant cursive, like a lady's dinner invitation. But the Witch's Abyss was a rough tavern deep in the bowels of Merivale. Not even the guards would drink in there. And how had somebody got all the way to her rooms to deliver it without being challenged?

If somebody meant to do her harm, they could have done so already. They could have poisoned the food on her small table, or waited for her to return and slit her throat. She whirled around, imagining an unseen assailant hiding behind her door.

There was nobody.

She knew she ought to tell somebody, but there was no one. Perhaps Theodric, if the thought of speaking to him again did not fill her with unspeakable rage.

Damn them all. She would go. Helana was a Sangreal, and she hunted and hawked as well as any man. And she was no coward.

The beer was cloudy and possibly stale, but Helana took a bold sip. The aroma made her eyes water, but the beer itself was sweet on her tongue, with a pleasantly bitter aftertaste. She had been in taverns before, but never by herself, and certainly never in one with sawdust covering the floor.

Jarhick would have liked it here, she thought. *He would have thought it exciting to linger here unrecognised.* The air was thick with the hubbub of men's low conversations and the cheap vapours of homemade smokesticks, while the barman polished tankards with a rag of questionable cleanliness, keeping a suspicious eye on his customers.

Helana kept her head low and her hood up. She did not believe she would be recognised – who would expect to see the king's daughter in here? – but that she was the only woman here and sitting alone was reason enough not to draw attention to herself.

From her corner table, she was able to discreetly watch the other customers, looking for any signs of her would-be companion. There was a pair by the door cloaked in the thick bearskins of the Adrari. The Adrari rarely came down to Merivale, and most lowland Erlanders could go their whole lives without seeing one in the flesh. The other drinkers kept their distance. Prejudice against the cliffside savages was rife, particularly among the sorts who frequented the Witch's Abyss: sister-marrying fish-fuckers, they might say.

At a small table near the bar sat an old man, hooded in magus robes, muttering to himself and staring intently at a coin balanced on its thin edge at the centre of the table. Some drinkers glanced at the man nervously, but Helana suspected that most magi were chancers and charlatans. The man sitting by the bar looked to be of that sort; his coin did not appear to be doing very much.

There was a commotion by the door, and Helana looked over sharply. A group of young men dressed for hogball saun-tered in, guffawing and slapping one another on the back. Hogball had once been played between rival villages over miles and miles of countryside, which usually just turned into brawls after the ball burst, so far as Helana understood. The game was more civilised now, played between the city's guilds, but was no less brutal for it.

Their arrival had distracted Helana from developments nearer her table, and she was startled when a man appeared in front of her.

'Buy you a drink, lover?' He peeled back his lips to reveal a row of yellow teeth, his voice thick with drink. 'The rest of this scum might not know a woman if she bit him on the cock, but ol' Garth knows, and he knows what a woman like you wants.'

Helana swallowed her disgust and tried to answer politely. 'I've got one, but thank you for the offer, sir.'

To Helana's horror, he took her reply as an invitation to sit down opposite her. 'I'll get the next one. Drink up.'

Helana fumbled for a lie. 'I'll be leaving when I finish this; my husband will be expecting me home.'

'Fuck off, you've not got a husband.' The man leant across

the table towards her, his mouth twisting angrily, exuding hot, stale breath. Helana gaped at him, suddenly regretting her decision to heed the note.

'Leave her alone, you old lech.' A younger man grabbed Garth by the collar and dragged him away, then threw a punch that sent him sprawling back towards Helana. Garth caught himself on the table, grabbed Helana's half-full tankard and swung it back towards the other man, catching him on the shoulder and sending a waterfall of ale over the next table. The three men sitting there rose angrily and moved towards the two combatants. Others were standing up as well, and suddenly what seemed like the whole inn were hurling their fists and whatever else they had to hand at one another, whether they were friend or foe.

Helana gawked. It had happened in a matter of seconds, and she had not even moved. Had the note summoning her here been someone's idea of a jest?

As if from nowhere, a man appeared at her elbow, shaven-headed and in his middle years. He gripped her arm with a rough hand. She barely heard his whisper over the chaos. 'Follow me.'

Helana did not need telling twice. While the brawl raged around them, the man led her swiftly to a door across the room, and up a set of narrow stairs to a short corridor with two doors on each side, presumably bedchambers for travellers. He knocked lightly at the first room on the left and pulled Helana through after him, shutting the door quickly behind them.

The room was brightly lit, and it took Helana's eyes a few moments to adjust from the gloom of the bar downstairs. She saw mismatched furniture and filthy windows, lit by a dozen candles that exposed the room's insufficiencies.

But it was the person sitting in one of the room's two chairs who brought true brightness to it: a woman, beautiful, in a tight-fitting dress of light blue silks and white lace, with burnt-copper hair flowing unbound down to a miniature waist. Helana might have guessed her age at no more than forty, but something in the shrewdness of her gaze put her in mind of somebody significantly older.

The woman stood and swept upon Helana, standing on her toes to kiss her on both cheeks. 'Princess Helana, it is wonderful to see you! I am sorry for the lengths I went to downstairs, but one cannot be too careful.' Her voice rose and fell like music. She returned to her chair and gestured for Helana to join her in the other.

Helana was not so naïve as to be taken in by such a display. That could have been Jarhick's mistake. 'Did you leave the note? Who are you?'

The woman smiled. 'If you come and sit down you will hear all.'

Helana did not move. 'If your answer satisfies me, I will sit down.'

At this, the woman laughed, a refined roar that tinkled melodically. 'Eryi's blood, there is no doubting who your father is. If you offered the man a gift of a fine horse he would grumble and count its teeth, and I see the apple has not fallen far from the tree. That said, to the eye you take after your mother, which is to both our good fortunes.'

Helana's gaze narrowed. She recognised this woman by reputation. Her chin jutted out in confrontation. 'I know you now. You are Lady Breta Prindian, my father's cousin.' Helana suddenly wished she had not turned her back on the man who had led her here. The Prindians were not to be trusted.

Breta Prindian beamed in confirmation. 'I am indeed, and I hope you now understand why I had to contrive this meeting. I am not welcome at your father's court, and it would not suit me to have him know I had spoken with you. I can only hope that the commotion downstairs was sufficient to divert any spies.' She cast a glance to her man by the door. 'Marius?'

Helana took the opportunity to turn and look at him. He had a look she knew; the man's short stubble, thick jaw, and broad chest screamed soldier, not to mention the sword and dagger at his belt. He was still by the door, standing with his arms folded. 'I saw no one, Lady.'

'Nor would you, if Hessian's wizard had a mind to be checking on the princess.'

The way she spoke so dismissively of her father without using his title immediately reminded Helana to whom she was speaking. This was the mother of Ranulf Prindian, who had butchered her mother's kin. She would likely tear Erland asunder to make her family kings again. She might even have had Jarhick killed, and now mean to do the same to Helana. 'Why are you here? If you plan to ask me to betray my father I won't do it, no matter what you've heard. Or do you mean to kill me?'

'By Eryi, no.' Breta Prindian looked genuinely vexed by the idea. 'I suppose you think I killed your brother as well?'

'That is the rumour,' said Helana.

'I know about rumours. Would I be here speaking to you if I had? I would be putting as much distance between us as possible. I should not be surprised though; I know of the whispers that still linger about my role in my eldest son's ill-considered rebellion.

'Folk are like this. They love to assume the worst of their lords, particularly if that lord is a lady. Presumably you have heard the rumour that I was responsible for Ranulf's rebellion, but never heard that Ranulf himself was responsible? People hate a woman who dares to dance with power. They say I am a shrew, a harridan, a witch, and folk never wonder if perhaps Ranulf was just a power-hungry fool. Had he listened to me, he would still live, and there would be none of this conflict between our families. I ask that you do not allow such talk to cloud your opinion of me.'

Helana thought on her own treatment by her father, and the cruel terms in which she heard spurned suitors spoke of her. There was truth in Lady Prindian's words. In a few decades the same suitors might name Helana a witch.

'Here is my knife.' Breta spun a small blade across the table towards Helana. 'If you believe that I killed your brother, then make an end of it. If that is what you think then you deserve your vengeance.'

'I will reserve my judgement.' Helana spun the knife back across the table. 'Why did you trick me here?'

'I wish to make peace with your father, but I need your help.'

CHAPTER 12

The squall rushed in from the bay in fierce gusts, whistling and roaring, sweeping in a cold rain from heavy black clouds that rolled over the water, thundering ominously and flashing purple lightning.

Tansa sheltered with Tam and Cag in the shadow of a bell-tower overlooking the Imperial enclave. The money from their theft at the playhouse had kept them fed for a fortnight, but that was gone now, and after the initial relief of having escaped, Tansa had made clear to Tam that she blamed him for the paucity of their takings.

'It was *you* who decided on the upper circle,' she had told him, several times. 'I was on the fourth of six when the curtain was pulled back; if you'd been with me we could have had twice as much.'

'It will be fine, Sis!' he had assured her, already joking with Cag over their close escape as if it had been a great adventure that had not nearly landed them all in jail. 'We'll be careful with it, and I've got a new plan in mind, one that can't fail; it will make the playhouse seem like no more than emptying a drunk's pockets.'

Tam's carefulness had lasted a week, until he had not come back to their rooftop one evening, and Tansa had had to drag him out of an inn where he was drunkenly regaling one of the tavern girls with an embellished story of their playhouse heist and his stolen kiss. He had also spent the last of their takings buying drinks for half the tavern. Once he sobered up, Tansa had angrily told him that, from now on, she would look after their money.

She had shared the last of their food with him all the same. He might be one of the greatest fools in Cliffark, but he was still her brother.

Then, she had discovered Tam had kept the Istlewick girl's bracelet. He had claimed it had been lost, until Tansa found it secreted inside a hidden pocket of his jerkin. After that, Cag had to intervene to stop her taking her fury out on Tam's face.

'We're here starving!' she had yelled at him. 'And you're walking around with a golden keepsake! Do you know how much coin that would fetch?'

'We can sell it if we have to,' Tam had insisted cheerfully. 'Just give me a chance; if this new plan doesn't come off, I promise you we can sell it.'

It was at least a relief to learn that Ciera Istlewick had married King Hessian and was on her way to Merivale. Her brother, though, had been morose at the news; Tansa could only guess he had been entertaining visions of sneaking into Cliffark Tower to return the trinket in a fit of gallantry. Tansa remained highly sceptical of his claim that Ciera had welcomed the kiss, telling him emphatically that if she ever caught him forcing himself on a girl she would cut his knackers off. That at least had wiped the smile of his face.

Their hunger and Tam's latest brilliant plan had led them to Cliffark's Imperial enclave, a vast complex near the harbour, surrounded by high black fences of wrought-iron bars topped with gleaming golden spikes, with guards making regular patrols along the inside. Within, there were verdant gardens unlike anything else in Cliffark, with rows upon rows of hedges and red, yellow, and purple flowers, strange birds with tails that spread in huge fans, and a hedge maze so tall even Cag might have got lost in it. Then, at the very centre, a colossal three-storey villa, built all in white, with elegant towers spiralling from a red tile roof. Even in the driving rain, it was a beautiful sight to look upon. It was rumoured the Imperium's lord administrator had transported the building materials specially from Ulvatia.

'What does the lord administrator do again?' asked Cag.

Tam shrugged. 'Trade or something. The merchants are always complaining he can undercut them or overpay their suppliers because Lord Istlewick grants him special tax rates. I heard he's the richest man in the world.'

Tansa snorted. 'That's no reason to rob him. If we get caught, they won't even bother with the jail; Cliffark law doesn't apply in there.'

'That's the point,' said Tam, grinning. 'You'd have to be mad to rob him, so he won't be expecting it.'

Tansa swore under her breath, taking in the immense wealth below them. The roof they were on was a little higher than the top of the fence, separated by a wide street. The take from a place like this might feed them for a year, provided she kept the money out of Tam's reach. 'And you think we can climb that fence without being seen? With the rain making it all slippery? It's got to be at least twelve feet high. Not even you can climb that.'

'The rain will help. Have you seen any guards walk past the last half-hour? They'll all be hiding under cover.'

'They could still be watching the gardens. And what's the plan once we get inside? There'll definitely be guards in the villa.'

'There.' Tam pointed to the nearest of the four towers.

'That window is slightly open. Get in, grab the first thing that shines, get out. Easy.' He left out, of course, the minor matter of scaling the walls.

'What do you want me to do?' asked Cag, to Tansa's annoyance seemingly already accepting that Tam's plan was agreed.

'You're going to boost us over the fence.'

'And how do you suppose we're getting out again if we need Cag to boost us over?' said Tansa. She hated how confident her brother sounded. The playhouse ought to have taught him caution.

He grinned at her in that infuriating way of his. 'We're not coming back over the fence. The entrance only has two guards on it; Cag's going to watch for us leaving the window, then take them by surprise so we've got a clear run back out.'

Tansa gritted her teeth. Her stomach rumbled from its meagre breakfast of stale bread and rainwater. At least Tam was not proposing to go in by himself. She could force him to leave if it became clear his plan would not work. 'Fine. But if I tell you we're leaving, we're leaving. No arguing.'

He raised two fingers to his forehead in mock salute. 'Good as gold. I promise.'

They made their way down to street level, taking a few moments' shelter from the rain under the eaves. The rain had grown heavier, and far out at sea Tansa saw the crackle of forked lightning, its roll of thunder crashing against Cliffark's waterfront seconds later. The Shrouded Sea was infamous for its storms. It was said that a generation ago, the pirate lord Captain Portes Stormcaller had been struck by lightning, leaving him with a dark red and purple motley all down his body and, some claimed, the power to call down squalls of dark rain and white lightning on his foes.

Tam looked at her hopefully, and Tansa gave a nod of agreement. The three of them scurried towards the fence, their feet slapping against the cobbles and throwing up flecks of water. At the fence, Cag set his back against it and effortlessly hefted Tam up, and then Tansa. She pulled herself atop the fence after Tam, and without waiting her brother leapt to the grass below. Tansa was more careful, manoeuvring herself between the spikes and down the other side, dropping the last six feet to the ground.

'We'll see you at the entrance,' said Tansa to Cag. 'Try not to kill anyone.' It would be just like Cag to hit someone over the head and accidentally move from theft to murder.

He left, and keeping themselves low Tansa and Tam scurried across the garden towards the villa. They saw no guards, but threw themselves beneath the first high hedge they came to and surveyed their surroundings.

'Would it not have been better,' said Tansa, 'to do this at night?'

'I heard the lord administrator's guards can see just as well at night as they do in the day,' whispered Tam. The administrator's black-cloaked Imperial guards were well known in Cliffark, with their strange, curved swords, dark ring mail, and grim countenances. Even the city's watchmen were reluctant to trouble them. 'And this way we know the lord administrator's out at the market.'

Tansa frowned. 'What does that have to do with it? Surely you don't think we're likely to run into him? This place is enormous.'

Tam did not reply, but cast a brief, guilty glance up to the slightly open window he had pointed to from the rooftop. That was all it took for Tansa to deduce what he had hidden from her, and before Tam could protest she seized him by the collar.

'Eryi's balls,' she hissed. 'That's his office, isn't it? You Norhai-cursed—'

'I told you we were going to steal from the lord administrator,' he protested, unable to keep the smirk off his face. 'What exactly did you think I meant?'

'I thought you meant...' She had thought he meant to steal something nobody would miss, not directly from the office of the second most powerful man in Cliffark, perhaps most powerful depending on one's opinion of Lord Istlewick. She released her grip on Tam's shirt. 'Next time you'll give me the whole story,' she hissed. 'Let's just get in there, grab something, and get out.'

Their clothes were soaked by the time they reached the wall of the villa, but still they saw no guards. Tansa looked back towards Cag watching them in the distance from across the street, his bulk visible even through the heavy rain, and then suddenly she found herself being hauled down and underneath a low hedge.

'What are you—'

She felt Tam's hand clamp over her mouth. He shushed her and pointed towards their right, where a pair of dark sentries, one man and one woman, had just rounded the corner around a hedge and were making their way along the side of the fence. Had they been just a minute or two later, or the guards earlier, she and Tam would have been seen for certain.

The hedge and the pounding rain gave them good cover, but even so Tansa could feel her heartbeat in her chest as they watched the two guards walk along the fence and eventually behind some high hedges and past the next corner.

When they were gone, Tam grinned at her. 'With all these hedges to hide behind he's practically begging someone to rob him.'

'Thanks for noticing them.'

The villa's ground floor was around eight foot high, below a lip a few handspans wide surrounding the floor above. Tansa looked up at the sheer white wall, slick with rain, silently wishing Cag was there to assist.

Tam was slightly over five and a half feet tall, but got himself up within the blink of an eye. He flung himself against the wall, pushed off with a foot and threw up a hand to clasp the top. He got his second hand up, and then shimmied himself up onto the lip, and sat looking down at Tansa with his feet dangling over the edge.

Tansa was the same height, but knew she could not match her brother's easy, limber grace and unlikely strength. She joined him at the third attempt, though it took a strong hand from Tam, and as quickly as they dared they edged around the thin strip of brick towards the lord administrator's tower.

She looked up at the window, some twelve feet above them. There was no helpful lip here. To her surprise though, Tam produced a length of good rope. 'Just give me a push up,' he said, 'then I'll throw this down to you.'

Tansa did as he suggested, though Tam barely needed the assistance, and with a firm grip of the rope she made swift progress up to the window. Tam had already lifted it, and they entered together, landing lightly upon a soft black carpet.

'Bit different to the outside,' said Tansa, examining the room. With the only source of light being the grey illumination from the window, the whole room was pitched in darkness. Black carpet, a large brown desk, a black chair, and a high, brown bookcase heaving with ledgers and a miscellany of other items she could not identify. She approached a clay bust placed on a shelf, a shrewd-faced old man with a hooked nose and fear-somely bushy brows, that could only be a likeness of the lord administrator himself.

'Ugly brute,' she muttered, meeting its cold eyes for a moment then turning to survey the rest of the room. A jewelled silk purse sat upon the desk, next to a closed ledger. Tansa picked it up, judged the solid weight in her palm, and unbut-toned it to examine within. Her eyes lit up at the contents, a cascade of silver and gold that almost spilt into her hands. She snapped it shut quickly. 'Tam, grab something and let's go.'

Her brother did not reply. Tansa looked up, and saw Tam

with his neck bent backwards peering at the very top of the bookshelf, high above them. She followed his eye, and spotted a small box of marbled, lacquered wood ornamented with gleaming gold edging. He was staring at it dumbly, his mouth hanging open and his eyes half-glazed over.

'Come on, just grab something.'

'I want the box.'

'There's countless things here you can take,' Tansa hissed in a forced whisper, suddenly mindful of being heard. 'Just pick something.' She pointed to a jewelled, golden-hilted dagger set upright in a holder on a lower shelf. 'That looks expensive.'

'I can get the box,' he insisted, still staring up at it. 'Just give me a boost.'

'We don't have time.' Tansa gripped and shook his shoulder. 'Why are you so fixated on it?'

'If it's that high up it's got to be valuable.'

'Or it's just been forgotten about.' Somewhere below them, Tansa heard the creak of a floorboard. 'We need to leave!'

Tam shook his head. 'I'll be five seconds.' He set a foot on the second shelf, and began to climb towards the box.

He would have made it, Tansa did not doubt, but despite its size, the shelf was not affixed to the wall. Two-thirds of the way up, Tam took a step and the stack of shelves creaked. 'Tam!' He paid her no heed, took another step, and with a groan the whole thing began to fall.

Tansa threw herself to the floor. With a mighty crash that shook the entire building, the bookshelf toppled into the desk, splitting wood and sending objects flying. The bust Tansa had admired broke to smithereens upon the carpet, while ledgers and all sorts slipped from their shelves onto the floor, some landing on Tansa.

She opened her eyes. A thick cloud of dust floated in the air, and a tale of destruction was spread all across the carpet. The room was still shaking with the impact. As the echoes of the crash faded, she heard confused shouts and running steps from the floor below, then heavy tread upon the stairs.

'Shit.' She looked for Tam, who had dived out of the way and was already on his feet, cradling the gilded box.

'I got it!' he declared.

Tansa had no time to berate him. 'Run!' Ducking beneath the ruined bookshelf, they ran for the window, and as she levered herself out, she caught the click of a lock behind her, and turned to catch a glimpse of a black-clad guardsman standing in the doorway.

Tam did not trouble to wait. He leapt from the window, and with a cry that was a mix of fear and adrenaline, Tansa jumped after him.

The ground rose to meet her, and she landed heavily, pain vibrating up her shins and knees. An enraged cry in a foreign tongue came from the window. Tansa cupped her hands to her mouth and yelled across the grounds to Cag, then without waiting to see if Tam was following, ran for the gate.

Rounding the corner of the villa, Tansa almost ran straight into the long arms of a lanky guardswoman, but slid beneath her and kept running. The rain had lightened to a drizzle, and all around she could hear the cries of alerted guards, and somewhere the blowing of a horn. Behind her, Tam whooped as he dodged around the same guard.

The gate was still some two-hundred-odd yards away, and there were sentries appearing from behind high hedges and running from the villa, closing in from both sides. Tansa's chest burnt as she willed a burst of speed from her legs.

But she could see already it would not be enough. There were six guards ahead of them, closing in and directly blocking their path to the gate. She risked a look behind, and saw two more chasing in their wake.

'This won't work!' yelled Tam from alongside her. 'Keep running!'

'What?' Tansa shouted back, as Tam veered away from her.

He ran left, towards the fence, holding their box high above his head and crying at the top of his lungs, 'I've got the box! I've got the box! Come on, you lead-footed Imperial bastards!'

For a moment Tansa considered going after him, then saw that four of the guards ahead were now running to intercept Tam, waving their swords and shouting incomprehensibly. That left only two in her path, both half a foot taller and several stone heavier than her, their arms spread wide as if attempting to corral an escaped sow.

Still running, twenty yards from them, Tansa drew her knife, and threw. It was a poor shot, striking hilt-first and catching only the edge of a square-headed guard's temple, but it was enough to stun him, and she flew under his outstretched arms and just beyond the second's grasping fingers.

The two gate guards were ready for her, but when Tansa was close Cag barrelled into one from his blindside, sending the man and his sword clattering to the cobbles. The second turned just in time to meet Cag's vicious running punch full on his jaw, sending him spinning. Without pause, Cag turned to lift the latch of the high double gate and flung it open.

'Run! Find Tam!' she called to him. He raced back the way he had come, as Tansa sped through the gates and went the other way, almost slipping on the rain-slick street as she turned a corner.

In her fist, the purse jangled heavily, and Tansa whooped with delight as she ran, her lungs burning and adrenaline coursing through her like fire. Behind, she heard the pounding of feet, and dared to look back. Two guards were after her, swords drawn, with two more following in hot pursuit. Tansa flew left down a narrow alley, nearly slipping over again on the cobbles, and leapt over an overturned barrel that blocked her path. There were more further down the alley, and Tansa knocked them over in her wake to cover her escape.

Emerging onto the next street, Tansa swung right. When she looked back, nobody was following her, but the cry of elation caught in her throat as the first pair of guards rounded the corner ahead, blocking her escape. She turned on her heel and started running back the other way, just as the second pair emerged from the alley and spotted her.

Cursing, Tansa hurtled down another alley, this one crowded with empty washing lines. She had to duck under them to pass, while the guards close behind hacked through them indiscriminately with their swords. As she emerged into another street, Tansa felt a guardsman's fingers grasping for her shoulder, narrowly failing to get a grip.

There was an inn to her right with wooden stairs leading up to a second level. Tansa leapt up them three at a time, took a running jump onto the banister, and propelled herself onto the tavern's gable roof, grabbing on with both arms and throwing a leg over to lever herself up.

She looked down, and saw two guards trotting up the stairs, seemingly no longer concerned by her flight.

'You're trapped, boy!' one of them called up in accented Erlish. He was breathing hard, and mopping at his forehead with a cloth. 'Throw us down what you stole, and we might let you go.'

The other, younger, guard laughed, displaying two golden teeth among the white. 'That's a girl, fool.' He added something in another tongue, and the first guard laughed along with him.

Tansa turned, scrabbled up the roof, and disappeared over the other side.

To her horror, she found the nearest roof was ten feet across from this one, and built half a floor higher. Too far to jump. Without a way down she was trapped. She scrambled to the edge and looked over. There was an open first-floor window she could drop down to, but if she slipped, she would fall into the street. With a silent prayer to both Eryi and the Norhai, Tansa dangled herself down from the roof edge. Stretching as far as she could, her toes found the windowsill, and she let go.

On a dry day, her old shoes might have found enough grip, but instead she slipped as she landed, and cartwheeled backwards towards the ground, head-first.

Tansa cried out in terror, but it caught in her throat as something grabbed her foot, and the back of her head thudded painfully against the tavern wall. She looked up. A woman was leaning out the window, holding her ankle with both hands.

'Hand!' the woman cried.

Tansa strained her stomach and reached towards her. The woman let one of her hands go, and Tansa was sure she would fall, but she grasped one of Tansa's wrists and then the other. Together, they pulled Tansa up and through the window, and Tansa collapsed on top of her.

'It's been a long time since I had a young man on top of me,' she said from underneath her. 'You owe me twice now.'

Tansa stood up quickly and checked that the purse was still in her pocket. It was, somehow. She heard a commotion from downstairs, and the shouts of patrons as guards forced their way inside. 'Hide me,' she whispered.

The woman was still lying on the floor. 'You're a girl! You should let your hair grow out. I'll hide you, if you split what you took with me.'

Tansa was in no position to argue. The woman stood and pointed to the bed, and Tansa dived underneath it, as the guards' feet pounded up the stairs.

To her shock, she heard the woman open the door.

'She went that way, through there!' She heard the guards run past the door and back outside. Unless Tansa was mistaken, the woman had just sent them back to the landing where she had climbed onto the roof.

'Come out then,' she said, when long enough had passed they could be sure the guards were not coming back. 'Let's count out what you owe. Reckon I should take three-fourths given I've saved your thieving hide twice now.'

Tansa sat with her at the dressing table and upended the purse's contents. A torrent of silver and gold coins poured out, all across the table, hundreds of them. Erlish golds and silvers, Æchenian florins, Imperial medallions, and half-a-hundred others that Tansa did not know the names for, with strange writing and holes in the middle.

The woman whistled. 'Who did you rob? Lord Istlewick? There's more here than this place turns over in a year.'

'How did they all fit?' Tansa wondered aloud.

'This is no off-the-loom purse.' The woman picked it up and examined it. She lit a smokestick, and offered one to Tansa, which she took gratefully. 'Might have been once. You've either robbed a magus, or a man so rich he has servants to wipe his arse.' She was shovelling the coins back into the purse, but it showed no signs of filling up. 'You should throw it away, into the bay. Or just drop it somewhere and don't look back.'

Tansa snatched the purse back, feeling a tingling sensation where she touched it. 'Are you mad? There's enough here to live on for years. You still want your half?'

'Give me the local coins. I can run them through this place without attracting too much attention. You can keep the foreign gold. I'd spend it carefully, not in Cliffark.'

Tansa poured the coins out again and split out the Erlish ones from the rest. She weighed up the sizes of the two collections and nodded to herself, shovelling her share off the table and back into the pouch. 'I'm keeping the purse.'

The woman laughed. 'Keep it. Magic brings folk nothing but trouble.'

Tansa left at nightfall. The woman had found her a small corner room at the inn, which she learnt was called the Siren's Storm, and Tansa had watched for hours from the edge of the window as Imperial guardsmen walked the street, growing more numerous with each passing hour. Occasionally, a blue-uniformed city watchman would appear, speak to them, and then be sent on their way. The black-garbed Imperials were all lean and long-limbed, and patrolled with a careful, competent eye. Tansa was surprised she had outpaced them for so long; she hoped Tam and Cag had been similarly fortunate.

When she was sure it was dark enough, she stepped out through the upper door, and leapt from the banister, landing silently on the cobbles.

Tansa walked around the inn and found the spot the woman had told her about, where a stack of crates was piled against a wall. She scaled them easily and crouched on the narrow brickwork, the next building within jumping reach.

She landed heavily, sending a loose tile spinning to the ground, breaking the night's silence. Tansa heard a shout from inside, but did not stop, moving swiftly across the terraces. Every fifth roof she paused to listen, waiting for the cry that would alert the soldiers to the shadow that slipped past them overhead.

None came.

Tansa dropped down to street level when she reached Pauper's Hole, a labyrinth of alleys and catacombs said to be the most dangerous hectare in the city. If she was being followed, they would never be able to track her through Pauper's.

She kept her hand on the purse, ready to run at the first scratch of a dagger being drawn. Thirty feet below was the hole the place was named for, an ancient well that locals liked to say had no bottom. Locals also liked to say that you could find anything in Pauper's. Anything except a body. The watchmen did not dare to walk these alleys. Dangerous as the Imperial guards looked, she would not have wagered one of them surviving a patrol through here either. Just the sight of their mail would be enough for one of the district's cut-throats to take them for a long walk underground.

Tansa saw nobody, but she knew they saw her.

She emerged on the other side up a set of stone steps, onto Market Road which ran between the city market and the harbour market. The cool night air filled her lungs, and Tansa realised she had been holding her breath. There was no one in sight.

When she returned to their spot, on the flat roof of a quiet one-storey inn sheltered between high rooves on each side, she was relieved to find Cag and Tam already waiting for her. Cag cantered across the roof and enveloped Tansa in a hug, nearly flattening her. Tam hung back warily, still clutching his Norhai-cursed box.

'Eryi's piss, what were you thinking?' she demanded, stalking across the roof towards her brother. 'You almost got us both killed!'

He smiled. 'We're fine though! Do you still have the purse?'

Tansa flew at Tam with her fists. 'I'm not bloody fine!' He raised his arms to shield himself before falling to the floor to escape her, but Tansa just sat on him and threw wild strikes at his head and shoulders while Tam flailed uselessly trying to fight her off. Eventually Cag pulled her away.

'You idiot! You total fucking idiot! We were going to escape without anyone seeing us, and then you had to grab that stupid box!'

'I'm sorry!' he protested. 'I saved us, didn't I? We'd never have got out if I hadn't gone for the fence.'

Tansa scowled. Her wretched brother was right. If left to her they would probably have both been captured. 'Worth it, I hope? Fancy box with lots of coins inside?'

Tam looked sheepish. 'It's empty. But I'm sure it's valuable, just look at it!'

'I'll give you valuable.' Tansa withdrew the purse from her pocket, and poured its contents into a pile at her feet.

Once Cag and Tam had seen the pile of coins, and Tansa had demonstrated twice how they could all fit inside the purse, their eyes were big as cartwheels.

Cag found his voice first. 'What are we going to do with it?'

'We can't spend it round here, we have to swap it,' said Tansa quickly, thinking of the woman's words. 'Wyatt down Pauper's does lending. I reckon he'd trade us it for regular gold.'

'That old crook?' Tam spat. 'He'd give us two silvers and shop us to the guards first chance he got.'

'We need to get out of Cliffark before the Imperials find us. The only other place we can trade those is Merivale.'

The next morning, Tansa left the roof, carrying a few of the more well-known Imperial coins. Her aim was to trade them for enough Erlish coin to buy their passage to Merivale. She insisted on going alone; one person would not attract so much attention as three.

Wyatt's premises were a cul-de-sac room in the catacombs of Pauper's Hole, guarded by a pair of mean-looking guards in motley armour, who leered at Tansa as she entered. She stuck her tongue out at them, and slapped one meatily when he reached out to rustle her hair.

The room was no less gloomy than the rest of the catacombs. The only thing that might have been called decoration was the dark wood, gold-banded chest in the corner. It was said Wyatt slept here as well, unable to move the chest and unwilling to leave it.

'Not seen you around much recently,' said Wyatt, as he

pretended to examine one of the medallions. 'But someone I know swears they saw you walking through Pauper's late last night when the rest of us were all hiding from those black bastards.'

Tansa shook her head. 'Wasn't me.'

'Well, I'll not name you a liar,' he said, making a great show of his charity with a big toothy smile. 'And if anyone asks, I'll likely say nothing, same you did. But I can't speak for all o' those round here. Lot of folk'll say anything for the right offer.'

Wyatt gave her a fifth of the coins' value, and Tansa was glad to take it. Later that day, she, Tam, and Cag stepped into the back of a horse-drawn cart with a dozen others, part of a caravan headed for Merivale.

CHAPTER 13

Piperskeep's great hall rang with the rough melodies of an eight-piece band. The pounding drums echoed off its thick walls, while a single fiddler cut through the din to lead a merry dance, straining to be heard over the guests' uproarious laughter and the clashing of cups as they toasted their new queen.

Ciera sat at the right-hand of the king's high-backed chair. Hessian had not yet emerged, leaving his man Theodric to send Ciera his apologies. It seemed odd that a man would miss his own wedding feast, but that accorded with what she had been told of him. His daughter Princess Tarvana was keeping her company instead.

'... and once you are settled here you will have to visit Lord Balyard and me at Prosbury. The gardens are delightful in summer, and you'll be glad of the peace after a few months of living in the noise of the city,' said Tarvana, smiling.

'My father's castle is set well away from Cliffark,' replied Ciera. Tarvana's kindness seemed genuine, but it was hard to believe that someone five years older than her could find so little to say. She had met Tarvana's husband Lord Balyard only briefly, and liked him even less: a sweaty, red-faced man with a paunch hanging over his belt, who had cast a cold up-and-down look over Ciera and given her only the merest courtesy. 'So far, the noise of Merivale has been a welcome change, but I would love to visit you there someday.'

When Ciera had arrived in Merivale a few days previously, so many people had lined the streets that it seemed as if the entire city had come out the welcome her. Children on their parents' shoulders had blown kisses to her, and tavern balconies had been crowded with rich and poor alike raising toasts in her name. Apprehensive as she was of her marriage, how could she not love the city after that welcome? After the cloistered safety of her life at Cliffark Tower, every citizen who waved to her was a wonder. They were clearly poorer than the citizens of Cliffark – many had been dressed in brown roughspun, and a stiff wind might have blown over some of the hovels she saw – but she would change that. At the gate she had heard guards charging a levy for entry per wheel, foot, or hoof; with such an erratic form of taxation it was no wonder the city did not prosper.

The people in the hall below her were another matter. While every second man was dressed in plain leather as if they had just dismounted a horse, the gowns of the women were a rainbow of colour, and even the lowliest serving girls wore wool dresses dyed the blood-red arms of the Sangreals. The pageantry and noise of the feast were almost overwhelming.

'My daughter, Caleste, was born earlier this year,' continued Tarvana. 'If you are with child soon, they would be nearly the same age. It would be lovely for Caleste to have a friend in the family!'

Ciera fumbled for words that might move the conversation on from speculation about her bearing the king's children, but Tarvana's eyes were drawn suddenly to something behind Ciera. Ciera followed her gaze, and turned to see an old man in rich robes of deep red entering the hall, in animated discussion with Lord Andrick and Theodric. He towered over both of

them, but was spindly next to Lord Andrick's brawn, with
rheumy eyes and sunken cheeks.

Ciera did not need the silence that had fallen over the hall
to know that this man was her husband. She had been warned
what to expect, but could not help being disappointed by his
obvious frailty, and by how *old* he was. He might have been
handsome once, but those days were long past. He looked at
her, and he quietened his companions with a gesture. He
approached, and bent his straight back to press his lips lightly to
the back of her hand.

'My Queen.' His voice was half a whisper. 'You are lovely
beyond words.' He sat next to her, and with a wave to the room
bid that the festivities continue.

Ciera's mouth was dry, and her heart was beating like a
blacksmith's hammer. What would they talk about? She had
been tutored in courtesy, but no lesson had prepared her for
having to converse with a king, wife to husband. Would he be
cross if she had nothing to say?

But to her relief, King Hessian proved unfailingly charming, asking gentle questions of what might be done to make her
feel comfortable in Merivale and whether they would need to
send for anything from Cliffark. Ciera chastised herself for her
foolishness. That her husband was old and a man people feared
did not make him any less kingly. The two of them supped
together on roast chicken and potatoes with black pepper, while
lords and ladies approached their table in ones and twos and
swore fealty to King Hessian, and to Queen Ciera. As each
well-wisher departed, Hessian sometimes made cruel japes
about them in Ciera's ear, about whose son was a simpleton and
who was being cuckolded by his groom, and she laughed
nervously along with him. *I will make him love me*, she
reminded herself.

Once the course was finished, the king stood to leave.
'Please excuse me, my dear. There are matters that require my

attention.' He gestured to Lord Andrick and Theodric, and the three of them left the hall.

Ciera could not help thinking it odd. What was so urgent that the king had to attend to it during his wedding?

Orsian was greatly enjoying this feast. Away from his father, he could relax, and celebrate a wedding the way one was meant to. He had wasted no time in joining Naeem's twin sons, Burik and Derik, in a drinking game, in which each of the three of them would splay their left hand on the table, while the man to his right would rapidly stab a blunt knife between each finger. Each round lasted until somebody missed and caught the other's finger, at which point they would both have to down half their ale, while the third hooted with laughter. The twins were old hands at the game, and Orsian was on his way to being good and drunk.

The disappointment was that Errian had not returned. He had last been seen riding at speed towards Thrumb, and there had been no news of him in weeks. His father had been furious not to find him in Merivale, doubly so when word reached him from Violet Hall that Errian had lied to his mother about having orders and ridden west in haste. Andrick had dispatched a dozen men with instructions to bring Errian back in chains if he would not comply. Orsian expected, though, that Errian was already in Thrumb, winning great victories. It should have been him. He reached for a fresh ale and took a long drink.

Even more disappointing was the absence of Helana. She lived in Piperskeep; where else could she possibly be on the day of her father's wedding feast? It had gone well between them last time, without any of his usual tongue-tied awkwardness, and he had hoped to speak with her again.

Trapped in his reverie, Orsian's knife suddenly caught

Burik's knuckle, drawing blood for the first time and earning a pained gasp, while Derik howled with laughter and gestured for them both to down their tankards.

As Orsian and Burik drank, Derik was already seizing another enormous flagon from a passing servant girl, and no sooner had Orsian replaced his tankard than he began immediately refilling it. 'More ale for the young lord!' Derik cried, laughing, lively spots of colour high on his cheeks.

Burik let out a deep belch. 'The young lord just stabbed me worse than he ever has with a sword.'

Orsian laughed along with them, forgetting his malaise and raising his tankard to smash against theirs, sending sudsy beer all over their hands and sleeves. 'I swear I've almost got the hang of it. One more round!'

———

'Where is my daughter?' Hessian raged, slamming his fist on the table in the small kitchen annexe they had found for their impromptu council.

Theodric looked genuinely troubled, which made the situation all the more concerning, Andrick thought. The wizard could sniff out secrets in a trough of slurry, but claimed to have no idea where Helana was.

'You tell me that Breta Prindian was seen crossing the Pale River a fortnight ago,' the king continued, 'but that nobody has seen her since, and now my daughter has disappeared. These two events are not coincidence!'

Theodric bowed his head and folded his hands up inside his robes. 'It may be unconnected, Majesty.'

Hessian shook his head and wagged a finger at Theodric. 'No, Theodric, you do not know Breta Prindian as I do. If she crossed the river she did it for a reason, like to kidnap my daughter.'

'That is not a task she would take on herself, no more than you would try to capture Rymond Prindian yourself,' said Andrick.

'I could have done no worse in that regard.' Hessian glared at Theodric. 'Find my daughter, and once you have her, find Breta Prindian. If she has so much as quenched her thirst in one of my streams I want her arrested for stealing.'

'Let me and Theodric deal with this,' said Andrick. 'It is not so urgent that you should miss your own wedding feast.' It was important that the attending lords saw Hessian, healthy and happily married.

Hessian grunted in grudging acceptance. 'Just keep me away from Lord Balyard. I pray my grandchildren do not end up so fat and useless as their sire.'

Andrick thought that a little uncharitable. Balyard was younger than him yet had long gone to seed, but there was a calculating intelligence behind his cold eyes.

A knock at the door interrupted them. 'Enter,' called Hessian. A nervous steward leant his head around the door.

'Forgive me, Majesty. There is a disturbance in the hall.'

The knife game had left Orsian's knuckles scarred and bleeding, and he excused himself from the twins to take a moment's recovery. He stepped through a side door to relieve himself in the yard, but as he went to piss was overcome by a torrent rising from his stomach. He crumpled forward and retched a trail of beery vomit against the wall.

He wiped his mouth with the back of his hand, grimacing. At least no one had seen. He cupped his hands in a nearby horse-trough and wolfed down water, then washed his face in it. When he felt sober enough, and was sure the stench did not linger on him, he stepped back into the hall, hoping his extended absence had not been noted.

To his good fortune, every head was turned towards the main entrance. Orsian stood on his toes to see Helana walking in, arm in arm with an older woman. They were speaking quietly with their heads together, as if they had taken a wrong turn on a stroll around the gardens and were unconcerned to have mistakenly disturbed several hundred wedding guests.

The room's atmosphere only added to the sense that there had been a mistake. The raucous conversations had stopped, and Orsian could sense the murmured asides and hostile eyes that followed the two women. Helana whispered something, and the older woman threw back her head and laughed, showing off a magnificent crown of unbound burnt-copper hair and a slender neck supported by an impossibly sharp collarbone.

They approached Ciera, and together dropped to their knees and kissed the back of her hand.

'My queen, I am Princess Helana.' Helana's voice was rich and ringing, cutting across the murmurs and reaching even those at the back of the hall. 'My companion is the Lady Breta Prindian, mother to Lord Rymond Prindian, and the king's cousin.'

Breta Prindian. Mother of the king's rival to the crown. The witch who had tricked her first son into an unwinnable war and left him to be driven slowly insane by his lonely death in an oubliette. Hated by King Hessian with a passion that wavered just next to madness. Orsian was fascinated.

He moved forward for a closer look, just in time to see his father re-enter the hall, followed closely by Hessian and Theodric. They all froze when they saw her.

'Lord Andrick!' Breta swept over to him, and stood on tiptoes to plant a kiss on his cheek. She looked magnificent in a sleek dress of Prindian green, showing off a miniscule waist and long, slender legs. 'It has been too long. When were we together last? The years have been good to you; you must tell me your secret.'

'The last time you saw him, he was breaking through the gate at Fallback Lodge while your kin fled from his sword.' Hessian loomed over her like an ogre, his lip curling and nostrils flaring. 'You are brave to come here, Lady Prindian. How did you get past my guards?'

'She was invited.' Helana stepped forward, appearing at Breta's elbow. 'By me.' She stared at her father, her back straight and her chin raised in defiance.

Hessian's eyes blazed, but before he could reply, Breta fell to her knees in front of him.

'Majesty. Accept my sincere apology for my deceit. I only wished to see my cousins, and to reaffirm my family's oath to you and to all those of the Blood. The Prindian family owes its survival to the Sangreal line. The lives of my forebears were bought with Meridival blood. We pledge our fealty to you, King Hessian; that we will pay to you a tenthweight of our yields twice annually; that we will endeavour to enforce your laws so far as they are accordant with our own; and that we will ride to defend your realms at your request. All we ask in return is that our people are defended from all foes, both native and foreign.'

Lady Breta was clearly no stranger to compelling people to listen to her. There was not a man or woman present who had not heard every word of the traditional oath. Hessian, though, looked down on her implacably, as if not a word had reached his ears. The room was still, as if spellbound, and for a moment Orsian thought the silence might stretch into eternity.

After an age, Lord Andrick touched his brother's elbow, and the look that passed between them seemed to lift the spell over the room. Hessian gave the smallest of nods. 'I accept your oath, Lady.' Breta kissed his outstretched hand and rose to her feet.

From her seat, Ciera stared. Her husband's face was tight and twisted, his eyes fixed upon Breta Prindian as if he were trying to strip the skin from her bones. He took his seat next to Ciera without a word, anger rolling off him in waves. She sat rigid, trying not to look at him. This was the man whose temper she had heard stories about.

Lord Andrick whispered something to a steward, and Lady Prindian was escorted as far from Hessian as possible. For the heir's mother to be hidden away towards an end of the high table was a plain insult, but anyone watching her would not have known it. She chatted amiably with her companions, complimented the serving girls, and when the band restarted she danced with Tarrik, Tarvana's young son, letting him lead her clumsily with unbridled enthusiasm, while she glided across the ground with girlish grace and flushed cheeks, laughing as Tarrik flailed his limbs exuberantly around the floor. Her delight was a clear contrast to the grey pallor of Ciera's new husband, the ghost at his own feast.

Lady Prindian was charming and beautiful, a queen in all but name. Ciera could not help but admire her effortless poise. She was brave as well; Ciera did not think she would ever be able to stand up against Lord Andrick and the king like that.

Lady Prindian stayed for the final two courses, but did not approach Ciera until Hessian was away from the table, distracted by a discussion with Theodric. 'My Queen.' She curtsied, extravagantly fanning out the hem of her dress, then seized two glasses of wine from a passing servant. 'Would you grant me the pleasure of your company? There is something I would like to show you.' She offered her a glass. 'We are cousins now, after all.'

Ciera hesitated, but accepted the wine and took Lady Prindian's hand, allowing herself to be led to the enormous stained-glass window behind the high table. It covered a whole side of the hall, twenty yards wide and at least as high, divided into eight panes.

The pane Breta Prindian led her to was partially hidden away in an alcove. 'This pane,' said Breta, gesturing upwards, 'shows the Accord, when my ancestor King Halord the Ninth handed his crown to Pedrian of the Meridivals.' It showed a blond man in green, kneeling and offering a crown to a dark-haired figure in red wearing a crown of his own. 'He had it melted down afterwards into a bronze dagger, and hacked off King Halord's head with it. Pedrian said Erland did not need two crowns, nor two kings.'

'But to the king you said the lives of your forebears were bought with Meridival lives,' Ciera said perplexedly. Her father had told her how Erland had been broken and reforged by the Sangreals of the Meridival tribe. Three hundred years ago, they had driven the Prindians out of East Erland, across the Pale River. Over a century later, the Imperium invaded West Erland, and the men of East Erland had driven them back, and claimed the West as well. She took a sip of her wine and started slightly at its cloying sweetness.

'In a sense, but they did not do it for love of us. They did not lift their swords until the Imperium reached the river, and we have been under their heel ever since.' Breta pointed upwards to the pane above, showing another man in red astride a horse with Eryispek in the background. 'King Darien. He ruled fifty years after Pedrian. When Halord's grandson declared West Erland independent, Darien prayed on Eryispek for twenty days and nights, bidding that his armies not lift a sword until Eryi had answered, even as the men of the West crossed the Pale River. When Darien came down from Eryispek, he gathered his armies and harried them all the way back to Irith, and when the rebels hid behind the walls he lit the whole city on fire. He killed the entire Prindian family, except a boy from a lower line still at the breast, my great-great-grandfather.

'Halord's grandson's name was burnt out of every record. My people call him Halord the Tenth, or Halord the Burnt. Your husband's people call King Darien "Darien the Divine", for in return for his prayers, Eryi blessed him with unnatural strength, virility, and life. He lived to be a hundred and ten and sired thirty children. I believe he is my and Hessian's most recent common ancestor.'

'Why are you telling me this?' asked Ciera, trying to shake the images of headless kings and charred corpses from her head. Lady Prindian's conversation was making her feel light-headed. She took another sip of wine to steady herself.

'To teach you something of the line your husband comes from, and the sort of man he is.'

'To turn me against him, you mean.' Ciera tore her eyes away from the window, making her vision swim. She could not deny that she feared her husband, but for all Breta Prindian's grace and geniality at the feast, she did not trust her. Ciera took a step back, and her legs almost gave way. The floor wavered beneath her, and the noise of the guests pulsed against the inside of her skull. Something was terribly wrong.

Lady Prindian was suddenly at her elbow. 'Are you well, child?' She ushered her towards a side door, but Ciera could not focus on it, nor make her legs work. 'You, the queen is unwell; help her.'

Strong hands seized and lifted Ciera. Her eyelids drooped, heavy as lead, clouding her vision. *The wine...* She struggled against the wave of warmth flowing through her limbs, slipping into darkness as she was carried from the hall.

Andrick watched Hessian carefully. His brother's mood was ever changeable, and today was no different. He had charmed his young wife as he might have thirty years ago, when his hair had still been golden and his body lithe rather than gaunt, then in council with Andrick and Theodric he had been raging, consumed with paranoia.

Or not paranoia, as it happened, because Breta Prindian had arrived, and it had sunk Hessian's mood further. He was not speaking to his wife now. He had eyes only for Lady Prindian.

Andrick shook his head. The girl would find being queen and wed to a much older man hard enough without Hessian being trapped in one of his black moods. After the weeks Andrick had been away to claim his bride, the king could at least have tried, but Hessian did not think like that; if he had he would not have been Hessian.

As well as the king, he was keeping a careful eye on the guests. Lady Prindian had brought half-a-dozen of her own guards with her, and there were those at the wedding who with a few drinks inside them would not be able to resist trying to goad a few West Erlanders into a fight.

When it happened, he was surprised to see it was Prindian men who were the instigators. One staggered and clumsily swung his tankard into a man's face, soaking him in beer.

Rather than apologising, the man and his two companions roared with laughter. 'You ought to be more careful,' said one of them. 'You owe my friend here a beer.'

Their red-faced victim mopped at his dripping face, and it took Andrick a moment to realise it was Lord Balyard. 'Careful, is it?' He swung his own tankard towards the other man's head, narrowly missing. Two other guests appeared, and suddenly the six of them were squaring up to one another, chest to chest.

Andrick did not see who threw the first punch, but he was there in seconds to push the two groups apart, almost taking a blow to his own face. After a struggle he eventually separated them. 'No more!' He dragged in two guards, forming a defensive barrier. 'These men are our guests.'

With a handkerchief, Lord Balyard wiped the beer from his flushed face. He had given as good as he got in the scuffle; no matter his other faults, the man was no coward. Balyard cast a withering look over the West Erlanders. 'I thought it was your job to defend us from the likes of these, Barrelbreaker, not the other way around,' he said scornfully, before he and his retainers retreated reluctantly to a table, staring daggers back at the West Erlanders.

'And you three should watch yourselves,' said Andrick, turning to the West Erlanders. They stalked off without a word towards the entrance, one of them clutching a hand to his bloodied nose.

Andrick watched them leave. He had expected Lady Prindian's guards to be on their best behaviour. He would have to report them to her and ask that they be disciplined.

'Lords!' A cry of alarm came from near the high table. Andrick turned, his hand immediately reaching for his sword. To his relief, he saw Hessian was safe, and looking just as startled as he was.

In a doorway, a pale guardsman in sweat-stained leathers leant awkwardly on his sword, breathing heavily. There was a collective gasp from the room. Blood was dripping onto the floor, dark and heavy, and the man's sleeve was soaked in it.

'My King...' His voice was weak. 'They took the queen... Prindian...'

There was a moment of confusion. Hessian instinctively looked at Andrick.

'Block the doors!' cried Theodric, rushing for the main entrance, while Hessian took up the same cry, looking around for Breta Prindian's green dress.

Andrick was already running for the exit, pushing aside

anyone in his way and grabbing two shocked members of the *Hymeriker*, still holding tankards of ale.

'After her,' he growled, shoving them towards the door. The three of them ran towards the yard.

But in the yard there was no sign of them.

'Horses!' Andrick demanded of nobody in particular. 'Three horses, or I'll wring your necks!' He collared a passing servant carrying a tray of cups, who shrieked and dropped them. 'Where did she go?'

The girl looked up at him wide-eyed. 'Who?'

'Breta Prindian, green dress!'

The girl pointed at the yard's western portcullis. Andrick vaulted a docile pony that a groom was leading towards somebody else. It whinnied indignantly, but Andrick slapped its flank and rode out of the keep and across the moat, tearing up mud and leaving the others to find their own mounts.

The streets here were broad and uncrowded. Andrick cursed. Had Breta Prindian gone a different way she might have found herself stuck in a narrow alley behind a cart, and he would have caught up with her in no time. There were fresh hoofprints in the mud, but Andrick ignored them, taking the fastest way to the Ram's Gate. Either he would catch them up or cut them off at the gate. He let loose a string of expletives at startled citizens blocking his path, and drove the pony on.

Behind him, a bell was ringing, ordering the guards to close the gates. But when Andrick arrived the Ram's Gate was open, and two guards on either side of it lay dead, hands gripping their swords halfway out of their scabbards.

Andrick grimaced. Breta Prindian had planned this perfectly. He spurred his horse on over the bridge.

Outside the city, he scanned the land ahead of him. There were a dozen riders, several larger figures flanking a smaller one with an unmistakable mane of copper hair. Squinting, Andrick thought he could make out that one horse was being led on a rope, with its rider strapped into the saddle and sat low with their arms wrapped around the horse's neck. *Ciera*.

Andrick judged the distance to be at least a quarter-mile. He could not have made up much ground on them at all; they may have actually increased their lead.

He stared down in annoyance at the docile pony. *Damn useless nag*. He could not catch them, but he could try to keep them in sight. Hopefully someone had the sense to send out a larger force, on proper horses. He rode on.

It had been cleverly done, he had to admit. The fight had distracted him and the entire hall while Breta Prindian spirited the queen out. But why had Ciera gone with her? And what was the Prindian plan; to capture Hessian's queen and so prevent him having an heir? It was as good as a declaration of war.

After barely a quarter of an hour in pursuit, his quarry had only lengthened their lead and were now small specks against the horizon. The sorry pony was exhausted, its head dipped and its breath coming low and laboured. Cursing, Andrick let the beast come to a stop and dismounted. He had no hope of catching them without reinforcements and a fresh mount. He looked back, hoping to see some sign of pursuit.

It was almost another half-hour before he saw them: the two *hymerikai* who had followed him from the hall, riding hard on proper Erland purebreds that could march for a day and a night and bite an enemy's face off when they arrived.

'Took your time, lads,' he said, irritated they had not caught him sooner. They were good warriors at least: a crafty veteran called Jack Bornaway and a young man named Drayen.

'Someone had barred the stable door and cut all the saddle girths, Lord!' replied Jack. 'It was a damn nightmare to sort out. We came as quick as we could.'

'By Eryi's balls.' Andrick clenched his fist in frustration.

Breta Prindian had thought of everything. 'One of you give me your horse; this one might as well have three legs.'

'No need, Lord, your boy followed us out.' Jack pointed back towards Merivale. 'He's brought your horse, and a pair of your hounds.'

A few minutes later, Orsian joined them, riding his own horse with Andrick's mountainous black steed Valour tethered to him, pulling at the rope grumpily and baring his teeth. Andrick's bitch Numa followed them with Gyrwulf, the largest of her last litter. 'Sorry,' said Orsian. 'Valour doesn't like being led.'

'Good lad, Orsian.' Andrick was thankful for his son's quick thinking; the boy had looked incapable of it when he had last seen him at the feast. He remounted on his own horse. 'Take the pony and head back; let them know which direction to go in.'

'They know to head west to the river,' said Orsian, his mouth set. 'I'm coming too.' His sword dangled in its scabbard, and he had a bow and quiver strung over his back.

Andrick looked at him levelly, remembering himself at that age, hot-headed and desperate for battle. Orsian was steadier than he had been, and if this was the Prindians' first act of war then he could not hold him back any longer. Whether Orsian was ready or not, and he suspected he was, blood would be shed in Erland this autumn.

'As you will. We ride fast, through the night if we must. And if they cross the Pale River we press into West Erland, with or without reinforcements.' Andrick slapped the pony on the rump and it shot off towards Merivale, far faster than it had with him on its back. 'Numa! Track!'

The two hounds sniffed the fresh hoofmarks in the grass at Andrick's feet, barked to each other, and set off at a run.

CHAPTER 14

They rode through the yellow haze of autumn, the sun hanging lower in the sky, blinding their eyes and casting long shadows in their wake. Past wild goats and docile sheep they galloped, the two hounds scattering them into the evening air, earning the shouted curses of whitebeard shepherds.

When the sun dipped below the horizon, they rode on, the hounds sniffing out their path while they followed under the cold grey moonlight. Orsian's clothes were soaked in sweat, and he shivered as the wind brushed his clammy skin. They had made good pace, and the tracks were fresh, but for many hours there was no sight of their quarry. Over every hillcrest he was sure they would finally glimpse them, but still Breta Prindian eluded them.

'They ride as if driven by demons,' he muttered.

'Not demons, Lord,' said Jack Bornaway. 'Your father.'

Finally, his father called them to a halt. 'That's enough for today. The horses need to rest, and if we lose their trail in the dark it's over. We'll ride on at dawn.'

'They could be only just ahead of us, Lord,' said Jack,

bending down to examine their hoofprints. 'What if they ride on through the night? We'll never catch them.'

'They'll need to rest as well. And if they have a fresh mount for Queen Ciera we may never catch her, whether we rest or not.'

Orsian was ready to ride on. His father said there were a dozen men among their quarry, and they were only four, so what better way to even the odds than to attack them by night? He kept quiet though; disobedience might cause his father to send him home again.

They lay down around a hastily assembled fire. Orsian did not sleep for a long time, his mind rushing with thoughts of the fight that would surely come on the morrow. He had heard some men say that their bowels turned to water the night before battle, but not Orsian. It was what he had been born for, and he was ready.

They rose early, but had no more luck the following day. The tracks they followed were clear, but still their quarry eluded them.

'It's impossible to know if we're gaining ground or not,' said Andrick, visibly frustrated. 'We'll ride through the night, as slow as we need to for the horses to manage. If they cross the river...'

Orsian knew what his father meant: if their enemy crossed the river with Queen Ciera, saving her would be almost impossible. They would have to ride into a likely hostile West Erland, just the four of them against half the country. There was no prospect of his father giving up though, no matter what stood in their path.

Orsian slept in the saddle, trusting his horse to follow the two hounds. If they were tired, they did not show it. One at a time, they would disappear to hunt while the other tracked, and return with stains of animal blood around their muzzles.

As the third day broke, they heard the first whisper of the Pale River. The ground ahead of them steepened to a crest, and Andrick gave a sharp whistle that caused the dogs to pull up, panting and growling restlessly. They dismounted in silence, and Orsian saw to the dogs and horses with water from his skin and a few apples.

Andrick beckoned them to him, and pointed over the ridge. 'Listen.'

Orsian strained his ears, and, hidden among a chorus of birdsong and the roar of the river, he caught the conversations of men on the wind. 'They've missed the ford,' he observed. 'They've come too far north.'

His father nodded. 'We're well south of Halord's Bridge as well. They're miles from where they need to be. Stick your head over that ridge. Keep your bow ready.'

Orsian notched an arrow and slinked up the ridge, lowering himself onto his elbows as he approached, ready to leap up with his bow drawn if he were seen. He poked his head over the top. The river was perhaps eighty yards away, flowing fast and roaring with white froth. The noise would be why their quarry had not heard their approach. There was a group of figures on the bank, and two in the water, struggling against the current to drag a rope to the other side.

He relaxed his grip on the bow. They were fools for trying to cross here. Other parts of the Pale River were hundreds of yards wide, but with a leisurely flow that allowed boatmen to ferry customers between the two banks. They were at a bend in the river perhaps thirty yards across, but the swift flow would make their crossing an ordeal, even with a rope. It was slower than usual due to the dry summer, but it was still strong enough to pull a man under and carry him north until he reached the sea or drowned.

On the near bank, Orsian recognised Breta Prindian's slender silhouette. The soldier next to her had a bundle strapped across the rump of his horse. *Ciera*. There was a rope running underneath to restrain her, though he saw no signs of struggle. Most of the soldiers had dismounted, letting their horses feed on the grass while they waited for their fellows to prepare the rope.

Orsian made a quick count. There were a dozen soldiers, armed and armoured. He shuffled back down the ridge.

'Twelve, as you said,' he informed his father.

Drayen looked at Andrick sharply. 'Can we fight twelve, Lord?'

'Makes no difference if it's twelve men or twelve magi,' Andrick growled. 'We are sworn to the king, and that means we rescue the queen, even if it ends in our deaths.'

He scrutinised the three of them, and Orsian could tell he was considering their odds. His pulse quickened, and his sword hand itched. He had never been so close to battle before. A small bubble of fear rose in his stomach. That was good, he had heard. Sometimes fear kept you alive.

'We'll make do with what we have,' said his father gruffly, touching his sword hilt for luck. 'We'll circle round and come up from the south. Orsian, you'll stay on the ridge. Once we're nearly on them, you start firing. Drayen, you stay on my right and cover any who try to get up the ridge. Orsian, how many arrows do you have?'

'But I want to fight!' said Orsian, dismayed. He had not come all this way to fire arrows from a safe distance; he needed to cross swords with somebody and prove himself.

His father's face was like stone. 'I'll ask again, and if you don't answer me you can turn around and ride back to Merivale. How many arrows do you have?'

Orsian obediently did a quick count of his quiver. 'Twelve,' he muttered, trying not to sound insolent.

'Make them count. If it turns against us, run for your horse and ride east. If I know Naeem there'll be another force only a few hours behind us.'

Jack looked at Orsian sceptically. 'Hope you can shoot straight with that bow, young Lord. If any of those arrows hit me you'll regret it.'

He was smiling, but Orsian was in no mood for jokes. 'I can shoot,' he replied defensively. His aim may not have been tested in combat, but he could hit a bullseye at a hundred yards. It could not be so different, could it?

The three of them rode south, with the two wolfhounds dogging Valour's heels, leaving Orsian alone.

He sighed, and loosed his sword in its scabbard. He wanted it ready, even if he was commanded to stay back. Drayen was only a few years older than him and had probably not yet swung his sword at a true enemy either, so there was a chance he might still be called upon. That was likely why his father had commanded Drayen to stay nearest Orsian, so he would have the benefit of arrow cover. He returned to his place on the ridge and waited.

By the time he saw the three of them riding up from the south, the two men in the water had made it to the other bank and were securing the rope to a tree stump. A lookout gave a cry of warning, and with a splash Breta Prindian plunged her horse into the water, gripping the rope as she spurred her skittish mount into the raging current. Behind her, one of the soldiers tried to drive the horse carrying Ciera into the water, but the beast refused to move.

Two soldiers had dared to run to their horses, and rode to flank their charging attackers. Orsian came to his feet and pulled his bowstring back. He tracked the path of the first horse with his bow.

Eryi, guide my arm.

He aimed just ahead of the rider, and the bow thrummed against his shoulder. The arrow whistled, and struck, sinking deep into the man's neck. He screamed, and the shocked horse reared up, throwing its rider into the air. He thudded heavily against the ground, and did not rise again.

The second rider whirled his horse around looking for the bowman, and by the time he saw Orsian, Drayen was already on him. He crashed into the other man's horse, and with a wild yell brought his sword down with where the man's collarbone met his throat with no armour to protect it, drawing a spurt of blood and a pained cry. A second thrust to the man's exposed neck sent him to the ground, blood pooling and mixing with the wet dirt of the riverbank.

Faced with a mounted foe and two snapping wolfhounds, the remaining soldiers fought a managed retreat, taking them to the edge of the water where the rope had been tied, protecting their lady's escape. To Orsian's dismay, one of them leapt onto the horse carrying Ciera and spurred it into the water. Cursing, Orsian fired at him, and missed. He broke from cover and raced towards the river.

His father did not seem to have noticed the man fleeing with Ciera. He brought Valour around, calling orders to Jack and Drayen, dragging his warhorse in a tight loop as the others followed in his wake. With a cry of 'Hessian!' he urged his stallion forward, his sword raised high and glinting gold in the dawnlight.

Even then, trapped between the roaring river and the screaming warrior, the Prindian soldiers held their line, weapons raised to meet the charge. The wild hooves and hulking chest of Andrick's steed crashed into them, flowing over them in a torrent of horseflesh, and those who bravely swung their weapons towards this terror were met by the song of steel, as Andrick's blade rushed down to meet them.

Orsian kept running towards the river, watching as Valour felled one man with a hoof to the head, and when another jumped forward with a thrust towards the horse's neck Andrick's own blade met him. As the hooves fell, his father's precise downward cut opened the man's throat. Jack drove a man back into the water, staining the surf pink, while another screamed to the sky as a wolfhound worried his neck, scattering dark droplets of blood.

How had none of them noticed the man escaping? Orsian raised his bow to his eye. The man was riding low on his horse, partly covered by Ciera's still body, giving him almost nothing to aim at. Orsian shot high, for the man's head.

The arrow arced through the air, but to Orsian's dismay struck deep in the horse's head. The animal screamed and flailed, its wound turning the river red with blood.

It had gone deep, right behind the eyes. Orsian watched helplessly as the horse's flailing grew weaker. It began to sink, leaving the man clinging to the rope, Ciera still tied to its rump. Her body sank beneath the water.

Barely thinking, Orsian ripped off his clothes, down to his undergarments, and gripped his knife between his teeth. There was still fighting, but he ran past and dived into the river.

The cold left him gasping, like being stabbed with needles. He was a strong swimmer, but the water was fast, and he had to fight against the current to keep to a straight line. Near where Ciera had gone under, he took a deep breath and dived.

He kept his eyes open, but the water was cloudy with silt, blinding him. He swam down towards the riverbed, reaching out every way he could with all his limbs, praying desperately that he would find her.

Orsian stayed under until his lungs burnt, but there was no sign of her. His body screamed for air, and he took one last stroke, ready to push off the bottom towards the surface.

His foot struck something hard and fleshy. He reached out with a hand. It was the horse's body. Orsian's lungs screamed in protest as he forced himself through the water, grasping for where he hoped Ciera would be.

He found her, and the rope that bound her to the horse.

There were black spots on his vision, and he cut through it with his knife as fast as he could. She came free, and gripping her tightly Orsian pushed off the bottom.

He came up into the sunlight, wheezing, taking long lung-fuls of air. It had never tasted so beautiful.

'Orsian!'

The call came from the bank. An end of rope landed a few feet away. Orsian looked towards the shore, and saw his father at the other end. He grabbed it, and holding Ciera's face above the water let himself be pulled in.

He laid her down on the bank and collapsed on all fours, rattling with cold and retching up water. Ciera was deathly pale, and her soaked chestnut hair clung to her skin like seaweed. He placed an ear to her mouth. She was not breathing.

Quickly he rolled her onto her back. He had seen this done once before, when a girl in Lordsferry had fallen into a pond. He tilted her head back, held her nose closed, then put his mouth over hers and gave two quick breaths, followed by hard, swift presses upon her chest.

Ciera's body jerked with each compression, but offered no sign of life, nor the second or third time Orsian tried. Desperately, he slammed a fist against her torso, putting all his strength behind it.

She coughed, and a torrent of water flooded out of her mouth. She kept coughing, and eventually began taking deep, desperate breaths. Her skin was tinged blue, and she was shivering.

Andrick rushed over, lifted her from the ground easily and wrapped her in a cloak. 'Eryi's balls, Orsian, she's alive!' He clapped him on the shoulder so hard it went numb.

Orsian tried to speak through his chattering teeth, and the result was unintelligible. He looked around the riverbank. It was littered with corpses, but he was relieved to see that Jack and Drayen lived. A bald prisoner knelt at Andrick's feet, with Andrick's sword laid against the back of his neck.

'Drayen!' called his father. 'Get a fire going for the queen.'

'Well fought, Lord Bastard!' Breta Prindian's voice reached them from across the river. She had reached the other bank, and was nonchalantly wringing water from her hair as if she had expected this day to negotiate a deep river with just a horse and a rope.

Orsian looked over at her. 'W-want me to p-put an arrow through her eye?' he managed to ask.

'No,' said Andrick. 'We do not kill unarmed women. Even her.'

'Honourable as ever, Lord Bastard!' she called across the water. 'Marius, kill the bastard's son!'

It was a useless threat. The man at Andrick's feet had been disarmed, and there was a slow drip of blood onto the ground from a wound in his hand. 'I surrendered, Lord,' he said, looking up at Orsian's father, with a hard gaze that was equal parts pride and submission. 'I won't give you no trouble.'

They rode home through a day and a night, all too exhausted to speak. On account of his honourable surrender the prisoner, Marius, was allowed his own horse, tied to Jack's mount.

Orsian had warmed up by the fire and been able to put his dry clothes back on. But reflecting on the events at the river warmed him far more than the fire. He had killed a man, and saved the queen's life! His father could not doubt him now; nobody could.

And yet... When he had seen the man's corpse he had thought he might throw up. It had been easy to kill at a distance, less so to meet the cold dead gaze of his victim. Would his nerve hold when he had to do it at the point of a sword?

Ciera sat behind Andrick, bound to him with a rope, passing in and out of consciousness. Whatever Breta Prindian had given her, it had been strong. At least she had stopped shivering. Despite her ordeal, the consensus was that she would live.

They were halfway home when they met Naeem, leading two hundred *hymerikai*. It had been intended as a warband, but turned to escort them home, and Andrick sent men ahead on fresh mounts to take the news to Hessian.

When they finally returned that night to Piperskeep, Theodric was waiting in the yard, flanked by a pair of guards holding torches.

'Is the queen well?' he asked immediately, wringing his hands.

'Tired and drugged,' said Andrick, 'but alive.'

'The king will be grateful,' said the magus, relief written across his face. Andrick lifted Ciera down from the horse and handed her to two waiting servants.

'What of Helana?' asked Orsian. She had brought Breta Prindian to the wedding feast; would Hessian punish her?

'She is under house arrest, confined to her chambers.'

However, when Theodric led Andrick and Orsian to Hessian's solar, Helana was there too, sitting at the window, with her legs crossed and hair unbound in casual defiance. Orsian could barely take his eyes off her. He was so transfixed it took him a moment to realise his father was finally allowing him an audience with the king.

'My daughter is to be confined to her chambers, but first she should know the consequences of her folly,' said Hessian, glaring at her. 'Are you happy now, dear daughter? If you were not of the Blood I would have you executed for treason.'

Helana laughed. 'Is it treason now to invite someone to a wedding?'

'It was a mistake, Helana,' said Andrick. 'You almost cost us everything. If not for Orsian, the queen would have drowned in the Pale River. What possessed you?'

Helana raised her chin and looked away.

Hessian advanced on her, and slapped her viciously across the face. Helana had not expected it; the blow sent her sprawling to the floor. She looked up at him in disbelief, a trail of blood trickling from her mouth.

'Stay there,' he snarled. 'If you stand I'll hit you again.'

Anger and defiance flushed across Helana's face. Orsian wanted to call out and stop her, but she stood, staring at Hessian.

He slapped her again, wildly, putting all his weight behind it. Helana fell hard, and let out a cry of pain as her head bounced against the stone. Orsian gaped. He wanted to run to her side, but fear kept him frozen to the spot. She stumbled to her feet again, pressing a hand to her face.

'Go on,' she said, laughing, fixing Hessian with a cold stare. 'Hit me again. Show everyone what a kind father you are.'

Hessian advanced on her, but Andrick placed a heavy hand on his shoulder. 'That's enough, Hessian.'

Hessian spun as if to turn his ire upon him, but his gaze found Orsian instead. 'Nephew! I am told you saved my wife. How can I ever thank you?' He wrapped him in an embrace so tight Orsian could feel the king's bones through his skin. He smelt of sickness and wine. Over his shoulder, Orsian saw Theodric handing Helana a cloth to wipe her face.

'It was my duty, Majesty,' Orsian managed to say, stammering slightly. 'Your gratitude is thanks enough.'

'Nonsense. You may take any horse you want from my stables.' He laughed and clapped, and whirled on the spot with his arms raised in triumph. 'Wine! Wine for my family! The Prindians have declared themselves, and nobody can name me faithless if I declare myself also. Rymond's head on a spike and a son at my wife's breast before next year is out. Let all the kingdom know them as traitors!'

Orsian stared at him. This was his king? This was who his father had sworn undying loyalty to, capricious as a cat and vengeful as a demon? He felt disgusted.

Hessian served the wine himself, including to Helana, his fit of temper seemingly forgotten. 'To family!' he called, drawing a mumbled response in kind. He took a long draught on his wine, and fixed Andrick with a stare. 'You have a prisoner?'

Andrick nodded. 'A Prindian soldier. He said his name was Marius.'

'I know him,' exclaimed Helana. She had returned to her window, and made no attempt to hide the angry handprint on her cheek. 'He was with Bre— Lady Prindian. When I met her at the inn.'

Hessian scowled at her. 'Silence!'

'We'll question him,' said Andrick. 'He may know something of the Prindian plan.'

'Send him to the dungeon first,' said Hessian. 'A few days there ought to loosen his tongue.' He turned his gaze upon Theodric. 'I had been meaning to ask you, Theodric. How is it that my own daughter was able to conspire with my enemy, who then killed my men and kidnapped my wife, and you were not able to prevent any of it?'

Helana made an indignant noise and opened her mouth to say something, but Orsian caught her eye in warning and she stayed silent.

Theodric had gone pale. 'I was watching her, as you told me.'

Helana could not hold her tongue this time. She fixed Theodric with a sharp stare, just like her father's. 'I knew it.'

'For your own safety,' said Theodric hastily. He was agitated, Orsian thought. He had always seemed so calm before, as if wearing some eerie mask. 'Can you blame me, after Jarhick, when you go somewhere like that? But when you went to the inn, I lost all trace of you.' He closed his eyes in concentration, and screwed them so tightly shut that Orsian swore he could feel faint tendrils of Theodric's magic reaching out.

He must have imagined it, for after a moment, Theodric opened his eyes. He swayed slightly, and Orsian hurried over to hold him upright. He pulled out a chair, and Theodric collapsed into it.

'I don't understand it,' he gasped weakly. 'Gone. I can't sense anything.'

Hessian stepped forward, and placed a hand on Theodric's shoulder. 'This was not the first time though, was it, my friend?' His voice was surprisingly gentle. 'A year ago, you would have felt the danger Jarhick faced, even from here. And here, at the wedding, you did not sense the Prindian scheme. You have lost something. How did I not see it?'

Orsian knew nothing of Theodric's magic, but the magus looked to be on the verge of tears. He buried his head in his hands. 'After Jarhick died, I thought there must be a Thrumb magus, unaccounted for. Then, when I found myself limited in other ways, I was not sure. There is so much I have simply not been able to explain: the Thrumb, the Lutums, Eryispek covered in mist all through the summer. There are tales of magi whose gift was blown out of them by freak accidents. I thought perhaps my powers were just waning.' He closed his eyes again, and Orsian again imagined he could feel his power reaching out. 'There is something wrong with my magic. There is something very wrong indeed.'

CHAPTER 15

The inn was a nameless shack. It was many miles from the next nearest inn, so to the handful of people who scraped a living from the thin soil near Erland's western border it was just 'The Inn'. The south-eastern wall was bare in places where wood had rotted away, exposing the five customers and the barman to the stiff breeze that rolled in over Erland's plains.

Rymond and Adfric hunched over a barrel in the corner, balancing on broken stools and nursing mugs of watery beer. Rymond kept the hood of his cloak up. Even in this bleak hinterland there could be those who recognised him.

When Rymond's mother had told him to gather men, he had thought she meant peasants from within his lands. He had not expected many hard days of riding to reach the very edge of West Erland, based on little more than gossip of some quarrel in the yard of Piperskeep.

Adfric had his cloak pulled back, displaying his scabbard for all the inn to see. 'Lord, I do not like this,' he murmured. His eyes did not leave the door across the bar. 'You've heard the tales of him; this Strovac Sigac could bring a handful of cut-throats in here and kill us both.'

Rymond ran a frustrated hand over his face. 'It was my mother's plan, not mine,' he said, not for the first time. Despite his mother's urging, his usually taciturn master-at-arms had cautioned Rymond against the journey every day since they had left Irith, and Rymond was sure his refusal to reconsider had committed Adfric to punishing him with increased ferocity in their early-morning sword practice. Rymond had the bruises to prove it. 'You raised no objection to her. What else would you have me do?'

'Find your allies elsewhere. Men like Sigac will not win your crown. They say he is a brute, a sadist, and entirely without honour, and the men who follow him are as godless as he is. If he is loyal to the Sangreals he will kill you, and if he is not, you have only gained a man who is just as likely to be disloyal to you.'

'Adfric, by that logic I should not try to convert anybody to my cause. I would enlist only true believers, and it would be me, you, and my mother standing alone against Hessian's horde. No man ever won a crown with the swords of righteous men alone. Even a dishonourable man may be bound to a bargain of mutual benefit. They say his Wild Brigade are second in skill only to the *Hymeriker*.'

'And second to no one in savagery, but you should be able to trust the men you ride to war with without reservation. You've spent too much time with those merchants, Lord, if you'll forgive me for saying so.'

Adfric had also been against Rymond speaking with his friends Dom and Will before they departed. His mother might have conceived this scheme, but Rymond could hatch schemes of his own just as well. Dom was prideful, as you would expect of a sea captain's son, and he had been stirred to stubbornness by his imprisonment and Rymond's refusal to see him after his release. Fortunately, Will was more forgiving, and even Adfric's steely eyes had not stopped him calling Rymond 'Majesty' and laughing about his captivity as if it had been a great adventure.

Eventually, Dom had been persuaded. Rymond had left him with four bags of gold and instructions: 'Go to the southern shores of Cylirien first,' he told him, 'where the Imperium rules only in name. Should that fail, you must go to Ffrisea, where the savages fight naked with logs. Bring me every willing man who can swing a weapon.' The air had been thick with Adfric's disapproval.

The inn door opened, and Rymond felt Adfric tense, like a dog smelling a wolf in his den. A man ducked under the doorway, and Rymond recognised Strovac Sigac by reputation. Six and a half feet tall, blond hair hanging loose to below his sledgehammer jaw. A mountain in leather and metal. He would have been the Erland warrior ideal, were it not for his eyes. They darted from corner to corner, small and rodent-like, shrouded by the shadow of his brow. They gave him a sly, malicious appearance: the face of a back-alley footpad, not a warrior. He had come alone.

Every face in the inn looked to the door, but seeing the size of the man and the sword at his hip they stared back down at their drinks. Only Rymond and Adfric met his eye. The blond giant frowned, but walked over to them, slapping down a few pieces of bronze on the bar and scooping up the fresh tankard that the barman had poured for another customer.

'I told your man *alone*,' he growled at Rymond.

'Lord Prindian does not require your permission to change his mind,' said Adfric.

'I don't require his permission to rip your fucking head off.'

Adfric was on his feet in a moment, and though the top of his head barely reached Sigac's chin, the larger man took half a step back, and both drew their swords up an inch, showing the dark steel in their scabbards.

'*Sit. Down,*' Rymond hissed. This was not how he had imagined his first attempt at an alliance going.

Adfric sheathed his blade and retook his seat, but his eyes did not leave Sigac. The big warrior remained standing, glaring at Rymond. A moment passed, and he joined them around the barrel.

'I hope none of these farmers are spies of the king's magus,' said Rymond, 'or we've just revealed ourselves and given him a fine tale.'

Sigac tapped a finger on his sword hilt. 'Sweet steel buys a man's silence. Once we're finished, I'll butcher every one of them.'

Rymond put a restraining hand on Adfric's shoulder. He was starting to think his master-at-arms might have been correct in his assessment of this meeting. 'Thank you for coming alone. I'm sorry I did not keep my word.'

Sigac shrugged. 'Lords rarely do. Why have you asked me here?'

Rymond assessed the man. That he had come this far suggested he knew why. Nevertheless, he took his hand off Adfric's shoulder, and glanced down at his sword, hoping it was loose in its scabbard. 'You rode west from Merivale with the Wild Brigade. I would have your allegiance, and theirs. The others you command too, if they'll follow you.'

Strovac looked at him carefully. 'I can set a price for my own sword, but I can't speak for the rest.'

Adfric chuckled. 'That's why he came alone. Doesn't trust his own men. No wonder: a true warrior knows a coward.'

Sigac's eyes flashed. 'Call me a coward again, old man, and I'll paint the walls with your entrails.' He looked back at Rymond. 'I want a lordship.'

Rymond had to laugh at his boldness. 'You could be the best killer in the kingdom, but no man's sword is worth a lordship.'

'Except Lord Andrick,' replied Strovac, sulkily. 'Give me a

lordship, lands, and free rein to take Andrick's head, and I'm yours.'

My mother would like him, but the man is half-mad. 'And how many men are you bringing in return for this lordship I am to conjure for you? Yourself?'

The big man thought for a moment, his beady pupils alive with calculation. 'Promise me a lordship, and I'll bring you every man of the three hundred in my Wild Brigade who'll agree to serve you. The rest I'll send above the clouds to meet Eryi.'

Half-mad, and five times as dangerous. The man spoke of murder as other men speak of meals. 'If I were to give a lordship to every man who could bring me three hundred warriors, I would give away half my kingdom before I've even taken it.' Rymond hoped that was true. If not, his cause was doomed. 'A few hundred will not buy you a lordship.'

The man took a long pull on his beer and swilled it around between his teeth. 'I can promise you three hundred. Maybe more.' His beady eyes glinted. 'Plus, a boon, something you can use.'

'I'd be a desperate man to make that bargain without knowing the boon.' Rymond was intrigued though. What boon could the man be speaking of?

'You are a desperate man, and I reckon the boon might be worth a lordship on its own.'

'Why would you turn on Hessian?' demanded Adfric. 'He gave you a keep, and, if tales are true, you are free to govern your own affairs, including your own band of warriors.'

Strovac looked at Adfric carefully, and for the first time Rymond caught something other than barely repressed fury in his almost mournful gaze. 'You've heard the rumour.'

It took Rymond a moment to comprehend what Strovac was speaking of. 'That you are his son?' he asked, stifling a laugh. 'I've heard the tale. I've also heard it was one you started yourself, though I can't imagine why. Surely better to have claimed what you have through your strength with a sword?'

Strovac's eyes flashed. 'It's fucking true. I nearly tore my mother in two when she birthed me. My stepfather knew right away I wasn't his. The little cunt never let me forget it, until I was big enough to fight back. I'd have killed him if my mother hadn't begged me not to. I was eleven.

'Hessian knows I'm his too, though he'd never admit it. So he gives me a crumbling castle in the marshes and makes use of my sword when it suits him. And he expects me to be grateful. Well, I'm bloody done with it, and that bastard brother of his. He takes everything, and all I get is a damp, draughty keep and him looking down his nose at me.'

Rymond tried to keep his face blank. He had no doubt Strovac believed his own tale, and there was a passing resemblance to Hessian, but he could not deny his own scepticism. No doubt there were women he had bedded who would tell their sons, rightly or wrongly, that Rymond Prindian was their father. Nevertheless, he nodded. 'Help me win the crown, and you'll have your revenge, and your lordship.'

The deal was not yet made then. It was another hour before both men were sufficiently satisfied by the terms to clasp the other's wrist. Strovac Sigac would bring three hundred warriors to Rymond's cause, with the proposed boon, and kill every Erlander engaged with the Thrumb who would not join them. In return, Lord Rymond would make him a lord, once he was king, with a keep, land, and servants, at a distance far but not too far from a major settlement, his activities subject to only limited oversight by Rymond.

'The Barrelbreaker's head is still mine though,' said Strovac as they clasped hands. 'And his wife. I want his wife.'

Rymond shook his head. He was almost regretting their bargain already. 'Another man's wife is not mine to give, and that is not the deal we made. Help me gain my crown, and I'll make you a lord, on the terms agreed. No more and no less.'

Strovac grunted, and his small eyes flicked around the room at the three other customers and the barman. They kept their heads down. 'I'd best start protecting that kingly arse of yours then.' He drew his sword.

He started with the man nearest them, a farmer in patched clothes facing the bar. Strovac's sword was in and out of the man's back before Rymond could blink.

The barman was next. He looked up in surprise as the sword arced towards him. He ducked, but the end of the blade caught him just below the eyes, and the sharp steel split one half of the man's head from the other.

The third man was still trying to rise as Strovac fell on him. He did not bother with the blade, just clobbered the top of the man's head with the hilt. Rymond heard bone crack, and the man slumped to the ground, gore leaking from the hole in his skull.

The fourth man had grabbed a fire poker from near his seat at the end of the bar, and parried a few strokes as Strovac rained down blows on him, retreating towards the fire to save himself from being crushed by the sword Strovac swung as easily as a hammer. The man was tall and rangy, but in the twilight of his years and no match for Strovac's ferocity. It ended when an overhand swing split the man's torso from shoulder to nipple. He had a moment to gasp, before Strovac twisted the blade and the light left his eyes.

'In the glade at the centre of Gwynæthwood,' said Strovac, withdrawing his sword and letting the man's corpse fall. 'The night before the new moon. You'll have your men.' Strovac Sigac wiped his blade on the dead man's tunic, opened the inn door, and disappeared into the night.

Rymond could only stare after him. He had not even moved

from his seat. *By Eryi*. It had taken Strovac only seconds to turn the inn into a mass grave.

Adfric had at least drawn his sword, though for what reason, Rymond did not know. 'That man will either win your crown,' he said, 'or kill us all.'

CHAPTER 16

Hrogo allowed himself to be dragged along by the two burly, black-clad guardsmen, shuffling his chained feet barely fast enough to avoid falling, his twisted back buckling under the weight of metal he wore. His master, Kvarm, had hundreds of these guards, each armed with a finely sharpened sabre, and deadly with it. Even without his chains, Hrogo could not have run anywhere, but it pleased the lord administrator to keep him hobbled. Hrogo had not attempted escape in decades, not since Kvarm had maimed his back and legs so badly he could barely walk. Now, the heavy chains were more to prevent someone kidnapping him rather than to stop anything Hrogo might have done.

His heart beat a little faster as they approached Kvarm's study. Since the break-in, his master's mood had been even blacker than usual, and Hrogo had to tread carefully to avoid his wrath. The guards who had been on duty had been flogged with such vigour that two of them had died.

The door to Kvarm's tower opened, and the guards flung Hrogo onto the floor like they were heaving a corpse into the sea. Hrogo's chains stopped him cushioning his fall, and though the carpet was soft and thick he landed painfully on his chest and face, driving the air from his lungs. He forced himself not to squeal with pain, and awkwardly pushed himself up to his knees with his bound hands.

His master was peering at him over his enormous, opulent desk, which was finally useable again after several strong servants had righted the bookshelf. The office had been cleaned, but some of the damage from the break-in could not be remedied; there were large chunks missing from the desk where the bookshelf had struck, and items damaged in the fall had been removed for repair, leaving the shelves half-empty.

Kvarm Murino was in his seventh decade, but in contrast to his dark study wore the vibrant, stylish colours of a younger man, a nod to his allegiance to the reformist factions in the Imperial Senate. With his handsome jaw and the lean physique of a man decades his junior, the clothes did not look out of place on him. Hrogo knew, though, that Kvarm did not particularly care for the reformers, nor his appearance. He wanted only to distance himself from Bovarch, his despised elder brother, a corpulent bear of a man who leaned heavily on tradition, and who to Kvarm's misfortune was also the current kzar of the Ulvatian Imperium.

That Bovarch was the elected kzar prevented Kvarm taking a seat in the Senate, and limited his influence to what he could garner through trade. Kvarm's creation of the enclave had ostensibly been to benefit the Imperium, but it mostly served as a way for him to cultivate wealth and influence away from his brother's interference. As many as one in six coins spent in Cliffark now found their way into Kvarm's pocket.

'Hrogo!' cried Kvarm, in a mocking approximation of the brotherly tone he took with other men of consequence. He seemed cheerful, but that could change in an instant. 'You are looking well, my friend; has your back untwisted slightly perhaps?'

Hrogo nodded silently, accepting the compliment, and Kvarm laughed. His dark eyes darted to the guards who had thrown Hrogo on the floor. 'You two. If you ever mistreat my property like that again, I will have you flogged. Leave us.'

The guards bowed respectfully and left without a word.

Crippled though he was, Hrogo was the only magus left to Kvarm – perhaps the only one in the whole Imperium – and thus valuable beyond measure. He was the fifth Hrogo to serve the Murinos, descended from the very first Hrogo, enslaved in secret after the Fourth Purge. As a child, he had been one of dozens of brothers and sisters, each even more pitiful than he, not even worthy of a name, their magic and their wits diluted by generations of inbreeding. Of the Murinos' attempts to breed more magi, Hrogo had been the only success.

That was all that kept him alive, whatever that was worth. He would be the last Hrogo. For years, Kvarm had forced him to copulate with an endless succession of slaves, in the hope one would produce a child with the gift. Not a single womb had quickened. Learning that Hrogo was likely infertile had so angered Kvarm he had broken half Hrogo's bones and left them to set awkwardly, leaving him with his twisted back and unsteady, loping gait.

It was a small thing to know you were the last, but it pleased Hrogo. Chances to thwart his master were rare. No descendant of his would endure the misery of life as a Murino slave.

'I am surrounded by half-wits,' Kvarm growled as the guards' footsteps receded down the stairs. 'Three years in this accursed city and my guards begin to forget what Imperial discipline looks like. Now sit down; looking at your twisted body trying to stand offends my eyes.' Hrogo obeyed, and Kvarm leant over the desk towards him with dark, penetrating eyes. 'Have you found it yet?'

Hrogo knew he dared not speak aloud what had been stolen. It had been one of the most valuable magical items in the

Murino collection. Taking ownership of most of his family's wealth, Hrogo included, had been the only perk Kvarm had gained from Bovarch forfeiting it by becoming kzar. If Bovarch found out about the theft it would cause Kvarm great embarrassment. Worse, there were enemies in Ulvatia who would not hesitate to use the knowledge of a lost magical item to move against Kvarm or even Bovarch, especially if it fell into the wrong hands.

Hrogo's existence was a jealously guarded secret. Banned books were one thing, but the family of the kzar owning an enslaved magus would be another matter entirely. If it became known to the citizens of Ulvatia, the Murinos could bring the whole Senate down with them. Hrogo's true nature was known only to Bovarch, Kvarm, and a powerful inner circle. So far as the guards knew, he was just a cripple, kept for their master's cruel amusement.

Hrogo licked his lips, considering his reply. He had known all along where the item was, but foiling Kvarm was one of the few pleasures of his wretched life. He had traced it all the way across and out of Cliffark, pleading ignorance, watching his master's temper burn higher and higher. The trick was never to let him reach the point where his anger overcame his assessment of Hrogo's value. That was when he started breaking bones.

Kvarm slammed both his fists down on his desk, shaking Hrogo in his chair. 'Answer me, idiot!'

Hrogo swallowed. It was time to start being useful. 'It is difficult, Master. The Mountain casts a great shadow, and I feel only the faintest trace of the item. I suspect it has passed to the other side of Eryispek. Most likely, it is in the capital, Merivale.'

Kvarm paused and made a slight grunt in acknowledgement, leaning back in his chair and steepling his fingers. Hrogo supposed that meant he was pleased with the answer, or at least not angry enough to start injuring his property. 'Then we must go to Merivale, though I am loath to do so. I do hate this country. The only vaguely civilised part of it is Cliffark. How these savages ever defeated the Imperium I will never know. If my brother was not so craven he would cross the mountains and crush them.'

Hrogo said nothing. It was best not to draw attention to yourself when Kvarm was thinking of his brother.

'Assuming you are correct,' continued Kvarm, 'when we reach Merivale, will you be able to locate it?'

Were he being truthful, Hrogo could have told Kvarm that the item was currently passing through a gate into Merivale. He could have even told him that there were three people with it, the same three who had robbed him, little more than children. Instead, he said, 'Maybe, Master. I will be nearer the item, but I will also be nearer the Mountain. I do not know how it might affect me.'

Kvarm waved a hand. 'Fine. I have two hundred men to search for it; not all of them can be as useless as those who let those accursed thieves escape. Once we are in Merivale, we will find them, and they will learn what it means to cross Kvarm Murino. The priority, though, is the item. That must be recovered at all costs. The very future of the Imperium rests on it.'

Truly, I pity the three who stole from him, thought Hrogo. If they knew anything of their victim, they would leave their takings behind and never stop running.

He had no intention of helping Kvarm any more than his survival required though. He would play the loyal slave, but a secret lurked deep within Hrogo's heart, so terrible that sometimes it scared him to think of it.

Hrogo had long ago given up on escape, or any respite from Kvarm's torment, other than death. His own demise was something he had contemplated, but one thought had always stayed his hand.

He would live to see Kvarm Murino dead.

There were ways with magic to kill a man, but Hrogo did not have enough faith in his skills to try them. Just one failed attempt would mean his slow and painful death. The cleanest way would be for Kvarm to die without anyone being able to link it to Hrogo.

And where better for that to occur than Merivale? The capital was deep in Erland, and said to be a filthy, barbarous city, with no love for the Imperium. In Merivale, a man like Kvarm Murino might find death quite easy to come by.

CHAPTER 17

'*This* is the capital?'

They had just dismounted from the wagon, after a month with nothing to look at except themselves, other travellers, and dark, rain-swept marshes. Tansa was not impressed by Merivale and was keen to make her displeasure known.

'It's barely a town! And why is it so muddy? And why does everyone look the same? And why is it so cold and smelly?' She could practically taste the stench of excrement and rotting meat. The mud threatened to steal her shoe with every step, and nine in ten people they could see had the same blond Erland look to them. The locals moved quickly, carrying curious bundles, throwing furtive glances at anyone who threatened to cross their path. In Cliffark, every man walked like a king, wearing his wealth. Men walked like these people only if they had something to hide. At home their nervous movements would have been an invitation for a robbery.

'It can't always be like this,' said Tam. 'Something must have happened.'

'What if it is though? What if this is as good as it gets?' Tansa was beginning to wish she had never stolen the purse.

'We'll go back, in a year or so,' said Tam. 'Or in six months, whenever it's safe,' he added quickly, seeing the look on Tansa's face. 'Or if you're in a hurry, you can get back in the wagon and go home now.'

Tansa was relieved to be free of the wagon, wherever they were. They could change their coins, lie low here for a few months, and let matters in Cliffark sort themselves out. The Imperials would not search for them forever.

They had planned to find someone to exchange their foreign coins as soon as they arrived, but had not considered how they would go about doing so. There could be no better invitation to a robbery than asking people where they could exchange money.

'I am sorry to bother you again, sir,' said Tansa, approaching the driver of their cart, flashing her most disarming smile. 'I was told to seek out my uncle when I arrived. He's a guard to a moneylender somewhere in the city, but I am afraid I don't know where. Would you be so kind as to point me in the direction of the city's moneylenders?'

The driver scowled at her. 'I'll want your share of the entry tax before I give you directions. Six legs, and your share of the wheels as well.' He named a figure so high that Tansa had to ask him to repeat it before she grudgingly handed over the coins. She could not imagine why anyone would willingly pay so much to enter Merivale.

'There's only one moneylender in Merivale,' the driver told her once the coins were stowed in his pocket, 'and he owns half my business. If your uncle really works for Hyland you can tell him from me that he's a money-grubbing scoundrel.' He left, without giving them directions.

Fortunately, one of the other passengers had overheard and was happy to oblige, pointing them westwards. 'Few streets to your left once you're in front of the Sanctuary of the Brides of Eryi,' she said, 'turn right at the man selling baked apples.'

The three of them trudged the way the driver had pointed, stepping carefully and breathing through their mouths. Tansa supposed they would get used to the smell, eventually.

The Sanctuary of the Brides of Eryi in Merivale was at least made of stone rather than sticks, but it was still unimpressive to children who had grown up in the shadow of the Temple to the Elements at Cliffark, which was glazed in white marble, blinding to look at when the sunlight bounced off the water.

'Why's it all so shit when the king lives here?' Tam asked.

They continued the way the man had suggested, and turned right at the baked apple seller. It was easy to spot the money-lender's premises; it was the only building with a pair of guards on the door.

A man in his middle years behind the counter appraised a sample of each of their currencies in turn, taking several minutes over the task. 'Well, you've quite a collection here,' he said, holding an Æchenian florin up to the light. 'A man wonders where you acquired it.'

'Inheritance,' said Tansa quickly. 'Our parents died, and we found this buried under their floorboards.' She felt Tam wince next to her at the obvious lie.

'Inheritance, is it?' The man leant forward, half a smile approaching his eyes. 'Well, that's a relief, don't see much foreign gold in these parts; not many ways to earn it honestly here. Of course, if it were stolen, I'd have to notify the authorities. You wouldn't be stupid enough to bring it in here, trying to tangle honest ol' me up in that, would you?' He winked. 'I'll give you one Erlish gold for every six by weight.'

'That's less than we'd have got—' started Tam indignantly, before Tansa quickly slapped a hand over his mouth.

The man scratched his head. 'Not sure what your friend was going to say, but by the look of him I'd say it was something stupid. My offer just dropped to one in seven.' Tansa swiftly accepted the second offer.

'Bastard,' spat Tam as they left, many Erlish coins heavier but many more ounces of gold lighter. 'Shook us down and spat us out.'

'Still more Erlish gold than I've ever seen in my life,' grinned Cag, lifting both Tam and Tansa into the air and twirling around on the spot, earning curious glances from passers-by. 'Let's go to an inn, or a hogball match! The driver told me the guilds all play each other, and half the time it ends up with both teams being thrown in jail!'

Tam grinned at his friend's enthusiasm. 'We will Cag, we will. First, let's see where the king lives.'

Cag frowned. 'I can see it from here,' he said, pointing north towards the dark stone behemoth that was by far the largest structure in sight, though dwarfed by Eryispek in the distance behind it. 'We've been able to see it ever since we arrived.'

'That's like saying you can see Eryispek from here so there's no reason to go there either,' replied Tam. 'I want a closer look.'

'We *can* see Eryispek from here,' Cag insisted. 'And not even that much of it; it was never that foggy in the paintings I saw in Cliffark.'

Tansa laughed, realising why her brother was so keen to go to Piperskeep. 'Let my brother be, Cag. He wants to try and see his beloved Queen Ciera.' She looked at Tam, her eyes glinting with sisterly malice. 'We can go, but if you even look as though you're planning to trick your way in or scale the wall or dress up as her maid or anything else I'll have you thrown in jail for your own safety.' She had sworn on the journey here that she was done with Tam's mad schemes. She had to protect him, not just from whatever dangers Merivale might pose but also from his own reckless whims.

She could tell by the look on his face that Tam did not feel that was fair. He had not mentioned Ciera once on the journey, but Tansa had learnt to tell when he was thinking about her, when his eyes went a bit misty and he looked to be staring at nothing. She had hoped he might have forgotten her by now.

They bought a round of baked apples as they tracked back the way they had come, then went back for seconds, and once their bellies groaned with fullness rather than hunger began wending their way towards Piperskeep. Merivale was a maze, and more than once they accidentally started walking down an alley only to realise there was no exit at the other end. They divided their coins three ways between them, to split the risk of a sudden mugging in the unfamiliar streets.

The poverty they saw made them all the more aware of that risk. In Cliffark, as urchins who slept outside, they had been among the lowest of the low. Here, their finer clothes marked them out as possibly wealthy outsiders, and Tansa was conscious to make sure the coins hidden about her person did not clink together. Some of the homes they saw were little more than hovels, built of straw and dried mud. More were made of wood, but perhaps only one in five were even partially forged from stone.

'I reckon we could buy the whole city and still have change for breakfast,' Tam whispered to her, then repeated the joke for Cag, who laughed loudly and drew curious looks.

As they moved up the hill towards the castle, the clothes became finer, and the homes less ramshackle, and eventually every building they saw was made from stone and at least two storeys high. The largest homes of all were behind gates manned by guards. There were entire roads closed to them, and nearly deserted except for the odd figure garbed in sleek silk and trailing an armed escort. They stared for a moment before one of the gate guards shouted at them to move along.

It made sense, Tansa thought. If you were wealthy you would want to be up the hill, nearer the protection of the castle, and with less water and waste flowing down on you, but that did not make the poverty she had seen any less unjust. 'How do they live like this,' asked Tansa, 'knowing that less than a mile away people are sleeping in mud and straw? I thought Cliffark was bad, but we never starved or walked around in dirty rags. The king should do something.'

'Cliffark's not all that,' said Tam. 'There's poor people there too; you just can't see them because they're all hiding underground in Pauper's.'

'Do you think we could buy a home now?' asked Cag. 'I like our rooftop, but it would be nice to live inside.'

'I don't think so,' said Tam. 'I like sleeping under the stars.'

Tansa rolled her eyes. 'But you prefer sleeping in a whore's bed. The money we have might get us two small rooms, but we'd still need to make a living after that. And it's much harder to be thieves if people know where to find you.'

They were approaching the castle now. They gazed up at its vast curtain wall, almost a hundred feet high in grey brick and black mortar, broken only by a gatehouse guarded by two soldiers keeping an eye on the collection of swollen-bellied beggars lying against the wall with their bowls out.

Tam bent down to catch a glimpse through the portcullis of the deep moat that divided the curtain wall from the inner wall, until a guard jabbed him in the stomach with the blunt end of his spear. Tam was caught by surprise and took a step back, wincing and cradling his abdomen.

'He was only looking,' protested Tansa.

'That's what looking gets you.' The guard flipped his spear over. 'If either of you look again you'll get the other end of this. King's orders are to kill anyone who tries to get in or looks suspicious. Lucky for you I'm merciful, or you'd be bleeding out with my spear in your gut.'

Their exchange was interrupted by a bellowing horn from inside the gate, forcing the guard to run back to his post. 'Raise the gate! Make way!' came the call from inside.

Tansa heard Tam give an intake of breath, and she crouched

down to look through, making out a collection of horses' legs. A mechanism creaked, and the portcullis began to rise.

A company of horsemen rode out, led by a barrel-chested black warhorse bearing an equally imposing man coated in mail and leather. Tansa's eyes, though, were drawn instead to the smaller figure behind him. It was Ciera Istlewick, her chestnut-brown hair tumbling artfully to below her shoulders. She glanced down from her horse as they passed, and for a second Tansa swore she saw her and Tam's eyes meet. A moment later, she was gone, as Ciera and her retinue disappeared in a cloud of dust.

'Well you've seen it now, and your lady love,' said Tansa, 'let's—' She looked around for her brother, but Tam was gone. She turned frantically, and saw him walking quickly after the riders. 'Tam!' she called. He glanced over his shoulder, waved, then broke into a run.

Ciera tried to look back, but Lord Andrick was setting a determined pace, and Tam was lost to view as her escort led her away from Piperskeep. What was he doing in Merivale? She was sure it was him. There had barely been a day when she had not thought of him, and every time she scolded herself for fixating on a boy she had been sure she would never see again, who had kissed her the day before her life had changed forever.

It had been weeks since her wedding, and that day continued to cast a shadow. She knew that she had been kidnapped, but she could not remember any of it, and nobody would tell her what had happened. Piperskeep was confusing and scary. The king's daughter Tarvana had returned to her husband's seat, and his other daughter Helana was still under house arrest. Her guards would tell her nothing. She had asked her new maid, but seemingly nobody outside the king's immediate circle knew any more than she did. There were rumours that Orsian Andrickson had killed Breta Prindian, and others swore Lord Andrick had slain a dozen armoured men just outside the city walls.

Ciera did not know what to believe. When she had finally found the courage to ask Hessian about it, her husband had wagged his finger at her warningly. 'Just be grateful you are safe, and do not concern yourself in my affairs. I already have a curious daughter. I will not tolerate a curious wife. It's that curiosity that got you kidnapped.'

The thought of Hessian made her shiver. His charm at the feast had been a mask, and it had slipped the moment he saw Breta Prindian. Almost every night, while she slept, the king would call on her. He did not knock, nor gently open her chamber door. His arrival was foreshadowed by the cold shriek of metal on stone, and her fireplace would open to reveal Hessian, covered in dust and carrying a glass of foul-smelling wine.

She had fought him at first, when he pushed her down onto the bed, but frail as he was he had overpowered her with a strength imbued with madness. Husbands were meant to be gentle with their wives, not rut them like dogs. He had never kissed her. He would not even look upon her face.

After the latest of these maulings, she had wiped away her tears and dared to broach the subject of trade in the city. She was sure reforming the city's peculiar method of charging entry would increase commerce, but first she wanted to understand the reasoning behind charging per wheel and leg. Hessian always seemed a little guilty afterwards, and so she thought he might be more amenable to her ideas, but he had scowled at her as though she had said something heinous. 'The best thing you can do for the city is start popping out heirs,' he snapped. 'When I want your opinions, I shall ask for them.'

She had sworn to make him love her, but how could a man so full of rage come to love anyone?

It was Orsian who had rescued her from being confined in her chamber. He had come to her this very morning, tapping at her door so quietly at first she had not heard him. When she had asked him why the king was now letting her outside the walls, he shrugged. 'I asked my father to speak with him. Didn't seem fair that you were stuck inside. Helana is under house arrest, not you.'

Ciera did not know the truth of the rumour about Orsian and Breta Prindian, but he did seem to carry himself differently since the wedding. On the journey from Cliffark, when she had first met him, he had dogged his father's steps like a miniature shadow, and spoke only when spoken to. He seemed taller, and when he spoke to the other men now he did so with the authority of a lord. He was behind her, forming the rearguard of her entourage. They had slowed to enter the narrow streets, allowing the milling citizens to leap back to clear their passage, and she was able to turn around to smile at him. He smiled and waved back.

There was the sudden screech of hooves on cobbles, and her front escort reined in their mounts, bringing all of them skidding to a halt. Ciera stood in her stirrups, and saw their way was blocked by a group of women wearing white robes.

The Brides of Eryi. The order was said to contain the most devout worshippers in all Erland, eschewing all material trappings for a life of prayer and contemplation. There had been a small chapter in Cliffark, who once a year would appear at the castle to try and persuade her father to put on a white robe and go on pilgrimage to Eryispek. He had always given them a meal and sent them on their way with a promise that he would go the next year, if his health improved. Ciera had heard they were more powerful in inner Erland, where the old superstitions still held sway.

She doubted the woman leading them would have been so easily dissuaded by her father's vague promises. She was tall and haughty, in her middle years, with a handsome strong-featured face and a noble bearing. Her brown hair was bound in a large bun on top of her head, accentuating the austere cheekbones of someone not accustomed to nor interested in life's comforts. She stared up at them in disdain, as if disappointed in them for not stopping sooner.

'That's the elder bride, Sister Velna,' Orsian whispered to Ciera, pulling his mount up next to hers. 'The king didn't ask her permission to marry you. She looks furious.'

Ciera did not get the chance to ask why the king would need permission to marry, not least from the leader of a cult of fanatics, because the sister was staring at Orsian with a look that could cut flesh.

'Who dares speak of me with such disrespect?' she demanded. 'Eryi hears *all*, and he has blessed me with the gift of perception. Eryi in his wisdom has also blessed me that I might speak with his voice, and if I am furious, it is because Eryi is furious.'

'Has Eryi granted you eyes in your head, Sister?' asked Lord Andrick dryly. Ciera had heard he had no patience for devout Eryians, and it was said the king's piousness stretched only as far as was needed to hold the loyalty of the commons. Having shared his bed, she did not doubt it. 'That's my son, the king's nephew, and you're not in your sanctuary now, so I invite you to consider who you are addressing.'

'Neither of you is of the Blood,' said the woman implacably. She fixed her gaze on Ciera. 'You are the new queen then. I should have been consulted before the marriage. You must come to my sanctuary and wash my feet, as proof of your devotion. Then you will be bathed and examined by my sisters. Only then will you be a fit mother to a prince, and without the traditional ritual I fear your womb will never quicken.'

'If Eryi speaks so clearly of his wishes,' countered Andrick, 'perhaps you could explain the mist that's covered Eryispek, and the mountain winds he sends to chill my bones.'

'The mist and the winds are proof of his displeasure; the weather will lift when the Sangreals make matters right with Eryi. You should show more respect, Andrick Barrelbreaker. You will know no peace above the clouds unless you mend your ungodly ways. Now, take me to the king.'

Ciera had not encountered many adherents to religion. The Brides of Eryi in Cliffark had been well-meaning but simple, lacking the fervour of this Sister Velna. Her father said that most preachers were seeking to take advantage of the gullible. Ciera could see that the elder bride was nothing of the sort. She was entirely sincere, fanatical to the point of madness. *She never has to justify anything, because she believes she speaks with the voice of a god.*

To Ciera's surprise, Andrick bowed his head in acquiescence. 'I would not tell Hessian it is his fault; even he would admit he cannot control the weather. I will take you though, Sister, provided your friends wait outside.' He looked to one of his men. 'Naeem, you have the command. Take Queen Ciera to the market, and do not let her out of your sight.' He turned his horse and trotted back towards Piperskeep, leaving the brides to follow in his wake.

'That was lucky,' said Orsian, keeping his horse alongside Ciera's as her six-strong escort led her deeper into Merivale's maze of streets. 'I was sure he would send you back to the keep.'

Ciera could not say she felt lucky when they reached the market. The markets in Cliffark were magnificent, fascinating events, where all the treasures of the known world could be bought for enough coin: purple silks from the Imperium; gold-and-glass oil lamps; many-coloured peppers that could set your mouth on fire. Merivale's market did not fare well in a comparison: a dozen drab stalls around a muddy square, manned by glum-looking men and their sour wives, selling turnips, roughspun yarn, and jewellery so crude it could have been made in a blacksmith's forge. People spent hours at the Cliffark markets; here the few customers she saw seemed to wish to stay no longer than they had to.

Orsian seemed to sense her unhappiness. 'It's not much,' he admitted as he helped her down from her horse. 'But the wine-seller might have something new, and sometimes there are Adrari here selling decorations carved from whalebone.'

The wineseller did not have anything new, but Ciera enjoyed the cup he sold her all the same. 'It's from Irith,' he confided to her in a whisper. 'Might be the last cask we see of it for a while.'

Both inside Piperskeep and out, there were rumours of war. She had wed for her father's sake, to save Cliffark from the wrath of her new husband, but the marriage seemed to have heightened the discord between Sangreal and Prindian, and Ciera was at the centre of it.

'What taxes do you pay to set up your stall here?'

The man looked hesitant. 'Well...' he began, then seemed to think better of it. 'You should ask the city reeve about that, my Queen, if you've concern about taxes. I swear I pay everything I'm asked.' The man excused himself quickly to busy himself with something at the rear of his stall, leaving Ciera to suspect that he had some sort of arrangement that lined the reeve's pocket and allowed the wineseller to evade the proper payments.

How much must the charge be if men would sooner break the law and risk hanging than pay it? Ciera asked herself. One could only pluck so many feathers before the goose began squawking. No wonder there were so few stalls in the market if the fee was so high.

She returned to walking about the market. 'What happened that day, at the river?' she asked Orsian, as he led her around the remaining stalls, her *Hymeriker* escort never far away.

Up close, Orsian seemed tired, perhaps even slightly unhappy, his mouth set in a stern line not unlike his father's. 'Sorry,' he said, 'my father said if the king wanted you to know, he would have told you.'

Ciera tried not to let her irritation show. *It's not fair*, she raged silently. *They brought me here, got me kidnapped, and now they won't tell me anything.*

A loud crash and the crack of splintering wood from the other side of the market shook Ciera from her brooding, and she and Orsian whipped round in surprise. Two men were brawling, throwing clumsy punches at one another, while a vendor cursed at them and tried vainly to hold up a cracked supporting pole one of them had just fallen into, which was in danger of breaking and taking his whole stall down with it.

Orsian cursed under his breath. 'Stay here,' he said, and walked towards the brawl. The *hymerikai* were already moving to separate the men and restore order.

'Psst,' came a soft voice. Alarmed, Ciera spun around looking for its source, and her heart leapt to see Tam, half-hidden behind a barrel.

'Tam!' she could not help herself exclaiming. 'How did you—?'

'Pickpocketed one of them, slipped it into the other's pocket, then told the first one I saw him rob him.' Tam grinned that gap-toothed smile Ciera had thought of so often.

'Still thieving then?' She tried to sound disapproving, but struggled to keep the smile off her face. A different city, but the same rogue.

'I had to. I wanted to give you this.' He reached out and pressed something into her hand. She opened her fist and found the bracelet that he had stolen off her wrist so many months ago. 'I should never have taken it, not after you saved me. I'm sorry.'

Ciera looked down at it, more touched than she could put into words. *He kept it, all these months, all the way from Clif-*

fark. 'Th-thank you,' she stammered. 'But you should keep it. Sell it. I have more trinkets than I know what to do with.' She thrust it back towards him, casting a worried glance towards the fight. Two *hymerikai* were keeping the brawlers apart while Orsian and another assisted the stallholder.

Tam reached out and took it, and for a heartbeat their fingers touched, sending a spark of lightning up Ciera's arm. 'I'll keep it,' he said, 'but only so I can come back and see you to return it again. Watch for me.'

'But—' Ciera tried to reply, but he was already turning away. She watched him run away down an alley, stuffing the bracelet into a pocket as he went, until he turned a corner and was lost from sight.

CHAPTER 18

'You should not have married her without permission,' said Sister Velna, scowling like she had just drunk vinegar. 'She must perform the traditional ritual, and you must do penance.' She stood in the king's tower solar, having refused his offer of a seat.

'It is not wise to speak to kings of permission,' replied Hessian. He also stood, on the other side of the table, leaning his long frame over the elder bride. 'I did not have time to seek your leave, Sister. You would have had me praying on my knees for half a year.'

Andrick waited silently near the door. Hessian's will was as stiff as cold iron, but the sister could match him in her stubbornness. In another lifetime, she might have made a worthy queen. Usually, Theodric would have played peacemaker, but he was absent, and Andrick had no illusions about his own talents for diplomacy, particularly where the viciously pious Sister Velna was concerned.

'One whole year,' she corrected him. 'Half for this marriage, and half for the last one you did not observe the requirements for.'

Hessian laughed, without amusement. 'You were not even the elder bride then. I made my arrangements with the old elder bride. Sister... Grunya?'

'Sister Grela,' offered Andrick.

Velna turned to scowl at him. 'It was Grecia, you godless heathen, and a more corrupt elder bride our order has never known.' She looked back to Hessian. 'You paid her a donation of gold and land in kind rather than prove your devotion. There can be no shortcuts.'

'Even so,' said Hessian, waving his hand carelessly, 'the matter of my old marriage is closed, and I cannot spend six months at prayer. I propose the following: you may borrow my new wife for a day, prod and poke her and whatever else, and after a son is born to me, I will go on pilgrimage.'

Velna's eyes narrowed in suspicion. 'You have promised to go on pilgrimage before.'

'Truly, Sister, I mean it.' Hessian held the palms of his hands together piously. 'If Eryi blesses me with a son, I swear I will do it.'

Velna's brow stayed furrowed, but after a moment she gave a satisfied nod. 'Very well, Majesty. Send the girl to me. She will be bathed and cleansed and readied to birth a prince. But you'll still do your penance, in the next life if necessary.'

Hessian inclined his head. 'If I have a son, I will walk to Eryispek barefoot. Shall I have Lord Andrick show you out?'

'No, thank you. I shall see myself out. The girl, at the Sanctuary, within the month.'

When she had left, Hessian slumped into his chair, and Andrick dropped into one the other side of the table.

'Mad old woman,' muttered Hessian. 'She dares to make demands of *me*! I should have her hanged and be done with it.'

'It could be worse, Brother,' Andrick replied, 'I should have thought you would prefer paying her in promises to paying her in gold. She may be your greatest ally. Obedience to Eryi and obedience to the king are two sides of one coin. So long as you make small noises of devotion, she will keep the commons on your side.'

It had been shrewd by Hessian. The elder bride had left satisfied she had extracted a concession from him, when in truth he had given her next to nothing. There were shades of the younger Hessian's nimbleness in the way he had manipulated her; few got the better of Sister Velna.

It was some distance from the night of Andrick's return to Merivale, when in his wrath Hessian had struck Helana. As foolish as the girl had been, Andrick was fond of his niece. But it was not his place to tell the king of Erland how to raise his own children. Hessian seemed calmer since then though. Perhaps marriage agreed with him.

'What will you do when you have a son, and she is knocking at your door demanding you remove your shoes and walk to Eryispek?'

Hessian snorted. 'Something will come up. She can hardly expect me to go on pilgrimage if we are at war.'

'The men will be ready. I've had Naeem and the rest drilling them till their blisters burst.' Andrick had the *Hymeriker* and a small standing force of regular soldiers, but after Breta Prindian's attempted kidnapping the word had gone out that every able-bodied man within a week's walk of Merivale must practise daily, not just weekly, with sword, spear, or bow. Instructions were sent to Hessian's nearest vassals to have their men do the same. Every day more farm boys arrived, eager for the three meals a day of the standing soldier.

'I don't doubt you, Brother,' said Hessian. 'You still believe we should wait?'

'Yes,' said Andrick, with certainty. 'We already have several hundred men inside West Erland with Sigac, and more with Errian.' His son had still not returned, nor the men Andrick had sent after him. As obstinate as Errian could be, it was not like

him to refuse a summons. It troubled Andrick that one of his
sons was so deep in Prindian land and had not sent word. The
boy must have been mad with grief for Jarhick. 'I have sent
more messengers. If Rymond marches, he'll do so with our men
at his back.'

Hessian nodded. 'As you will.' He reclined contentedly in
his chair.

There was silence for a few seconds, before Andrick leant
forward over the table with questioning eyes. 'Majesty, what of
Marius, the man we captured? Has he said anything of the
Prindians?' He was Andrick's prisoner, technically, but since he
had been sent to the dungeon he had seen neither hide nor hair
of him.

Hessian's hand moved to a jug of wine. 'It is not your
concern. The prisoner is being dealt with.'

Andrick swallowed. The man was a warrior, and he had
surrendered willingly once he realised his position was hopeless. He ought to be treated with honour. 'Respectfully, Brother,
I believe it is my concern. He surrendered to me and thereby
placed himself into my care. He remains my prisoner.' He could
not look at Hessian as he spoke, but felt the king's eyes on him.
When he looked up, it was like staring into clouds on the cusp
of a storm, flickering between malevolence and amusement.

'As you will,' said Hessian. He stood, and gestured for
Andrick to do the same. 'I would not want you to worry for the
man. Come.'

Hessian picked up a stray candle and strode towards the
bookshelf, which was littered with histories and ancient maps,
and reached high to a thick green volume. Andrick heard the
creak of a mechanism as he pulled it, and the bookshelf rotated
a few degrees clockwise, revealing a slim gap in the wall.

'This way, Brother.'

Andrick gaped, but Hessian did not wait for him, so he
followed him sideways through the gap, and immediately had to

duck under a beam. Ahead of him, he could make out Hessian's stooped shadow turning to descend a narrow staircase carved into the wall.

'My solar was also the solar of King Piper,' said Hessian as they made their way down. 'When he had the castle built, he had these stairways made, accessible only to him. Ten successive generations of Sangreals have walked these stairs, passing the secret down from father to son. Consider it a token of my regard.'

Andrick did not understand how this could be true – Piper's three grandsons had fought a bloody civil war among themselves that had ended with a new king on the throne, and he did not imagine that whichever of them had held the crown first had passed down the secret before being executed – but he followed in silence, ducking under beams and low stones and sweeping cobwebs out of his path, breathing shallowly in the musty air.

They must have descended over a hundred feet when Hessian placed his candle in a sconce and pulled. With a groan, a section of wall rotated, revealing a dark room with four corridors branching off from it, lit by torches. The air was warm and heavy, and Andrick could hear the slow drip of condensation falling from the ceiling.

'They were gifted, our ancestors,' said Hessian, as they walked through the open wall. 'Theodric swears this is no magic, just a mechanism, but how could just that lever move that heavy stone? Our stonemasons cannot make anything half as clever.'

'This is the lowest dungeon,' observed Andrick, his breath coming short in the thick moisture that made his clothes feel drenched in sweat. This was where Ranulf Prindian had met his end.

'There is one more level below this,' said Hessian, 'but the staircase collapsed. The builders say we cannot excavate without destabilising the foundations. Best not to dwell on the poor souls we left down there.'

Andrick felt a cold shiver run up his spine. Could the vengeful spirit of Ranulf Prindian still linger down here?

Hessian led him through the catacombs, foul water dripping from the stone, and the cadaverous stench of lives extinguished in the dark stalking their steps from locked doors with huge keyholes. Their candle flickered in the moist air, and Andrick feared they might be plunged into darkness at any moment.

At the end of a winding corridor, they reached another door, with the same gaping keyhole as those they had passed. Hessian pulled a large key from beneath his robe, and bent down to the lock.

In the days and weeks to come, Andrick would relive many times in his mind the moment that his brother opened the door. Andrick knew of his implacability, his mercilessness, his cruelty, but this was the first time he had seen with his own eyes to where Hessian's dark heart led.

The cell was small, made smaller by the dark corners the solitary candle did not reach. It stank like a battlefield: all the piss and shit that men voided when their hearts hammered in their chests and their blood ran hot with fear.

But even on the deathliest of fields, Andrick had never seen a creature as pitiable as the one in the middle of that room.

Marius hung from the ceiling by his wrists, naked, his bloody toes barely touching the floor. His chin was slumped against his chest, and his pale torso glistened with a film of dried dark vomit. Over the manacles, his fingers curled lifelessly, showing his maimed fingertips and missing nails.

Andrick gaped. For a moment he thought the poor man was dead, until he saw spit bubble on his lips as he took the barest of breaths. He would never argue that Ranulf Prindian had not earnt the end he had met in this darkness, but Marius' only crime was being sworn to Breta Prindian.

Theodric was sitting to one side at a table, a deck of cards arrayed in front of him, looking up in surprise at the interruption. 'Majesty? You are early today.'

Hessian seemed equally surprised to see Theodric. 'You are early as well. Are you sleeping here, in this filth? Where is Hop?'

Hop was the keep's ancient and hobbled dungeon-keeper, there since before Andrick was a boy. Once Andrick had been caught filching bread from the kitchens, and Hop had threatened to drop him upside down in an oubliette and drown him. Even then he had seemed old. Andrick had not laid eyes on him in years. He doubted the passage of time had made him any less cruel or meticulous in his work.

'He likes to drink after work and sleep through till night,' said Theodric. 'His apprentice usually watches Marius in the day. I sent him away; I wanted some time alone with him.'

'And you've learnt nothing,' said Andrick. He stared stonily at Theodric. He had thought better of him than this. 'This man is only a soldier. What could you hope to learn from him? This is madness.'

'We had to know, Andrick,' said Theodric. 'What if my malady is the fault of the Prindians and this man knows something? But I confess, I believe you are right. I have probed this man's mind with all the magic I know, and it has returned nothing. All we know is that he is scared enough to be honest; he does not lie in the hope that we will stop.'

Hessian appraised the suspended body with a sneer. 'Then he is deceiving you. He plotted with Breta Prindian to kidnap my bride. He must know something. This will continue until he breaks, or your magic reveals something.'

'I fear it will do no good, Majesty. I beg your leave to release him and tend to his wounds.'

'It was not a request, wizard. While he threatens my kingdom, he will know no peace. If your magic can neither prevent nor explain anything that has occurred these last months, you must make yourself useful in other ways. This man will die down here.'

'No, he will not,' said Andrick, making up his mind. He had obeyed his king without question for four decades, even in Hessian's darkest moments, but he would not condone this. At least Theodric seemed to have come to his senses. Andrick stepped between Hessian and Marius' hanging body, arms folded in front of him. 'The man is my prisoner, and I reclaim him. We will release him from this place, and he will go with Theodric.'

Behind him, the man stirred, mumbling and grasping for purchase with his feet.

Hessian looked down at Andrick, one eyebrow raised, a small smile playing around his lips. 'Is this the hill on which you make your stand, Brother? The life of a traitor who tried to steal my wife? You swore an oath to serve me.'

'I swore an oath to protect you as well, my King, and in this I am protecting you from yourself.' Andrick stretched for the ceiling and released the chain that held Marius there. The soldier's limp body slumped into his arms. 'I would expect this of Strovac Sigac, but never of you.'

Hessian stared at him, seemingly shocked to muteness that Andrick would follow through with his disobedience. It did not last long. His eyes narrowed dangerously, like a hawk sighting a vole. 'Then you are released from my service. You are removed from your position as *balhymeri*, to be replaced with Strovac Sigac. At least I can rely on his loyalty to me. I need strong men, not soft, old men who have forgotten how we treat our enemies. What say you to that?'

Andrick said nothing, but steadied his nerve to hold Hessian's gaze. He slowly unbuckled his sword, and held it out hilt-first towards Hessian. 'I am ever your servant, Brother.' When

Hessian failed to take it, he placed the sword on the floor. 'If you think I have betrayed you, strike me dead.'

Nobody moved. The sword stayed at rest on the dungeon floor. Hessian looked down at it, but he did not reach for it.

'Then never question my loyalty again.' Andrick walked to the door and left, carrying Marius like a side of meat. 'I am going to Violet Hall. I will return when you have need of me.'

CHAPTER 19

The glade was silent, lit softly by the thinnest sliver of moonlight, but the dark woods around them chattered with life. Rymond heard the chirping of crickets, and from the trees the occasional screech of an owl. Somewhere to the north, two foxes wailed their mating cry.

They were in Gwynæthwood, where it was said Algareth, the first king to unite West Erland, had won the heart of a wood-nymph, who had blessed him with the strength to unite the tribes. The Prindian line was supposedly descended from Algareth and Gwynæth, but Rymond did not believe such legends, nor in nymphs. Algareth had lived hundreds of years before Rymond's earliest recorded ancestor, and all stories of him were preserved solely in song. He wondered if Strovac had known of the wood's significance to his family when choosing this particular meeting place.

He and Adfric were mounted, with twenty horsemen behind them and eighty men on foot, mostly scattered around the edges of the clearing with long spears at the ready for a mounted charge. Having seen the limits of Strovac Sigac's mercy at the inn, Rymond was taking no chances.

Beside him, Adfric eyed the woods for signs of movement, alert for any snapped twig or rustling of bushes. The grizzled veteran had a sour look on his face. After they had left the inn, he had unendingly counselled Rymond that Strovac could not be trusted. 'Lord, you are tying your plough to a wild horse,' he had said. 'It may do the work, but eventually will grow tired of the yoke and trample you.'

'A man is not a horse, Adfric,' Rymond had told him. 'As long as there is a chance of victory, he will fight for that lordship.'

Rymond wished he felt as sure now as he had then of Strovac's motivation. It would have been hard enough to keep faith with any stranger to keep a bargain that saw both of you committing treason, but to trust the word of a man who had slaughtered a whole inn as easily as he might have swatted a fly was another matter. If Strovac had thought that display at the inn would make Rymond more inclined to trust him, he was entirely mistaken.

For all Rymond knew, Strovac could at that moment be encircling the woods with his Wild Brigade. Adfric said their own men were brave and willing, but untested, and they would not stand against a superior and more experienced force. Rymond was relying on Strovac's word, and his enmity with the Barrelbreaker.

'You seem restless, Lord,' said Adfric. 'It is not too late to leave this place.'

Rymond fought his own urge to run. 'There could be a thousand reasons he is late.'

'A thousand reasons, or a thousand soldiers?'

Rymond ignored him. The old man's chastening tone was beginning to grate on him. It was almost enough to make him wish for his mother's lofty disapproval. If this was an ambush, he would let Adfric die before he shared a cell with him.

Somewhere behind them a twig snapped in the distance,

and they both turned with their hands on their sword hilts, as the men around them brought up their spears and rushed into a defensive position.

Rymond held his breath.

After a silence, a wolf howled, marking its territory, but too wary to come near a gathering of armed men.

For Eryi's sake, thought Rymond. If Strovac Sigac could have seen them sitting here in the dark shitting themselves he would have laughed himself stupid. Some king he would make; Rymond doubted that Hessian would be afraid of a wolf howling in the dark.

Had Jarhick not got himself killed, Rymond could have been sitting in his chambers with a pair of whores, or out drinking with Will and Dom. He had sworn off drink since his abduction, for the most part, but the current situation was more precarious than anything he might have done in his cups. Perhaps sobriety did not suit him.

He had received a letter from Dom two days earlier.

Your Cylirien mercenaries and Ffrisean warriors await you in Irith. Come home and take them to war before they kill each other and burn the city down.

It boded well that Dom had encountered success so much sooner than Rymond expected.

'Lord Rymond.' The voice came from behind him, and Rymond nearly fell out of his saddle in shock. He whirled his horse around, drawing his sword, and heard the sharp sound of dozens of others doing the same.

He was met by the vast frame and rictus grin of Strovac Sigac, seemingly unconcerned by the collection of blades pointed at him.

'How did you get here?' demanded Adfric. 'We have men all around this clearing.'

Strovac insolently thumbed the hilt of his sheathed sword. 'My stepfather and his father were huntsmen for the old king. I was stalking deer before I could walk. I could have spent the whole night wandering around this camp and your men would never have seen me.'

His light-footed approach to the glade complemented the easy grace with a blade Rymond had seen in the inn. It was a plausible tale, but Rymond suspected that Strovac's family had in fact been poachers, rather than huntsmen.

'You're late,' said Adfric. 'And had I seen you sneaking into our camp, I would not have asked your name before I rode you down. If we are not already at war we will be soon. This is not the time for your childish japes.'

Strovac shrugged. 'You might have tried. You are too old for war, greybeard. Go home to your wife.'

'Quiet, both of you,' said Rymond. 'Strovac, what of our bargain? You promised hundreds of men, and I see only you.'

Strovac rolled his eyes. 'I have them. I could hardly bring all of them through the woods. Follow me.' He turned and began striding southward.

Shrugging to Adfric, who looked outraged, Rymond followed Strovac at a distance, squinting through the darkness to keep his large frame in focus, and with his guards in tight formation around him. Adfric bravely went ahead of them, holding a ready hand on his sword hilt. Behind them came their infantry, crashing through the undergrowth like a drunken bear. If this was an ambush, then they were walking right into it.

Approaching the wood's edge, they saw many fires ahead of them, like orange lanterns dancing behind the trees. There were enough that Rymond knew they were certainly outnumbered, but the brazenness of the fires made him doubt an ambush, and he signalled to his guard to quicken their pace. They burst from the wood onto the plains, the firelight casting long wraith-like shadows across the trees.

Rymond saw the shapes of men crowded around the flames, within thirty yards of them, and judging by the fires there were several hundred more than he had anticipated. He squinted through the gloom, and alongside the ranks of Erlander men-at-arms, he swore he could see men with their hair styled in long plaits: the Thrumb.

Adfric had seen them as well, and turned his horse on Strovac, his hand already moving to his sword hilt. 'Thrumb! Is that who you mean to betray us to? I knew you were a cowardly—'

'Strovac,' called Rymond, cutting shrilly across Adfric, 'I see here many more men than you had promised. Before I thank you, I would ask that you name your intentions.'

Strovac was grinning again, recognising their discomfort and relishing it. 'I brought two hundred and ninety-two Erlanders at last count. But I reckon you'll forgive me for being eight short.'

From the fires behind him emerged a man on horseback, in his middle years but powerfully built, with a broad, windburnt face. His hair hung in six great plaits around his scalp, and he was clean-shaven save for a moustache that dropped to below his chin. A sickle-shaped scar ran from beneath his right eye to the left corner of his mouth. He was garbed in a cloak of silver-blue wolf pelt, and held himself straight as a spear in the saddle.

'Lord Prindian,' said Strovac, 'may I introduce you to the noble Chieftain Ba'an of Thrumbalto, Master of Trees and Talker to Winds, who has agreed to take up your cause.'

Rymond stifled his urge to gape at the man, and bowed low from his horse. 'Well met, Chieftain Ba'an. I am glad to learn of your support, and I thank you for it. However, I must ask what I can have done to earn it.'

The chieftain indicated towards Strovac. 'Lord Strovac told me of your agreement.' His voice was low and rasping. 'That he will become Lord of the Fortlands. We agreed he will marry one of my daughters. It will serve me well to have a blood ally in the lands that neighbour mine.'

Lord of the Fortlands? Rymond had never agreed to that. The land Strovac would take when he came into his lordship had never been discussed. Such a title would make Strovac one of the most powerful men in West Erland.

He caught Strovac's insolent eye, and understood that he had been led like a child. To refuse him now would break faith with the Thrumb, and he and Adfric and the rest of them would be butchered by the overwhelming strength of Strovac and Chieftain Ba'an. Rymond had no choice but to agree.

'Between us, Chieftain Ba'an and I bring over five hundred men,' said Strovac, 'each one eager to press your claim against the capricious and tyrannical King Hessian.' *And to kill you if you refuse me*, went the unspoken threat. Strovac raised a questioning eyebrow towards Rymond, who gave the tightest of nods in response.

The deal was made, and the dice were cast. Adfric's face was thunderous.

'We brought something else for you as well,' said Strovac. 'Bring him up!'

From somewhere, a hooded figure with hands bound behind him was retrieved, and four of Strovac's men dragged him towards Rymond. The man struggled all the way, stumbling as he tried to fight his jailers with his head and shoulders and feet. He wore the remnants of fine clothing, reduced to rags. With vicious blows to his shoulders and kicks to the backs of his legs his captors forced him to his knees at Rymond's feet.

Strovac approached, and tore off the man's hood. The face underneath was young, with features not unlike Rymond's own, with matted blond hair down beyond his shoulders and a filthy-looking rag shoved in his mouth. His face was a motley of bruises old and new.

'The boon I promised you,' said Strovac. 'I present Errian, the first son of Lord Andrick Barrelbreaker.'

CHAPTER 20

Helana woke in her chair, a book lying open in her lap. She looked around, momentarily forgetting where she was, before she recognised Theodric's austere room. It was not much like one would imagine a magus' bedchamber, not so different from any other room in the keep: the same monolithic stone walls, with a large feather bed and a table and chairs. There were no familiars, nor oddly coloured potions in jars, nor mirrors through which one could step to another world. He had his study though, and he had warned her that any attempt to open it would cause her arm to break out in painful hives. She was not sure if he was joking or not.

Theodric's bed was currently occupied by Marius, still rarely awake, and incomprehensible when he was, even weeks after his release from the dungeons. The flesh had melted from his once heavy face, leaving behind gaunt furrows covered by a messy brown beard, and his eyes were framed by deep shadows. Helana was still under house arrest, and to stop herself losing her mind filled her hours caring for the unconscious man, spooning water into his mouth and ensuring he was warm, like nursing a baby bird back to health.

Having been ignored by her father her entire life, Helana was not used to being denied her freedom. Confinement did not suit her, but she felt some responsibility for Marius' welfare. It had taken all Theodric's powers of persuasion to stop her confronting her father about his treatment. He was merely a pawn of Lady Prindian, as she had been.

There had been a note waiting on her pillow that night, after the feast. *I am sorry. I can only hope you will understand. Visit me in Irith when you can.*

Helana shook her head angrily and stepped to the window, dragging a comb through her sleep-tangled hair. The note made the deceit no less painful. For the first time, Helana had thought she had someone who understood her, as a mother might have. She should never have trusted Breta Prindian. She had been taken in by her beauty and her charm, her desire for peace, and their common adversary in her father.

Instinctively, she touched her cheek, at the bruise her father had left her. Though it had faded now, it was still slightly tender. He should not have hit her, and she should not have stood for it. She should have got to her feet ready to strike him back, not daring him to do it again. But at that moment, for all her defiance, she had been afraid of him, and she hated herself for it. Old and infirm as he was, his blows had set her ears ringing. And not one of them had come to her aid, except Theodric with his handkerchief. Not even Orsian.

A door handle clicked behind her, and Theodric emerged from his study. He had been up all night again; she could tell by the blue bags under his eyes and the grey fuzz on his jawline. Even before Marius' arrival she doubted the bed had got much use.

'Trouble sleeping, Theodric?'

The magus sighed, and collapsed into a chair on the other side of his bed. 'I have much to trouble me, Princess.'

'I've decided I hate that word. Just call me Helana.' It was a useless title, with no power that did not derive from her father. 'What troubles you?'

Theodric gave a thin smile. 'Everything. Everything since your brother went to fight the Thrumb. Errian was meant to go with him until the Lutums attacked Basseton, but would then they both be dead, or both alive? And why were the Thrumb making incursions into Erland, and where are the Lutums? And is the fog that covers Eryispek only weather as your father thinks, or something else?' He rubbed at his face. 'It's all connected, I am sure of it, but whatever has been set in motion I am powerless to stop it.' He sighed and looked down at Marius. 'I cannot sleep, and yet our guest sleeps like a man who has not slept in years. Any change in him overnight?'

'I was dozing myself until the birds starting singing,' said Helana. 'I believe he stirred once or twice. His fingernails are starting to grow back.'

Theodric said nothing, though Helana thought he might have winced slightly. She had been almost as angry with him as she had been with her father. It would have been obvious to anyone that Marius was not a confidant of the Prindians, but it seemed Theodric had done little to dissuade Hessian.

'Nothing to say, Theodric?'

'Nothing that would correct the injustice, still your anger, nor grow his fingernails back. Not a trick I've learnt, I'm afraid. I healed his back at least.'

Helana opened her mouth to reply, but Theodric paused her with a raised hand. 'I am too tired to keep having the same argument with you,' he said. 'I obeyed your father, as I am sworn to. And if I were you I would not antagonise him further. He thinks he let you off lightly.'

Helana snorted. 'He has already imprisoned me. What will he do? Have me whipped through the streets?' Her father was cruel, but he was not stupid. Mad, possibly.

'Just know that he has not forgotten that he intends for you to marry. He may have been diverted by you invoking Rymond Prindian's name, but he is still considering prospective husbands for you.'

'Let him try,' said Helana, with more confidence than she felt. If she refused, would a priest be brave enough to defy Hessian? Of course not; he would choose a tame one. Who would speak up for her if it happened?

Before Theodric could reply, there was a sudden gasp from the bed. Thrashing against the bedsheets, Marius woke, wide-eyed and alarmed, with a great breath as if he wanted to pull the whole room into his lungs.

Helana rushed to the bed. 'Loosen them, before he hurts himself!' The two of them worked to untuck the sheets, and Marius rose and pushed himself up against the bedstead, panting.

'Eryi's balls, where am I?' he gasped. His already pallid face whitened a shade when he saw Theodric. 'You! You—'

'You're safe, Marius, I swear. You're in Piperskeep, in Merivale,' said Helana. She spoke gently, as she might have to a child. 'My father thought you were someone you are not, but I promise you're safe now.'

Marius blinked at her. 'Lord Andrick promised me safe conduct, he said—' Anger stirred behind his suddenly sharp eyes. He tried to rise, but pulled up, wincing. 'By the pissing Norhai, my back hurts.' He stretched his shoulder out, grimacing. 'Help me get up, please. And give me some bloody clothes.'

'We can't let him,' said Theodric, alarmed, perhaps as much by the soldier's rough manner as by him being awake. 'What if he—'

'What if he what?' demanded Helana, turning on him. 'Are you afraid of an unarmed man wearing a nightshirt? Is he going to kill us and fight his way out of Piperskeep?'

With Theodric's reluctant assistance, she helped Marius to

a chair, and the magus found a pair of roughspun trousers and a loose-fitting tunic to replace the man's nightgown.

'That's better,' he wheezed as he lowered himself into a chair. 'Eryi's shit, I feel terrible.' He let out a bitter, barking laugh. 'Hessian's hospitality is just as I was told.'

'I'll fetch you some food,' said Theodric, clearly of the view that Marius was too weak to be a danger to Helana and eager to extricate himself. He left quickly.

'I am so sorry,' said Helana. 'My father—'

'Don't speak,' said Marius, his eyes tight with pain. 'Just give me a moment.'

For several minutes, Marius sat in silence, taking deep breaths, but when servants brought bread and soup for him, he tore into it hungrily. Helana watched him. Now Marius was awake, she wanted to ask him about Breta Prindian. Was the note genuine, or just more deceit?

'That's better,' he said, setting aside the soup when he was finished. 'Though I feel about a hundred years older than when I left Irith.' He looked down at his torso. He had been broad and brawny when Helana had met him, but confinement had reduced him to little more than skin and bone. 'Is there more food? I could barely lift a sword in this condition.'

Helana sent for more food and, as she watched him eat, decided that her curiosity could not wait. 'Did Breta Prindian tell you what she was going to do?' she asked.

Marius paused with a rasher of bacon halfway to his mouth. 'Of course.' He looked at her uncompromisingly. 'I'm her sworn man, or I was. Who do you think sneaked in and left the note on your pillow about the inn? She did like you though, genuinely. Did she not tell you she wished she had a daughter like you?'

Helana remembered that; it had been the day of the feast. Had Breta meant it, or was it just more of her manipulation? If Breta thought Helana would make a good hostage she did not know her father. It did not matter particularly, while she was trapped here. Her father would not be sanctioning any journeys to Irith, especially while she was under house arrest and they were on the brink of war.

CHAPTER 21

The day was still. The remnants of the first frost gave a silver dusting to the green lands, with not even a gust of wind to break the stillness. The way was a winding hill path, and so the watchman of Violet Hall heard the approach of horses before he saw them, and sent a runner to the small barracks for twenty men with bows to join him on the battlements above the main gate. By the time he returned, the watchman had sighted the high banner that went before the horsemen, and sent the runner to raise the flag of three barrels over the hall and have the kitchen prepare a feast. The man blew a long note on his horn, deep enough to rattle the frost from the walls, and behind him the yard burst into activity.

Lord Andrick Barrelbreaker had returned home.

Lady Viratia was the first out to greet her husband. No sooner had Lord Andrick dismounted than his wife was there beside him, and he swept her off the ground in a wild embrace. The servants and guards grinned and exchanged looks; it pleased them that their lord and lady were still as eager as newlyweds for one another.

'You are away for so long,' said Viratia when they finally broke apart, 'and then you return without notice, and covered in dirt. My dress will need to be beaten and washed.'

Andrick laughed, lifting and whirling her round by her waist. 'I do not care, I am home, and you will not need that dress.' He called to a servant. 'Bring wine and meat to our chamber, which I do not mean to leave again until tomorrow. Food and beer for my men also.' He threw Viratia over his shoulder and walked from the yard, through the keep's entrance and upstairs to their chamber.

When they were finished, Andrick lit candles, poured the wine, and brought a plate of food to bed for them to share. He made a pile of plump pillows, and drew Viratia to him, wrapping her under his arm, smelling her deep blonde hair and savouring the warmth of her body.

'I often wondered when we were younger,' said Viratia, 'whether age and lordship might change you. But you still behave like a wild boy, riding off for months at a time and making a scene in the yard when you return. What am I to do with you?'

'Kiss me.'

And so she did.

'I had hoped you would attend the wedding,' said Andrick. 'Did the invitation not reach you?'

'It did.'

'Why did you not come?'

Viratia was silent for a moment, resting her head on Andrick's broad torso and staring into nothing, twirling his thick chest hair around her finger. 'I could not bear to see that poor girl wedded to the king,' she said eventually. 'What she will endure... What would you say if it were Pherri?'

Andrick laughed at that. 'We should be so lucky. Finding a husband for Pherri will be my greatest battle.'

Viratia slapped his stomach in rebuke. 'Do not make it into a joke. Do you not remember what it was like when my father tried to marry me to Lord Storaut? I was terrified.'

'I remember.' Andrick grinned wolfishly. 'I broke into your father's keep and stole you. We were married the next morning, by a travelling priest I had found on the road. I wonder what became of him.'

Viratia smiled back at him, remembering fondly. 'My father knew your mind. That's why he placed four guards at my door.'

'They tried to arrest me. It did not end well for them.'

It was an old tale, one they had shared a hundred times or more, but it had never grown dull. After their wedding, they had ridden north to Hessian's lands by the sea. He had been Prince Hessian then. They had been tracked there a week later by Viratia's irate father, Lord Brithwell, and an equally angry Lord Storaut.

'They stood there, twenty armed men at their back,' she said, smiling. 'You were still half a boy, but you walked out to meet them alone.'

'I remember,' said Andrick. '"Lords, I am sorry, but we are wed. I will settle this by the sword with either of you, to satisfaction."' He could not help grinning at the memory of it. 'By the Norhai I was a vain and foolish young man. Your father was purple with rage; I thought he might actually accept. Lord Storaut as well, though it was me who put him in his seat by killing his nephew! The man never even thanked me for it.'

'My father was no fool,' Viratia replied. 'For all his faults, I hope Eryi treats him well above the clouds. He had seen what you could do with a blade. It would have been folly.'

Andrick kissed her. 'That day, fighting for your hand, even a thousand men could not have laid steel on me.'

Hessian had been wroth with Andrick, for he was also against the match, but had made clear to the two lords he would not tolerate any retribution against his half-brother, and placated them with generous offers of land. Hessian's father, the old king, had been less forgiving. For marrying without leave, Andrick was banished from Erland for five years. Two years later though, the old king was dead, and Hessian bid Andrick return to help him secure his crown, then gave him Violet Hall for his seat.

Done with reminiscing, they returned to the subject of Hessian's new bride, once Andrick had relit the fire and refilled their wine.

'The girl is a small thing,' said Andrick, 'but well-suited to court. What would you have Hessian do, Viratia? He needs an heir.'

'I understand the need for an heir, but that makes me no less troubled. He is old enough to be her grandfather, Andrick. I know he is the king, but even as a young man he left me feeling... peculiar. I have never liked the way he looks at me.'

'Who can blame him?' Andrick kissed her neck and by mistake spilt a dribble of cold wine onto her breast. Viratia shrieked, and Andrick laughed in delight. She tried to hit him, but he blocked the blow and held her wrist in his hand.

'I mean it, Andrick,' Viratia said sternly. 'I am of a mind to come to court and make sure she is not mistreated. That is what I ought to have done before the wedding. Ancient laws be damned, Hessian should be able to name Tarvana's boy, Tarrik, as the heir, and there would be no need for this.'

Hessian shook his head. 'It is not the law that stops Hessian doing that, but that the country would tear itself in two after he died. Half the lords would declare for Tarrik and half would declare for Rymond. It would be war.'

'It will be war anyway,' Viratia replied. 'The gossip is that Lord Rymond has not been seen in Irith for weeks. They say he has crossed the sea and is raising mercenaries.'

'Theodric tells a different tale. Rymond has left Irith, but remains in Erland.'

'But you agree that war is coming. And yet you are here, not at Hessian's side or riding to battle. What happened?'

Andrick sighed. He had expected Hessian to send for him once he had calmed down, but the summons never came. Perhaps he had truly meant it. Andrick had left that evening, his heart heavy with guilt. His brother needed him. 'We had a disagreement,' he said eventually. 'I am afraid I can say no more.'

'Really? Well I reserve my wifely right to ask you about it when you have had more wine.' Viratia stood to rearrange the blazing firewood, and the sight of her moving naked about their room put Hessian out of Andrick's mind. 'You always put too much on,' she said, examining the fire. 'This will collapse any moment and fill our room with smoke. What would the servants say if you set fire to our own chamber?'

'That the old lord still has it?'

She flung a pillow across the room at him, narrowly missing his head and sending a cup tumbling from the table and spilling wine all over their sheets. They looked at one another, and both collapsed into laughter. Andrick threw the pillow back towards her, narrowly missing the fire.

When Viratia returned to the bed, Andrick pulled her towards him again and covered her laughing mouth with kisses.

She smiled at him bewitchingly. 'So soon, my love? You old lords are full of surprises.'

'I have been too long away,' said Andrick, drawing his wife closer to him, 'with many miles on horseback spent thinking of you.'

Later, as she lay once more in her husband's arms, Viratia spoke again. 'My love?'

'Yes?' Andrick replied sleepily.

'When this war with the Prindians is done, I believe you should retire. You have spent three decades fighting Hessian's wars. Nobody has given more to his crown than you. I want you here, with me.'

'Hessian dismissed me. I am no longer the *balhymeri*.'

'He will send for you again.'

'And I might refuse him.' If Hessian could dismiss him, then he could refuse Hessian. Though even as he thought it, he knew it was false. It was his choice, but it was a choice he had made decades ago. Young as he had been, loyalty was not a decision he had taken lightly, and he did not take it lightly now.

'You will go, because for reasons I have never understood you love him. I beg you, make it the last time. Win the war, and ask him to release you from his service. You have raised two strong sons capable of stepping into your boots. Let them guard the king and train his men and fight his battles.'

Andrick thought on it. If he won the war, and the bride he had chosen for Hessian proved fertile, there was nothing Hessian would refuse him. He could ask for Naeem to be made *balhymeri*, with Errian to succeed him once he was older.

But what then? He could live another twenty years, and Viratia ruled his land well enough without him. War was all he had ever been good at, and he still swung a sword and rode a horse better than anyone.

Or he had. But what if that were no longer true? There were perhaps two dozen men in the *Hymeriker* older than him, Naeem among them, and though they had lost none of their bravery, most were best-suited to guard duty. The bright reflexes and boundless resilience of youth did not last forever. If Andrick walked too far, his knee pained him, and if he sat for too long his back would spasm when he stood. It would not be Rymond Prindian, but there might come a time when he crossed swords with somebody fast enough to kill him, and that grew more likely with every passing day.

He would have thought about it more, but the heady satisfaction of a bellyful of wine and the warmth of his wife beside him had left him sleepy. He never felt half so content as when he was at home with Viratia. Perhaps she was all he needed. 'If I agree to consider it, will you let me sleep?'

'I might.'

'Then I will think about it,' he said, his eyelids beginning to droop, 'but only because I love you.'

Pherri was at the rear of Violet Hall with Delara, and had not heard the horn blowing or the commotion in the yard. It was her former nursery, where the toys and trinkets of her childhood still littered the shelves, but Pherri preferred to think of it as her study, where she sat at her small desk and read her books.

While her parents greeted one another after their months apart, she was engaged in a spirited debate with Delara.

'But if Eryispek is endless,' asked Pherri, 'then why are the sides of it not vertical? It may be steep, but it is sloped all the way up as far as I can tell.' Delara's initial refusal to discuss Eryispek did not appear to extend to debating the nature of its existence.

'It is sloped all the way, and it is endless,' said Delara implacably. This was the third time in a week they had had this discussion, and Pherri's tutor had remained steadfast in her explanation, hunched patiently over her staff like a weather-beaten gargoyle.

'So it is sloped, and endless, and it has no summit?'

'It has a summit, but no man or woman has ever seen it.'

Pherri slapped her hand on the table in frustration. 'But that doesn't make any sense! It can't be all three things; I'm not sure it can even be two of them!' Da'ri had taught her geometry; it was preposterous. She tried to picture what Eryispek must look like above the clouds, but it remained irritatingly beyond her imagination.

'It is best not to dwell on these things, Pherri,' said Delara, tapping her staff on the floor as if to reinforce her point. 'Just accept that it is. It is unlikely you will ever go to the Mountain, never mind walk into the higher reaches.'

'But how do you know all this? And where do you think the Lutums have gone?'

Delara's mouth formed to reply, when suddenly the door opened, and the head of a young man with a wild mane of black curls appeared.

'Orsian!' cried Pherri, and raced from her chair to him. He swept her from the floor so she could wrap her tiny arms around his neck. 'You're home!'

'Of course, little Sister.' He grinned at her, holding her out in front of him by her armpits. 'You've grown.'

She hadn't; she was still small for her eleven years, but Orsian seemed taller than before and had filled out around his chest and arms. He had lifted Pherri easily.

Delara coughed from behind Pherri, and they both turned to look at her. 'Who are you?' she asked. 'You've interrupted our lesson.'

Orsian lowered Pherri to the floor. 'I'm Orsian, Pherri's brother. Where's Da'ri?'

Pherri had tried not to think of Da'ri. She had not been plagued by dreams thanks to Delara's medicine, but she still sometimes felt a pang of sadness when she walked past his old rooms. 'I'll tell you later,' she said to Orsian, trying not to cry. 'This is Delara, my new tutor.'

Orsian nodded to her, oblivious that anything was amiss. 'Pleasure to meet you, Delara. Might you end your lessons early today? I've not seen Pherri in months, and I don't know how long I'll be able to stay.'

After a few moments' pause, Delara nodded her agreement. 'Pherri, I will speak with you tomorrow.' She swept past them and out of the room without another word.

'She's quite... abrupt,' said Orsian. 'Where did you find her?'

'Errian brought her back from Basseton,' said Pherri. 'She was a servant to the lord there. She helps with tasks Tammas can't manage any more, and Mother thought it might be good to have a woman tutor me.'

'She's barely younger than Tammas, but never mind. Shall we take a walk along the walls?' He opened the door and the two of them departed towards the outside.

While they walked the battlements, Orsian filled in Pherri on his adventures with their father since they had left Violet Hall. There was a restlessness to him, Pherri thought, as if he was waiting for something and Violet Hall was just an interlude.

While he told of the fight at the Pale River, Pherri realised what he was waiting for. War. It made her sad. Her brother was becoming a man, and he would have to kill other men or be killed himself. It had never quite seemed real when he had only practised in the yard.

'Did you feel anything?' she asked, when he told her of the man he had killed with his bow. She wanted him to regret it. Men were cruel, but Orsian was different. He had to be.

Orsian hesitated. 'Let's stop here for a bit.' They were on the western wall, looking out towards the Pale River. He leant against the battlements.

He was silent for a time. There was a low mist over the land, wrapping it in a white cloak. Pherri watched the flocks of birds, flying south for sunnier climes. In the months to come, East Erland would freeze. Perhaps if war were averted for the next month, Orsian would stay here for the winter.

'Pride,' said Orsian eventually, without looking at her. 'That's what I felt. It was a good shot, and he was trying to kill Father and his men. But then I saw his body, and all I could think about was whether he had a family, and if somewhere there is a boy barely younger than me who somebody will have to tell that his father isn't coming home again.'

Pherri hugged him. He would always be her brother, no matter how many men he killed, but she was relieved. He was nothing like Errian. 'If it's your life or theirs you have to,' she said. 'Otherwise somebody will have to tell me that you are dead.'

'I will do what I must,' he said solemnly. 'I've dreamt all my life of fighting alongside Father, for Erland. But the king...' He sighed. 'It is best I do not speak of him. Tell me of Da'ri. Did he return to Thrumb?'

Pherri bit her lip. She had thought often of what it would mean to tell Orsian what had happened. He would be as furious with Errian as she was, but Orsian was a man now, with a sword. What if Orsian killed him? Or worse, what if Errian killed Orsian?

Orsian laughed at her silence. 'Come on Pherri, you can tell me. I know it can't have been easy for him here, but you must miss him.'

'He's dead,' she whispered. 'Errian killed him.'

She took a breath, and told Orsian the whole sorry tale: the cockfighting, the drunk townspeople, and Errian carrying her away while they murdered Da'ri. He stared at her, lost for words.

'That bastard,' growled Orsian when she had finished. His eyes clouded with cold fury. 'I'll kill him.'

'No!' said Pherri, grabbing Orsian's hand as if to stop him drawing his sword right there. Her eyes filled with tears, and this time she could not stop them. She buried herself in Orsian's chest, weeping so hard she could not speak. Da'ri was dead, because of her brother, and her other brother would soon ride to war. It was too much to bear.

Orsian held her, letting her tears soak his shirt, as still and patient as a priest.

Da'ri was dead, and it pained Pherri so deep in her soul that it was like a mortal wound. She thought the tears might last forever – all the grief she had somehow held back gushing out of her in a torrent.

And then, just when Pherri thought the flow of tears might never end, she stopped sobbing. She sniffed, and wiped her nose on the back of her hand. 'Sorry,' she said, with a small smile. 'I don't know what happened to me.'

Orsian knelt down to wipe the tears from her cheeks. 'Something awful happened to you, Pherri. I'm sorry I wasn't here. I've always hated Errian, but this... what he did was evil. He should pay for his crime.'

'You can't kill him. Mother would never forgive you.'

Orsian gave her a slight smile. 'I've often thought of it, but sadly you're right. He will face justice though, I promise.'

But to Pherri, it did not seem to matter quite so much now, now Orsian was here. Her brother understood. She felt lighter, as if her tears had lifted some great weight from her. Da'ri was dead, and no amount of bloodletting between her brothers would change that. She hoped he was with his gods, the Thrumb's mysterious forest deities. She considered for a moment telling Orsian of Da'ri's final letter, but some instinct held her back: she liked having a final secret to share with Da'ri, and Orsian might insist they tell their parents. She had come only slightly further since her successful translation of it: the Thrumb's ancient brethren on the western slope could be the Adrari, but there was little information in Violet Hall's library about them, and Delara certainly was not interested in discussing them.

For a time, they instead talked quietly of small matters,

and watched the sunset draw a blanket of shadow over the country. As it grew dark, they retired to Pherri's room, preferring to leave the communal areas for the servants and soldiers to enjoy away from the eyes of their lords. They played a few slow games of chess, while talking lightly of their memories of Da'ri and laughing. Orsian had taken some wine from the kitchens, and gave a cup to Pherri under a promise that she would not tell their parents. Pherri won the first three games, but by the fourth she was yawning openly and could barely keep her eyes open. Orsian won with a triumphant checkmate, before lifting his sister over his shoulder and putting her to bed.

Pherri woke before a faltering campfire that seemed to give off more smoke than heat, wrapped in ragged furs.

Her limbs felt leaden, and her feet so cold and wet she could not feel her toes. Through a shifting curtain of snow, she saw others around the failing fire, dressed as she was, with gaunt, haggard faces. She reached up to touch her own face, and felt cold, cavernous cheeks like those of a corpse.

She remembered her chess games with Orsian, and being put to bed, and realised this was a dream. She had forgotten to drink Delara's medicine. *Wake up*, she urged herself. She had to leave, before the doe with the sharp blue eyes found her.

'It's no bloody use,' grumbled a hunched old man next to her, with his hood pulled forward so only the tight skin of his gaunt jawline was visible. He threw a dead twig frustratedly into the fire, but it refused to catch aflame. 'Boy's doomed us all.'

'Be patient,' said another man across the fire, younger than the first, though barely less emaciated. 'The Mountain has chosen him. The Norhai will make their will known to him. They are testing us.'

'Patient?' scoffed a woman. Unlike the men, she was standing, with a hunting bow clasped in one hand. 'We've not eaten in three days, more than half of us are dead, and all he does is stand there staring at nothing!' She pointed behind Pherri, and Pherri turned to follow her finger.

Past a succession of struggling fires and huddled figures wrapped in furs, a man stood with his back to them atop a steep slope, silhouetted against a mountain of snow that stretched endlessly into the sky. A great white fleece straddled his neck, and he looked to be in better health than the rest of them, with powerful shoulders and arms taut with muscle.

Then something rose over the Mountain beyond him, and Pherri recoiled, too scared even to scream.

A man's shadowy face loomed over her like an enormous moon, until it filled her vision. His features were indistinct, shifting like smoke, but his cold blue eyes shone like moonlight upon an icy pool, pinning her to the snow. Pherri raised her face to the sky and screamed, but her voice was lost on the rising wind.

She woke, clawing at her tangled bedsheets as she struggled for breath. She threw off the sheets, and with shaking fingers reached for a match.

The wick caught, and Pherri looked wildly around the room, stepping fearfully from her bed to the floor. Sweat flooded her skin, and blood pumped in her ears.

But there was nobody there. To be sure, she drew back the curtain. Nothing stirred outside. She was alone, in her room, and Violet Hall was silent.

She tried to picture again the face she had seen, until fear filled her heart and she had to put out her hand to steady herself. She shook her head, as if to shake the dream from her mind. And that was all it was: a dream. She had been disturbed since Da'ri's murder, and any connection between the man who wore white fur in her dream and the Lutum rebel called Gelick Whitedoe was surely nothing to be concerned by. Everyone's dreams had strange connections with the real world. She had to keep drinking Delara's medicine.

It was in a jar under her bed. She poured herself a thimble-ful, and drank it. It seemed to calm her, or at least it got her hands to stop shaking.

Pherri wrapped herself tightly in her blankets and slammed her eyes shut, determined to fade into dreamless sleep. But sleep did not come for a long time. Just memories of snow, and the shadowy man with pale blue eyes.

CHAPTER 22

Rymond sat at the head of the long table, trying to look comfortable, as the heir to the kingdom might. In truth he wanted to disappear to his room and not come out for at least the rest of the day.

To think that only a few hours ago he had been glad to be back in Irith, where he could sleep in a warm feather bed, with a ready supply of his favourite smokesticks. He had inhaled the first with relish, but now he felt as if the smoke was the only thing holding him together.

How was this his war council? Of the seven at the table with him, somehow he had found six for whom he had less affection than the seventh, his mother, and none of them could agree on anything.

His mother wanted to crown him the king of West Erland and tumble the bridges into the river. Adfric proposed they march for Halord's Bridge in force and dare Hessian to meet them. Strovac Sigac wanted to challenge Lord Andrick to single combat, as if that would settle anything. Chieftain Ba'an watched all but said little, an unreadable expression on his weather-beaten face.

Even had it not been a dreadful idea, Rymond was loath to give Strovac anything. The big warrior's behaviour on the march back to Irith had almost had their whole fragile coalition coming to blows, and cost Strovac the little finger of his left hand.

A few nights into their march, Strovac and some of his brutes had visited Errian, who was chained to the central pole of a tent beside Rymond's own. Rymond chose not to imagine what Strovac might have had planned for Errian, but it was clear he had underestimated the strength of this son of the Barrelbreaker, who in the ensuing scuffle had somehow broken a man's arm and got hold of a sword.

Fortunately, Rymond had been woken by the noise and raced towards the disturbance. Inside, he had found one of Strovac's men dead, and two others wounded. Though the rest had together managed to wrench the sword from Errian's grip, he had Strovac's hand locked between his teeth. Rymond's guards had restored order, but a bruised and bloodied Errian had defiantly spat out the remains of Strovac's smallest finger.

Strovac's angry demands that Errian's hand be cut off in retribution had fallen on deaf ears. Rymond had never been easily stirred to anger, but his rage at Strovac actually seemed to have cowed the man, and had his followers begging for Rymond's mercy. Adfric had counselled him to execute every single one, but Rymond knew his authority with Strovac and his Wild Brigade hung by a fine thread. He had ordered that neither Strovac nor his men would come within fifty feet of Errian, and doubled his guard. Strovac had been a sulking child ever since, insolent in responding to commands and glowering at Rymond when he thought he was not looking.

And then there were the three newcomers at the table. Old Lord Storaut, in the winter of his life, spear-thin with pale, watery eyes and white eyebrows thick as gorse. Even in his youth he had never been much of a warrior, but he was rich enough to garb his soldiers in matching mail and helmets, with silver-on-blue cloaks about their necks. Like all old men, he counselled patience, that they ought to wait until more lords had answered the call before they took the field.

Chieftain Arka of the Ffriseans did not counsel patience, nor did he speak any Erlish, but he did have the advantage of being the largest man Rymond had ever seen. He was perhaps a hand's-breadth taller than Strovac, and broader across the chest, with a thick bear-like pelt covering his bare torso and a fierce black beard. He seemed to understand Erlish, but spoke only in the guttural language of Ffrisea, with deep grunts from his throat that the terrified translator at his shoulder had to interpret for the rest of them.

The Ffriseans Arka had brought were all large men, and fought not with iron or steel but with great lengths of wood as thick as their vast arms. On their introduction, the translator had told Rymond that they hoped to collect many enemy scalps to gift to their wives. He had elected not to ask how they scalped their enemies without blades.

Arka wished to barricade Hessian inside Merivale, and have his Ffriseans force their way in and kill all who opposed them. The best Rymond could have said was that it was a better plan than Strovac's.

Finally there was Captain-General Gruenla, the leader of the Cylirien mercenaries, who Rymond had been surprised to discover was a woman. Naturally, she was the most interesting of the guests at the table. She was unremarkably plain, but her dark green eyes had held Rymond's gaze flirtatiously when they were introduced, and that she had a sword and dagger tucked into her belt and was clad in armour only increased her allure. When they marched he would have to try to ensure their tents were next to one another.

Gruenla suggested an attack on Hessian's fortress at

Carthred as an act of provocation, an idea to which Lord
Storaut took exception.

'Come now,' he said loftily, 'Carthred has no strategic significance. Lord Rymond, you cannot take the advice of a foreign,
lowborn woman who does not know our lands.'

Gruenla did not reply, but fixed her gaze on Storaut until he
was forced to look away.

Of the plans available, Rymond actually liked Gruenla's
most. Adfric's would just leave them freezing on Halord's
Bridge waiting for something to happen; Lord Storaut's would
only give Hessian a chance to build up his own forces; Arka's
and Strovac's were not genuine options; and his mother's plan
to crown him would only increase the Sangreal perception of
the threat without him even taking to the field against them. If
they struck Carthred and then faded away into the winter mists
they would bloody Hessian's nose with no chance for him to
counter. The Sangreals were no fools who would go to war in
winter.

Rymond sighed, and rubbed his face. The coming winter
made their bickering largely pointless. Unless there was some
plan they could execute in the next fortnight, any attack would
have to wait until spring. That was what made attacking
Carthred at least feasible.

But what if there were some way to harm Hessian through
winter, and perhaps beyond? By spring, their armies would be
so large they would eat the land to ruin wherever they marched.
Right at this moment, peasants would be bringing the last of the
harvest in, ready to be carted to the city. Hessian might need to
hold some food back for a spring campaign, as might Rymond. It
would be a lean winter, in both West and East Erland.

A small smile tickled at Rymond's lips. He might be new to
warfare, but he could not help but think he had a better idea
than all of them. Perhaps now they were sufficiently tired of
arguing to listen.

They ought to obey him anyway, as their uncrowned monarch, but Rymond was aware that he was the youngest at the table, and had the least experience of war. He had to tread carefully, and flatter them all sufficiently to believe their voice had been heard.

He rose from his chair to draw their attention, and after a moment they stopped their discussions to look at him.

'Lord Storaut,' he began, speaking quickly before their arguments could restart, 'in time, others will come, but already I feel the bite of winter. If we wait, we will have no chance to strike until spring. Strovac, Chieftain Arka, nobody doubts your bravery, nor the ferocity of the Ffriseans, but you should be put to better use than risky single combat or a direct attack against Merivale.

'Mother, I will be crowned in time, but not until we have shown we have the strength to oppose Hessian. To do otherwise would be to invite him to bring all his power against us. Captain Gruenla, Carthred is a fine target, which we must consider when spring comes.

'Adfric is right. Halord's Bridge is the key to East Erland. Across that bridge sit acres and acres of good farmland, watered by the Pale River.' He leant over the table, and ran his finger across three specks on the map, just south of the bridge. 'The settlements of Southton, Ditchford, and Imberwych. Large villages, or small towns, whichever pleases you.'

Strovac snorted. 'I passed through Imberwych on my way west and there was nothing large about it. Didn't even have an inn.'

'But what all three towns do have are vast granaries, which right now will be full to bursting with the harvests of all the smaller villages within twenty miles. Before winter, much of that grain will be transported by barge, down the Little River to Merivale to be sold, and a fraction must also be given in homage to Hessian.

'We have a chance for one assault before winter, and I propose that the most damaging attack would be on their stores. Our own harvest has been poor, and I doubt East Erland's has been any better. It will already be a lean winter. If we burn those granaries, we might kill more East Erlanders through the months of winter than in a single battle. At the very least, the price of bread in Merivale will soar, and Hessian might demand his lords provide more food to Merivale, or buy more from further east. Both would weaken him.

'That is my proposal. We ride hard for Halord's Bridge and cross into the breadbasket of East Erland. Burn the granaries, and kill any farmers or millers who stand in our way.'

Adfric looked up at him, frowning. 'Is that honourable? We would be butchering peasants whom you hope to one day rule.'

'Honour fled the stable the day Hessian tried to have my son kidnapped,' said Breta. 'Come spring those peasants might be in Lord Andrick's army, armed with spears, not scythes.'

'The Barrelbreaker might ride out and meet us,' added Strovac, rubbing his jaw. 'If he does, we can tempt them to battle where the ground favours us.'

Strovac agreed with little else Rymond or anyone else said, so from that perspective it had to be a good plan. Rymond turned to the others at the table. 'What say the rest of you?'

Lord Storaut was nodding thoughtfully. 'Early glory for us, and a hard winter for Hessian and the Barrelbreaker. It suits me well.'

The rest murmured encouragingly, though Adfric remained silent for a moment. He looked to be choosing his words carefully.

'If you do this,' he said eventually, 'there is no going back. Hessian will shed no tears for farmers, but a king who cannot protect his people is no king at all. There will be no settlement, no second Accord between East and West. Hessian and his brother will chase you until they have your head on a spike. It will be your life, or theirs. If you are prepared for that, then this is a fine plan.'

'I am,' said Rymond. Hessian had shown his ruthlessness. Now it was Rymond's turn to show his. Let East Erland feel the consequences of Hessian plotting to kidnap him. They would turn the Pale River red with farmers' blood. 'Hessian gives no quarter, and nor shall we.'

That evening, their discussions concluded, Rymond returned to his own chambers, which he had missed greatly. He poured himself a glass of wine filled to the brim and collapsed into his chair, closing his eyes to the headache around his temples.

They had all agreed with him, and the meeting had concluded with Strovac slamming his knife into the map, obliterating Halord's Bridge where they would cross into the east. Adfric had shaken his hand, and the savage Ffrisean Arka had slapped him on the back so hard that Rymond thought he would throw up his breakfast. Even his mother had looked approving.

He had shown them he had what it took to lead. So why did he just feel empty? Where was the triumph he ought to feel?

He had to stir the idea around his head a few times before he realised why. It was because he felt used. Except for the dutiful, dull Adfric, they were all using him. Strovac wanted a lordship. Gruenla he was paying. Even for his mother he was only a means to an end.

What he needed was loyalty, and not of Adfric's sort. Friends, not allies or servants. He downed his wine, and collected his hooded cloak from the wall. He swung it about his shoulders and stepped into the corridor.

He sneaked out of the castle, down some servant stairs he

had disobediently used as a child, and through the darkness out into Irith.

He looked in the Smoking Sow first, and all through the New Quarter. The taverns and streets were alive with gossip of the convergence of armies in the town. The whole citizenry seemed to know that they would march to war tomorrow. Rymond saw some of his own men, stumbling arm in arm across the road holding one another upright. He smiled, and pulled his hood lower over his brow.

His search eventually led him to the Blushing Bride, a tavern of ill-repute in the Old City. It was still early for a haunt like the Bride, and there were only a handful of other drinkers, many of them hooded as Rymond was, so his garb did not attract the odd looks it had in other more savoury establishments. The floor was covered with sawdust, and a sow with a litter of piglets had made her home in a corner, giving the inn a powerful farmyard scent.

It was here that Rymond found what he sought: Will and Dom, at a corner table laughing over a pitcher of ale, Will deep in the telling of a story while Dom drank hungrily between cackles of laughter.

Rymond smiled. It cheered his heart to see them both. He approached and sat down at a third stool without a word, and when they looked up at the intrusion pulled back his hood enough that they could see his features.

'Ry!' Will smiled in delight, and Rymond had to urgently put a finger to his lips to silence him. Dom's tanned face, however, stayed impassive, still obviously indignant over his brief imprisonment.

'I came to say thanks,' said Rymond to Dom. 'The Cyliriens and the Ffriseans look like fierce fighters. And they didn't burn the city down.'

'You shouldn't be here,' said Dom, not looking at him. 'That hood won't do you any good when you're sitting here with us.

Everyone knows about you being kidnapped, and I'm sure this isn't the first time that bloke over there has been watching us.' His eyes moved past Rymond, who turned his head to glimpse through the corner of his eye another hooded man hunched over a table by himself.

Rymond shifted warily on his stool. 'I'll keep my wits about me.'

'It's not you I'm concerned about. If you get kidnapped again in our company Will and I will swing from the gallows.'

'Eryi's teeth, Dom, we were in jail for less than twelve hours!' laughed Will. He did not bother to lower his voice, and Rymond had to shush him again insistently. 'Ry never asked to be kidnapped, and since then you've sailed to Cylirien and Ffrisea for him, so you can drop the indignance.'

'I took a contract,' said Dom stubbornly, 'as sailors do every day.' He took a drink of his ale. 'And for less than I might have if it had been anyone else. Was fearful I'd be thrown in jail again if I refused.'

'If you want more, I can give it to you,' said Rymond. 'But I came here hoping to make you a better offer than mere gold. We've been friends for a decade, ever since I paid Will to sneak me a mug of ale out the back of here and he gave me a mug of your piss. I ride to war tomorrow, and I want you both at my side.'

Immediately, Will slammed his palm down, shaking the table and spilling beer over the side of his mug. 'I'm in.' He slapped Dom on the back and put his arm around him. 'Come on, Dom, we'll make King Hessian mess his breeches and stick our mate King Ry on the throne. What an adventure!'

'Why are you always in such a bloody hurry, Will?' said Rymond. 'You've not even let me tell you the best part.' He reached over, took a sip of Will's ale, and leant in towards them. 'Everyone else is with me because they want something. My mother wants to piss on Hessian's grave and restore the rightful line. Strovac Sigac wants me to make him a lord. You two are my best friends, and you've never asked anything of me. So, when I take the throne, I mean to make you both lords as well.'

Dom nearly choked on his beer. 'Don't think you need to make me a lord just because I'm your bastard cousin. I'm happy as a sailor.'

Rymond had to laugh at that. 'Is this you happy, Dom? You being my cousin has nothing to do with it. I never got to choose my family. My father was a drunken oaf, and my brother was a vicious oaf. I'll make you a lord because you're my friend.'

'You can stick your pride up your bum, Dom,' said Will. '*Lord Willam Holdfell* and *Lord Dominac D'bure*. The girls will be lifting their skirts like we've got cocks made of sugar. Just say yes, and we'll celebrate with a drink.'

Dom took a sip of beer and swilled it around his mouth, and eventually he grinned. 'All right then.'

'Yes!' cried Will, leaping to his feet and gesturing towards the bar. 'Barman! A bottle of your finest wine, and another of your second finest! We're drinking like lords tonight!'

Rymond grinned, not even bothering to try and quieten his friend. He had a plan that would strike fear into East Erland, and he would be taking his friends with him. Perhaps becoming king would not be so bad after all.

CHAPTER 23

They rode through the night, while a torrent of icy rain fell mercilessly upon them, soaking them to their skin. The sky rumbled angrily overhead, and their torches flickered under the downpour, threatening to plunge them into pitch black at any moment.

Orsian gasped and shivered inside his cloak, leaning in close to his horse's mane and speaking soothing words in its ear. The dawn was still hours away, but he trusted his mount to follow his father through the darkness, out in front and setting their party a punishing pace.

They had been abed when the message came. A rider without a banner, standing below the gate and shouting to all who would listen that he must speak with Lord Andrick. Naeem had recognised the man immediately: a soldier, in the service of Errian, gaunt and sweat-stained, and smelling like the lowliest of beggars.

He had almost collapsed when they opened the gate, and there in the yard he had told them his tale, of how they had made camp with Strovac Sigac's band, then how they had been butchered in the night and Errian taken captive.

They had been on the road within the hour, racing back to
Merivale to take word to Hessian and prepare for battle. Whatever his father's quarrel with the king, it had been forgotten as
soon as he heard Errian was captured. He rode like a man
possessed, heedless of the thundering rainstorm that threatened
to drown them before they even reached Piperskeep.

Orsian had been ready to kill Errian for what he had done
to Da'ri and to Pherri, but there was no time to think of that
now. He too had wanted to ride off to fight the Thrumb, as his
brother had done. It could have been him at the mercy of
Strovac Sigac and the Prindians. They might kill Errian as
vengeance for Ranulf's death sixteen years ago, or worse. As
much as Orsian hated him, that was not a fate anyone deserved.

Pherri had woken with the rest of them, and had hugged
Orsian fiercely while he readied his horse. He had reassured her
he would be home again soon. Whether or not they could free
Errian, it was almost winter, and no one went to war in the
Erlish winter.

If he lived that long. Orsian clenched his reins, and touched
a hand to his sword hilt for reassurance. He was sure he was
ready; he had killed a man now. But killing a man at a hundred
yards was not the same as gutting them with a sword with their
hot breath in your face and battle raging around you. If he hesitated when the moment came, he was dead. He held out his
hand to test his nerve, but even in riding gloves the wind and
rain chilled his skin, and he could not stop it from shaking.

Hours later, as day broke, Orsian rode behind his father
through the King's Gate at a gallop, trailed by a train of two
hundred men. They rode up the Castle Road in lines five
abreast, scattering citizens and guards alike. Orsian carried his
father's standard, and above Andrick's flag fluttered the king's
own blood-red banner.

At Piperskeep, the guards did not hesitate to allow them
entry, leaping out of their way to raise the portcullis. Orsian

suspected they were under orders to watch for his father and admit him without question. Whatever their disagreement, the king relied upon him.

Sure enough, Theodric was waiting for them in the yard, his face pale with worry and his hands thrust deep within his robes.

'How have you arrived so soon?' asked Theodric when he hailed them. 'Our messenger should only have reached Violet Hall this morning.'

'Never mind that,' said Andrick, dismounting. 'Is Strovac allied with the Prindians? Do they mean to attack?'

'We should speak inside,' said Theodric. 'The king will wish to speak with you himself.'

Andrick took a few quick strides, and before Theodric could raise his hands in defence had gripped him around the collar and lifted him off his feet. 'They have my son,' he growled, his face tight with fury. 'Tell me, Theodric.'

Orsian gaped. Theodric looked as alarmed as he had ever seen him, his ethereal serenity dissolved by his father holding him a foot off the ground. Few men dared to lay a hand upon the king's magus, lest they have their hands scalded or their bowels turned to liquid.

'Two thousand men rode from Irith,' spluttered Theodric. 'Less than a week ago. We think they are riding for Halord's Bridge.'

Andrick dropped Theodric, and the magus stumbled side-ways to keep his balance. 'Do you have men ready to ride?'

'Six hundred, with the *Hymeriker*, plus your men here. Lady Gough is marching from Tallowton with another thousand.'

Orsian knew of Lady Gough. She was a young widow, ruling her late father's lands not far from Merivale. Her thousand would likely be horseless peasants armed with hoes and rakes.

'They are all to assemble outside the King's Gate,' said

Andrick. 'We ride for Halord's Bridge.' He turned away from Theodric towards his men.

'Lord Andrick, would it not be better—'

Andrick turned back, his eyes blazing. 'Better to what?'

'Wait.' Theodric had regained some composure. He replaced his hands in the deep pockets of his robes and drew himself to his full height. 'They have three times our force. When Lady Gough arrives we will not be so outnumbered.'

His father's expression was so fierce that Orsian thought he might be about to grab Theodric around the throat. 'Listen here, you shit-stain of a wizard. I've been winning battles against the odds for thirty years. I may not be able to explain Eryispek, or the Lutums, or why you're as useless as a three-legged horse, but I know how to win a war, and it's got little to do with numbers, and even less to do with anything you know. So you stick to magic or whatever the fuck it is you do around here now, and I'll stick to war, and we'll give that Prindian boy such a scare he'll never leave Irith again. Understood?'

Theodric swallowed, and nodded, suitably chastised. 'Understood, Lord.'

Andrick turned to his men. 'You are dismissed. Kiss your wife and children, have a meal at a tavern, fuck your favourite whore, do as you please. Just be outside the King's Gate in two hours.'

Orsian thought it was testament to their loyalty that not a single man grumbled, even after their mad moonlit ride. The quicker and cannier among them were already turning tail to ride into the city and make the most of their last hours of leisure.

Andrick nodded to Theodric. 'Now I will see Hessian.' He strode into the keep, without a backward glance.

As Orsian followed him, he heard Naeem lingering to apologise to Theodric. 'Sorry about that, Lord. But if he's like that to you, just imagine how he treats them not on his side.'

As they entered the keep, his father seemed surprised that Orsian was still there. 'My command applies to you as well. The next two hours are yours. I suggest you do whatever you would regret dying and having left undone.' He turned on his heel and walked away, his steps echoing on the stone floor.

Orsian stared after him for a moment. His father was right. They were riding to war, and for now vastly outnumbered. His father's *Hymeriker* were the finest soldiers in the land, perhaps the world, but there was a chance they could all be dead within a week. The Prindians had the numbers, and Strovac Sigac was well-versed in warfare. Orsian's mouth felt like dried-out leather.

He was relieved his father was not taking him to the king. His father had always spoken of his brother reverently, as if he possessed some wisdom beyond men's understanding, but Orsian had seen the truth now. Hessian might be his king, but he was no leader. No wonder his father had kept him away from Hessian for so long. Orsian was prepared to spend as little time with him as possible.

What did he want to do for the next two hours? He could join the men in one of Merivale's taverns, but what he wanted most was to see Helana. She was still under house arrest, so sure to be in the keep. He doubted imprisonment agreed with her.

He walked towards Helana's rooms, his stomach knotted with nerves. Would she blame him for not intervening when Hessian had struck her? He could feel his palms sweating. He tried to wipe them on his clothes, but managed only to gather dirt and grime from the road. Wiping them on each other just seemed to make the sweating worse. In the end he ran his hands through his hair, drying them but leaving his hair greasy.

He arrived at her room and knocked.

Helana opened the door. She still kept her vigil of black in honour of Prince Jarhick. Today she wore a simple dress of black velvet that clung to her and fell enticingly below her knee.

Orsian thought it suited her, framing her willowy figure and accenting her high cheekbones. When he finished admiring her and finally met her eye, she was looking at him with a knowing smile, and he blushed in embarrassment.

'You ride to war,' she said, with what might have been a hint of disapproval.

He nodded. 'Soon. I thought I would visit you before we leave.'

'Thank you.' She smiled at him, making his stomach flip. 'I've been losing my mind in here; the guards won't even let me outside the keep for a walk.' She gestured inside. 'Will you take a cup of wine with me before you leave?'

Orsian followed her in, relieved that she seemed pleased to see him. She had not mentioned that he had stood by while the king struck her, so presumably did not hate him for it.

They sat together at Helana's table, and she poured them wine. Orsian took a sip. It was sweet and sharp, honeyed with a hint of lemon.

'I heard about Errian,' she said. 'Do you think you can free him?'

'I don't know.' Orsian did not want to think about Errian. Part of him still thought his brother might deserve a period of imprisonment. 'They have three times our number, and they've probably left Errian in Irith. He could be rotting in a dungeon, or dead already.'

Helana shook her head. 'I spent hours speaking with Lady Prindian. She is not some bloodthirsty harpy intent on spilling Sangreal blood, whatever my father may think.'

Orsian looked at her in confusion, knowing it must show on his face. 'But Breta Prindian tricked you,' he said slowly. 'She tried to kidnap the queen. They've gathered an army and captured Errian. They want to destroy us.'

'She blames my father. She says he tried to kidnap Lord Rymond.'

'She would say that.' Orsian shook his head, irritated. He had thought Helana would feel horribly guilty for her role in Ciera's kidnapping, but evidently not. 'This war started the day you let Breta Prindian into Piperskeep.'

Helana's cheeks flushed. 'I paid for that. You were there when my father humiliated me. And now I am confined to the castle, like a criminal.'

'Eryi's balls, Helana! Had it been anyone else he'd have sent them to the dungeon!'

'I did what I thought was best!' Helana rose to her feet. They were both shouting now. Orsian did not understand what had happened. 'I just want peace, Orsian, so that nobody else will feel how I did when I was told Jarhick would not be coming home. Already my father is dragging peasants from their fields and their villages, boys who've never held a sword. Not everyone is born and raised for war like you.'

The face of the man he had shot flashed before Orsian's eyes, but he pushed it from his thoughts. 'This is the Prindians' war,' he said. 'They started this. We have to show strength. Otherwise Erland is lost. If the Imperium invades, we'll be too divided to fight back.'

'Oh come on, Orsian,' Helana scoffed. 'The Imperium invasion was centuries ago! You can't really think that a united Erland is all that stands between us and slavery? My father wants to rule all of Erland because it suits him, not because of some high-minded idea about protecting people.'

Orsian spluttered, trying to think of a reply. He wanted to connect the selfish, capricious Hessian he knew with the belief that he wanted Erland to stand together to protect his subjects, but the two things went together like oil and water. Keeping Erland under Hessian's rule was nothing to do with keeping them safe; only a fool would believe that.

He downed his wine and stood, shaking his head as if that realisation could be shaken off like a flea. 'I have to go,' he said.

'I can't think about this. My father commands me to fight, and that's what I have to do. I'm good at it. I'm fighting for Erland. For all of us.' The words felt hollow on his lips.

To his surprise, his words somehow seemed to steal the wind from Helana's sails. Her face fell. She looked sad, and scared, and beautiful. 'I'm sorry,' she said. 'You must do what you think is right.'

To Orsian's surprise, she closed the gap between them and locked him in a fierce embrace, as if she meant to hold him all the way to Halord's Bridge. 'Just come back safely. I am running out of black clothes.'

'I will. I promise.' Orsian pulled away from her slightly, and their eyes met. Helana's were emerald green, glistening with faint tears. He was close enough to see each delicate eyelash, and smell her perfume, like smoke and wildflowers.

He remembered what his father had said: to do what he would regret leaving undone. His heart was beating so hard he was sure she could hear it.

He kissed her, lightly on the mouth, and she did not stop him. Her lips were soft as down. He savoured the feeling, wishing it would last forever, before he wrenched himself away from her.

'Just in case you don't,' she whispered.

───────────

As he climbed the stairs to the solar, Andrick wondered what he would say to Hessian. Truthfully, the king's barb that he was going soft had hurt more than the questioning of his loyalty, because he had worried it might be true. He was no stranger to the cruelty men could inflict on each other, particularly Hessian. Andrick had forced Ranulf Prindian into the oubliette himself, ignoring his desperate, bestial screams. But what if Hessian's justice was cruelty for its own sake? It had weighed on him, in a way it never had before, as did many things. As a young man, he had never worried about anything, but as he aged every threat was something to be balanced against the danger it posed to his family, and measured against his own power to resist it.

That fear had dissipated now. Errian's imprisonment and the force led by Rymond Prindian had killed his uncertainty. The fear he had for his family only hardened his will, and the fire for battle still blazed.

But as they said farewell in the yard of Violet Hall, he had given Viratia his promise: this was to be his last war. A man could not fight both his enemies and the stream of time forever. He had seen in the flesh what happened when a man fought beyond his prime, when the old Lord Storaut, the pride of West Erland, had crossed blades with a boy of sixteen, and Andrick had parried two dozen strokes before burying his sword in the older man's neck. Storaut had been five years younger than Andrick was now. There were ways he could serve Hessian and Erland without standing in a shield wall.

He had been right about Marius. Hessian may believe that the public perception of his honour and righteousness stemmed from the authority of the crown he wore, but Andrick had spent a lifetime among fighting men, and knew different. Men knew of Hessian's penchant for cruelty, but they believed it was justified, derived from an iron sense of justice and of what was right for Erland. But using a blameless soldier as a lightning rod for his hatred of the Prindians was the behaviour of a tyrant. There had never been a popular rebellion in Erland, but enough kings had lost the crown because men swore their sword to another. If they were to defeat this new Prindian threat, they would need every sword they could muster.

His thoughts had led him to the top of the stairs. He nodded to the guards, knocked twice, and entered.

He was surprised to discover that Hessian was not alone.

He sat at the table with a man dressed richly in the stylish silks of an Imperial merchant, sharing a jug of wine.

Hessian and the merchant looked up at the intrusion. 'Lord Kvarm,' said Hessian to the man, 'my brother, Lord Andrick.'

The foreign lord stood and extended his hand to Andrick. He was old, but wore his years well. 'Lord Barrelbreaker,' he said, in heavily accented Erlish, 'it is an honour. Even in the Imperium we know of your legend.'

'The honour is mine, Lord Kvarm.'

'Just Kvarm will do, Lord. Your king does me the honour of a title that I have no claim to. I am a mere merchant.'

'You may leave us, Lord Kvarm,' said Hessian from the table, with a casual wave towards the door. 'Your request is granted, provided your men behave themselves. I hope you find whatever it is you are looking for.'

Kvarm seemed slightly startled by his dismissal, but took it well, giving a low bow to Hessian and leaving through the door.

'Who was that?' asked Andrick.

'Kvarm is the lord administrator of the Imperial enclave in Cliffark, one of the richest men in the world. It is the first I've heard of this enclave, but I suppose I will have to forgive Lord Istlewick for granting the Imperium a presence in his city now we are family, provided he pays the right taxes. Kvarm and I had an interesting discussion. He has lost something of great value: a purse, he claims, though I suspect there is more to it. He asked permission for his men to search the city for it. I'll have Theodric keep an eye on them. He even offered me a reward if it were found. He is unmarried – odd for a man his age – but I have asked if he would consider Helana as a bride. It may serve us well to have such an ally in the Imperium.'

Andrick nodded. He had little interest in the affairs of wealthy Imperials.

A silence fell between them. Andrick looked around the

room, and noted that the sword he had left at Hessian's feet was now mounted above the door to his private sanctum. His eyes lingered on it. 'Remember that sword you gave me when we were young? It still rests on the wall over the door to my and Viratia's bedroom. It was too valuable for me to use.'

'You never seemed that comfortable with it. I am surprised you didn't take it down after I had left.' Hessian smiled, remembering. 'I knew it was only put there for my benefit. It was an outrageous gift, but you earnt it.'

'My daughter is fascinated by it. Her old tutor said it was valuable enough to ransom me if I were ever captured.'

'If you are here to ask my permission to offer it in ransom of Errian, you do not need it. I know what it is to lose a son.'

'Never,' said Andrick. The Prindians had no need of gold. 'I will free Errian with the old, battered sword above your door, if you will allow me to take it.'

Hessian stood, and retrieved the sword from its mount himself. He handed it to Andrick hilt-first.

'Will you ride today?'

'Yes. With your leave, my King.'

'You have it, of course, my *Balhymeri*.'

The two of them clasped wrists. Neither apologised. Their quarrel was no longer important.

'Theodric says the Prindian boy rides with over two thousand,' said Hessian. 'Can you defeat so many without reinforcements?'

'If Strovac Sigac has the command, they will fight fiercely, but I have beaten worse odds, against better men. If we can reach Halord's Bridge before they cross, we have the advantage. If not, we must do what we can.' East Erland's grain stores were the Prindian target, Andrick was sure of it. He had debated sending men directly from Violet Hall to guard the bridge, but they would have been too few to make a difference.

'Curse Strovac, that treacherous dog,' spat Hessian. 'I should have listened to you. I want Strovac alive. Prindian you can kill. Chieftain Ba'an as well, if it is true he rides with them. But the world must see how King Hessian punishes turncoats.'

Andrick knew Sigac would never let himself be captured. The man had enough cruelty in him to imagine the fate that would await him. 'Will you ride out with us? It would give courage to the men if they could see you.'

'I may need to be reminded which end of the horse I am supposed to be facing, but I will do my part.'

Outside the King's Gate, Andrick and Hessian sat on their horses together, faced by eight hundred mounted men, all wrapped warmly against the autumn winds. Hessian had not been seen outside the keep in half a year, and men strained their necks to catch a better view of him. He had been dressed for battle in the red and gold armour of his youth, though he would not ride with them beyond the first mile of their journey.

The king surveyed their force and gave a satisfied nod, then leant towards Andrick and Orsian, speaking in an undertone. 'Andrick, I would not see you lose two sons in service of my cause. If you want to leave Orsian here, all would understand.'

No sooner had the words left his lips than Orsian replied for himself. 'No,' he said forcefully. Andrick and Hessian looked at him. 'I want to fight.'

Hessian nodded sagely. 'All young men want to fight. If that is your wish and your father's, I withdraw my suggestion. You sound just like he did at your age.'

'Orsian,' said Andrick, 'go and check with the supply carts that they have enough feed for the horses. We will need their strength if we are to beat Prindian to the bridge.'

When he had left, Andrick looked back to Hessian. 'Orsian

would never forgive me if I left him here. I raised him and Errian knowing one day they might give their lives for Erland, but it is their mother who worries me. I never considered how I would tell Viratia should that come to pass.' He offered a silent prayer to Eryi that Errian still lived, and that Orsian's courage was not misplaced. He would not be able to hide his second son behind a ridge armed with a bow if it came to battle with the Prindians.

Hessian nodded. 'May Eryi lend speed to your horses, Brother. I shall not delay you.'

He raised his arm, and in unison the whispers from the soldiers fell away, all eagerly awaiting the king's words.

Hessian spoke from low in his gut, loud enough that every man could hear. 'Men of Erland. I shall not delay you. I know you have many miles to ride, and scant time in which to do it.

'Hundreds of years ago, when the Meridivals journeyed across the Sorrowlands, it was an exodus from tyranny in the south. And when my ancestor King Pedrian rode into West Erland, he did so because of tyranny from the north. It is the same tyranny that threatens us today. Lord Prindian and his followers seek to divide this land, and if they were to succeed, we would be a vassal state of the Imperium within a lifetime. But that will not come to pass. Not because I will that it will not be so, but because of *you*.

'Just a moment ago, I made Lord Andrick an offer: he could leave his second son, Orsian, here at Merivale, where he would be safe. Orsian refused me, without hesitation, as if he would sooner die than be left behind. And I thought to myself: if that is the hunger of every man here, what army in the world could defeat them? So, I ask you now, is there any man here who would have accepted?'

The men howled their denials. 'No! Never!'

'As I thought! Then ride now, and remember what you fight for. Freedom for Erland!'

'ERLAND! ERLAND! ERLAND!' Their voices echoed off Merivale's walls like thunder, booming like a hundred bells, loud enough to shake the earth beneath their feet. 'HESSIAN KING! HESSIAN KING! HESSIAN KING! HESSIAN KING!'

INTERLUDE

There were days when he woke up with no memory of the day before, nor sometimes the day prior to that. Even on the days he could remember, there were hours he could not account for, like reading his life as a book with pages torn out.

At least the others did not seem to notice the wandering of his mind. Or more likely they were too hungry to care. After Basseton, Gelick had led all the Lutums, near to five hundred men, women, and children, up the Mountain. Barely a tenth of them remained. The rest had frozen to death in the night, or gone hunting and never returned, or been slain in an argument over whatever meagre food they had found that day.

Even when the tribe had first come up the Mountain, food had been scarce. Within weeks, there were no rabbits, nor wild goats, nor much of anything, and several times they had been forced to set out again in search of more plentiful hunting grounds. With all their wandering, Gelick could not be sure which side they were on. He knew only that they seemed to be getting higher. The cold winds were rising, and the snowy squalls that could stop a man seeing beyond a yard in front of him becoming more frequent. They existed in a sort of half-life, speaking only when needed, and at night huddling together for warmth.

Today though was the calmest they had known in weeks, and for once they had been able to start a fire large enough to warm them all, which they sat around as a rabbit slowly cooked in front of them. Mad Errek had even taken off his furs, and was sitting cross-legged and shirtless, grinning like a loon.

The weather was such that Gelick could for once look outwards, all the way down the rush of the distant Pale River, proof that they were on the western side. This was Adrari land, but he did not fear them. There were enough Lutums to make a fight of it, and it would be easier to feed themselves if a few were struck down by the Adrari's whalebone axes. The extra meat might also be useful, in time.

'*You have nothing to fear from death.*'

The voice was suddenly there again, clashing inside his head like the strings of a mistuned harp. It had been with him ever since he had killed the doe. Sometimes it might go days without speaking, but it always returned. 'Did you kill the others?' Gelick mumbled. If anyone asked, he would deny having said anything.

'*They have more purpose in death than they would have in life.*'

'Who are you to decide that?' Occasionally, Gelick's anger towards the voice would rise. It had convinced him to commit a massacre, to drive away the worshippers of the false man-god, to purify the Mountain, and instead of glory it had led them into the White to die. The pride he had felt returning home with a white doe over his shoulders felt from a different age. He had thought the voice one of the Norhai, making their will plain to him through the Mountain, the pillar that held up the sky and the Norhai's embodiment on earth at the centre of all existence. He still thought it, sometimes, in his few more hopeful moments. 'Who are you truly? Why are you doing this to me?'

'*You will know more pain, before the end, worse than this cold. Nothing has value if not hard-won. You should be glad for those who have died. An icy death is preferable to many others.*'

'Have you died?'

'*A thousand times or more.*'

'You speak in riddles,' hissed Gelick. 'What do you want from me?'

No reply. The voice was gone.

Gelick looked around at all the Lutums who remained, some of them among the very first who had taken up his call for rebellion. They sat and stood around the fire, in various states of weakness. The frailest of them were nearest to it, some of them so close Gelick thought their clothes might singe. Parius, a distant cousin, had his feet almost in the fire. His toes had begun turning blue a week earlier, and its tinge was now creeping up his foot.

Gelick felt a pang of guilt for the hardship they were willing to endure for him. He had returned from his trial in the wilderness preaching the Way of the Mountain with fiery certainty, urged on by the whispers in his head. The voice had told him it would set him on a path of righteousness, to restore the line of mountain kings and cast out the non-believers. *A lie.* The whole tribe had taken up the cry, convinced by the corpse of the white doe he carried: a rare beast, almost mythical, and surely a sign of the Mountain's favour. When they had asked him what to do, it had been the voice who told him: '*You will ride to Basseton.*'

Gelick's blackouts had begun after Basseton, but when he thought of that day, it was like watching through somebody else's eyes, looking down on himself as he wrote a tale of death in other men's blood. By the end he had barely been able to lift his axe. Only once he came to his senses had he realised the horror he had wrought. Wild dogs fighting over stripped bodies, charred corpses with stakes driven through them. And then he had set the ruins alight. The smell of blood and burning still lingered in his nostrils.

The tribe had been giddy over their victory, and for three nights they drank and danced amidst the ruins. That had lasted until the stores ran dry. Then, after days of asking Gelick what they were to do next, they heard that a force from Merivale was riding to retake Basseton, greater in number and armed with steel. Their wood and bronze was no match for steel – their ancestors had learnt that – but some were eager to stay and fight. The voice had been absent from Gelick's thoughts for most of what occurred at Basseton, until it had told him they must flee up the Mountain, to purify themselves for the fight that was yet to come. Foolishly, he had listened, and so had the Lutums.

Gelick silently cursed the damnable voice.

His stomach rumbled. Hunger gnawed at him, like a rat chewing him out from in. Gelick's mouth salivated at the rabbit over the fire. They had not eaten cooked meat in weeks, surviving on gristly uncooked flesh ripped straight off the bone. The rabbit was a poor, stringy thing, and by the time it was shared out between them it would barely be a mouthful each, but they could boil the bones into a thin broth and go to sleep with at least some warmth in their bellies.

'It is faith that will sustain you, not broth.'

'Can we eat faith? Leave me alone.'

The voice gave a grim, coughing cackle. 'Fine words, but you would not have survived this long without me. See how even as your companions' muscles wither with hunger and their hands and feet rot, your stomach remains firm and your limbs strong?'

It was true, Gelick had to admit. He was faring better than all of them, even Mad Errek, who claimed not to feel the cold. He flexed his fingers, feeling the strong muscles that ran through his arm. His body seemed not to have lost even an inch of flesh.

When the rabbit was cooked and its meat divided, Gelick gave his share to Parius, now weeping over the pain in his toes and trying desperately to rub some feeling back into them. When the broth came, Gelick gave that to Parius too.

'*A waste. That one is not long for this world. I do what I can to sustain you, but the flesh still needs food.*'

Gelick had had enough. 'Every one of them followed me up here, and I'll be damned if I lose another one to the cold. If I'm so damn important, you'll find a way to keep me alive.'

The voice did not speak again that day. Gelick felt like he had regained some authority over his own mind, and his body, though it ached with hunger.

The next morning though, Parius did not rise. Gelick pulled back his cousin's hood to find him dead, his face frozen in the features of sleep.

The familiar cackling echoed around his skull. '*I told you. A waste of good rabbit.*'

The winds were rising again, and the camp regretted wasting the clear day sitting by the fire when they might have been hunting. By late afternoon, they were back around the fire, while Yunesa, yet another cousin, tried desperately to blow life back into the previous night's embers.

The others huddled around to form a barrier, but could not stop the wind dousing the fire with sleet and cold air. In the end, they dragged Parius' stiff body to it and propped it up against the wind. Eventually their sad fire sparked into life.

Gelick retreated to the outer edge of their circle to convene with the voice. 'You killed him.'

'*The cold killed him. Let it be a lesson.*'

'Help us then. I cannot watch my friends die one by one. What must I do to save them?'

The voice gave no reply.

'Why are you doing this?'

He could sense the voice's irritation in his head. '*The first part of my plan is already in motion. The prince is dead, because the one who would have saved him rode to Basseton. Does that mean anything to you? Do you feel better for having been learnt it? I thought not. You are my servant, and my goals are not for you to understand. Serve me well, and you will be rewarded. That is all you need to know.'*

CHAPTER 24

The air was thick with the stench of burning thatch. Heavy clouds of smoke hung in the sky, smothering the land in shadow. Fire crackled like feet upon dry twigs, while somewhere a child or an animal screamed.

Rymond wiped his watering eyes against the smoke. He had lost count now of the granaries, homes, and flocks they had ravaged. Endless pounds of grain burnt to ashes, and butchered livestock left to rot in the fields.

He looked down at the peasants on their knees before him, the dregs of Ditchford, or what remained of the settlement. They were pitiful, really. Ragged clothes soiled with dirt, and not a spark of defiance among them. How had the likes of these conquered his ancestors?

'The prisoners, Lord?' asked Adfric, for a second time.

Rymond shook his head. He would have to rule these people one day, and yet he had taken everything from them. Everything except their lives. Many of them would starve this winter. Perhaps killing them now was a mercy?

'Leave them,' he heard himself say. 'We've done what we came for. The ones who might fight are already dead.'

There had been a few young men, armed with pitchforks and barring their way to the granary. The rising plumes of smoke on the horizon would have been warning enough to them of what was to come. Brave, for peasants. Strovac had seen to them in a hurry, and found the rest hiding in the woods.

The assault had not been entirely without loss. One strapping peasant boy had slain a member of the Wild Brigade with a hoe and injured two more, and Strovac had made a point of not killing him and instead bringing him before Rymond, his hands bound and his face a motley of blood and bruises.

Strovac stood over him, his sword laid against the nape of his neck. 'I want this one,' he told Rymond, his smile stretching to a hungry grimace. The peasant tried to stand, but with a boot to the back Strovac pushed him face-first into the dirt. 'I won't need him long.'

Rymond appraised the situation. This was war, but there were limits. He would not be known as Lord Rymond, Torturer of Peasants. 'Pull him up.'

When Strovac's only response was a hard look, Adfric moved forward to help the boy back to his knees, and when Rymond spoke it was the peasant he addressed. 'A hoe is a poor weapon. If I spare you and put a sword in your hand, will you join me?'

The boy spat out a glob of blood. 'S'pose I'd rather fight for you than die over a pile of grain.'

Rymond nodded. 'Adfric, see to it.'

Strovac was seething. 'He killed one of my men!'

'If your men cannot defeat a peasant armed with a hoe, they're of no use to anybody.'

Strovac did not trouble to reply, but merely stared at him sulkily as the peasant's bonds were removed, simmering rage rolling off him like a noxious miasma. Rymond did not believe Strovac cared particularly about his man's death – he had been left to feed the crows with the rest of the corpses – but he could never resist the opportunity to torment somebody. It was why he was such an effective killer; he held no affection or sympathy towards anybody.

'There is still Imberwych, Lord,' said Adfric, pointing northward to the settlement nearest Halord's Bridge, just visible on a hill several miles away through the early evening gloom.

They had passed by Imberwych on the way to Southton and Ditchford, on account of the town being easier to approach from the south due to the angle of the hill on which it rested. Through a spyglass, several undefended granaries could be seen beneath the shadow of a squat wooden fort, but the settlement appeared to be deserted, presumably because its people had chosen to flee. The Lord of Southton – a lord in the very lowest sense of the word – had tried to shelter his commonfolk within the town's wooden fort. Strovac had set the structure on fire, and they had fled in terror straight onto the swords of the Wild Brigade. The fort at Ditchford was built in stone, but the lord had not troubled to bring his peasants within the protection of his walls, and they had died for it.

Rymond turned to look up at the fort again, where through the curtain of rising smoke the Lord of Ditchford stood hunched on a balcony, casting his eye down upon the slaughter of the folk he had been charged to protect. Rymond was tempted for a moment to train his archers upon the distant figure.

'Lord?' asked Adfric. 'Shall we proceed to Imberwych?'

After a moment, Rymond shook his head. The heavy stench of blood and burning was threatening to upend his stomach. There might still be Imberwych peasants in the vicinity; he would be merciful and give them the chance to escape. More merciful than he had been here. 'Tomorrow. It's growing dark. We'll send men tomorrow to fire the granaries on the way through. It won't even take the morning.'

Adfric's frown showed what he thought of that. 'I suggest

we don't delay, Lord. The longer we tarry the more likely it is we'll have to face Lord Andrick.'

Strovac snorted. 'Coward. Andrick and Hessian are probably still putting their boots on.'

'Underestimate Lord Andrick at your peril,' warned Adfric. 'If word has reached Merivale he won't be far away.'

Adfric's prediction made Rymond momentarily nervous. They did not want to be caught on the wrong side of the river when Merivale roused itself. 'Send out more scouts,' commanded Rymond. 'Two pairs in each direction.' If Andrick was approaching, they would have known by now, but there was no harm in caution.

No scouts disturbed him that evening, and Rymond went to bed content after a skinful of wine, secure in the knowledge that they were at most a half-day's ride from the bridge. He went to sleep dreaming of a comfortable winter in Irith, warmed by his log fire and the image of Hessian spending the cold days desperately trying to feed his people.

It felt like he had barely shut his eyes when he was shocked awake by the deep noise of a horn, so nearby it seemed to rattle his eyes in their sockets. Rymond sat up with a start. Surely they were not being attacked; they had scouts and sentries to warn them. He pulled a robe about himself and raced outside, barefoot.

It was early. The sun was still barely a sliver in the east. Predawn dew twinkled in the half-light, and pricked coldly at Rymond's feet. He shivered in the chill air.

There were men outside his tent, staring north, at their route towards Halord's Bridge. Rymond followed their gaze, and what he saw made his blood run cold.

A brown-on-green standard fluttered over Imberwych, while men rushed to and fro with spades and great wooden stakes, fortifying their position.

Andrick Barrelbreaker had come.

Rymond looked frantically for Adfric and found him quickly, already awake and barking orders for tents to be pulled down and fires quenched. 'Adfric!' Rymond raced over to him, as dignified as he could manage wearing little more than a robe. 'How did he sneak up on us? What of our scouts?'

'Expect he killed them, Lord,' said Adfric. He sounded almost admiring. 'He must have spotted us and set his camp in the dark. It was heavy cloud last night. Our sentries wouldn't have seen a thing.'

They had come to pillage, not to fight Andrick Barrelbreaker. Rymond cursed himself for not retreating over Halord's Bridge the night before. The granaries of Imberwych represented perhaps three-tenths of the grain he had wanted to destroy. What madness had possessed him to leave them?

'We can go around them, can't we?'

Adfric stroked his jaw. 'We could, but if they give chase they could tear our rear to shreds. It can be done, but our losses might be significant.' Rymond's heart sank. 'He must have half-killed their horses to get here,' Adfric added, shaking his head in disbelief.

Rymond heard a snort behind him and turned to see Strovac approaching, already in his armour and binding back his long hair. 'If he's so bloody brilliant, why's he not brought more men?' the giant warrior asked. 'There's no more than a thousand at that camp. We should be attacking, not talking about fleeing.'

Adfric looked at him scornfully. 'That's the *Hymeriker*, and in case you hadn't noticed, they're on a hill. If they slow us down, how far behind them do you think a larger force is?'

Strovac shrugged. 'We have the numbers. We'll charge them and drive them down the slope. All it takes is one man to turn his heel and the rest will follow.'

Rymond stroked his fresh stubble. He needed to dress, but first he had to make a decision. The East Erlanders had a strong position, but he had the numbers, and he had Errian, a valuable hostage, though he was miles away in Irith. Strovac seemed to like their chances. What if they could attack? If he could capture or even kill Lord Andrick he would rob Hessian of his greatest asset. They could burn the remaining granaries, and if the winter was mild – though there seemed little prospect of that – he might gather an army in West Erland large enough to march on Merivale and win the war by spring.

'Adfric, raise the white flag below my standard. I would parley with Lord Andrick.'

'Lord,' said Adfric, surprise visible on his face, 'I do not believe there are any terms he would accept.'

'No,' agreed Rymond, 'but I wish to take a measure of the man.' Famed as Andrick the Barrelbreaker was, Rymond had close to three times his number. Why should he feel daunted?

As the sun rose, Orsian stifled a yawn, and looked up from his shovel, over a trench now many feet deep. They had set their shelters and fires, strengthened their flanks with pits and tar-coated spikes, and polished their weapons until they could have shaved in them. Their position was as fortified as they could hope for after only a night's work, and if his father was correct, the Prindians would not be able to resist an attack.

Now they waited. Many a man looked longingly in the direction of Halord's Bridge, only a few hours' ride away. The bridge was the key to Erland – every child knew that; where hundreds of years ago twenty thousand of their ancestors had defied an empire – and they had eschewed it in favour of this barren hillcrest.

It had been his father's decision. 'We've come too late – the time to take Halord's Bridge was before they crossed,' he had said. 'Now if they arrive at the bridge and find it barred they'll be free to take the granaries, and plunder our countryside all along the river. We need to tempt them to battle, and defend the remaining grain. When they see how few we are, they won't be able to resist, and we'll have the high ground. We can stand firm and watch the corpses pile up.'

Orsian had no reason to doubt his father, but they were eight hundred, while the Prindians they thought numbered over two thousand. Reinforcements were still days away. His stomach rumbled apprehensively. His father knew war better than any man alive, but to judge by the number of men rushing to their latrine ditch he was not the only one with reservations.

Perhaps Errian's imprisonment was playing on his father's mind. Orsian did not believe he would have given up the security of Halord's Bridge unless he hoped to tempt the West Erlanders to parley. But Errian was likely hundreds of miles away, trapped in a Prindian dungeon.

He had no love for his brother. Had their roles been reversed, he suspected Errian might have actively counselled their father to take a strategy that might lead to Orsian's death. Orsian, though, would do no such thing. It was not his place to argue with his father, the *balhymeri* and greatest warrior in Erland for three decades, no matter Orsian's own feelings towards Errian.

They had ridden hard from Merivale, pushing themselves and their horses to near exhaustion, and yet they had been too late. Tendrils of smoke spiralled from all along the river where the Prindians had struck, filling the air with the stench of butchered meat and burnt grain. It would be a hard winter in East Erland, no matter the battle's outcome.

At least he would spend it at Piperskeep, with Helana. Orsian smiled. The memory of her kiss had sustained him all the ride from Merivale, as if she had gifted him the power of flight. He would stay alive for her, and if they could defeat the Prindians she would surely speak no more of peace, nor of Lady Breta.

'Orsian!' The sudden call of his name broke Orsian's reverie. His father was striding towards him, accompanied by Naeem. Andrick shouted to a group of warriors as he passed, ordering them to dig their part of the trench deeper. 'They've raised the white flag. Let's see what this Prindian brat has to say for himself.'

They rode out together, Orsian bearing his father's banner.

Andrick assessed the four men who waited for them. Old Lord Storaut he knew from decades past, corpse-gaunt and older even than Hessian. Viratia had been promised to him, until she and Andrick had eloped. As expected, when their eyes met, Storaut's glittered darkly with contempt. Did old men never tire of youthful quarrels? Andrick nodded and smiled in mock friendliness. Storaut scowled.

Next to him was Adfric, master-at-arms of Irith. Andrick recalled him from Fallback Lodge, the last stand of Ranulf Prindian's short-lived rebellion. A decent soldier, but not a man to make armies fear or revere him. They greeted each other like the old soldiers they were: a brief glance taking in the lines of age, the greying of hair, old wounds.

He had never met Rymond Prindian as an adult. Their one encounter had been at Fallback Lodge when Rymond was just a child, snivelling behind his mother's skirts. He was a slim and handsome youth, with the golden hair of the Prindians. His windburnt face suggested he had spent more time outdoors recently than he was used to. The years had not made him a soldier; he sat his horse like a young lord gone courting.

And, next to Rymond, the hulking frame of Strovac Sigac,

holding the Prindian banner. He sneered at Andrick as their eyes met. They held each other's gaze, with no attempt to hide their loathing.

I should have killed you when I had the chance.

'Do you know what the king does to those who betray him, Strovac?' He ought to have greeted Rymond first, but Andrick preferred to address Strovac. 'Ranulf Prindian screamed like a pig for two weeks.' His eyes flickered to Rymond, looking for a reaction, but the youth's handsome face was a mask of indifference. 'We may struggle to find an oubliette big enough, but I am sure we can make alternative arrangements.'

Strovac laughed back at him. 'Fine words, for a man whose son is my prisoner. He's unharmed, for the most part.'

'For all I know you've killed him already.' He did not believe they would, but an accusation was the swiftest way to learn the truth.

Rymond interrupted before Strovac could reply. 'Lord Errian is under my protection. He is at Irith, and I swear he will be well treated.'

'The sworn oath of a traitor.' Andrick spat on the ground between them. 'What is your protection worth, Lord Rymond? I see only a vain and idle boy, with a shadow where a man's beard ought to be.'

Rymond ignored the jibe. 'I raised the white flag so that we could negotiate Errian's release.'

'Make me an offer then.'

'We shall return Errian to you unharmed, and allow you and your men to leave here in peace. In return, you and the House of Sangreal shall agree that West Erland is a free and independent kingdom, comprising all lands from the Pale River to the western edge of the Fortlands, with never a single coin to be paid in tax, nor any oath of fealty made to King Hessian or his descendants. And he shall name me his heir, in the event he dies without male issue.'

Next to Andrick, Naeem laughed. The offer was absurd. 'I admire your ambition, Lord,' said Andrick. He stroked his beard, listening for a moment to the whistling wind that followed the Pale River. 'I have a counterproposal. You shall free Errian, and you and all who follow you shall swear a solemn oath to never again take up arms against your rightful king, pay ten thousand gold pieces in compensation, and provide suitable hostages as a promise of your good behaviour. In return, we shall let you leave in peace.'

'You cannot be serious,' scoffed Rymond. 'You have one-third of the men, and you're not on the bridge!'

Andrick smiled. 'How foolish of me! Let's call it fifty thousand. When men whisper that I feared to face the mighty Lord Rymond, I would like to be able to point to the size of the settlement.'

'As you wish, Lord.' Rymond took up his reins to turn his horse around. 'My first offer stands. If at any time you decide that you value the lives of your men more than your pride, just raise the white flag.' He rode back towards his army, followed by his three companions. Andrick turned his horse and rode back towards their hillock, Orsian and Naeem following in his wake.

It was a risk, Andrick knew. Their odds would have been better on Halord's Bridge, or with more men, but for the sake of East Erland, the remaining granaries needed to be protected. And, if the battle went their way, he might end the war in a day: take Prindian captive, and exchange him for Errian, a promise of peace and submission, and a generous settlement of gold. He had won battles against worse odds.

They will send their horses against our flanks first, hoping we flee and can be chased down. More fool them when they did. His men were disciplined, and too sturdy to be frightened by horses' hooves. They had long poles and spears, and were stubborn the way only Erlanders could be. They would never turn.

Once that failed, Prindian would have to send his foot against them. *We will fight as they did in the old times, in a shield wall, with the enemy's foul breath in our noses and our own piss and shit in our breeches.* The outcome then was less certain. The difference in numbers would count for little at first, but as the day grew long and their sword arms grew tired, Prindian could send fresh men against them. Andrick would be at the front and in the centre, where the fighting was thickest. As long as he stood, their wall would hold.

Rymond tried to take regular breaths, and to control his hammering heart. Lord Andrick Barrelbreaker was just as fearsome in the flesh as his reputation. For a moment Rymond had felt like a boy again, hiding behind his mother while this warrior cut apart his brother's army. But he had not baulked, and who would dare doubt him now he had faced Andrick down and rejected his offer of peace?

The four of them retired to Rymond's tent where a table had been erected, leaving grooms with their horses close by, in case Lord Andrick was minded to attempt a surprise attack. The word went around that there would be battle, and the camp was alive with panicked shouts and the clash of steel as men tested their weapons.

Rymond spoke first. 'Andrick tempts us with victory, and I've a good mind to seize it. We can send the Cyliriens first to hammer his centre. Mercenaries should prove their worth, and each one who falls is one less to pay. The Ffriseans can go as well. As they engage, we'll send Storaut's cavalry against their flanks. If either flank breaks, we can turn their whole force and trap them.' He turned to his master-at-arms. 'How do you like my plan, Adfric?'

Adfric stroked his whiskers. 'It's a fine plan. Lock the centre up and attack the flanks. Were you actually listening when I taught you tactics?'

Rymond smiled in satisfaction. He had in part taken inspiration from the Barrelbreaker's tactics at the Battle of Andrick's Hill. He could not attack from behind as Andrick had done that day, but he could strike hard at the less experienced troops on the flanks. If one side broke the battle would turn into a rout.

Storaut was nodding. Only Strovac seemed troubled, frowning slightly and squinting his beady eyes in the direction of the East Erlanders, as if he could see their force through the tent's canvas. 'I don't like it. The Cyliriens won't break through, so you're sacrificing them and assuming you can break through with a cavalry charge at the flank, which they'll have fortified to stop us going around them. If that fails, we'll have to climb over a mound of dead mercenaries to strike at their centre.'

'What would you have us do?' asked Adfric scornfully. 'Do you still want to challenge Barrelbreaker to single combat so you can settle your private war?'

'Andrick will place himself at the centre, where the fighting will be fiercest. Let me lead men there on foot, and we'll meet them on their own terms. It will be bloody work, but eventually our numbers will tell, and if I kill Barrelbreaker the battle is won. The cavalry should hang back, to keep their flanks honest and stop them coming around us.'

Adfric had been listening to this mirthlessly, but when Strovac finished speaking he openly laughed. 'Lord, ignore him. Strovac still seeks only personal glory, as ever.'

Rymond agreed with Adfric. Strovac's plan seemed driven by his own desires, but the man was so capricious and conceited it was possible he did not even realise that himself. He did not, though, want to risk offending him when battle was so near, so chose his words carefully. 'Lord Strovac, no man here doubts your bravery. You are among the most important men in this army. You and your men should hold back, ready to reinforce if necessary, should something not go as we plan.'

He had expected Strovac to sulk, or throw out an angry retort, but the man only shrugged. 'As you will, Lord.' He stalked from the tent, insolently taking a flagon of beer from the table on his way. 'My men and I will be ready.'

CHAPTER 25

Andrick arranged his men in lines six deep, protected at either end by the defences at their flanks. The front two rows would fight at close quarters, with the third and fourth ready to step in as men fell. The back two rows were where he had placed their best archers. From his place at the centre, he watched men on foot come to the front of the Prindian host, with a troop of horsemen either side of them. Squinting, Andrick identified the infantry from their motley armour as Cylirien mercenaries, and the handful of hirsute and shirtless men among them could only be Ffriseans.

If the mercenaries were to attack their centre, the two groups of cavalry would charge their flanks, to try and turn their small force. He had placed less experienced men there, where the fighting was not usually so fierce. Andrick looked warily at their left. The defences there were not as fortified as those on the right, with fewer spikes and a shallower trench.

'Naeem.'

'Yes, Lord?'

'Go to the left wing. Join the third or fourth row and lend heart to the men in front of you. Take Orsian with you.'

'Yes, Lord.'

As he left, Andrick grabbed Naeem's shoulder to whisper to him. 'If the boy dies before you do, I swear I'll haunt you.'

Naeem grinned back at him and clasped his wrist. 'None of us are dying today. One sniff of blood and that green Prindian boy will piss himself.'

Andrick was less sure of that. The boy was green, but he had not disgraced himself during the parley. There had been a defiance in him, like one of whom nothing is expected who seeks to prove others wrong. He was no fighter though; he would not be there crossing blades when the shield walls met.

Naeem somehow always maintained a cheerful façade before combat, but that was rare. Since it had become clear they would do battle, the sounds and smells of men shitting into their clothes had become more common as the hour approached. With the Prindian forces now preparing to attack, the smell was insufferable.

They never wrote about this part in the histories. Andrick savoured the stench. It had been too long since he had held a sword and faced men who wanted to kill him. He drew his short sword and tested its edge, a single bead of blood forming as it sliced his fingertip.

'Men!' he cried. 'Shield wall! Flanks – keep the long spears ready!'

The *Hymeriker* were already packed tightly together, but now squeezed in even closer, locking their shields together in front of them. Those in the second row stepped forward to fill the gaps above, creating a lattice of iron-banded wood.

Andrick stood in the middle of the front row. He had kept his helmet off and would not don it until the last moment. He wanted the enemy drawn to the centre by his presence, where his hardened warriors were.

The idea of the shield wall was that the men in the front rows would hold the line while carving up the attacker with

swords and knives from behind the protection of their shields.
The men behind them had spears that could be thrust through
any gaps, and there were also longer spears that were effective
against a horse charge.

From across the field came the black beat of marching
drums, and the slow advance of the mercenaries began. Andrick
felt a small knot of fear in his stomach. Good. A healthy fear of
death kept a man alive. All along the line, he heard the angry
challenges of his men, straitening to a single call given in a
hundred voices.

'ER-LAND ER-LAND ER-LAND. ER-LAND ER-LAND
ER-LAND.'

Their wall was now so tight he had only the slimmest sickle
of light between the shields through which to see. He felt the
hum of pounding feet through the ground as hundreds of
soldiers all broke into a run, less than two hundred yards away.
He chanced a glimpse of them, and saw that the wild Ffriseans
had made their way to the front of the advance, bearing their
huge wooden weapons and screaming a war cry. They were a
hundred yards away, and running straight up the slope towards
their centre.

'Any man steps back from this line, I'll cut his balls off!'

Fifty yards. Andrick steadied his breathing, and checked for
the grip of his longsword, in case the line should break. Arrows
flew overhead, but Andrick did not look to see if any of
them hit.

Twenty yards. The Ffriseans accelerated to a sprint, and
gave a war cry that could curdle the blood.

Eryi lend strength to my arm, and to Orsian's.

'Hold! Hold!'

The Ffriseans smashed against their shields, splintering
wood and rattling steel. Andrick had known cavalry charges
that struck with less force. The impact drove the breath from his

lungs. His shield was pushed back against his shoulder, and the air filled with cries of anger, fear, and pain. His feet strained in the soft ground against the drive of the Ffriseans, and all along the line he saw soldiers struggling against the weight of these huge bestial men, crying out as they pushed back against them.

They were driven back several yards, but the line held.

Andrick felt the beat of fists and heavy wooden staffs against his shield. It was pressed against his nose, with no gaps through which he might slice his shortsword into unprotected flesh, but at the edge of his vision he saw the thrust of a spear from behind him, and heard a grunt of pain as it found its mark.

There were new cries, as the Cyliriens caught up with the Ffriseans and began hacking at their shield wall with swords and axes. Andrick felt the weight relent from his shield as the man who had been speared withdrew, and pushed, calling for those around him to do the same, pressing up from his knees and driving his shield forward. He glimpsed a lightly armoured shin at his shield's lower rim, and lashed out with his sword. There was a scream, and the man ahead of him went down.

He swung his head left and right. All along the line, men had steadied themselves against that initial onslaught, and were finding gaps where they could strike out at their foe. Andrick raised his voice to the thick air, straining to be heard over the screams and the sharp clang of steel. '*One – two – three – push!*'

To both sides of him men screamed wordlessly as they drove forward. Those in the line behind leant in, lending their strength. As one, they stepped forward, swallowing up the prone and wounded bodies of foes who were swiftly dispatched by downward thrusts of shield and spear. Andrick's men screamed in triumph, while arrows whirred overhead and dropped onto the defenceless mercenaries who had failed to break an inch in the Erlish shield wall.

Andrick felt no triumph. They would have to repel another

hundred such assaults before the day was won. He filled his lungs again. '*Brace!*'

———

On the left flank, Orsian had been standing with Naeem in the third row when the cavalry charge cannoned into them. The long spears did their job, forcing their assailants' mounts to rear up whinnying in terror or be impaled upon them, sending their riders flying. Some were propelled by their horses' own momentum, and sailed through the air to land behind the shield wall, where they were slain as they lay winded, or left wailing at their broken legs and cracked ribs.

Orsian had already killed one man, slitting his throat with his shortsword while he lay on the ground, screaming down at the shinbone protruding below his knee. He had not hesitated. In the heat and the noise of battle there had been no time to think about it.

He felt exhilarated. His face was already slick with sweat, and his armour covered in mud and other men's blood, but his sword was as light as a feather in his hand, as much a part of him as his arm itself. Every breath he took was to be savoured, a wordless defiance of the death that reigned all around him. He had trained half his life for this. All those hours and years in the practice yard. This was what he had longed for. This was what he had been born for.

But the enemy were many, and for every foe foiled by a long spear four more crashed against their line, horseshoes smashing against their shields. Ten yards away, a man was forced to the ground under the weight of the assault, to be crushed beneath the hooves, and then riders in the blue armour of Lord Storaut were through, driving into the gap, fanning out and causing chaos as some men tried to flee and others to move forward.

'*Close that gap! Close that gap!*' Orsian grabbed Naeem by the shoulder and drew his longsword, running heedlessly towards the man who had fallen.

Orsian leapt into it, taking a horseman's spearpoint on his shield. He swung his sword into a gap in the rider's armour at the elbow, cutting his forearm to the bone. Blood sprayed into Orsian's face, and the man screamed, his horse rearing in terror. As the man came back to earth, fear flashed across his face, but Orsian paid it no heed. He thrust his sword up, finding flesh at the man's neck between helmet and armour.

The rider fell, dead before he hit the ground, as his horse turned from the scene of blood and terror before it and raced for the safety of the Prindian camp.

Orsian screamed, lifting his bloodstained sword high over his head in challenge. This flank would not break. Not as long as he had a blade and an arm to wield it. Stepping into the shield wall he shouted for others to join it. He chanced a glance behind him, and saw Naeem and others pulling the riders who had broken through from their horses with sheer weight of numbers. All along the left flank men were cheering, roaring defiance as Lord Storaut's horsemen wheeled around for another charge.

———

Andrick's arm was numb where a Ffrisean had swung his huge staff straight into the centre of his shield, and he could feel the steady drip of blood running down his face from his temple, though whether it was his or not he could not tell. It felt like hours since the battle had started, but the sun had barely moved in the sky.

As a young man I could have done this all day.

At least a hundred Cyliriens and Ffriseans lay dead, with so many wounded that he was yelling orders not to bring them into the killing ground inside their shield wall by advancing, lest they stretch their line too thin and offer space at the flanks. Near a dozen he had wounded or slain himself, with quick thrusts of his shortsword under the rim of his shield, finding gaps in the armour at the knee, thigh, and groin. Many more had been killed by the spears of the back rows, as the mercenaries threw themselves against the unyielding shields of the first.

The shoves against their shields were weaker now, as men were having to climb over the bodies of their comrades to reach them. To his left, Andrick saw one of the surviving Ffriseans make a desperate running leap over the shield wall, landing in a roll and coming up swinging his staff. Two men took vicious blows to the head that sent them spinning to the ground, but in an instant the Ffrisean was overwhelmed by swords, and fell to a knee, bleeding from half-a-dozen wounds.

All the while, their attackers also had to contend with arrow fire. The rate had slowed as their shafts depleted, and men had to fumble in the mud for the few that remained, but at this range, with so many enemies inhibited by the bodies on the ground, they could barely miss.

There was no order shouted but together the mercenaries turned tail, as if they had all decided that their assault was hopeless. A few Ffriseans remained, swinging their staffs senselessly against the shields, but soon realised the futility of this and ran, looking over their shoulders and listening for the whirr of an arrow aimed at their backs.

Andrick looked to the flanks. He saw many more dead and wounded being pulled back from the shield wall than at the centre, but they had held the line. He prayed that Orsian was not among the casualties. The horsemen had wheeled around, preparing for another charge, but at the sight of their centre retreating they too galloped for the safety of the Prindian camp.

The East Erlanders cheered and shook their weapons in triumph, while beardless boys ran forward from behind the lines to slit the throats of dying men and retrieve unbroken arrow shafts.

Andrick smiled grimly. No war had ever been won with mercenaries. He was certain Strovac Sigac had not been among the charge. If he had been, he would have made a beeline for their centre. The true test was to come, with Strovac Sigac and his Wild Brigade, men who had trained with the same weapons and drilled the same drills as his own, who would not be so foolhardy as to senselessly throw themselves against a shield wall.

Orsian's sword was drenched in blood all the way to the hilt, and felt so heavy he could barely lift it. It was easier to focus on that ache than the pain in his shoulder, which had been struck by a flail and hurt to move.

He could not recall how, but he had ended up in the second row, holding his shield high against the mass of cavalry, while they drove down with spears and hooves. He had swung his sword when he could, but mostly the press of bodies and horses had been too tight, and he exerted all his energy into keeping his shield straight under the onslaught, and sucking in musty air hot with blood and sweat. Naeem had been behind him with a spear, and more than once he had saved Orsian's life with it, not least when he had thrust it into the face of the man with the flail who had been about to swing it back towards Orsian's head.

For that time, nothing else existed. Just the need to hold his shield and keep it locked with the others.

He was vaguely aware that the steady press of attack on the other side of his shield had ceased, and then Naeem was shouting in his face, though Orsian barely heard him.

'Orsian! Orsian!'

Orsian shook his head like a dog trying to throw off a flea, and suddenly a sense of his surroundings returned. There were screams of pain and triumph, men offering prayers and crying desperately for their mothers as they pressed their hands to wounds that pulsed thick crimson blood, and even men with no visible injuries were collapsing onto the sodden ground, taking deep breaths and blinking at the sky with wide eyes.

'Orsian! Are you hurt?' Naeem was shaking him.

He shook his head. 'No. Just my shoulder. It will be fine.'

The horsemen had retreated, and as the shield wall came apart Orsian saw they too had taken heavy losses. Dozens of men lay in the mud, either dead or dying. There was a Prindian soldier with his legs trapped under his dead mount, screaming in agony and trying to replace his innards into the huge gash in his belly.

Orsian stepped forward and thrust his sword point down through the man's neck. The man's screams ended, and Orsian fell to his knees and vomited.

Rymond watched in stunned disbelief, Adfric silent at his side. He had ridden as close as he dared to the battle, and watched in horror as the desperate mercenaries flung themselves against the anvil of the Sangreal shield wall and barely dented it a yard. For every one of Hessian's who fell, four or more of his own went down, by sword and spear and arrow. For a time, he had thought Lord Storaut's cavalry would turn the enemy flank, but no matter how many times they charged the shield wall stood, bending but never breaking.

Captain-General Gruenla approached him, dragging her right leg, where the fletch of an arrow protruded from her calf.

'Lord.' She dropped to a knee, though Rymond saw it pained her to do so. 'My lads are done. Fifty or more dead, and another hundred-odd won't fight again today.'

Rymond nodded. 'They fought bravely. Now get yourself seen to.'

'It's nothing, Lord,' she grimaced. 'Some bastard caught me with an arrow while we were retreating.' She hobbled away.

Rymond resisted the urge to draw his sword and slam it to the ground in frustration. What a fool she must think him to throw her men's lives away so carelessly. Many nights he had imagined sneaking into her tent, but she could hardly be expected to accept the advances of a man who had wounded and killed almost half her company. He felt an even greater fool for thinking about that while men lay dying and his kingship and perhaps his life hung by a thread.

At least they still outnumbered the East Erlanders. But what if they were expecting reinforcements?

Rymond had not heard his approach, but the hulking figure of Strovac suddenly appeared at his side. In silence, Strovac stared at the battle scene, where boys from the opposing army were running between the bodies, sorting through corpses for men's throats to slit, while the East Erlanders leant on their shields and slapped each other on the back for still being among the living. Rymond was sure Strovac's reticence was a rebuke for choosing his own plan over his. Even in silence the man was insufferable.

He knew, back in the tent. Rymond had thought it odd when Strovac left without making a scene. He had predicted the plan would fail, and rather than trying to persuade anyone otherwise had chosen to let it, to increase his own importance to their cause. Rymond needed Strovac, but as soon as the throne was his he would find a way to strip the slippery bastard of his new title.

'Strovac?'

'Yes, Lord?'

Rymond saw a wriggling smile playing around in Strovac's mouth, like a worm caught in a beak. 'Your plan. Will it still work?'

The man made a show of pursing his lips as if he had not already thought about it. 'They are well entrenched there, and the bodies will make it more difficult, but they might be low on arrows. We need to hit them in the rear to make an end of this.'

'We've already had scouts check their rear,' said Adfric. 'The other side of the hill is steeper, and it's just as fortified as their flanks. You couldn't even march an army up there, never mind mount an attack.'

'You let me worry about that.' Strovac gave a thin smile. 'Sometimes, all you need is a few brave men. We'll hit them in the centre. Give me command of the Thrumb; we'll need archers backing us up. And have Storaut's men watching the flanks.'

―――――――

Andrick had remained at the centre, conducting his forces in the clearing of the ground, and preparing for the next assault. The badly wounded were dragged back to camp for arrows to be pulled and wounds to be sewn. There were mercifully few broken bones. Those who could fight on were treated where they stood, having bleeding foreheads bound and dislocated fingers pulled back into joint. Skins of water and wine were passed around quickly, to soothe men's dry throats and tired limbs.

Word had been passed along the line that Orsian lived, and had distinguished himself by filling a break in the line when for a moment it looked as though they might be overrun. Andrick allowed himself a moment of pride, and relief, in the small part of his mind that was not wholly focused on the battle.

So far, they had thrown back a force many times larger than their own, but unless Rymond and his council took leave of their senses they were unlikely ever to be able to take the fight to the Prindians. Too much energy had already been expended in the first assault, and there would be more to come. He resisted the urge to wonder if he would have been better to hold the bridge. The battlefield was no place for doubt.

A drum began beating across the field. Not the tinny drum of the mercenaries, but the thick rolling bass of Erland, that shook the earth and set crows flying. His men knew that drum. It was the sound that woke them from deep sleep and ordered them to march to war. Their drum. But on this day, it meant Strovac Sigac, taking the field with his band of brigands and traitors. He turned his eyes towards the noise, and sure enough saw a looming figure at the front of an army, standing a head taller than every man around him.

Andrick removed his helmet, and strode to the front of the line, to the point where he thought Strovac would join the fray. He cupped his hands to his mouth.

'*Here, you treacherous cunt!*'

Hessian wanted him to bring Sigac before him in chains, but Andrick knew he would be lucky to get that choice. If the man was brave enough to face him, Andrick would not hesitate to kill him.

Sigac began his march up the slope. Not as the mercenaries had done, in the wild charge of an open field, but in tight rows, with shields held in front of them. Alongside them rode Lord Storaut's horsemen, also keeping their discipline. Already Andrick anticipated this was to be a harder fight.

'*No quarter for traitors!*' he cried, and the men yelled their challenge towards the advancing army, and as their own drums began they took up the war cry.

'ER-LAND ER-LAND ER-LAND! HESSIAN KING!
HESSIAN KING!
'ANDRICK! BARRELBREAKER! ANDRICK! BARREL-
BREAKER!'

Twenty yards from their position, the Prindian shield wall
accelerated as one into a steady run, still slow enough to be
orderly. A stray arrow flew from the back to thud against a
shield, and Andrick shouted back a rebuke to the fool who had
wasted it.

The shield walls crashed together, hard enough to splinter
wood and bend iron. Andrick's feet slid in the mud. The whole
centre began to move under the enemy's weight, threatening to
bend their line like a bow. He sensed an opening and lashed out
with his sword, and felt the skin and muscle of a man's calf split
under its edge. He roared in defiance as the man screamed, and
the advance slowed as other blades carved into what gaps they
could find.

'HOLD... HOLD... HOLD... FORWARD!'

The whole line moved as they had been trained, pushing
with their legs and driving the Prindians back. The rows behind
them followed, jabbing their spears wildly at their foe's flesh.

Over the smashing of wood on wood and the screams of
wounded men, Andrick thought he heard the singing of steel
somewhere around the edges of Strovac's force, where if their
line was holding there ought to be calm. In a moment of respite,
he grabbed the man behind him and thrust him into the front-
line with a shield, and withdrew behind him to survey the field.

What he saw filled him with dread. Without a foe to fight,
men from their flanks had advanced to engage Strovac's force,
leaving themselves open to a cavalry charge that would take
them in the side.

'Flanks pull back! Flanks pull back!'

He was not sure if they heard him, but they heard the
cavalry thundering towards them. Both flanks rushed back into

line, barely in time to brace themselves against a second round of cavalry charges.

He looked across the line for Strovac Sigac, and such was his size was able to recognise him even half-hidden behind a shield. His strength and reach made him a colossus in a shield wall. Andrick watched him drive into their line with his shield, and when the man opposite stumbled Strovac's arm sprang out and pulled the man inside the Prindian lines, where he was driven to the floor under an onslaught of blades.

Andrick grabbed a fallen shield and ploughed into the line to fill the gap. He kept his head and helmet low behind the shield, hiding himself. He felt a sword strike against the iron rim, and had to brace himself against the heavy thump of a shield.

Sensing his moment, he broke a step forward from the line and thrust his sword through a gap in the enemy shield wall. He felt the point find flesh at the armour's weak elbow joint, and the roar from Strovac Sigac as it bit into his left arm served as proof he had found his mark.

There were vicious thrusts in retaliation from Strovac and the man next to him. Andrick danced around one and blocked the other with his sword before sliding it down the other man's blade to cleave his fingers at the knuckle. He barely got his other hand up in time to catch a spear point on the rim of his shield then dived back into line, locking his shield in with the others. It had taken barely five seconds.

He allowed himself a smile at the blood dripping down his sword. This was what he had been born to do. All around, men were looking to him, roaring their pride in their commander who had waltzed between the lines and wounded their greatest foe with the grace and speed of a falcon swooping from the sky.

Orsian had been among those yelling at the men who had rushed to attack the narrow enemy's vulnerable flank to get back. The men had ploughed on, deaf to their calls, until the thunder of hooves sent them racing back to the line. Those not fast enough fell, sprouting arrows and spears from their backs. After that, nobody made the same mistake, and the cavalry seemed content to hang back, close enough to chase them down if necessary but too far for an arrow to be accurately aimed. Most were glad of the rest, but some crowded into the centre, eager to bolster it and find more victims for their swords. Naeem had stopped Orsian joining them – 'Your father told us to go here and hold the flank, and that's what we'll do until we hear otherwise.'

The fighting at the centre looked fierce. Orsian saw bodies being dragged back with limbs hanging loose, and on both sides there were men dead, fallen facedown with blood pooling into the wet ground underneath them. Strovac Sigac's men were having to climb over the prone corpses of the first assault, and so despite their numbers could not easily overcome the East Erlander position.

Watching it was worse than fighting. The horrors of death and maiming had barely seemed real when he had been in the thick of combat, with his senses on a knife-edge and his blood running hot as flames. Now, outside the fury of battle, there was no escaping that every scream and every wound belonged to men, men just as desperate to live as he was.

He was squatting on his haunches, behind their line, unsuccessfully trying to repair an arrow with a bent head.

A man he did not know crouched to his eye level. 'You're the Barrelbreaker's lad.' It was not a question. 'You look just like him.'

Orsian lifted his eyes briefly from the arrow shaft. 'So they say.'

The warrior never got the chance to reply. A horse

suddenly galloped past them, terrified eyes rolling in its head. It caught the man in the back of the skull with a hoof and he fell, unconscious or dead.

Orsian stood and looked in panic towards their rear, where the horse had come from. Amidst the sounds of battle, he heard a loudening rumble, beginning to shake the dry earth. Others were turning to look too, and as Orsian realised what was happening he felt a dawning sense of horror.

There were other horses, dozens of them, riding straight for the rear of their shield wall in a thunder of hooves, as men dived out of their way to avoid being trampled and abandoned their place in line. He grabbed his shield and had to protect himself with it almost immediately as a braying horse reared up wildly in front of him and nearly struck him in the head.

What was happening? The horses were riderless, and had appeared from behind them.

Suddenly Naeem was there, bellowing at everyone to get their shields up and hold the line. 'Fire!' he yelled at Orsian, pointing towards their rear.

Orsian stared. Orange flames were flickering at their camp. The horses riding down on them were their own, panicked by the fire and with no care but to escape it.

'They've set our horse lines on fire!' Naeem bellowed over the chaos. A huge stallion burst towards them, churning up mud, and Naeem only narrowly pushed Orsian out of the way and onto the ground.

'If they charge us now, we're done for,' said Orsian, shoving Naeem off him to rise, wiping mud from his face. Their shield wall was already beginning to disintegrate as their warriors scattered to evade the bolting horses. 'We need to pull back.'

Naeem shook his head. 'We need to hold the flank. We'll turn the spears on them.'

As Naeem finished speaking, it became clear they were already too late for either. They heard the war cry of charging cavalry, and faced with an assault from both sides their left flank was falling back in disorder. To their credit, many of the warriors kept their shields together, but they had nowhere to go except towards their own centre, stretching the line and abandoning the protection of the trenches and spikes at their left side.

'Hold the line!' Orsian and Naeem shouted frantically, pushing against the weight of men, trying to drive them back towards the flank. Orsian felt a moment of terror as he realised there was nothing he could do, and the rush of fleeing men swept over them in a tide.

Andrick found himself stumbling rightwards. As the flank careened into the centre every man to his left was stepping back, and in the confusion they collided with one another like rocks becoming an avalanche, struggling to keep their feet.

Swept along with them, he lost sight of Strovac. Instinct took over, and he was yelling to all who would listen to keep the line and fall back in good order.

The Wild Brigade were taking advantage of the confusion, driving into their faltering shield wall and pushing them back further. To make things worse, at the other end Sangreal men were rotating forward to keep the line straight, and the whole army was starting to pivot anti-clockwise, abandoning the ground they had chosen.

Andrick forced his way towards them, flinging men aside and screaming at the line of shields to pull back with the rest, strong-arming those who failed to listen. Others eventually heard him and took up the task.

Somehow they turned what might have been a rout into a mere catastrophe. They held the line in retreat, but lost the protection of spikes and pits at their left flank, and at the right the obstacles were no longer angled to defend them.

Their shield wall reformed and stabilised, and Andrick breathed a sigh of relief. That retreat had been enough to save them was pure fortune. The Prindian centre must have hesitated, perhaps robbed of heart by the wounding of Strovac Sigac, and had the other force of horsemen not been caught on their heels they might have crashed into the temporarily exposed right flank and crushed them between three sides.

But now the Prindian shield wall had reformed, and was advancing on their position. Hundreds of yards away, Lord Rymond's reserve was cantering to join them. They had taken heavy losses but still outnumbered Andrick's force comfortably, and without obstacles at the left flank could strike with fresh soldiers in a dozen places all along the shield wall.

Andrick shook his head grimly. 'Any man who flees will die at my hand!' he roared. Not a man even looked back, and they screamed curses of defiance across the ground that separated the armies. Andrick stalked along the line, calling out at shields that were too low and for chinks of air through which a sword or spear might be thrust to be tightened up. Men struggling with wounds were pulled back and replaced. He had said that they could hold this patch of land until Eryispek crumbled to dust. Now he would have to prove it.

He ran into Naeem and Orsian coming the other way along the line. Naeem was hobbling, carried between Orsian and his son Derik.

'Report,' said Andrick to Orsian.

Orsian was caked with mud and blood, but bright-eyed, and he spoke clearly. 'They set fire to our horse lines and the horses scattered straight into us. It must have been a small group of them going around our rear.'

Andrick listened stony-faced as his son told him what had happened. Without the protection of the pits and spikes on their left the Prindians could flank them easily with a larger force. If they attacked with sufficient numbers it would not matter that they had so far held the right and the centre.

'Lord,' said Naeem. He winced as he struggled to place weight on his ankle. 'If I were to suggest that you and Orsian take two horses each and race for Merivale, would you consider it?'

'*Are* you suggesting it?' Andrick could see their situation was dire, and to make their stand on this hill had been his plan. He was not going to abandon his men. Would Strovac and Rymond Prindian accept his surrender in return for his men's lives? Rymond might, but Strovac would more likely kill them all anyway.

'I'm suggesting you consider it.'

'Then I'm suggesting you consider keeping your suggestions to yourself. Though if you want to try it I won't stop you. You can't fight with that leg.'

Naeem laughed, pushing Orsian and Derik aside and using his sword like a walking stick. 'I've watched my wife birth nine children, and each one still lives. I've lost half an ear and a nose but I'm still here as well. Face facts, Lord, the Norhai love me. I'll be the last man standing on this battlefield, leg or no leg.'

Andrick raised an eyebrow. 'Call it a wager. The first of us to die here serves the ale above the clouds. Agreed?'

Naeem grinned. 'Agreed.'

Orsian felt a bubble of fear rise in his parched throat as Naeem and his father clasped wrists. Was their position so terrible? It must have been for Naeem to suggest they try to escape.

Their position had all but collapsed, but perhaps there was still hope. Strovac Sigac's warriors were taking their time with their advance, waiting for reinforcements while the cavalry milled around behind them awaiting an order to charge. Orsian took a deep breath, checked for his sword, and grabbed a discarded spear, ready to take a place in the line. There would be no flanks this time, just the hot and bloody work of the shield wall, alongside his father.

He looked back towards what remained of their left flank, the now useless pits and wooden spikes they had put so much faith in. They had coated the spikes in tar, to impede any West Erlanders brave enough to cross their trench and attempt to manoeuvre their way through.

Still the Storaut cavalry hung back, waiting.

A spark flashed in Orsian's mind. He looked back further, towards where the fire had begun. A whole section of their hastily assembled camp was now smouldering, while a few horses that had not fled milled around, chewing at the grass. He could turn the fire against the Prindians. All he needed was a torch.

He slapped Derik on the shoulder, then Burik. 'Come with me.' He ran, not looking back to see if they were following, the confused calls of Naeem and his father echoing in his ears.

Orsian weaved through their lines towards the remnants of their left flank. He ran in the direction of the spikes, not daring to look to see if the Storaut horsemen were riding towards him. The spikes were sticky with pitch, and heavy, connected by thick logs, but he grabbed one and managed to snap part of it away. He ran towards the fire.

Orsian had not been prepared for the heat of their smouldering camp, and the thick smog that made it hard to see. Coughing on bitter smoke, his lungs burning, he thrust the end of the tar-coated spike into the nearest fire, and it burst into flames instantly, billowing acrid fumes.

It was then that Orsian realised he ought to have protected his hands with something. They were both sticky with black pitch, and when the fire worked its way down the wood his skin would be next. Too late now. He ran back towards the spikes, his makeshift torch held out in front of him like a flaming standard.

The Storaut horsemen were riding now, their blue cloaks fluttering together like a rippling pond. Not in a mad charge, but at a disciplined canter, content to take their time encircling the East Erlanders.

Orsian reached the spikes just as the torch burnt down to his hand. He suppressed a scream as his skin began to sear, threw the torch into the spikes, and plunged his hand into the cool earth, gritting his teeth against the fiery agony.

The fire licked at the wood, spreading all along the row of spikes, hungrily devouring the tar. The horsemen were barely twenty yards away from him now, but instead of charging towards him their mounts reared up, neighing in fear as the fire reached them, filling their nostrils with smoke.

The horses tried to turn away from the smoke, while their riders attempted to spur them on. Some were able to hold their mounts on course, but others had less success, perhaps just as eager as their horses to escape the flames. Soon their advance was in chaos, as horses veered away into one another and riders struggled to keep their saddles.

Some managed to ride on, but barely enough to bother a shield wall. They were still enough to cut Orsian down where he stood on the open ground though. He looked towards the tightly packed battle line, and to his relief saw Derik and Burik, beckoning him to a gap in the row of shields.

Orsian ran and dived inside the East Erland line. He lay on the cool ground, coughing and wheezing from the heavy smoke, savouring the cleaner air and cradling his burnt hand. He could only hope it would be enough.

Andrick lashed out with his sword, hemmed in so tightly he could see nothing beyond the wood of his shield. In the fury of battle he did not know whether he struck anything. Sensing victory, Strovac Sigac's Wild Brigade were fighting like men possessed, raining down blows with sword and axe against their shield wall and driving them back inch by inch with sheer weight of numbers. Other men's blood dripped down his face, mixing with his sweat like a river meeting the sea.

He did not know where Orsian was. His son had raced towards the camp, deaf to Andrick's commands. Naeem assured him Orsian had distinguished himself in the fighting before their flank collapsed. It was unthinkable that he would flee. What was he doing?

The pressure against him eased, and Andrick risked lifting his head to look over his shield. His eyes found what he sought. He had lost him in the confusion of their retreat, but there was no mistaking the vast frame of Strovac Sigac, bellowing his fury as he smashed his shield against that of the man opposite, almost breaking the Sangreal shield wall single-handed. If the wound Andrick had dealt him troubled him, Strovac gave no sign of it. The man was a force of nature in a shield wall, like a bull among rams.

Andrick was less than ten yards away. He needed to get to him. If he could wound him again it might steal heart from his warriors once more, and give them time to deal with the horsemen who would soon batter their left and perhaps their rear. Why were the Storaut cavalry delaying? He thought he could hear fighting in that direction and smell burning pitch, but there was no movement of their line to suggest that their flank was beset by the weight of a cavalry charge.

Something smashed against his shield and forced him back half a step, pressing it back against his shoulder. Andrick cursed. He would never get to Strovac without risking this part of their wall breaking. There was no prospect of taking him by surprise again.

'Strovac!' He drove up from his knees to free his shield and called down the line to him. 'Here, you snivelling dog!'

Over the noise of battle, Andrick's words reached him. Strovac looked over his shield, and through a gap in their wall almost took a spear to the face. He grabbed it, whip-fast, and yanked it from his assailant's hand.

'Barrelbreaker!' Strovac reached behind him, dragged forward another warrior to take his place, and stalked along the line towards Andrick.

Andrick waited, listening as Strovac forced a man away to take a place opposite him. He risked a glance over his shield, and had to duck back as Strovac lashed out towards him with the spear. Its sharp point scraped against his helmet. A second spear thrust punched against his shield, almost splitting the heavy wood like parchment.

It should not have been possible for a man to be that strong and that quick. Andrick realised he had been lucky before; if Strovac had seen him coming he would never have escaped with his life. In the shield wall his skill counted for little against Strovac's strength and reach. He had to be careful. The spear was thrust against his shield again, hard enough to rattle his shoulder.

Strovac laughed, high and giddily. 'I'll have your head on a spike, Barrelbreaker!' From somewhere he had seized an axe. He swung it down, lodging it in the top rim of Andrick's shield and trying to pull it down and away from him. It was an old trick, and Andrick was wise to it. He let his shield tilt slightly, and lashed out over the top with his sword, but Strovac was too fast again and pulled back.

'Keep that shield tight!' Andrick shouted back angrily to the man to his rear who held the one above his. He glanced behind, and to his shock saw Naeem, crouching in the third row holding a spear. 'Get back, Naeem!' The man could barely walk; he had no business here. 'Get that leg seen to!'

'If we all die, what's the point?' Naeem gripped his spear tightly. 'You go high; I'll go low.'

Andrick understood immediately. He turned back, just in time to catch another of Strovac's crashing axe blows on his shield. The axe caught in the wood, and Andrick twisted his shield, pulling the axe head with it, and drove his sword through the gap towards Strovac's exposed shoulder.

Strovac released the axe, and raised his shield to catch Andrick's blow on the rim, clashing iron upon steel. A spear flashed, and this time Andrick was not fast enough. It collided with the edge of his shield, and sliced into his shoulder at the collarbone.

Naeem had been ready. His own spear flashed forward, barely a handspan above the grass churned to mud. Andrick kept his face pressed against his shield, but heard a howl of pain as it punctured Strovac's boot and embedded in his ankle.

Naeem held tight, twisting and pushing as Strovac howled. Wood splintered, and when Naeem pulled his spear back it was broken, the head left behind in Strovac's leg.

Andrick did not hesitate. 'Push!' Warm, iron-scented blood was dripping down his face and arm. His shoulder felt like it was on fire. 'Push, you miserable dogs!'

They were exhausted, outnumbered, choking down the hot, black smoke that hung over the field like a blanket, but the warriors of East Erland obeyed. They moved as one, screaming curses into the faces of their enemy through bloodied lips, howling a war cry as yard by yard they reclaimed the ground they had lost. The Prindians were falling back. Andrick looked around frantically for Strovac Sigac, and saw him hobbling away from the shield wall supported by two men. He gave a howl of triumph and drove his men on. '*Push, damn you!*'

It was his East Erlanders' turn to sense victory. They

pushed once more, and the Prindian forces retreated before them, stepping back towards the slope with their shield wall in disarray.

'*Push!*'

They drove forward again, and the Prindians began to turn. It was all the encouragement his men needed. Orders forgotten, they broke from the shield wall and ran after them, howling curses.

Andrick would have liked nothing more than to join them. Somehow they had turned the tide, but there was still the matter of the Storaut cavalry on their exposed left flank. He turned, coughing against the smoke and pressing a hand to his shoulder. His wound was pulsing blood, but did not seem too deep. It would need cleaning with hot wine when this was over.

But where there ought to have been fierce fighting, there was only smoke, so thick he could barely see. He saw shadows of men on horseback, fewer than there should have been, turning in confusion as they tried to fight or flee, driven back by Sangreal spears. Their flank was more than holding; they were winning.

Andrick walked towards them, his eyes streaming from the smoke, as more and more of his warriors ran past him after the fleeing Wild Brigade. The spikes they had set over their trenches had been reduced to little more than ashes. Had the Prindians done that themselves? What madman had thought to set their defences on fire?

'Lord Andrick!'

Three men were stumbling towards him, one supported between the others, all smeared with blood and dirt and their hair plastered to their heads with sweat. He stared blankly at them before he realised that the central figure was Orsian, supported between Burik and Derik.

'Orsian!'

Andrick raced towards them. Naeem's boys released Orsian, and his son fell to a knee.

'Maddest thing I've ever seen!' cried Burik.

'Damn near set himself on fire!' added Derik.

Orsian was covered in ash, there was a bright gash of blood across his forehead, and the skin of his left hand was cracked and burnt. But he was alive, breathing shallowly against the smoke, with the bright eyes and flushed cheeks of a man who had fought until he had no more to give, and won.

CHAPTER 26

Ciera sat at the edge of her bed, too numb to rage or to cry. Hessian had just been with her, arriving as he did from his secret fireplace entrance, and leaving as soon as the deed was done.

She had thought it might become easier to bear with time, but it had only got worse. It had been a girl's foolish notion to think that Hessian might come to love her. She did not believe he was capable of loving anyone. To him she was merely a chamber pot, a vessel that would bear him a son. He did not even bother to speak to her sometimes, just slipped into her bed without a word, and claimed her with the indifference of a man butchering meat. She had learnt the hard way it was better not to fight, or to say anything to him, whether it be gentle enquiries about his day or weightier matters like how he meant to feed Merivale this winter after the poor harvest.

There would be no shortage of food if he had removed the milling levy, and ensured the price paid to farmers was fair, she thought fiercely. The taxes and tribute demanded by Piperskeep had already sown the seeds of the harsh winter to come. Merivale would starve because of Hessian's failure, and his war could only make things worse.

He had spoken to her tonight, after he was finished.

'I am sorry, you know,' he had told her. He seemed diminished, as if their cold embrace had leached the rage from him. 'But we must do our duty.'

His words only made it worse. He did not hate her; he just did not care. His apology was worth nothing. Did he think his brutality could be undone by words, or justified by his desire for an heir? She had said nothing in reply, letting his words hang in the air until he left.

She would endure it. What else could she do? She was trapped with him, trapped until he died.

There was a sudden, gentle tapping at her window. Ciera looked up, and her anger with Hessian immediately ebbed away as something lighter rose within her. She held a candle up towards the window, and revealed Tam's face through the glass, with that unmistakable cocky smile and the gap between his front teeth.

It had not been like this the first time, weeks ago, two nights after she had met him at the market. She had thought the tapping must be a bird, or a rodent, for nobody could be at her window. When it continued, fear seized her heart, and she wondered if it was some malevolent Sangreal ghost, sent to torment her. But it had been Tam, her salvation, the only person who made Merivale bearable.

'I hope I didn't startle you,' he said once she had let him inside. He was shivering. There was a sheen of frost on the glass and Ciera could feel the chill air through the window. 'Thank you for not being asleep.'

'What would you have done if I had been?' said Ciera admonishingly. She ushered him to a chair and began searching for warm clothing to give him. 'Climbed back down again? I still don't understand how you get inside the walls.'

'It's easy. I climb the outer wall, and on the north side there's a stone gutter connecting it to the inner wall. Then I climb down to the yard and up again to your window. Once I get to the top of the stable the keep wall is no problem.' He grinned. 'The harder part is making sure Tansa doesn't catch me. She's started working at an inn now; she shouldn't be back for hours.'

Ciera could detect the falseness of his modesty. *He does all that, just to see me.* She handed him a thick blanket she had found in her trunk. Their fingers brushed as he took it, quickening her heart despite his icy fingertips. 'The king was here only ten minutes ago; you could have been caught. I told you only to come when you see the candle in my window.'

After the first time, she had sworn to herself it would never happen again. Then he had come a second time, and she had relented, and suggested the candle. He had ignored her idea of course, just as he ignored laws, and her marriage, and the fear he ought to have felt.

Ciera stepped towards him, her heart pounding. She pulled Tam from the chair and kissed him. Not as they had in Cliffark, that momentary brushing of his lips against hers, but full on the mouth, with the taste of his warm breath on her tongue and the smoke of the city in her nostrils. He had one hand in her hair, the other in the small of her back pressing her body against his. Through the thin material of her nightgown she could feel the heat of him, warming the night's chill from his bones.

I know this is wrong. I just want something that is mine. She pulled him towards the bed, tugging at the buttons of his shirt and lifting the nightgown over her head.

After, they slept front to back, Tam's arms holding Ciera tightly to him, and for only the third time since she had arrived at Piperskeep, she felt safe.

It was still dark when Ciera woke, with the warmth of

Tam's slight body pressed against her back, his hands cupped around her breasts.

Ciera supposed she ought to feel regret, but she regretted nothing. At her father's behest she had married a man who wanted nothing from her but an heir. Nothing in her life was for her, but this was. She had earnt her moments of selfishness.

The heir though... What if Tam got a child on her? Would they know? What if the child came out looking like Tam? She pushed the worry from her mind. Babies looked like babies. It would be years before it could be said a child looked like anyone. Hessian could be long dead by then, and who would challenge her?

She elbowed Tam sharply in the chest, startling him awake. 'Do you need to leave?'

Tam looked to the nearly burnt-out candle by the bed. 'Shit. Yes. I should just make it back before Tansa.' He roused quickly, with the reactions of someone who had learnt to survive on the hard streets of Cliffark. 'I'll go back out the window.'

He rolled out of bed and began collecting his clothes from the floor. Ciera stood, wrapping the blanket around her. She felt strangely conscious of her nakedness.

'Can I visit you again?' he asked, pulling at his boot. 'I'll watch for the candle this time, I promise.'

Ciera paused. In Cliffark, she could have run away with him. Cut her hair off and changed clothes. They would never have found her.

'Or you could come with me?' he asked, as if reading her mind.

She shook her head. 'You know I can't.' They would chase her to the ends of the earth. She and Hessian were bound, and without her he would have no heir. 'And you should not come here again.' Saying it was like a knife in her heart, as it had been the first time, and the second time.

Tam nodded, disappointment written across his face. 'I understand.' He stood before Ciera in his reclaimed clothes, looking even more dishevelled than when he had arrived. 'What if we were still in Cliffark, and you weren't married?'

Ciera walked to Tam and kissed him gently. 'There is no answer to that question that will satisfy either of us.'

'I wish I had stolen you from the playhouse, not the bracelet.' From a shoulder bag she had not noticed before, he produced something, a box, finely carved and edged with gold, and placed it in her hands. 'You said you had lots of jewellery. I thought you might like a box for them.' He climbed through the window, smiled back at her, and disappeared into the darkness.

Ciera covered her face with her hands, fighting the urge to call out to him, to tell him she would go with him, to say they should go to Cliffark and across the sea and never look back.

But if they were caught, Hessian would kill them. She would have to be strong this time, for both their sakes, no matter how bad it got.

***

Days later, Ciera stood in front of the Sanctuary of the Brides of Eryi, covered in a heavy cloak against the cold and fidgeting from foot to foot. From a horse, on the day of her arrival, the streets of Merivale had felt friendly and welcoming, but standing stationary on the ground she could hear just as many pleading cries for bread as there were calls wishing Eryi's blessing upon their new queen. She had no food on her, and even if she had, she feared what some of the crowd might have done if she started sharing it. She was glad of the armed guard arrayed behind her, though they were boys barely older than her, too young to ride to war with Lord Andrick.

Her stomach lurched, and she held a fist to her mouth to stop her breakfast rising back up. She always felt anxious these days, and being required to attend upon the Brides of Eryi to be poked and prodded like a cow for market did not help matters.

Their temple was unimpressive compared to the riches of Cliffark. It was forged in grey stone, like many other buildings in Merivale, with an unambitious rectangular shape and no ornamentation save wooden double doors carved with scenes of pilgrims ascending the Mountain. Those at least gave it an element of grandeur, such was the detail in the carved figures, and the imposing impression of Eryispek. The doors faced the true Eryispek to the north, so the brides could pray in sight of it from inside their Sanctuary.

The double doors opened, revealing a pair of small, elderly women, clad in white, their wizened faces shadowed in the gloom of the Sanctuary's interior.

'The elder bride is ready for you now,' croaked the older, uglier one.

With small, deliberate steps, Ciera walked inside.

'It is an honour to meet you, Majesty,' said the younger bride, closing the doors behind her. 'I remember when Queen Elyana came here, over twenty years ago. I was young then, but I remember it like it was yesterday. I cried for days when she passed.'

The younger bride's words were met with a vicious slap from the other, snapping her head back, fierce enough to draw blood. 'She is not truly a queen yet, Bertha!' The other woman pulled her hand back for another slap. 'Not till the traditions have been observed. Mind your servile tongue.'

The second cowered, clasping her hand to her bloody nose. 'Yes, Sister, I'm sorry Sister.'

The two women immediately set Ciera on edge. Her father had always thought that those who dedicated their life to religion were strange, and between the first's gushing praise and the second's violent impatience it was hard to disagree with his assessment.

They will have nothing from me. I have given away too much of myself already.

They guided her through simple corridors, immaculately swept and without a single cobweb. It was not a large building, and they were soon facing the elder bride Velna. She was kneeling, facing north towards Eryispek, with her palms together in prayer.

'Queen Ciera,' she said, rising. 'It is an honour to welcome you to our Sanctuary.' She gave the smallest of curtsies. 'The king has taken you as his bride, but before you can be considered truly our queen and fit to bear royal children we must observe the formalities. I know the king sees these as an inconvenience, but I would hope we can agree on their necessity.'

Ciera understood that she was expected to agree, and nodded slightly. But what gave this woman the right to speak to her like that? She had already taken the king as her husband, so why was she expected to endure further humiliation from these white-robed cultists?

The elder bride eyed Ciera appraisingly. 'You are proud. Pride may serve you well outside these walls, but not while you are here. Eryi has no need of proud brides, nor proud queens. Sisters, leave us.'

The old women departed, leaving Ciera alone with this pious, thin-lipped harridan.

'Do you pray to Eryi?' Sister Velna asked. She moved to sit on her bed, and took off her shoes.

'Sometimes.'

'And what do you pray for?'

Truthfully, Ciera never prayed. Not since she had left Cliffark. 'I pray for my father,' she said. 'And my mother. I pray for our country to prevail in the war and for the winter to be mild.'

'Not for the king?'

'And for the king.' If she had prayed for him at all, it would have been for his death.

Velna smiled thinly. 'Good. Not all marriages can be as happy as mine. Now you must prove your humility before Eryi by bathing my feet. Then you shall be bathed and examined by four of my sisters to ensure your suitability as our queen. If you look outside the door, you should find soap and water.'

Reluctantly, Ciera stepped out and returned with a bowl of water, fortified with soap. It stank of oils, and made her feel slightly dizzy. She suddenly gagged and had to cover her mouth, her stomach threatening to spill itself. A small ripple of vomit rose in her throat. She swallowed it and retched, almost dropping the bowl.

Velna rose quickly and helped Ciera to the bed, easing her down onto it. 'Are you well, child?' she asked, unexpectedly tender. 'You're very pale.'

'Yes, fine,' Ciera replied weakly. 'I must not have eaten enough this morning.'

Velna frowned, and her hand went to Ciera's stomach, cupping it with her palm. 'You are with child!' she exclaimed. 'And so soon! You must be delighted.'

Ciera stared at her blankly. With child? 'You mean...?'

'Did you not know?' Sister Velna gave a slight laugh, pressing her hand upon Ciera's stomach. 'I know the signs. Congratulations.'

Ciera's head swam as she tried to remember her last cycle. With horror, she realised it had been before Tam had visited her for the first time. Hessian called on her often, but what if the babe was Tam's? What if the child were born with the broad, honest face of a commoner? Her head felt too heavy, as if she might faint at any moment.

'Child? Are you quite all right?'

Ciera closed her eyes, holding back tears, thinking quickly. 'Yes. I'm fine. I just did not know.' She could not let the elder bride see her doubts. She had been the first to realise she was pregnant; who knew how acute her powers of observation were?

'If I complete the rituals, and it's a boy, will he still be the king's heir?'

'Yes.' Velna placed a hand upon Ciera's shoulder and looked her in the eye. 'Have no fear, child. Here, we give praise to Eryi, but our rituals do not change the facts of this realm. You are the king's wife, and you carry his child. The child is of the Blood.'

Tears began to run down Ciera's face. 'Will the others know, when they wash and examine me?'

'I expect so. They can recognise the signs as well as I. Why would you not want them to know? When you tell the king I am sure he will be singing it from the ramparts of Piperskeep.'

Ciera denied the image of Tam that rose unbidden to the forefront of her mind. 'I will have to tell him, won't I?'

The elder bride laughed. 'Of course, girl. The child that grows inside you may be his heir, may someday wear his crown. Why on earth would you not tell him?' She paused, looking at the tears rolling down Ciera's cheeks. 'Is he... ungentle, with you?'

Ciera sniffed, blinking back her tears. How did Sister Velna seem to know everything? What if she told people? The king would punish her if he found out. 'It is not as I expected,' she said weakly. 'Please do not let anybody know.'

The sister sighed. 'It seldom is,' she said, taking Ciera's hand in hers. 'Many a woman here remembers what it is to carry the child of a man who forced her.'

Ciera looked at her, astonished. 'But they are brides of Eryi.'

Velna sat down next to her, looking older than she had when Ciera had met her in the town. Ciera fixated on a strand of brown hair that had come loose from her bun. 'Do you know how our order came to exist, Ciera? When the name of Eryi first spread across our country, it was common for converts to go on pilgrimage to Eryispek. It was especially common among young women, seeking to bring meaning to their hard lives serving husbands and bearing their children.

'One such woman went on pilgrimage fleeing her betrothed, who she did not wish to marry. Her name was Arna. When he followed her and tried to retrieve her by force, she fought him, and with the help of her fellow travellers sent him running from Eryispek. Arna declared that day she would never submit to the will of any man, but only to the will of Eryi. Many other women took up her cry, and the Brides of Eryi were born.

'So I know, Ciera. Every sister of mine knows the cruelty of men. My advice to you, though, is to tell the king. If he knows you are with child, he may consider himself satisfied, and leave you alone.

'However, it is your choice, so I will keep your secret. We shall tell the brides that you washed my feet and I consider Eryi satisfied, with no need for your examination.'

Ciera sniffed. 'Thank you, Sister,' she said, her voice thick with gratitude. She felt better. The sister was right; with a child growing inside her perhaps the king would leave her alone. And she had been with Hessian many more times than she had been with Tam; what were the chances of the child being his? 'And what if it is a girl?'

'I shall pray that you birth a son. For your sake, and for the sake of peace in Erland.'

That night, in bed, Ciera dreamt. She was back at Cliffark, at the window of her father's high solar, looking over the city and the bay below. The sky was dark, but the sea shimmered under the light of an invisible moon, rippling like copper passed over a flame. She turned to the room, where her father sat with his back to her, bald and bowlegged. She called for him, but he made no reply.

She heard the cold shriek of metal on stone, and woke, bolt upright and eyes wide, watching Hessian emerge from where her fireplace had been, wine clutched in his hand and cobwebs in his hair.

'I am with child,' she said, without thinking. *Please don't let him touch me again.*

Hessian stopped, frozen by the fireplace. 'You're sure?' His voice was as cold as the creaking hinge of his secret door.

'The elder bride said it is so. I have no reason to doubt her.' *Please let him leave me alone.*

He studied her, fixing her with his blue-grey eyes. It was as if he turned her inside out with his stare, picking his bony fingers through her deepest thoughts and desires, looking for a lie. The effect was terrifying. Breta Prindian was surely the greatest fool alive to start a war with this empty ghost of a man.

'Do you think that if I believe you I will stop visiting you?'

'Do you believe me?' Her voice sounded small next to his, swallowed by the high ceiling of her bedroom.

'Yes.' His tone was enough to tell her he still required an answer.

'I do not know,' she said. 'You could be gentler with me perhaps?' she asked, growing bolder. 'My mother told me the first few months can be the most dangerous.' Her mother had said no such thing.

Hessian was silent for a moment, and then smiled. The effect was stunning, lifting the years from him in a flash of thin lips and yellowing teeth. 'You are with child! My dear, you wondrous, beautiful creature!' He rushed to the bed, and embraced her.

Ciera quivered in his grasp, astonished. It was as though he had become a different man. He was almost kind.

He pulled back suddenly, alarm on his face. 'I'm sorry, the moment took me. I will not ever touch you unless you permit me. Do you need anything?'

Ciera shook her head. 'Just sleep. Perhaps we could speak in the morning?'

The king nodded. 'Yes, yes. My sincere apologies for waking you. I will call on you tomorrow.'

'There is one thing.' She thought quickly. He would never be more amenable to her requests than he was now. It was too late for any change in the city's taxation to make a difference, but she could do something. 'I've seen what it's like in Merivale, and it will only get worse. We can't stop people starving if there's not enough food, but we can ease their burden. Allow the commoners to hunt for game in your forest this winter.' It was a small measure, but it was all she could think of.

'I am not blind, Ciera. I know the city's troubles. But I cannot have a hundred common citizens treading through my woods, disturbing the hunters who take game for my table.' He paused for a moment. 'A proclamation will go out that anyone believing themselves capable may present themselves to the huntsman Yarl. If he agrees, they may hunt. Though no boars or deer.'

He had heard her, and to Ciera that was progress. Hessian remained sitting on the bed, and took a sip of his wine. 'I am sorry, you know. I know I hurt you, but it was... it was only so I could produce an heir. Since Elyana died... I have not been able to...' He hung his head, the years waxing back upon his face. 'Perhaps I have just been alone too long.'

Finally, he rose to leave. For the first time, he walked to the door rather than the fireplace, but as he reached for the handle turned back to Ciera. 'I don't suppose... is it too soon to say whether it is a boy?'

Ciera nodded. 'It is too soon.' As she spoke, she realised she had been holding her breath.

He nodded stiffly. 'No, of course. Too soon. Goodnight.' He fumbled with the handle and slipped out of the door.

After he left, to Ciera's surprise she found herself smiling. He would not touch her during her pregnancy, and he had listened to her! If the forest idea went well, then in spring he might listen to her on other matters, and if she gave him a boy perhaps he might consider her of sufficient import to actively seek her counsel.

Yet, as she sat thinking about it, somehow his sudden kindness only made it worse. That he could be so cruel... and then justify it by his desire for an heir! She should not have to endure his cruelty to get him to listen to her, and if the child was a girl it would all begin again. And if it was a boy, what then? Would she be forced to watch this man raise him to rule, and to all the cruelty and capriciousness that went with that?

But she could not leave. While she held the promise of a true-born heir, Hessian would hunt her to the ends of the earth. She would not deny her unborn child a kingdom for life as a fugitive.

She cried herself to sleep, and dreamt of Tam.

CHAPTER 27

It was nearing midnight, and the Witch's Abyss was packed to the rafters. Every stool was occupied, and every table haloed by a ring of blue smog rising from the smokesticks of its occupants. The fabled blue smokes of the east were usually far beyond the means of common men, but the barman was selling them cheaply, and no man had the poor sense to ask where they had come from.

Tansa moved lithely from table to table, taking orders and collecting cups, a sheen of sweat on her brow. Their time in Merivale had been a sharp lesson. Everything here cost many times more than in Cliffark, which made their fortune seem meagre in comparison. The citizens of Merivale were not so poor as they had thought; Merivale was just expensive. They had soon realised their haul of gold would not be enough to last them the six months to a year they expected to stay here, and with none of them inclined to thievery in this strange city where they knew no hidey-holes or shortcuts, they had decided to look for honest work.

All they had found was inn-work – it seemed ale was the only thing that came cheaply in Merivale – and Tansa knew it had to be her to take it. Cag was too much of an oddity – a giant with the mind of a boy and the eagerness of a puppy – and Tam would inevitably end up filching something.

Thus, Tansa had come to the Witch's Abyss, weaving her way between the tightly packed tables six evenings a week, bearing trays of beer and avoiding the gropes and lewd comments. With the price of food rising as winter drew in, she made barely enough to feed herself, but it would help see them through the season, and leave them enough left over to return to Cliffark. It was a disappointing outcome, after their initial excitement at discovering how much money they had stolen, but she was just relieved they would survive the winter and hopefully get back to Cliffark unharmed.

At least they were no longer sleeping on a roof. Innkeeps were suspicious folk, and none had been willing to let a room to youths who could not explain their purpose in Merivale. It was winter now, and the nights in Merivale were cold, particularly so much closer to Eryispek. They had made their home on the top floor of a deserted manor, next to one of the gated streets.

The barman worked her hard, but there were some benefits to being in the Witch's Abyss. She could listen in on the conversations and catch titbits of choice gossip that she would never have heard otherwise. Much of the talk was of the battle that was said to have occurred near the Pale River, and the winter which the old folk swore was shaping up to be the coldest they had known in thirty years, though it was barely past autumn. There were also strange tales coming down from Eryispek, of missing tribes and storms that dissipated as quickly as they appeared.

There was even talk of Ciera Istlewick. Tam was less prone to uncharacteristic melancholic silences now, which Tansa took as an indication he was beginning to forget about her. She had been furious with him for running off that day outside Piperskeep, but he had sworn to her he had lost her escort's trail before he got the chance to attempt to speak to the new queen.

'I'm telling you,' she heard one old soak say, his cheeks and nose purple with broken veins, 'that girl went into that castle and never came out! I hear the king's got her locked up in a pillory so he can dump his seed in her whenever the mood takes him.'

'That's a load of bollocks,' Tansa said as she passed, 'I saw her leaving the castle on a fine horse barely a month ago.'

The man turned in his chair to scowl at her. 'You calling me a liar? Bloody servant girl, I won't have it!' He swiped for her, but Tansa was too quick, and she ducked away towards the bar.

'You can get me another drink while you're there!' the man called after her.

Tansa cursed inwardly. Getting into disagreements with the customers was an invitation to being out the door with no work. The ogling and lecherous comments were part of working in an inn, but for some reason the ridiculous stories men told about women troubled her more.

'Tansa!' The barman thrust a tray of short drinks into her hands as she approached. 'Here's some free whiskies for the young masons over there. I've got a packet on the fletchers at the hogball tomorrow and I've a mind to get those masons nice and pissed.'

She looked down at the drinks. 'Have you put anything else in them?'

'Never you mind what's in them! Just hand them over and wish them luck for tomorrow.'

Tansa rolled her eyes. The barman had even forgotten to remove the vial of powdered drowshroom from the tray, a mild poison that would put a man to sleep, and cause unfortunate stomach problems if mixed with strong liquor. She said nothing and pocketed it – who knew when she might fancy adding a little something extra to the drink of a troublesome customer?

As she approached the table she caught fragments of a story one of the masons was telling.

'Strangest thing... Wanted to know about comings and goings... Told him to ask a guard...' The man paused his story when he caught sight of Tansa with the whiskies, and chuckled. 'Those whiskies on the house? Tell that barman of yours he'll have to do better than that to stop us thrashing the fletchers tomorrow!'

The whole table laughed as Tansa placed the tray on the table.

'Here, girl,' said the storyteller, a kettle-bellied mason a few years older than the others. 'Have you seen any of what I'm telling these about? Men in black, strange accents, funny swords, going about asking odd questions?'

Tansa's mind raced with panic. What were Imperial guards doing here? Surely not looking for her and Tam and Cag?

She shook her head. 'Not had any in here. What did they want?' she asked, trying to sound casual.

'Information about Merivale's ins and outs,' said the mason, 'whether there were any ways out except for the three gates. They've been watching them all day. Surprised the guards haven't dealt with them yet.'

'Those fellows in black?' A man at the next table with a guardsman's uniform peeking out under his cloak turned his head to them. 'My brother-in-law works the gates. They've been told they aren't to be interfered with; they're the private army of some Imperial lord. He reckons they're looking for somebody.' The guard took a sip on his ale. 'Don't like it myself. It's our job to guard Merivale and catch troublemakers. These foreign buggers will only get in our way.'

'You lot couldn't catch a cold,' scoffed one of the masons. 'And the Imperium don't have lords; they have senators, so you're wrong about that too.'

It was unwise to talk back to a guard, especially one who

had been drinking, and Tansa retreated to the bar before the matter got ugly, letting the guard's angry retort be swallowed by the din of the inn. How had the Imperials tracked them to Merivale? They had not spent any of the coins, and she was sure the moneychanger would not sell them out when he was complicit. All they had to link them to the theft was the purse and the ridiculous box that Tam was still holding onto.

The *magic* purse. Tansa cursed. She remembered the words of the woman who had saved her: '*Magic brings folk nothing but trouble.*' It was hidden under one of the floorboards of the house they were squatting in. Could the Imperials track it there? She had to warn Cag and Tam. She ripped her apron off and threw it over the bar, and rushed out of the inn with her cloak, ignoring the barman's confused shouts.

Somehow she had not seen them when she arrived for work, but there were a pair of black-clad Imperials on the street outside, their foreign blades hanging naked at their waists, glinting menacingly in the light of the braziers. Tansa kept her head low and hooded, walking at a pace she hoped looked natural. She felt their eyes following her, and breathed a sigh of relief as she turned the corner.

Her relief was short-lived. There were two more on the next street, and two again the street after that.

Another street over, she reached the wide thoroughfare of the Castle Road, running all the way northward from the King's Gate to Piperskeep. This was busier, and though there were still Imperials keeping watch, she did not feel their gaze on her so much, as their eyes followed the bent figures of the locals.

Tansa slowed her pace as she approached the gated streets, turning around regularly to scour the street behind for any pursuit. She saw nobody, and began to breathe a little easier. She felt slightly foolish; she could have stayed at the inn and tried to learn more. They might not be here for her at all.

She looked forward again, just as a group of three Imperial

guards were passing her. Tansa's eye caught a guard's, and a sliver of familiarity passed between them, as Tansa remembered flinging the blunt end of a knife into the man's temple.

'That's her!' cried the guard, thrusting his hand towards Tansa as if he could reach out and grab her from across the twenty yards of cobbles that separated them.

The Imperials ran straight for her.

For a moment, Tansa was frozen like a rabbit who had wandered into a wolf's den. Then she ran, terror pumping blood around her ears and lending speed to her feet.

She made a beeline for the gate to her left, barely dodging a guard's outstretched hand. She was lucky. The bars were narrow, but scarecrow-thin as she was she slid between them, slipping free from her cloak as strong fingers grasped at her. Tansa ran down the deserted street, steps echoing off the cobbles against the high stone houses.

She chanced a look back, and saw that the slimmest of her pursuers had been able to slide between the bars, leaving her companions behind.

Tansa kept running, praying to Eryi there would be another gate she could slip through at the other end of the street. She spared another glance behind her, and to her dismay the woman had closed the gap between them and drawn her blade. She moved like a cat, her light steps masked by the noise of Tansa's own panicked gait. There was no hope of outrunning her. Tansa veered right, making for a set of steps that snaked up the side of a house all the way to the roof.

Tansa did not dare look back again. She ran, her feet pounding so heavily on the stairs she was sure anyone inside would hear her. She emerged into a roof garden, and with horror realised her mistake. This house had a flat roof, while all the rooves adjacent to it were high and sloping, covered in slick slate tiles. If she lost her grip, a fall from here would kill her, or deliver her straight into the hands of the administrator's men.

She glanced back, and saw a flash of black cloth and hard steel turning the corner.

Tansa ran for the edge.

She leapt, and crashed heavily against the next roof. She pressed her fingertips against the slate, straining for the friction that would stop her slipping to a messy death on the cobbles. The roof's apex was just yards above her, but when she instinctively reached for it she started to slide. She scrambled desperately with her feet for purchase, and her boot thudded against something solid that gave way, just as her other foot found a row of guttering. She jammed her toe against it, slowing her fall, almost crying with relief.

She could not rest now though. If the woman was bold enough to follow Tansa would make an easy target.

But when she looked back, there was no sign of the woman on the roof garden, and her thin steel blade was resting just next to Tansa's right leg, caught in the gutter. Immediately Tansa realised what she must have kicked with her boot. She awkwardly adjusted herself to look down at the ground.

Far below, in an alley that ran between the houses, was the woman's body, her lifeless limbs arrayed like those of a discarded puppet, dark blood flowing like deltas between the cobbles.

I must have kicked her just as she landed, before she could use her sword.

Straining with all her limbs, Tansa pulled herself up to the roof's summit. She looked down at the sword. She had never held one, and it seemed a waste to leave it. A blade might come in useful if she encountered more Imperials; it would be useless against trained soldiers, but it was better than going unarmed. She toyed with reaching down with her foot for it and dragging it up to her.

Footfall sounded on the cobbles below, and with a sinking feeling Tansa realised the Imperials must have found a way through. The alley running between the two houses had its own gate, but to her dismay she heard a shout, and people began running towards the body. Someone had seen it.

Agitated shouts in a foreign tongue floated up to the roof. Tansa grimaced. They would know she was up here, and they would find the stairs soon enough. She gave up on reaching for the sword.

Tansa looked around. There was no hope of an escape over the houses on this street. Each leap would be as treacherous as the last, and the Imperials would dog her every step. But the gap between this house and the next street was not much larger than the one she had just jumped, and it would be from apex to apex, giving her something to grab onto. In the next street she could jump from house to house along that row. Dangerous, but in the dark it might be enough to lose the attention of her pursuers.

Tansa jumped, and reached the next roof easily, and from there leapt along the new row of houses, vaulting from roof to roof. The clattering of slate was deafening, cutting like a knife through the night's silence. Tansa cringed at every heavy landing, hoping the dark would mask her whereabouts. But the darkness brought its own dangers as well. When the moon slipped behind a cloud, she could rely only on the distant glow of the street braziers by which to measure her jumps.

Eventually she reached the larger house that marked the end of the street, with a main entrance looking down the whole road back towards the gate. She breathed a sigh of relief.

Tansa looked across the city, weighing up how to return to Tam and Cag, and whether it was worth the risk of them being drawn into this. The Imperials would be searching the area and every gated street they could access. She did not believe that they could trace the purse to precisely their room – if that were possible they would have done so as soon as they arrived in

Merivale – but if they picked up her trail again she would lead them straight to her companions.

Eventually, after half an hour sitting in silence and with no sign of pursuit, Tansa decided she could risk going home. She was frozen by this point, without the cloak she had shed in her escape, and a light snow had begun to fall. Cautiously, she made her way along the rooves, ever watchful and alert for Imperials and any sound from the ground that might mean she had been seen.

By the time she made it back, her teeth were chattering, and her numb fingers struggled on the window latch. Cag helped to bundle her inside.

'G-g-get me a cl-cloak,' she managed to say. A full fire was too conspicuous in what ought to have been an unoccupied house, so Cag wrapped her in several layers of cloaks and blankets they had found in the property.

It took Tansa several minutes to warm up, with Cag watching her all the while, concern written across his face.

'What happened?' he asked, once he appeared to have decided that Tansa was warm enough to speak.

'Imperials.' Tansa swiftly told him everything, from the rumours in the pub to her mad escape across the rooftops. She looked around, suddenly realising that Tam was not there. He would have been full of questions by now. 'Where's Tam?' she asked.

Cag's guileless face took on a guilty look. 'He's out. I'm not sure. At an inn probably. I don't know. Do you want some food?'

Tansa's face hardened. 'I swear, Cag, if you lie to me after the night I've had—'

She jumped as the window creaked behind her, and turned to see Tam sliding into the room. He looked no less shocked to see Tansa than she was to see him.

'Tansa,' he said, turning his surprise into a smile. 'I thought—'

The cold forgotten, Tansa came to her feet and strode towards him. 'Where have you been?'

'Just at the inn. Not the friendliest crowd, so I came home.'

'What was the name of the inn?'

Tam swallowed. 'The Black Dandelion.'

Tansa looked at him through narrow eyes. 'I don't believe you.' She rounded on Cag. 'Cag, I swear if you—'

'It's the truth!' said Cag, backing away from her slightly.

'Why didn't you go with him?'

He shrugged his massive shoulders. 'Didn't fancy it. Bit tired.'

Tansa sighed and gave a long, exasperated breath through her nostrils. She could not trust the pair of them with anything. She looked back at Tam. 'I've never seen you come home from a tavern anything but drunk out of your mind.'

'It's cold out. Sobered me up.'

'Eryi's balls it did.' She turned to Cag, who was pale with worry. She dreaded the day he realised he was a foot taller than her and likely strong enough to throw her clear over a building. 'I swear, Cag, if you don't—'

'He's been going to see Ciera!' the boy blurted out fearfully.

Tam dived for the window, but Tansa was quicker, and this time she would not let Cag pull her off. She leapt on top of Tam and slapped him in the face as hard as she could. 'You.' *Slap.* 'Fucking.' *Slap.* 'IDIOT!' *Slap.* He opened his mouth to protest and so she slapped him again. 'I'm out all hours of the night working to keep us all fed, and you're... what? Sneaking over the castle walls? If they catch you—'

'They won't!' he protested feebly. 'I love her, Tansa. I—'

'Shut up.' Reluctantly, she got off her brother. For as long as she could remember, Tam had been all she cared about in the world, yet for all they had survived together he seemed determined to throw his life away on this girl, and it hurt as if she had been punched in the stomach.

'I will not watch you hang,' she told him, holding back tears, 'but that's where you're headed if you don't stop this.' At least she could now believe that the girl had kissed him back. She had believed him ever since she had seen how they looked at one another on their first day in Merivale. The madness would pass, she was sure of it. She just had to get him back to Cliffark. 'I'm not going back to the inn,' she said quietly. 'Too much risk with the Imperials out there. I'll go out once a day for food, and you two can't leave at all. Once the winter's over and people start travelling again, we'll get a passage back to Cliffark.'

'But—'

'But nothing.' She glared Tam into silence, then looked at Cag. 'Cag, if Tam tries to leave, I want you to break his arm.' Defeated, he nodded mutely. 'I don't know if they can track us here, but we're getting rid of the purse, and the box. I'll go out tonight and hide them somewhere far from here. Tam, give me the box.'

He came to his feet; his cheeks were an angry pink where she had slapped him, but somehow he still had a sheepish smile on his face. 'I gave it to Ciera.'

'Of course.' She rubbed her face with her hands. She was exhausted. 'That might be the first sensible thing you've done since we arrived in Merivale.'

CHAPTER 28

Orsian winced as he reapplied a poultice to his blistered hand. He had barely felt it while fighting for his life against Lord Storaut's horsemen, but days later the pain had been maddening. The poultice stung and itched, but it at least gave some respite.

They were returning to Merivale. Many days' ride, especially with so many men having lost their horses when Strovac's men had sneaked into their camp and set it afire. Their mood had been jubilant after the battle, but now had turned sombre, blackened by the weather, and the realisation of what victory had earnt them.

Rymond Prindian and Strovac Sigac had escaped, and they lacked the men to pursue them across Halord's Bridge into West Erland. Less than seven-tenths of their warriors had escaped alive and uninjured. Meanwhile, they had learnt the extent of the Prindian destruction. A harvest that might have fed thousands had been reduced to ashes, and their victory could not regrow crops, nor sate the anger of farmers who blamed Merivale for not coming to their aid sooner.

It had already been a poor harvest. If King Hessian could

not buy food from elsewhere, the city would starve this winter. Food in winter would not come cheap, and every coin spent was a coin less to be used upon the war. They might reach the spring with the king's treasury reduced to cobwebs and dust.

It was a strange sort of victory, Orsian reflected bitterly. They had beaten back a far greater force, and he had distinguished himself, perhaps saving them from defeat, and yet still the Prindians had struck the greater blow.

And now there was no prospect of Errian being freed before spring, when they could resume the war. Not having his brother around did not trouble him, but he knew it did his father.

When they stopped for the night, still a day's ride from Merivale, Orsian built his own fire and sat at it alone, eating the broth brought to him by a servant, barely tasting it. A cold sleet was blowing into their camp at a steep angle, and so Orsian placed himself near the fire. Despite its warmth, he found himself shivering. It had been the late days of autumn when they had left, but this was unquestionably winter.

'With the look on your face you might think we'd lost.'

Orsian looked up to see Naeem standing over him. 'Didn't we?'

'Wars are not won in a day, Orsian,' said Naeem, taking a seat on the ground. 'We taught the Prindian lad a hard lesson, and Strovac Sigac. We bled them more than they did us, and they fled the field.'

'By the skin of our teeth.'

Naeem grinned. 'Well, it's you we've got to thank for that.' He clapped Orsian hard between the shoulder blades. 'Setting our own defences on fire. I never saw the like, but it worked.

'You carry too much worry, lad. Focus on the good you did, not on the parts you can't control. Yes, it will be a lean winter, but we saved Imberwych and its grain stores, and that could make all the difference. I know your father's proud of you.' Naeem clapped him again on the shoulder and stood to leave.

'We'll get Errian back, and next time your father will gut that traitor Strovac like a pig, unless I get to him first.'

Orsian could not help the quiet smile that spread across his face as Naeem left. He had earnt the gratitude of the entire *Hymeriker* with his quick thinking, and more importantly the respect of his father. It had been worth a burnt hand, even if they had not been able to capture Rymond Prindian.

And now he would return to Merivale a hero, and alive to see Helana. His heart leapt to think of her. She had kissed him, despite their disagreement, and now they would spend the winter together. He imagined telling her about the battle. She could not fail to be impressed by how he had distinguished himself.

He went to sleep that night smiling, despite the cold.

No horns nor heraldry greeted their return to Merivale, nor any of the citizens. The cold sleet had become a colder snow, blowing in off Eryispek in spiralling sheets that left men blinded. The signs pointed towards an arduous, bitter winter.

The snowstorm receded as Orsian and his father rode into the yard, the bulk of the keep forming a protective barrier between them and Eryispek. Orsian was surprised to see Hessian already waiting for them outside, his spindly body draped in thick red furs, surrounded by four servants bearing flaming torches to warm him.

Andrick dismounted and knelt before him. 'Majesty, we were able to save Imberwych and its granaries, but Southton and Ditchford were already put to the torch by the time we arrived. The Prindians fled the field, but Rymond Prindian and Strovac Sigac escaped. We believe they have returned to Irith for the winter. I beg your leave to muster a force and take the fight to West Erland in the spring.'

They could go no sooner. A hard winter would slow and starve an army, and if the ground froze it would cause much discomfort for their horses, but Orsian's father had told him he was confident that in three months of winter he could gather a force of men that would make Rymond Prindian tremble.

'Rise, Brother.' Andrick stood, and Hessian embraced him. 'You will take the field against Prindian again, once winter is over. Come to my solar. You too, Orsian.'

They followed him inside, and up the high staircase towards Hessian's private rooms. A creeping chill seeped through the walls as they climbed, and they wrapped their furs tightly around themselves.

A fire was already burning in the solar, and unusually Hessian had all the windows closed. He dismissed the servants who had been tending the fire, and served them wine himself.

He did not wait for them to speak, nor did he ask about the battle. 'Ciera is with child,' he said, with a grin that melted the years from his face. 'An heir may grow inside her! There is hope yet. You were right, Andrick.' He embraced his brother, laughing joyously, and then to Orsian's surprise embraced him also. He could feel the king's sharp ribs through his furs.

'Congratulations, Brother!' Andrick's delight was open and genuine. He raised his glass. 'To Queen Ciera, and to bold King Hessian!' They drank.

Orsian raised his glass with them. There was no guarantee of it being a boy, but Orsian supposed that Hessian could still get a woman with child was reason enough to celebrate.

'Do not tell anyone yet,' said the king. 'Andrick, you may tell Viratia, but no others, and certainly not Helana, or she's likely to start hysterically shouting it from the battlements. Theodric knows of course, and Sister Velna – no doubt she will want to prod and poke at the child when it is born – but otherwise this is our secret. Now, tell me of the battle.'

Andrick left out none of the details, speaking honestly of how near they had come to disaster, how both Rymond Prindian and Strovac Sigac had evaded them, and how Merivale might starve this winter.

Hessian nodded silently when he had finished, and sipped his wine. Orsian waited for the outburst that would follow.

'You are too hard on yourself,' said Hessian evenly. 'You drove them from the field, despite your numbers, and you wounded Sigac. I am only sorry we do not have any prisoners we can exchange for Errian. If I can negotiate his release, I will.'

Orsian was stunned. Where was the angry, capricious Hessian he had known before? *If it is the hope of an heir that cheers him, we must pray for a boy.*

Andrick nodded. 'Thank you, Brother. What of feeding the city this winter? Are we able to bring grain from elsewhere?'

Hessian frowned, and rubbed at his gaunt jaw. 'It was a poor harvest to begin with. The price of food is already rising. That you saved Imberwych will make a difference, but not enough without further action. Lord Kvarm may be able to help.' He sipped his wine again, pausing thoughtfully. 'Orsian, leave us. Have the kitchens send two extra barrels of ale to the barracks for the men. And well done, it sounds as if we have you to thank for our victory.'

With a spring in his step, Orsian left, heading towards the kitchens. He had done as he hoped: distinguished himself in battle, and become known to the king. If they could win the war and he fought well, his future would be secure. Perhaps one day, Hessian's unborn son would make him the *balhymeri*, to replace his father.

What he really wanted, though, was to see Helana. He called to a servant who was lighting wall sconces, and told him to pass the king's orders to the kitchen. The warriors lucky enough to return would be up drinking for hours yet, more than enough time for him to go to the barracks himself and make sure the additional barrels had been delivered.

He remembered walking to see her before they had left for battle, with a heartbeat that would not slow and his palms slick with sweat. He did not feel that now; he felt confident, sure of himself. She had kissed him, and now he was returning, as a proven warrior. As soon as she opened the door he would take her in his arms and kiss her again.

He knocked confidently at her door. He heard a loud bang inside, cursing, and something heavy being dragged across the floor. He was about to force the door when Helana opened it.

'Orsian!' she exclaimed in surprise. Unusually, she wore a black, hooded travelling cloak, lined with fur. 'You're back!'

He smiled. 'I am. Can I come in?'

She hesitated. 'It's not a good time. Can it wait until morning?'

Orsian studied her. Her hood was dry, and in any case she was not allowed to leave the keep. 'Where are you going?'

'Nowhere,' she said, unconvincingly. 'I just put this on against the cold.'

Orsian frowned. He could feel the heat of her fire, even from the doorway. 'I don't believe you.' He looked around the door, past Helana. Her room was in disarray, with clothes strewn about everywhere and a heavy-looking travel sack on the floor, half-hidden behind a trunk that she must have been searching through just before he arrived.

'Where are you going?' he asked again.

Helana cursed under her breath. 'I'm leaving, Orsian,' she said, heavily. 'I can't handle being trapped here any longer, and now my father is threatening to marry me to some lord from the Imperium, even older than he is. I can't stay here.'

Orsian stared at her. Leaving? 'But he can't marry you against your will,' he said slowly. 'Not even a king has that power.'

'He is using my own words against me. I said I would marry Rymond Prindian for the sake of Erland, and now he says that for the sake of Erland I must marry for an alliance. I won't do it, though. I won't be shipped off to the Imperium like a sack of meat.'

Orsian barely heard her after the words *Rymond Prindian*. She had offered to marry him? He felt like he had been stabbed. 'Marry Prindian?' Anger rose in his chest. 'Eryi's balls, Helana, do you know how many East Erlanders will starve this winter because of what he's done? How many men died because of him?'

'I only said it to upset my father, but it might bring peace at least.' She looked up and down the corridor. 'Quick, you better come inside before someone hears us.' She pulled him inside and shut the door behind her.

When the door closed, Orsian immediately moved to kiss her. He was still angry, but if he showed her how much he cared for her perhaps she would not leave.

Helana put two hands on his chest and pushed him away, taking a step backwards. 'What are you doing?'

Orsian grinned. 'Kissing you.'

Helana looked at him as if he were stupid. 'Eryi's balls, Orsian, did you not hear what I just said? I'm leaving. I'm not going to stand around kissing you.'

'Then don't leave.'

Helana turned away from him, opened her trunk and began rummaging through it, not bothering to reply. This was not going the way Orsian had hoped. *Rymond Prindian*. The anger rose in him again. It felt strange; he almost never got angry. 'Would you kiss me if I were Rymond Prindian?' He felt disgusted. 'You don't even know him.'

'You were just telling me a moment ago how many people have died because of this mad vendetta of my father's. What better reason to marry would there be? And who else would I marry?'

Orsian's mouth went dry. He wanted to ask her, there and then. His father had won his mother's hand fighting. He could do the same: prove himself worthy to Hessian of his daughter's hand by fighting for him.

Helana paused her rummaging, and turned towards him. 'You?' she said incredulously, as if reading his mind. 'Did you take a hit to the head during your battle? We're cousins, Orsian! And you're a child!'

Orsian bristled. 'I'm only a bit younger than you, and I'm a man now.'

'You think killing people makes you a man?'

'So you'd have married Rymond Prindian, who wants to kill us all, but not me?' Tears sprang to Orsian's eyes, and he wiped them away with his sleeve.

Helana's face softened. He thought he even saw her smile slightly. 'By the Norhai, Orsian. I care for you, deeply, but think of what you're saying. If we were free, then maybe, but we aren't. You'll be fighting my father's wars for decades, even after he's gone. I love your mother, but do you see me doing as she does for your father, waiting at home for months on end for you to return? Until we have peace, none of us is free.

'I saw the men returning up the Castle Road, with the wounded carried in carts. How many dozens of children will be told today that their fathers are dead? And how many more will die this winter with no food? Is it a price worth paying? Have you never thought of being anything other than a sword for my father?'

Orsian felt all the pride seep out of him like a leaking wineskin. Being a warrior was all he had ever wanted, all he was, and now the woman he loved scorned him for it. 'Where will you go?' he asked, trying to stop his voice from cracking.

'I don't know yet. East maybe. I have never been to Cliffark, but it's large enough for me to get lost in until this Imperial my father wants me to marry leaves.' She shoved more clothes and a wheel of cheese into her travel sack and pulled it closed. 'I have to go; there's a stableboy waiting with my horse.' She wrapped her cloak around her and pulled her hood forward. 'If they ask you, will you tell them you didn't see me?'

Orsian nodded mutely. He could run and tell the guards, but then Helana might never speak to him again. 'Will you come back?'

'Someday.' She stepped forward and kissed him on the cheek. 'Don't go getting yourself killed. Goodbye, Orsian.'

Orsian watched her, all the way down the corridor. Helana reached the next door, waved back to him, and was gone.

CHAPTER 29

The huntswoman Creya was waiting where Helana had asked her to be, outside the forest, with two horses bearing saddlebags.

'You sure about this?' she asked as Helana approached.

Helana nodded. 'As sure as I am likely to get.'

Creya gave a small grunt, as though she had won a bet with herself. 'If you think you can bring peace, I'll take you as far as Halord's Bridge. For the sake of Yarl and my boys. They were given their uniforms this morning. Never thought I'd see the day. Thank you.'

Helana acknowledged Creya's thanks with a small nod. Merivale's guards were exempt from being dragged to war in service to their king, being required to keep order in the city. A healthy bribe to their commander had been enough to secure the entry of Creya's husband and sons into his company, though strictly the two youngest sons were too young, and her husband Yarl too old.

'How did you get out here anyway?' asked Creya.

'Told the gate guard if he let me out I'd show him my tits when I came back.'

Creya cackled. 'They'll show him the hangman's noose once they realise. Men are fools.'

The huntswoman led the two horses into the undergrowth, with Helana following close behind. Through the forest was far from the quickest route out of Merivale, but it would ensure they were not seen.

Once they emerged from the forest into open fields, they rode south and west, to join up with a stream that fed the Pale River. They had no map, but Helana trusted Creya to know the way.

Helana was not riding east to Cliffark as she had told Orsian. She was going west, to Irith, to see Breta Prindian.

Did that make her a fool, or a traitor, or both? Not that it mattered. Anything was better than staying a prisoner in Piperskeep waiting to be sold by her father.

Yes, Breta Prindian had deceived her, but if she had spoken truly about the attempt to kidnap her son then her father had deceived an entire country, and started a war. And where else was she to go? She knew nobody outside Merivale. This time when she saw Breta, she would demand the truth.

The stream was frozen solid in places, and weaved across the land like a great silver-blue snake. There were more direct routes west, but Creya trusted the river, and Helana trusted Creya. Helana shivered, and drew her many furs closer around her, squinting through the gloom to keep sight of the huntswoman. Night fell early in winter, and she was already relying on the glint of moonlight against the ice of the stream to show her the way.

Orsian would have known the way. He might even have shown her, but she could never have told him she was going west. He would have tried to stop her, and when they eventually realised she was missing he would not have been able to keep it to himself. This way, if anyone came searching, they would go the wrong way.

She followed Creya through the night, to the point of exhaustion, until a heavy shadow of cloud blew across the moon and it became too dark to go on.

'We'll stop here,' said Creya. 'Can't have these breaking a leg.' She patted the neck of her horse.

They found a shepherd's hut, unoccupied, and tethered the horses outside with blankets across their backs. Inside, Creya managed to get a fire going, and Helana settled down for the night wrapped in all her clothes, shivering, despite the fire.

When she woke the next morning, it was still dark, and the white mist of her breath hung in the air like smoke. They broke their fast on hard bread and cheese, which Helana hoped would last her to Irith, and she fed her horse a bare handful of oats. When it realised there were no more, the mare whickered and nibbled at Helana's hand.

'Sorry,' she said, hugging the mare and patting her neck soothingly. Her name was Mitra, and Helana supposed she was used to more generous rations in the Piperskeep stables. She was Helana's, or more accurately her father's. *Might as well add horse theft to my list of crimes, along with escape and treachery.*

'You sure you still want to do this?' asked Creya, crunching the frost-glazed grass under her boots. 'No shame in turning back.'

Helana heard the implication under her words: Helana might hunt with her, but she was still a noblewoman, accustomed to a feather bed and servants bringing her meals. 'I'm fine,' she replied, swinging herself up into the saddle.

'Why?'

The simplicity of Creya's question threw Helana for a moment. 'For peace,' she said, with some uncertainty. 'If I marry Rymond Prindian the war might be averted.'

Her response set Creya off into loud and long laughter, at odds with the morning's icy stillness, far longer than Helana thought she deserved. 'Peace!' she exclaimed, wiping a tear from her eye. 'Girl, I never meant for you to sell yourself to some lordly fop. You've already done enough for me and the boys.'

'But I'm not doing it for you,' said Helana, puzzled. 'I'm doing it for all of Erland, for all the mothers and sons.'

Creya shrugged, seemingly unimpressed. 'I never claimed to speak for all Erland, I only spoke for me. Never even told the boys; idiots would have thought I was calling them cowards or something. Do what you want, Princess, but Eryi's balls, don't make yourself a whore to peace. In ten years' time there'll be another war over something else, and if not, people die anyway, whether it be a chill, or a fever, a fall from a roof, or simply because they looked at the wrong man funny in a tavern. War or not, life is hard and often short. These sons you reckon you're saving don't sleep on a bed of feathers in sheets spun from gold, believe me. Put you and yours first, girl, like the rest of us. Sacrificing your own happiness for the sake of a kingdom is too much luxury, even for you.'

That had not been the response Helana had been expecting. She certainly did not think of any of this as a luxury. 'I will do what I must,' she said quietly.

'Aye, you do that.'

It snowed little the next few days, but a grey winter sky hung low over Erland, smothering the land to a frigid stillness. They saw nobody – few were desperate enough to cross Erland in winter – and the whistling of the soft wind through the bare-limbed trees was a constant reminder to Helana of how alone she was, even with Creya at her side.

When needed, they broke through the river ice so the horses could drink, and cupped water in their shivering hands for themselves. When it reached Helana's empty stomach she felt as though it were freezing her from inside to out. One night, they slept in a barn, and another, under a bush. In Piperskeep, Helana would have lain under a pile of furs, with a hot coal pan to warm the sheets and a fire roaring in the hearth.

Nevertheless, by the middle of the third day, Helana could not keep the smile off her face. No one was coming after her. She was free to ride wherever she pleased, free to find some dark forest and live off the land, or follow the Pale River north to Whitewater and take a ship across the sea, maybe cut her hair short and get taken on as a ship's boy.

But she had resolved herself to a course. She was doing her duty to the people of Erland. Helana set her mouth in a hard line, and rode on.

Finally they reached Halord's Bridge. Helana had seen it before, but even so it did not fail to take her breath away. It was hundreds of feet wide, wrought in stone, supported by grand arches that plunged dramatically into the churning rush of the Pale River. Unlike the stream they had followed, the river had not frozen; if she were to fall in it would carry her north all the way to Whitewater and the Shrouded Sea. How had Halord of West Erland built such a thing? It was majestic, and yet somehow a little unsettling. This was where her ancestor King Pedrian had stood against the might of the Imperium and thrown them back. The whistling of the wind under the arches was like soldiers' screams. She breathed in the air, and a faint stench of soot and sulphur filled her nostrils. Foul humours, blown north from the Sorrowlands.

'This is where I leave you,' said Creya, extending her arm for Helana to clasp. 'I hope you know what you're doing, because I sure don't. Good hunting.'

'Thank you,' said Helana, taking her arm. 'For everything. Safe journey back.'

Creya grunted. 'And to you.' She looked studiously towards the sky. 'Snow's coming. Be safe, Princess.' She turned her horse, and rode away with neither a wave nor a backwards glance.

Helana wiped faint tears from her eyes. She was not sad to see Creya leave, only aware that once she crossed Halord's

Bridge there would be no going back. She urged Mitra onward.

On the bridge, Mitra's horseshoes clacked loudly against the cobbled stone. The sound only made Helana feel more alone, and the cold mist that closed in around her even more so. A single snowflake landed on her nose. She looked up, and another landed in her mouth. Creya had been right, almost to the second.

She had thought it might feel different on the other side, but West Erland looked no more alive than the East. Also, she could no longer rely on Creya to guide her way. She knew Irith was to the north-west, but did not know how far.

Helana stopped to go through her packs. She ought to have brought a map, but all she had was warm clothing, her remaining food, and a small fortune in gold. What good had she thought gold would do her, with nowhere to spend it? And why had she not thought to pack a map? She cursed her own stupidity. It was just the sort of mistake a spoilt princess would make her first time travelling alone.

Her head whipped back at the creaking sound of wheels on the bridge. The silhouette of a cart appeared in the mist, rolling steadily towards her. Helana looked around for somewhere she might hide, but there was nowhere. It could not be that her father had already sent out pursuers and caught up with her; it just wasn't possible. And why would they have a cart? She waited, ready to set Mitra into a gallop at the first sign of hostility.

As the cart came closer, she saw it was pulled by two donkeys, urged on by a man with a long switch sitting at the front of the cart. There was a strong stench to him, like rotted meat, even at a distance.

Nevertheless, Helana breathed a sigh of relief when he came into focus. He was no soldier of her father's, just a peasant, wearing filthy clothes, with a hare lip and one cloudy eye.

He squinted at her through his one good eye. 'A girl. What's a girl doing 'ere by 'ersel'?'

He spoke like he was chewing mud. Helana hoped he was not simple as well as ugly. 'I'm travelling to Irith, but I'm not sure of the way.'

The man looked at her confusedly, tilting his head to one side. 'Eh? I got not a word o' that.'

Helana had to repeat herself thrice, including gesturing vaguely to the north-west before she could make herself understood. The stench of the man was overpowering. She was tempted to shove him in the river just to clean him up a bit.

'Irith!' The man slapped his thigh jovially, finally understanding. 'What you going to Irith for? I'm a-headed that way.'

'My business is my own. Can I ride with you?'

The man beamed, peeling back his hare lip to reveal a row of crooked yellow teeth. 'O' course! Stay upwind o' me though. Got a bit of a stench 'ere.'

As she fell in alongside the man's cart, she risked a peek inside. He had dozens of sacks, each roughly the size of a man, pulled tightly closed with string. It was the man's cargo that stank. She could almost see the fumes rising off them.

Helana realised immediately what the man was carrying. She raised a hand to her mouth, just managing to turn her gag into a cough. Corpses. Dozens of them, from the battle. Just the thought was enough to make her gag again.

She looked at the man, and his eyes met hers. 'I'm a blackmaster,' he said solemnly. 'The families'll claim 'em.' He nodded backwards at his cargo. 'For burnin'. And if they don't, the farmers will. Good fertiliser, corpses. Good pig feed too, if you can stomach the thought o' that.'

He was somehow more coherent talking about his work. Helana thought she had preferred him when they could barely understand one another. She tried not to retch, and did not dare look inside the man's cart again.

It was for men and boys like these that she was doing this. They had died hundreds of miles from their homes, for the sake of lords' squabbling. No doubt there was a very similar sort of man riding into Merivale with a cart of East Erland bodies.

'How will the families claim them?'

The man sucked at his teeth. 'I'll lay 'em out. The bodies are free for the families to claim, or they can pay me in silver for a burnin'. It's no easy task, burnin' a body proper.'

Trust the Norhai that the first West Erlander she met stood to profit from the war. *If Creya was here she would laugh herself dead.* 'The war is good business for you then.'

He gave her an odd look. 'There's never a shortage o' dead. I prefer when it's the old'uns. Got no children myself, but most of these are of an age wi' my sister's young'uns.' He shrugged. 'Better wi' me than left to rot, and a man has to make a livin'. If I had another trade I'd take it, but this is all I know.'

Helana was relieved by this. Not everyone was so hard-hearted as Creya; this man at least might thank her for peace between the Sangreals and the Prindians. She nodded. 'You're a good man. I didn't mean to suggest otherwise.'

The man grunted, hacking up phlegm and then swallowing it. 'I dunno 'bout that. Man's a man, as I see it.'

They rode in silence for a time, Helana keeping her eyes up and away from the man's cart. West Erland so far looked no different to East Erland, just endless miles of frost-dusted grass. Eventually they stopped, next to a pond the man seemed to know, where he filled his waterskin and Helana drank from her cupped hands. The man handed her a spare skin, which Helana thanked him for, and washed thoroughly before she drank from it.

'You got a babe on the way?' he asked.

Helana looked at him sharply. 'No!'

'I meant naught by it,' replied the man hastily. 'You don't look it. Just thought you might have lain with some West Erland boy and come seeking him to marry you.' He scrutinised her, up and down. 'You don't look the sort though. You a noble?'

'A lord's bastard,' said Helana, the lie coming easily. 'His new wife doesn't like me, so he's sent me to look for my mother.'

The man spat. 'Damn shame that. Folk should look after their own.' He wiped his hand against his filthy cloak and extended his arm to her. 'I'm Carid. These two are Auric and Eric.' He gestured to his two donkeys, who were lapping at the pond where Carid had broken open the ice.

'Elyana,' said Helana hastily, choosing her mother's name. There must be dozens of girls around her age in Erland named for her mother. 'How far to Irith?'

'A week's ride, if the weather holds.' It was still snowing gently.

Fortunately for them both, the weather did hold, and it was barely a week later that they crested a hill, and Helana had her first sight of Irith.

She had expected a town much like Merivale, built upon a slope, surrounded by high walls and with a great castle like Piperskeep at its summit. But Irith was flat, and its walls were barely half the height of Merivale's. Irith Castle was squat and flat-roofed, set away from the town on a slight incline. It did not look particularly intimidating; no wonder her ancestors had conquered West Erland.

'D'you know where you're going?' asked Carid as they approached the gate. His cargo had begun to smell even more as their journey went on. Now even his even-tempered donkeys snorted irritably when he hitched the cart to them, and Mitra would go nowhere near it.

'Vaguely,' said Helana, wishing she had picked a less interesting deceit. Carid had been full of questions on their journey, to the point that Helana had had to invent an entire backstory for herself and her make-believe family. It troubled her to lie to him; his simple decency put him ahead of most men she knew.

He was no fool either; she suspected he knew she was more than she let on, but he never pushed her on it. 'Thank you for your help. I'd never have made it here without you.'

'Don't mention it, least I could do. You'll want to go ahead o' me at the gate. The guards know me, but they'll still make a great fuss about the bodies.'

Helana had been worried about being questioned by the guards, but the one she passed was young, barely older than her. He looked her up and down admiringly, then waved her through. Feeling daring, Helana blew him a kiss as she rode past, and the boy blushed crimson, in a way that reminded her momentarily of Orsian.

She had tried not to think of Orsian, lest she confuse herself. He was brave, and honest, and she admired that, but by Eryi, if he was not one of the greatest fools she had ever met. He had seen her father up close in a way few would, seen his madness and his cruelty, and still he somehow thought that him being king was something worth fighting for. He would come to his senses one day, she hoped.

The differences between Irith and Merivale were even starker inside the walls. Every street was cobbled, and she passed a market, still thriving despite the chill, that by the look of the customers' clothes was used by both rich and poor alike. Even the homes made of wattle and daub were clean and upright, and when she had to veer Mitra out of the way to avoid a child, the mother smiled and waved to her. In Merivale she would have been facing a string of curses.

Inns in Irith were plentiful, and looked more welcoming than those in Merivale. She would have struggled to find anywhere as loathsome as the Witch's Abyss. After weaving through the streets for less than an hour, Helana eventually settled on an inn named the Smoking Sow, and dismounted to lead Mitra around the back, where a sullen but energetic stableboy took the reins from her.

Inside, the inn was small and cosy, with a roaring fire surrounded by several soft chairs, currently occupied. The customers, all men, looked up as she entered, but when Helana did not meet their eyes they returned to their drinks.

'Room for you, miss?' the barman asked when she approached him. 'You look like you've come a long way.' He was built like a barrel, with a thick set of auburn whiskers, and his apron was immaculate.

'Your largest, please, and a hot bath.' It was the longest she had ever gone without a bath, and after a week in the company of several dozen corpses, she felt she would need at least two before she felt clean again. 'And a bottle of your best wine.'

Helana had spent a long time thinking about how she would act when she got to Irith, and how to approach Breta Prindian – she could hardly just stroll up to the castle – and had determined that she would act like any visiting lady seeking an audience: spend a lot of gold and make a lot of noise.

She knew there were dangers inherent in this idea. There was always the chance somebody would recognise her, or that Breta Prindian would decide that she would be an effective hostage, but she might have drawn just as much attention attempting to be secretive.

She slapped two heavy gold coins down on the bar. 'And send for a seamstress. I'll want her in my room after I've bathed.' She could tell by the silence behind her that every ear in the room was listening. 'The same one Lady Prindian uses.'

The barman's eyebrow raised slightly, but otherwise he gave no indication that she had said anything unusual. 'Follow me please, Lady.'

The largest room took up the whole of the inn's top floor, with a separate room for a bath, which the barman filled himself from four massive pails carried between him and two struggling servant girls. Helana resisted the urge to help them; it would have looked unusual after her display downstairs.

She looked around the room admiringly. It was more luxurious than anything she had known in Piperskeep. The four-poster bed could have slept six, and the floor was covered in lush sheep's wool. She removed her shoes and ran her bare toes through it, grinning like a child.

She thanked the barman as he left, and slipped a coin each to the wide-eyed servant girls. Then she threw her filthy clothes into a corner, replaced them with a robe, and stepped into the bathroom. She undressed again and slipped into the bath.

It was hot and steaming enough to turn her skin pink, but she did not wait for it to cool down. She had been cold for over a week, with a chill that had got deep into her bones, and she meant to wring every last morsel of heat from this bath.

Between the warmth of the water and the enervating qualities of her wine, Helana soon regretted that she had made arrangements for a seamstress to attend her. She would have happily got into bed in the middle of the afternoon and dozed until morning. Nevertheless, having scrubbed herself clean, after a time she stood from the bath, and draped her robe around her once more.

Helana stepped into her bedroom, and gasped to see Breta Prindian sat in the corner, rooting through her travel bags.

She looked as immaculate as Helana recalled. Somehow even the luxury of her room seemed diminished by comparison to her. She was dressed for winter, in bright white furs trimmed with silver, and a shimmering circlet that kept her perfectly coiffed hair bound in ornate plaits.

Coming to her feet, Breta swept upon Helana in a cloud of perfume. 'It is wonderful to see you,' she said, planting a delicate kiss on each of Helana's cheeks. 'Genuinely, just wonderful. I am so sorry about last time.'

Helana was immediately conscious of how shabby and underdressed she was next to Breta Prindian, wearing the inn's robe and with her soaking-wet hair dripping water onto the carpet. 'How did you get in here?'

'Here, child.' Breta reached into Helana's pack and pulled out a dress, before shaking it out to remove the creases and passing it to Helana. 'You were right to send for a seamstress; the gowns in Irith are far better than anything you will find in Merivale.'

She averted her eyes, allowing Helana to pull the dress over herself. Her hair was still sopping wet, so she wrapped it in a towel. 'How did you get in here?' she asked again. 'And more importantly, how did you find me?' She had barely been in Irith for an hour. It had been her intent to see Breta Prindian, but not to summon her to her room like some demon.

'I received word a few days ago that you had left Merivale, heading west,' she said, sitting down and helping herself to a glass of Helana's wine. 'I assumed you were coming to Irith, and then both the man you travelled with and the innkeeper sent word to me confirming it. Nothing happens in West Erland without me knowing about it.'

Helana could only be astounded by the reach of Breta's knowledge and informants. She had barely even known herself that she would be leaving Merivale until she had done it. And smelly, corpse-selling Carid, of all people, had her ear?

Her confusion seemed to amuse Breta Prindian. 'He was quite taken with you, Carid. It troubled him to sell you out, but the taste of gold is hard to resist. I suggest you choose a better alias next time. Elyana, indeed.' She chuckled melodically. 'Don't just stand there gaping at me. You're cleverer than that. We can save ourselves some time here: I'm going to tell you what I think has happened, and you can just tell me if I'm right.'

Helana nodded mutely.

'Your father has tried to marry you to somebody undesirable. You have correctly judged that I am well-disposed to you, and will see you as of little value as a hostage due to your father's obvious dislike for you, and so with nowhere else to go you have come to Irith, as I hoped you would eventually. Am I close?'

Helana cursed silently to herself. 'And I want peace,' she added, defiantly. 'Between our families.'

Breta laughed dismissively. 'It is a little late for that, I fear.'

'You lied to me. We could have had peace if you had not tried to kidnap Queen Ciera.'

'And maybe if Hessian had not tried to kidnap my son.'

'You can't win,' said Helana. 'Not against my uncle.'

Breta's lips curled. 'Rymond did not shame himself in battle, from what I hear, and this new warrior of his, Strovac, seems to believe himself Halord the First reincarnated. And while war has its price, so does peace. The question is whether it is a price you are willing to pay.'

Helana took a deep breath. She knew to what Breta Prindian referred, but that did not make it any easier. 'You want me to marry Lord Rymond.'

'That is why you are here, is it not?' Breta smirked. 'Marriage. The eternal price of peace. I married for peace. My husband was from another Prindian branch, and our two families fought like cats in a bag until someone had the good sense to wed us.' She sipped her wine. 'It was a disaster, of course. The best thing about him was the Prindian name, and that was already mine.

'However, it did bring peace. Whether the same would be true in this case, I doubt. Do you truly believe your father would lay down arms if you married my son? We know he holds you in little regard.'

'Yes.' Helana swallowed, wanting it to be true. 'If Rymond swore the necessary oath of fealty, yes. He would not like it, but my uncle and Lord Theodric would make him see sense, and my uncle would not lead an army against my husband if he had sworn himself to peace.'

Breta gave a small laugh. 'Your uncle would do whatever Hessian told him. Hessian is more of a father to him than a brother, really. He does have honour though; I will allow you that.' She brushed her fingers absent-mindedly across her wine glass. 'Very well, child. I will entertain this madness, but only because it amuses me. If it is truly your wish to marry, come to the castle with me. You are free to try and persuade my son.'

CHAPTER 30

The library of Piperskeep was musty and dry, the air dense with the dust of undisturbed books, set on tight shelves with coats of grime thick enough to write in. The stacks were unlit, dark as a moonless night. There were candles, but the librarian guarded them with the jealousy of a mother cat, sitting over a small flame by the entrance.

Pherri had not been allowed a candle. The ancient librarian with hair sprouting from his ears and nose had told her she was too young to be trusted, with an angry croak which implied that if it were up to him, no children would be permitted in the library at all. Pherri had accepted this without complaint. Though the library was on a lower floor, she had been able to find a table with a small window over it at ground level that offered a chink of light through the snow and ice that covered it. If she held her face close to the page she could just make out the words.

It was several weeks since Orsian and her father's return to Merivale. Her mother had decided that if the war meant the king needed Andrick at his side, they would all see out the winter together in the city, and in any case, the routes back to

Violet Hall were now covered in thick and treacherous snow. Her mother said she had never known a winter like it, with snowfall so heavy and the winds from Eryispek so fierce that the blizzards could leave a man unable to see more than a foot in front of him.

Pherri had not been to Piperskeep before. Her home Violet Hall was the largest building she had been in, but the keep dwarfed it, and she felt pleasantly forgotten in its vastness. Initially, she had kept up her lessons with Delara, working in the old woman's room, but her tutor had been unwell the last few days, leaving Pherri free to explore the castle alone.

She had discovered the library a week ago, and so far the only other person she had seen here was the librarian, always hunched over the same small desk. She wondered if he slept there as well, or ate, or used the latrine.

Reading books was a welcome relief to poring over Da'ri's letter, which she had begun to do less of late. It troubled her still, but there was nothing she could do. Jarhick and Da'ri were both dead, the Lutums still missing, and if anything was imprisoned on Eryispek, it could stay there.

This library was much larger than Violet Hall's. She had counted the stacks and paced out their length, and estimated that there were at least ten thousand books here, far more than she could hope to read over the winter. She had focused on learning more about distant lands where the sun never set, or where three moons could be seen in the sky. Her favourites were books about the Imperium, of which the only ones at Violet Hall had been Da'ri's. She read that in Ulvatia there was a library that held over a million books.

The more she read of the Imperium, the more she thought it sounded preferable to Erland. They had mastered the transportation of water, so any man could take a drink from a pipe that serviced his home, and dispose of waste by an alternative pipe. It made Pherri wonder why the Imperium was their enemy; if they controlled things in Erland everything would be much simpler.

Today though, she was in the mood for something more light-hearted. The week before, she had read a book of seafaring tales written by the captain of a merchant ship out of Cliffark, and fancied something similar. So when she arrived at the library she raced down the stacks trying to remember which section it had come from.

Pherri turned the corner down the stack she thought it had been, and collided with something head-first. She crashed backwards into the stone floor and lay there, stars swimming before her eyes.

'I am so sorry. Please, let me help you.' The voice was kindly, and she took the outstretched hand that was offered to her. It belonged to an old, bald man, draped in midnight-blue robes. He was smiling down at her bemusedly. 'You should be careful, Lady Pherri. It is lucky for you I am only a small man. Are you well? Should I fetch your mother?'

'No, no,' said Pherri quickly. 'I'm fine. I was searching for a book.' She looked at the man, who had a twinkle of mischief in his brown eyes. 'You're the king's wizard!' she exclaimed. She recognised him from Orsian's stories.

The man chuckled. 'We prefer *magi*, or *magus* if it is the singular. I am the king's magus, Theodric.' He extended his arm and Pherri clasped his wrist with her tiny hand. 'What book were you looking for?'

Pherri squirmed in embarrassment, wishing he had found her racing for another history rather than children's tales. 'Last week I read a book of stories written by a captain from Cliffark,' she said, 'I thought I would enjoy something like that.'

'*Sea Stories* by Captain Shurgill?'

'Yes, that one!'

Theodric grinned broadly, bringing out dimples and wrinkles around his deep-set eyes. 'A fine book. If you are looking for something similar, I believe Shurgill did write a second one.' He lifted a candle he held in a clay plot. 'Shall I help you find it?'

Pherri ended up following Theodric up and down several of the stacks, describing books of a sort she might find interesting so Theodric could pick out suitable titles. The magus pulled a small trolley behind him on which he placed Pherri's books next to his own selection. Together they chose for her the second book of sea stories, a collection of folk tales, a history of Merivale, and three books on the Ulvatian Imperium. Theodric seemed delighted to have a young companion interested in books, which pleased Pherri as much as it puzzled her.

'Lord Theodric, my brother says men are frightened of you, but you don't seem very scary.'

Theodric chuckled again. He laughed easily, far more than her father or brothers. 'Men fear what they do not understand, and little is understood of the magi. But a little fear can be useful, so I do my best not to shatter their illusion with mundane truths. I am just a man with some small skills at magic, nothing for anyone to be afraid of, least of all you.'

Pherri nodded seriously, satisfied by this explanation. 'Are there books on magic here? Is that what you read?'

'Not here,' said Theodric, shaking his head. 'Not anywhere.' He put his hands on his knees and lowered his face towards her. 'Would you like to come and read with me in my study? I have some of my own books, including on the Imperium.'

'Yes, but I'm not sure we're allowed to take the books out of the library. The librarian told me to read at one of the desks.'

Theodric stood up, frowning. 'But you don't even have a lantern.' He did not wait for a reply but instead shouted towards the librarian. 'Luthius, did you tell Lady Pherri she could not take books out of the library?' He strode purposefully towards the desk, his hands deep in his robes.

'That privilege is for the king's family and his councillors only,' replied the librarian in a supercilious tone, looking back at

Theodric over the top of his half-moon glasses. 'Anyway, don't tell me you think that child is actually reading the books?'

Theodric bristled. 'She *is* the king's family, you dunderhead. And you've not given her a lantern either! Do you expect her to read in the dark?'

Luthius smiled with the patience of a man addressing an infant. 'Yes, but she's not actually *reading* the books, is she? She is a child.' He leant back with an air of superiority, but his face blanched with terror when in the blink of an eye Theodric was standing over him. He bent down to whisper something in Luthius' ear, and the blood drained from the librarian's face.

Moments later, Luthius was standing on shaky legs, begging Pherri's forgiveness, falling over himself to say that it had all just been a misunderstanding. He even bowed as she and Theodric left with their trolley of books. 'Enjoy the books, Lady Pherri!' he called after them. 'Do come back when you need more.' She instinctively waved back in thanks, but Theodric ignored him.

'Honestly!' said Theodric as they turned a corner. He paused to grab a passing servant, and instructed him to transport the books to his room. 'That man does not have the sense he was born with.'

'What did you say to him?' Pherri asked. They climbed the stairs, which Pherri tried to take two at a time while clinging to the banister.

'Just an ounce of fear,' said Theodric smiling knowingly. 'Imagine though, suggesting the king's niece cannot read! The king has had men thrown out into the streets for less, and Luthius would not survive outside the library. He needed a sharp reminder that it is not his personal fiefdom.'

'I don't mind.' Pherri was not keen on the idea of grudges. People did not choose who they were, and if it gave Luthius pleasure to exert control over the library it was not doing any harm. 'I expect most people can't read. You're the first other person I've seen using the library.'

'Most of the court have servants bring them books. I usually send a boy for them during the night, when I get most of my reading done, but what he has brought back recently has not met my requirements. When your mother requires a new book, she has them bring it with her breakfast so she can read in bed.'

Pherri did not volunteer that she had not known she could do this, nor that her mother made use of the library. She decided that she would continue to get her own books, at least for now.

They had reached Theodric's room, and when he opened the door she was disappointed to discover it was not so different from anywhere else in the keep. There were no animals, nor oddly coloured potions in jars, nor mirrors through which one could step to another world. Nothing that would in any way suggest there was anything unusual about Theodric, which to be fair was much what he had told her.

A second man, older than Theodric, with rat-tails for hair and a squashed face, was hunched over the table reading something, and looked up in surprise as they entered.

'Georald, my assistant,' said Theodric. 'He has some talent with magic, or at least a little. Together we are deciphering the old stories, looking for the truth in the tales.'

'Your room doesn't look much like a wiz— like a magus' room,' said Pherri.

Theodric chuckled. 'No, I suppose it doesn't. I don't wish to scare the servants, though given the state of the place I am sure they are too scared to clean it anyway. Would you like to see my study? That's where I keep my wand and my pointy hat.'

Pherri nodded and followed him, not sure if he was serious. He led her to a thin door that she had thought must be a cupboard. 'You must never touch this door,' he said warningly to her as he unlocked it. 'I am sure you would not, but your father and mother would never forgive me if I did not warn you.'

The door opened into a square room, with high shelves

straining under the weight of the books they supported. There were three desks arranged adjacently, which struck Pherri as odd, but her eyes were drawn to the pair of small black and white dogs curled up together on a bed in a corner.

'Puppies!' she exclaimed, and raced over to them. She knelt down to pet one, but when she touched its coat her hand met nothing solid, passing through as if there was nothing there. It felt like dipping her hand in cold water, and she pulled it back, frowning. 'What are they?' she asked as she turned to Theodric, who was looking at her strangely, a confused frown on his forehead.

'Shadowhounds,' he said. 'They do not take visible form unless somebody enters without my permission. You're not meant to be able to see them; I must have made a mistake.' He walked over, knelt down, and ran his fingers around the dogs' bed, his eyes closed in concentration. He finished, and looked at her as if to say something, but instead stood without a word, a troubled expression on his face.

Pherri was worried; had she broken something? She couldn't see how, but she could be clumsy, and perhaps magic things were easy to break? She shouldn't have touched anything without asking.

Theodric took a book from his shelf and leafed through it at his desk, his fingers a blur. When he found the right page, he read quickly, his eyes roving across the page. Pherri stayed where she was. Next to her, one of the shadowhounds mewled in its sleep and clutched at its sister with his hind paws. Pherri had decided that they were definitely siblings, one boy and one girl.

Theodric finished his reading and stood, hands buried in the folds of his robes. 'Pherri, do you know anything about your father's mother?'

Pherri shook her head. 'Father has never spoken of her. I've only met my mother's mother, and her father, before he died.'

'Nothing unusual about either of them?'

Pherri shook her head again. Her mother's father had ignored her, but her mother's mother had treated her well, trying to win her favour with gifts of dolls and sweets. Pherri had not been interested, but she had appreciated the intent. 'My grandmother is kind. She looks like Mother.'

Theodric pursed his lips. 'Pherri... I am not quite sure how to put this... is there anything unusual or *magical* about anyone else in your family? Your father, for all his undoubted talents, is about as far from a magus as a man can be, but I wonder if there is anything I might have overlooked in your brothers, or your mother.'

Pherri chewed at the inside of her mouth, thinking. 'Orsian can juggle, and wiggle his ears,' she said eventually. 'Errian can't do anything.'

Theodric was silent for a few moments. The air of the room felt very still, and not a single sound from outside penetrated its walls. Pherri realised she was absent-mindedly stroking where one of the dog's fur ought to have been.

'Pherri,' he finally said, 'I believe you may have some talent for magic.'

Pherri looked at him curiously, trying to work out if he was serious. She decided that he was. Theodric spoke as if this were a very significant moment for him. Pherri did not fully grasp why. All the magic she had seen so far was the two shadowhounds, and they were asleep and not even real. It did not seem all that different to Orsian's juggling, or a man she had once seen do tricks with cards.

'It is the only explanation,' Theodric continued. 'Only a magus would be able to see them.' He produced a coin from inside his robe. 'Here, let me test you.' He threw it over, and Pherri caught it. On one side, it had a picture of a young King Hessian in profile; on the other, a crude etching of Eryispek.

'I want you to toss it in the air,' he said, 'and call "heads" or "tails" before it lands.'

This seemed slightly silly to Pherri, but she did as he asked, flicking the coin in the air. 'Heads,' she said as it tumbled, and held out her palm. It landed in her hand, heads-side up.

'Heads,' she said to Theodric.

'Do it again,' he replied, eyes fixed on her.

She called 'heads' again, and it came up heads, and then two more times. After these four goes, she decided it must be a trick coin, and so called 'tails' so she would be wrong. It landed tails-side up. After that, she tried alternating, but every time she called the coin correctly.

'Ten times in a row...' mumbled Theodric when he had finally let her finish. 'Do you know what the chances are of calling a coin correctly ten times in a row?'

Pherri chewed her lip. 'One in a thousand?' she suggested. There was an odd tingling in her hand, like she had slept on it too long.

'Near enough.'

Pherri shrugged, feeling uncomfortable under his scrutinising eyes. 'I'm just lucky. I bet I couldn't do it again.'

'Try it.'

Pherri flicked the coin in the air again. As it reached its highest point, she said 'heads', but in her mind thought *tails*.

The coin landed in her palm, resting on its narrow side, neither heads nor tails. Pherri stared at the coin in disbelief, and at his desk Theodric began clapping enthusiastically.

'Well done! Well done! You said "heads" but thought "tails", yes?'

Pherri bit her lip and nodded, worried that she might cry. What was happening?

'It's nothing to be scared of! The coin waits for your decision. Say or think which way you want it to land, and it will do so.'

Heads, thought Pherri. Without so much as a quiver the coin fell, and the young King Hessian looked up at her.

'Well done, Pherri. Now, come and sit down,' said Theodric, indicating a second chair he had pulled up opposite him at the desk. 'Do you feel tired? Shall I send for some food?'

Pherri did feel tired. The tingling she had felt in her hand had now enveloped her whole arm in a numbness, as if it was no longer part of her body. The exercise of repeatedly flipping a coin had taken more out of her than it should have.

She nodded. 'Yes please.'

Theodric pulled on a cord that hung behind his desk, and somewhere far away below them Pherri thought she heard a bell ring.

'That is how they used to test for magi in the old Imperium, before the purges,' said Theodric. 'It's also said that it was how the first magus to come to Erland was discovered. He would travel around, betting men he could call more coins correctly out of five than them. He was clever enough to never win by more than he needed to, but eventually he was discovered, in this very city no less. The tale is that the citizens tore his head off with their bare hands and burnt it, while the body was thrown to the dogs. Fortunately, we live in more civilised times, and the few magi who remain do not waste their time cheating people.' He took a drink from a cup of water, flavoured with lemon. Pherri realised she had one also, and sipped at it. She was sure the cups had not been there a moment before.

'You've barely said anything since I asked you to flip the coin,' he observed.

'It's a lot to take in,' Pherri replied. 'An hour ago, I had never met a magus, or read much about them, and then you were there in the library, and you're not scary, and then you're saying I must be a magus, and then the coin was strange. And I don't think I understand what a magus is. I had thought them people who could do unexplainable things, but then you made it sound as if you just did tricks and people were silly to be afraid of you, but being a magus is obviously important. What did I do? How does it work?'

Theodric nodded, listening patiently. 'Forgive me,' he said. 'I got carried away. What you just demonstrated is what the ancient magi of the Imperium called *phisika*; the act of influencing the physical world by ensuring a particular outcome or path. It is the first of five disciplines. It expends energy, as you have discovered, which depends upon the physical effort involved, and the likelihood of the sought event. Ensuring a twenty-sided die lands on a particular number is significantly harder than selecting the side of a coin.

'It also requires will, which it is no surprise you have in abundance, given your family; your parents, and your uncle, are among the most hard-willed people you are ever likely to encounter.'

'What else can it do?' asked Pherri. There had to be more to it than just flipping coins and throwing dice.

Theodric stroked his chin. 'I can cause things to move from one place to a different place. Like so.' He raised one eyebrow slightly.

To her shock, Pherri felt a piece of warm crusty bread appear in her mouth, and instinctively started chewing. 'It tastes just like real bread!' she exclaimed.

Theodric beamed. 'That's because it is. I believe our food is here.'

He left the room momentarily and returned bearing a wide plate, overburdened with bread, roast chicken, potatoes, and all manner of other morsels. The two of them ate in silence, savouring their feast. Pherri found her appetite was greater than she could ever recall, and piled her plate high.

'You will learn that magic expends a lot of energy,' said Theodric when he had finished his plate. 'In moving that bread to your mouth I used many times the energy it would have taken to simply pick it up and deliver it to you, because there are so few other realities in which the bread was already in your mouth.'

'There are other realities?' asked Pherri, pausing mid-bite to stare at Theodric.

'Infinite numbers of them, so the theory goes. You and I are having this exact conversation in endless other realities, and each decision you take creates more of them, with divergent paths. By flipping a coin and choosing the outcome, you created a settled path and closed our reality to the alternative.'

Pherri frowned. 'But flipping a coin is not like moving bread through the air. Anyone can flip a coin.'

'That is simply a question of likelihood. A coin is easiest because there are only two outcomes; in half of realities it will be heads, and in the other half tails. There were realities in which you already had the bread, and that is the path I chose.'

Pherri closed her eyes, trying to wrap her head around it. If what Theodric said was true, even by choosing to think about it she was creating a new path. 'So in flipping a coin and choosing the outcome, do I use twice as much energy as I would to flip it normally? Why has it made me so tired?'

'You flipped it ten times, one after the other, for which there were over a thousand possible outcomes. You expended the equivalent energy to flipping it ten times *over a thousand times*, or ten times flipping a coin a thousand times the weight. What you did making the coin stand on its edge is more complicated... you made something that had virtually zero likelihood occur while leaving both the usual outcomes open to taking place. Had you held it on that edge you would have found yourself struggling for breath after a time.

'I'm not sure you realise just how astounding this is, Pherri. You have no apparent ancestors who were magi, no significant previous knowledge, and yet you held that coin on its edge as if you had practised. Have you ever done things and found that you had unexplainable success or luck at them?'

Pherri thought of her younger childhood. She could not recall learning to read; the books had been there, and she had read them. It had always been easy for her to cultivate plants and ensure they grew in the way she wished. And Da'ri had told her he had never met a child as gifted with figures. Had those been magic?

Theodric did not wait for her to reply. 'Would you be interested in learning more?'

'Yes.' The word was out of her mouth before Pherri had even thought about it. Of course she would. Her life did not need to be like her mother's, with a home and children to organise and a husband to wait for. She would be a magus. Theodric had said there were five disciplines; what were the others? Even *phisika* was beyond anything she had ever learnt with Da'ri or Delara. 'More than anything.'

That night, Pherri lay in her bed, tossing and turning, playing the spinning coin over again in her mind and resisting the urge to try it once more. Disappointingly, Theodric had ended their impromptu first lesson there and then, and made her promise that she would not practise without his supervision. He had told her to rest well and return to his rooms early the next day.

But she was too excited to sleep. She could have drunk some of Delara's potion, but it always made her feel a little groggy first thing in the morning, and she wanted to be as fresh as possible for her first proper lesson.

It was not so late that there was no activity in the castle. If Pherri opened her ice-coated window she could hear the clamour of guardsmen in the yard below, warming themselves against the snow with a barrel of ale after their evening meal, and if she pressed her ear to the stone floor she could make out snippets of a conversation between a man and a woman on the level below.

For a lack of sleep and anything else to do, she decided to go and see Orsian. She was sure he would be excited to hear about her being a magus. Perhaps Orsian could be one as well.

There were guards posted in the corridor, but with what she thought was a dignified wave she told them she had to speak to her brother about something, and walked confidently past them before they could disagree.

Orsian's room was just around the corner. She knocked twice.

'Who is it?' Orsian's voice was muffled by the door, but he sounded awake, if slightly alarmed.

'Pherri,' she replied. She heard the patter of Orsian's bare feet on the cold stone. He opened the door a crack and peeked his head out.

'You shouldn't be up this late.'

Pherri sensed she had interrupted him. 'Why? What are you doing?'

'It doesn't matter. Just come in before you get me in trouble.'

'Why would I get you in trouble?' she asked, once she was inside and Orsian had closed the door behind him. Orsian's room was the same dull grey stone and dark mortar as her own, but he had decorated his with a map of Erland on one wall and their father's coat of arms on another, with a sword mounted above it. 'I'm the one wandering the keep after I'm meant to be abed.'

'Father's had me rising before dawn these last few days to spar with recruits from the villages,' said Orsian. 'That's why you've not seen me. Some of the new recruits have been quarrying stones since before I was born, and when they hit you, you stay hit. Not to mention how cross they are to be here because it's the only way to feed themselves, and they just love to take it

out on the son of the Barrelbreaker. And it's colder than
Eryispek out there; I thought my feet were going to fall off.'
Orsian spoke with vehement bitterness he had obviously been
storing up for days. 'And meanwhile Errian rots in a cell under
Irith. Winter or not, our focus should be on freeing him.' He
slumped into a cushioned chair behind a table, on which rested
a second map of Erland weighed down at the corners by a pair
of candles and two mugs of ale, which he had pinned with
makeshift flags made from needles and small pieces of cloth.

'Sorry,' he said. 'Been holding that in for hours. Better here
than where Errian is. And at least I've got a fire.' He pointed
towards the hearth, which was burning handsomely.

Pherri frowned. Orsian probably cared about as much as
she did that Errian had been captured. Better him than any of
the rest of their family, and no less than he deserved. Something
else was bothering her brother.

'I met Lord Theodric today,' she said, changing the subject
and taking a seat opposite Orsian. 'He was nice. He showed me
his rooms.'

'Really?' said Orsian in surprise, lowering his ale to the table
too hard and causing it to foam. He had to drink swiftly to save
his map. 'That's brave of you. I'd wager most folk who go in
there don't come out again.'

Pherri shrugged. 'It's not as strange as you would think. But
he showed me something.' She pulled a coin from her pocket
and placed it on the table. 'Flip it, and call it.'

'Why?' Orsian looked at her quizzically.

'I'll tell you after.'

Orsian shrugged. He took the coin and flipped it in the air.
'Heads.' He let it clatter onto the table, head side up. He looked
at Pherri. 'What now?'

'Do it again.'

Pherri made Orsian do it four more times, of which he
called two heads and two tails, two correctly and two incor-

rectly. Pherri nodded, satisfied that whatever it was that Theodric thought remarkable about her, Orsian did not possess it.

'Watch this,' she said. Pherri felt slightly guilty after her promise to Theodric, but he had only told her not to *practise*. This wasn't practice; she already knew she could do it. She flipped the coin ten times in quick succession. *Heads, heads, tails, heads, tails, tails, tails, heads, tails, heads.* As she had known would happen, every time the coin landed in her favour.

Orsian stared open-mouthed, as if trying to work out a riddle. 'Is it a trick coin?' he asked when Pherri had finished. 'Why doesn't it work for me?'

'Theodric says it's because I'm a magus.' Pherri flipped the coin again, letting her mind rest simultaneously on both heads and tails. It landed sideways on the table, fixed on its thin edge. Pherri waited for a few moments before she called it. 'Heads.' The coin fell.

Orsian paled, staring dumbly at King Hessian's golden visage, with just a hint of fear, Pherri thought. 'Eryi's blood. You are a magus.' His tone was almost accusatory, as if she had cheated him somehow. 'Did you just learn that today?'

'Not much to learn. I just call it and the coin falls. It's quite tiring actually.' She could feel a weary tingling in her fingers, and picked up one of Orsian's mugs of ale to take a sip. She had not tasted beer before, and had to raise a closed hand to her lips to stop herself gagging it back up.

Orsian frowned. 'It's a powerful thing to be messing around with.'

Pherri nodded.

Orsian paused to take a long draught on his ale, and Pherri copied him, trying not to cough. 'It was the magi who first formed the Imperium; they bent men to their will for hundreds of years to build Ulvatia. It's not just flipping coins, Pherri; this is dangerous.'

Pherri frowned. 'The magi of the Imperium are long dead.'

'All the more reason not to be messing around with it! Do you think people fear Theodric because he can decide the way a coin lands? It's not safe, Pherri. You should stay away from him.'

Pherri could not understand why her brother was being like this. What business of his was it who she spent time with? He was allowed to play with swords and fight in a war; that was far more unsafe than what she was doing with Theodric. 'I won't. It's interesting. I want to be a magus.'

'What for? People will be afraid of you. Mother wouldn't like it either.'

Pherri laughed. 'Why should Mother mind? I've always had tutors.'

'This is different. What Theodric can do is unnatural.'

'You don't even understand what Theodric can do!' Pherri threw her hands up in exasperation. This was not like Orsian; they never argued. 'Theodric is giving me a chance to be something. Don't you want me to be happy?'

'I want you to be safe. What would your life be like? Nobody is going to want to marry a magus, and Errian won't let you stay at Violet Hall when he inherits.'

Pherri shook her head. She had never realised before, but Orsian really was terribly unimaginative. 'It's easy for you. All you've ever wanted to be is a warrior. What if I don't want to be just some lord's wife when I grow up?'

Orsian blinked at her. 'You know I would never force you to marry anybody. I'm just telling you how it is.'

'How it *is* is not necessarily the only way it can be.'

'What do you mean?'

Pherri tried not to show her frustration. 'I mean you're not required to be a perfect copy of Father, and I will never be a perfect copy of Mother. Don't you want to be free? Have you ever considered *not* being a warrior?'

Orsian's face fell, and it was several moments before he spoke again. 'None of us is free, Pherri,' he said sadly. He took a long drink on his ale, replaced his mug heavily, and stood up abruptly. 'You should go. I have to be up early again tomorrow. You should speak to Mother before you see Theodric again.'

Pherri nodded, though she had no intention of doing anything of the sort. 'Goodnight, Orsian.'

She walked back to her room. What in Eryi's name had got into her brother?

CHAPTER 31

Rymond's return to Irith was a blur of inebriation. He had lost hundreds of men in East Erland, but had they prevailed each life would have been well spent. It had been within his grasp, until some madman had set their flank on fire.

During their retreat, he had resolved to wipe that day from his memory by drinking until he could not even remember his name. He pulled Dom and Will along with him, and together they had made their stand in Rymond's chambers, with a steady stream of servants fetching wines from the cellar and women from the town to join them. It had been just like the old days, before he had got into his head the foolish notion that he wanted to be king.

Many days later, he woke in his chair, with flecks of vomit trapped in his beard and a girl passed out in his lap. He stumbled to the balcony, swaying, and threw up again, the contents of his stomach melting the morning frost.

The chill air was enough to sober him up. The wind raged in his ears, and he could smell the sour stench of days-old liquor on his breath. He looked back into his chambers, where Will was asleep cradling a wine bottle to his chest and Dom was tangled up with another girl, and began to feel a little disgusted with himself. This was not the behaviour of a man who hoped to be king. There was shame in defeat, but drinking himself into a stupor was worse. He had done what he set out to do, had he not? A few hundred dead, mostly mercenaries, did not change that. East Erlanders would starve this winter, and Andrick Barrelbreaker had not broken him. Next time he would do better. Next time he would win.

He left the room as it was, and despite his pounding head took the time to dress in one of his finest doublets, and had a servant comb his hair till it shone. He descended to his lower chambers, which were annexed to the hall where the Lord of Irith was supposed to settle disputes and dispense justice. He had done precious little of either recently.

To his surprise, he found his mother there, resplendent as ever in a green silk dress with a plunging neckline and dripping in jewellery, already sitting at the table with Adfric and Strovac. Adfric too had the bagged eyes of someone who had found solace in drink. Strovac looked like himself: hard and mean and petty.

'Well this is a pleasant surprise,' his mother greeted him. 'Just the three days staring at the bottom of a bottle. Perhaps you are not so much your father's son as I thought. He'd have been corralled in a tavern for at least a week.'

'Nice to see you as well, Mother.' He did not feel up to sparring with her. 'What are you doing here?' he asked Adfric.

Adfric looked sheepish. 'I was planning our campaign for spring, Lord.'

'You're both pathetic,' scolded his mother. 'Do you think Lord Andrick has spent the last three days drunk because he failed to stop over half the granaries being burnt, or do you think he's mustering men and planning for war? There will be many more deaths and perhaps defeats before this is settled. Pull yourselves together.'

Rymond rubbed at his temple. He hated that she was right. 'Very well. Where do you propose we begin?'

'We should begin by reflecting on our success.' Her words were such a surprise that they were more sobering than a cold bath. Rymond could not recall the last time she had praised anything he did. 'It had already been a poor harvest. The price of milled grain in Merivale is up three-fifths on what it was last year, and you might have cut the supply by a tenth. Hessian could add to the city's woes by increasing his garrison, and all signs point to an unusually cold winter which would swell the city's population further, and their demand for bread. In short, your attack has exacerbated what was already a troubling situation for Hessian, just as you planned.'

Rymond was genuinely lost for words. He tried to thank her, but all that came out was a croak.

'As for matters here,' she continued, 'Lord Strovac has done much of what needs to be done.' She nodded approvingly to the giant opposite her. 'Families have been informed of their losses, and your mercenaries have been found appropriate lodgings. Lord Storaut's men will winter with him, but he has sworn to return on the first day of the new spring.'

Rymond was astonished and annoyed that Strovac had assisted with any of those things, but tried not to show it. He had expected the man to be wroth after taking a wound in the battle and fleeing the field, and to take it out on somebody poor and unsuspecting. He needed to stop underestimating the man. It was impressive enough that his wound did not seem to trouble him, but he was also more cunning than Rymond had given him credit for. Useful too, if you watched him warily and let him have his head occasionally, like a bad-tempered but tireless horse. He seemed to have gained his mother's favour, and recognition of his as-yet landless title.

'Lord Sigac has shown his worth on the battlefield as well,' said Rymond. 'His cunning and bravery turned the tide. He'd have won a famous victory if not for the fire.' *That ought to keep him happy.*

'Well he didn't,' said Breta plainly. 'And when the chance to kill Andrick presented itself he somehow took a spear to the leg.' Strovac's face fell. 'There's no use wondering *what if*. You held three times their number, and yet you wasted good men trying to break open their shield wall piece by piece using mercenaries and savages who could have been put to better use. Had I been there I would not have allowed it.'

Rymond could feel his headache strengthening. He resisted the urge to send for wine and instead seized an apple from the table, taking a huge bite to stop himself snapping something back at her.

'At least you left the Barrelbreaker boy here,' she said.

Rymond almost choked on his apple. He had forgotten about Errian. 'Where is he?' he asked with a cough as he tried to swallow, his eyes darting to Strovac. If Errian had been harmed Rymond would have his head.

'On the highest floor of the guest wing,' Breta replied. 'We've given over the whole floor to him.'

'Is that necessary?' asked Adfric. 'He is a prisoner, not a guest.'

'He is nobility,' said Breta, as if that settled the matter. 'He may be the son of a foreign whore's bastard, but we shall treat him as befits his rank. I assure you he's quite safe. There are six guards, and he is given nothing that could be used as a weapon, not even cutlery for meals.' She looked pointedly at Rymond. 'You should go and speak with him.'

'Have you gone mad?' Strovac spluttered. 'He is a prisoner! Clap him in irons, put him in the dungeon, and start sending body parts to his father.' He licked his lips. 'I'll do it myself.' His eyes were predatory, like a fox stalking a henhouse, and the hand where only a stump of his little finger remained curled into a fist.

Breta did not even bother to look at him. 'We are not Hessian, throwing our enemies into an oubliette to be eaten by rats. We will treat him with civility. You do not rule in Irith, *Lord*, and you would do well to remember that what is given can be taken away.' She dragged his title out to two syllables, a reminder that while she may use it as a courtesy, he was lord of nothing and nowhere save what the Prindians could offer him. While Hessian ruled in Merivale, Strovac's meagre lands in East Erland were forfeit.

Strovac said nothing in reply, and kept his eyes respectfully neutral, but his mouth was set like he was chewing a nettle.

When there were no further objections, Breta Prindian nodded with finality, considering the matter settled. 'I am glad we all agree.' She lifted some sheets of vellum from the seat next to her and passed them towards Rymond. 'These are the letters calling your vassal lords to arms, and some further ones asking the other lords of the West to support your claim. We will be ready to march in numbers as soon as spring arrives. I have messengers ready, so add your mark and seal and have Adfric make the arrangements. Now if you'll excuse me, I will hold court today.' She stood abruptly from the table, requiring that the three men rise with her, and glided from the room towards the main hall in a sweep of green silk.

Rymond sighed, and cursed himself for wasting three days and letting his mother seize control. It was as if he were still a boy, sent to bed without supper. Would he still be bending to her whims when he became king? If he was truly to rule, he would have to challenge her at some point, but it would not be today, while his headache gave no sign of abating.

Once the letters were signed and sealed, he climbed the stairs to the guest wing. The highest floor was one of the most opulent, walls decked with ornate tapestries showing the Prindian ancestry, and the floors covered in thick green carpet that warmed one's feet, even in deepest winter. Usually, this floor would be held by a whole family or a collection of visiting dignitaries. To give the entire floor over to one man was unheard of, particularly a prisoner. Irith Castle's dungeons were not as low and dark as those in Piperskeep, but no prisoner had ever escaped. If Errian would not cooperate, Rymond resolved that a few days down there might make him more agreeable. He took six guards as an escort. There were six watching Errian already, but Rymond was taking no chances.

He knocked at the main bedroom, and entered without waiting.

Inside, Errian stood at the window, with his back to the door. On the road he had been filthy, but now wore a clean and simple leather jerkin over a red doublet, with dark trousers and high black boots, as if dressed for a day's hunting. His beard had been trimmed as well. His arms rested behind his back, but Rymond sensed the coiled fury that lurked within.

Rymond spoke first. 'The window doesn't open, if you were wondering.'

To Rymond's surprise, Errian replied. 'I know, I've tried.' He turned slowly to face Rymond, his face set in defiance. Defeat and imprisonment had not stolen his pride. 'Not that it would do me much good so many floors up.' He took in the six guards at Rymond's back, each resting a hand on their sword hilts. 'Are you here to kill me? At least let me die with a sword in my hand. Fifty gold says I kill three of them before they're able to stick me.'

Rymond had never noticed while they were on the march, but with his bruises fading and dressed like a lord again he was shocked by how much the man reminded him of Prince Jarhick. He was shorter, and broader across the shoulder, with his hair left fashionably long, but had the same sharp, handsome features and steely eyes. 'You look like Jarhick,' he said without thinking.

Errian's face flushed with anger, and he took a step towards

Rymond. He might have taken another, but the guards flashed steel from their scabbards to warn him back. 'You do not speak his name. Jarhick was like a brother to me. You never knew him.'

Rymond raised a placating hand. 'Forgive me.' He was glad to have so many guards with him. He gestured behind him, where a white-faced servant nervously held a tray bearing a jug of wine and a plate of bread and meat. 'Will you drink with me?'

Errian shrugged. 'Your castle. If you want to drink here, I can hardly stop you. Maybe I'll join you, maybe I won't.'

Rymond sat at the room's table, poured two cups of wine, and set the bread between them. Errian was eyeing them hungrily, and once he had seen Rymond take a sip joined him, still radiating hostility.

The guards were standing a little distance from them, but Rymond could see Errian admiring their swords as he sipped his wine. Rymond touched the knife at his belt, sure that he could reach it in time if Errian tried anything.

'Did you kill Jarhick?' Errian asked. 'I'll know if you lie.'

Rymond shook his head. 'No. I thought it was my mother, but she denies it also. Did you know Hessian tried to have me kidnapped?'

'Don't blame him,' said Errian, 'seeing as how you've broken faith and are trying to steal the crown. As things stand it's yours anyway when he dies, but no chance of that now.'

'Before he tried to kidnap me I wanted no part of it. But he forced my hand. I'll never be safe while he rules.'

Errian shrugged. 'You're hardly going to say, "I heard Jarhick was dead and decided I couldn't risk Hessian siring another son before he died." I'll listen to your reasons, but they'll make you no less a traitor.' He took a piece of bread and chewed it insolently. 'Not that it will be worth anything. As soon as spring comes my father will take the field again, and your head will be on a spike.'

'I'd have defeated him, if he had not set his flank on fire.' It sounded weak as he said it, like a child making excuses for losing a game.

Errian snorted. 'And if I hadn't been fool enough to trust Strovac Sigac I wouldn't be here. Every arsehole alive has an excuse.'

Rymond conceded the point. 'We will settle it in the spring.'

Errian nodded. 'And I mean to be there when we do. What ransom will it take for my release? I have some of my own wealth, and if I cannot afford it my father may agree your price. Or even the king.'

'There will be no ransom,' said Rymond. 'You may write to your family, and receive their letters, but until I win the war you will not leave this castle.' He tried to keep his voice firm, and held his eyes fixed on Errian's, watching for any sudden movement that might suggest an attack. Errian held his gaze steady and his limbs still, so Rymond continued. 'If you require anything during your imprisonment, you only have to ask, and I will do what I can to provide it.'

Errian leant back, scratching his neck thoughtfully and swirling his wine. 'Paper and quill. More wine. A few hours in the yard each day to practise my swordwork. The freedom of the castle.'

He grew bolder with each request. Rymond gave a small smile. 'The first two I can provide. The third, perhaps, though it will only be a wooden training sword. The fourth though... never.'

Errian inclined his head. 'Better than I expected. And do you swear to keep that animal Strovac Sigac away from me? If I see him, it will end in one of our deaths. He caught me unaware before, but next time I mean to kill him. How is his finger? Sweetest meal I ever tasted.'

'Your father wounded him too, but the man is relentless.' Rymond did not reveal his own ambivalence towards the man.

He trusted his guards for the most part, but speaking ill of his finest warrior would make fine gossip for the garrison.

'Shame he did not kill him.'

The next day, Rymond ordered Strovac to seek lodgings in the city. Having Strovac and Errian in the same vicinity for the months of winter was too much to risk. Rymond did not want to lose either one of them, though for all his bluster he was sure that Errian would have come off worse if it had come to blows, with or without swords.

Chieftain Ba'an and his Thrumb had elected to winter in Irith rather than brave the snows and return home. Ba'an had sworn he would not leave until Strovac honoured their agreement to marry his daughter, and Strovac appeared to be in no rush to do so.

Rymond was not wholly sure what to make of Ba'an and his Thrumb. They dressed similarly to Erlanders, but all had drooping moustaches and wore their hair in six long plaits. They spoke accented Erlish almost as well as the natives, but claimed to build their homes in the high trees of Thrumb rather than on the ground. They had not disgraced themselves in battle, but nor had they distinguished themselves; their numbers seemed barely depleted, which might indicate either competence or cowardice. Ba'an himself said little, even when directly questioned by Rymond one day when Rymond invited him for dinner.

'I trust you are satisfied with Strovac as a son-in-law?' Rymond attempted as an opening gambit.

He thought he might have detected a slight quirk of the lip stretch the chieftain's ugly sickle scar, but otherwise Ba'an's face barely moved. 'I have eight daughters. They all must marry someone.'

'And do you hope to find more potential matches during your time in Erland?' Rymond could not believe that the mere prospect of Strovac as a son-in-law had been enough to tempt Ba'an to war.

'I hope to protect my people by keeping you between us and Hessian.' Ba'an did not elaborate further.

Conversing with Ba'an was about as enjoyable as pulling out one's fingernails, and no more illuminating. Rymond did not invite him back.

The Thrumb's presence did not go unnoticed. For many, they were a greater enemy than the East Erlanders, and in the first few weeks there was blood in the snow on more than one occasion between the Thrumb and the men of Irith. Rymond and his mother punished the perpetrators, and those who showed they could not be trusted were ejected from the castle and sent to the city barracks. After the first few examples, men learnt to hold their temper.

Later that month, Rymond's mother summoned him to her chambers, filling him with a sense of foreboding. He had wrested some control back from her by expelling Strovac from the castle, but she retained her grip over the household, and the servants, and most egregiously of all she continued to hold court and adjudicate on disputes, which as Lord of Irith was Rymond's duty by right.

She had held onto the lord's chambers as well, which were far larger than Rymond's own, but removed every trace of her deceased husband, to the point it was impossible to tell a man had ever lived in them at all. There were mirrors on every wall of the antechamber, sweet-smelling candles on every surface, and the ceiling was painted like the night's sky, with hundreds of delicately etched stars. A roaring fire was permanently attended to by a servant, with a pile of chopped wood that was refilled every morning. There was even a hidden door, if one knew where to look, with stairs behind it allowing food to be brought straight up from the kitchens.

She had told him to dress as if it were his coronation, which had confused Rymond, but he had done as she asked. He wore his most polished boots, a doublet of Prindian green, with an emerald necklace on a gold chain, and a black wool cape from his shoulders. He arrived after his mother's appointed time, having elected to stay in his room with a glass of wine, simply for the pleasure of making her wait. He knocked, and entered without giving her a chance to answer; it was his castle after all.

To his surprise, his mother was not alone, and the beauty of the woman standing next to her stopped him in his tracks.

She was young, but tall, of a height with Rymond, with long black hair, cheekbones as sharp and straight as stiletto blades, and big dark green eyes like chips of jade. Heavy furs hung from her shoulders, and a sleek red dress was cinched at her waist, emphasising her graceful figure. She looked up at Rymond, her dark lips unsmiling, her proud chin slightly raised.

'Rymond,' said his mother. Rymond realised he was gawping, and shut his mouth. He turned to close the door behind him, giving himself a chance to regain his composure. Who was this girl?

His mother answered his question. 'I have the pleasure of introducing Princess Helana Sangreal.'

Had Rymond not already been lost for words, that revelation would have done it. 'It is a pleasure to meet you, Lady,' he managed to splutter, through a mouth that seemed simultaneously too wet and too dry. Feeling like an idiot, he stepped forward and bent from the waist to lay a kiss on the back of her hand. 'Welcome to Irith Castle,' he added, as if welcoming his enemy's daughter to his home was the most natural thing in the world.

'And a pleasure to meet you also, Lord.' Her smile was pure icy courtesy.

Breta also smiled, apparently satisfied. 'I have arranged for you to have dinner together in the lower hall. The servants do not know Helana's identity, so take care to be discreet.'

Rymond nodded, but as they bid goodbye to his mother he could not help feeling uneasy. What was his mother's game here? Helana remained cold towards him, making no attempt to converse.

The table in the lower hall had been set for them with the first of what Rymond was told by a servant would be eight courses, pickled herring with onions. Rymond pulled Helana's chair out for her, earning what he thought might be the flicker of a smile.

'Quite the feast, for winter,' she said finally, serving wine and herring for herself.

'Our stores are well stocked,' said Rymond.

She wrinkled her nose. 'Not so much in Merivale, thanks to you.'

'I did what I had to do. Our families are at war.'

'My father won't starve. Others will.'

'When I am king, all will be fed their fair share.' He was past feeling guilty about what he had done on the other side of the river. It was no more than Hessian would have done.

That finally drew a smile from her. 'When you are king?' She laughed. She looked so beautiful Rymond almost forgot to feel insulted. 'I heard my cousin pulled your breeches down and lit your arse on fire.'

There was something pleasing about hearing a young woman of high birth use vulgarity. Rymond poured himself some wine, unable to help the smile playing about his lips. 'Next time I will be more careful. And I have two hostages: I have Errian, and now I have you.'

'You can ask your mother how my father feels about me. I'm no value to you as a prisoner.'

'I wouldn't dare try it. You seem more dangerous than Lord Errian.'

'And better with a blade.' She speared the last herring with her knife, as if to prove the point.

'A mercenary captain of mine is a woman; she's dangerous as well. But if you're not a prisoner, why are you here?'

Helana arched an eyebrow. 'I'm here to save your life.'

'I wasn't aware it needed saving.'

'It will, once winter is over. My uncle beat you when you had three times the men. Once he gathers his army you won't have a prayer.'

'How do you mean to save me? As my champion?'

'As your bride.'

Rymond had been taking a sip of wine, but ended up spluttering it back into his glass. He dabbed at his dripping chin with a cloth, feeling immensely foolish as a pair of servants arrived with a second course of buttered broccoli.

'What do you mean?' he asked when he had finally recovered some dignity. He drank more wine, carefully this time.

'I saw the men coming back from the battle, or rather those that didn't,' she said seriously, setting down her cutlery. 'You'll lose, eventually, but not before the people of Erland have had their lives torn apart. I want peace, Rymond. Even if it means getting married.'

He smirked, recovering some of his composure. 'How romantic.'

She smirked back at him. 'If my father had his way I'd be married to some Imperial with half his teeth missing. Romance is not an option for me.'

Rymond stalled for time, drinking more wine and busying himself with slicing the broccoli stems, while Helana stared serenely, smiling at him with her wine-stained lips, her eyes deep and large enough to drown in. By Eryi, she was beautiful. Would it be madder to say yes, or madder to say no?

'You don't have to decide now,' she said, as if reading his mind. 'I'm here for the winter, at your mother's invitation.'

Rymond was struck by the strangeness of this conversation. He could not recall speaking so honestly with a woman, ever.

Within an hour of meeting him, Helana had proposed marriage, and been entirely open about her motivation.

'I will think on it,' he said carefully. 'Suppose I decide I can win?'

Helana shrugged. 'Then best of luck to you. I'm offering you peace and security, and the chance to avoid facing my uncle again.'

They did not speak of marriage again after that. Rymond steered them on to safer topics, such as hunting, and Helana's impressive wintry journey across Erland. After five more courses, and another bottle of wine, he showed her to her chambers. To his disappointment, she did not invite him in, and he had to settle for a chaste kiss on the cheek.

In his own chambers, he collapsed into his bed with a sigh. He could not deny the girl had charmed him, and she was offering him a way out of this war that involved no risk of dying on the point of Andrick Barrelbreaker's sword. He would still be the heir, and if by some miracle Hessian had a son, he would live with that.

Marriage to her though... There was something in Helana's forthrightness that reminded him of his mother. And that chilled him to his very soul.

CHAPTER 32

Pherri focused upon the birdcage that sat on Theodric's desk, sweat beading on her forehead. This was the third day in a row she had tried to make a bird appear, and still nothing.

She had learnt quickly that there was more to magic than *phisika*. That had come easily. By the end of her first full day with Theodric she had been able to move small objects from one side of the room to the other. She had also learnt its limits: *phisika* could not create matter from nothing, nor be used to achieve what was physically impossible, and it could only affect objects in the magus' immediate vicinity.

Now, though, she was attempting *shadika*, another discipline used to draw something from another reality, or at least the form of it, into their own. Theodric assured her that somewhere, in another world, there was a bird in the cage, and that with sufficient focus she would be able to summon a spectral shadow of it. So far, she had summoned not even as much as a feather. Every day she felt herself getting closer, but every morning was like starting afresh, as if all her progress had dissolved overnight. It was maddening, like trying to understand

Delara's explanation of the endlessness of Eryispek all over again.

When Theodric had first explained *shadika* to her, she had excitedly thought that with one of Da'ri's possessions she might be able to summon a shadow of her old tutor and speak with him, but Theodric said that calling upon the shadows of the dead was absolutely forbidden.

'It is too much for a human mind to bear,' he had told her. 'The ancient magi of the Imperium could do it – there are even tales that they could give the dead corporeal form – but summoning a human mind as well as a human form is beyond our limits, I am afraid. The shadow of your tutor would be a drooling idiot, practically incapable of speech. Birds and dogs are simpler creatures, fortunately for us.'

She had become distracted again. She renewed her focus, straining to the point where her vision vibrated with two images of the cage, as if there were a second one just behind the first. She thought she saw the shadow of a bird flicker, and then it was gone. With a gasp, Pherri collapsed to her knees, breathing heavily.

'Here,' said Theodric, bending down and handing her a plate of food. 'You did well. I thought you had it for a moment.'

'I thought so too,' gasped Pherri. His understanding tone made her failure all the more difficult. Her fingers trembled as she tried to pick up the food. 'What's even the point of it? It seems useless next to *phisika*.'

'Less showy perhaps,' said Theodric easily. 'Many of its secrets are lost to us, but it has its uses: my shadowhounds are *shadika*, and they protect my study without me having to worry about feeding them. It is no surprise you find it difficult: *shadika* requires focus, not will, which is often hard at your age. You are making progress, however it may feel.'

'I never seem to get any better at it.' Pherri did not want his kind words. She wanted to summon a bird into that accursed cage. 'What's the third discipline? Is that any easier?'

Theodric smiled. 'In a sense perhaps. *Inflika* requires only a negligible amount of energy, but you need both focus and will, and it is much harder to practise. It is the act of altering somebody's perception; making them see something, or changing what they believe they have seen.'

'Could you make me believe I had summoned a shadowbird? I might find it easier if I thought I had already done it.'

Theodric's laugh was interrupted by a timid knock at the door. He frowned. 'What is it, Georald?'

'It's a summons for Pherri,' came the muffled reply. 'From her mother.'

Theodric looked at her. 'I am guessing you did not tell your mother about our lessons?'

Pherri bit her lip. 'She never asked.' How had she known to find her here?

'Well, I suspect she has found out. Run along. I'll join you soon.'

Pherri headed downstairs. Her mother's rooms were on the floor below Pherri's, the expectation being that Pherri would be supervised by Delara and have half-a-dozen servants to call upon, but Delara had barely left her room their whole time in Merivale due to her mystery illness. Pherri doubted her mother would mind – it had always been at Pherri's insistence that she had a tutor, rather than at her mother's urging – but she might take a poor view of her instead learning the ways of the magi from Theodric.

Pherri knocked, and her mother's voice beckoned her in. Pherri opened the door, and the grassy scent of fresh tea filled her nostrils. Her mother was at the table, with two others, obscured by the steam rising from the pot. Once her eyes adjusted, Pherri realised they were Orsian and Delara. Her heart sank. She had not thought Orsian would actually tell on her.

'Come and sit with us please, Pherri,' said her mother.

As slowly as she could manage, Pherri walked to the table and took a seat opposite the three of them. Orsian looked troubled. Delara looked furious.

'Did I give you permission to dismiss Delara?' asked her mother.

'I didn't dismiss her, she's been ill!'

'Deceit!' barked Delara. 'You told me you would read in the library until I recovered.'

'What difference does it make?' said Pherri, stung by the accusation. Delara did not seem particularly ill now. 'I didn't break any rules.'

'Even so,' said her mother, 'Orsian has told me of your new tutor, and it is not appropriate.'

Pherri shot a dirty look at Orsian, who at least had the good grace to look ashamed. 'But I want to learn!' she pleaded. 'Theodric says I can be a magus. That's what I want.'

Delara coughed dismissively. She did look slightly unwell, Pherri thought, her skin as pale and worn as wrinkled parchment. 'You cannot be the judge of what you want. You are too young to make that decision. Had I known that's what you were doing I would have resumed your lessons straight away and told that wizard to leave you alone.'

'But you didn't know,' said Viratia icily. 'And that is part of the problem. I will discipline my own daughter, Delara.'

'You do not understand the danger, Lady,' said Delara, not to be diverted. 'Magic corrupts all that it touches. You should send her away from this place; that magus of the king's is not to be trusted.'

Pherri was mystified. What could Delara have against Theodric?

Viratia sighed. 'Delara has said she will return to Violet

Hall with you, and I agree that would be for the best. You will leave as soon as the snow clears, but until then you are to stay away from Lord Theodric.'

'But that's not fair!' said Orsian. 'I only wanted Pherri to be safe; you don't have to send her away.'

Pherri was shocked into silence. Theodric had opened a new way of life to her, a new way of thinking about the world, and it was being ripped away. There was no point even arguing; once her mother had set her mind to something she did not change it. She wanted to cry.

There was a sudden knock at the door, making all of them jump. It was not the apologetic tap-tap of a servant bringing refreshments, but a forceful rap that rattled the handle, demanding admission. Viratia put her tea down angrily, spilling pools of it onto her saucer. 'Who could that be?' She rose and walked to the door, and opened it to reveal Theodric, standing calmly, a little half-smile on his face.

'You are not wanted, wizard,' said Delara with a scowl. 'Pherri is leaving.'

Theodric stared back at her curiously. 'And what do you know of wizards, whoever you are?'

'Enough.'

'Enough to brew this, you mean.' Theodric lifted a jar of something: the potion Delara had given Pherri that she kept under her bed.

Delara grunted dismissively. 'That's a sleeping draught. Lady Viratia gave me permission to brew it for Pherri after she had nightmares.'

'And it is not your concern, Lord Theodric,' said Viratia, distaste plain on her face. 'Pherri will return to Violet Hall tomorrow. Whatever you have been filling her head with, you can stop.'

Theodric smiled, as if he had not heard her, and raised the jar to his nose. 'And do your sleeping draughts usually contain bogroot?' He coughed. 'It's the most awful stench, if you know it's there.'

'What's bogroot?' asked Pherri. She had thought Theodric might save her with some clever argument. Why was he talking about bogroot, whatever that was?

'A common herb,' said Delara. 'It brings a restful sleep.'

'In small quantities.' Theodric walked to the table and slammed the jar down in front of her. 'There is enough bogroot in there to fell a horse. Or, to blow the magic right out of somebody.'

'What are you talking about?' said Viratia, looking at the jar. She lifted it to her lips and gagged. 'That does smell foul.'

'This woman has been plying your daughter with a herb to deaden her to other worlds,' said Theodric, with a flourish, his eyes trained on Delara. 'It made no sense to me. The few students I have had in the past were strongest in the morning, when they were rested. But Pherri's focus improves throughout the day, and then every morning it is as though she has gone backwards. Now I know why.'

'Nonsense,' spat Delara. 'That's a perfectly normal dose of bogroot.'

'You tried to poison my sister?' said Orsian, an angry blush on his cheeks, rising from his chair and resting a hand on his sword hilt. 'What sort of tutor are you?'

'That's enough, Orsian,' said Viratia sharply. 'If you draw that sword I will have you sent back to Violet Hall as well. Delara, I demand you explain to me what is going on. And that is not just a sleeping draught, so do not lie to me.'

Pherri stared in confusion at Delara. By the look on her face, what Theodric said must be true. What had she been drinking for all these months? And why?

'It was for her own good,' said Delara, her weathered face set in defiance. She levered herself slowly to her feet with her cane, shuffled towards the window, and stared towards the endless shadow of Eryispek, shrouded in a blanket of snow and mist. 'Have you ever been on the Mountain, Lord Theodric?'

'I confess I have not.'

'The Mountain is the centre of every living being on this earth. From the lowest larvae to the highest king. If you were to stand upon its slope, you would live through the rise and fall of empires, whole centuries in the flicker of a moment, as easily as you might blink your eye. My people remember, but you lowlanders forget. My great-grandmother—'

'Your people?' interrupted Viratia sharply. 'You told me you were a servant to the Lord of Basseton!'

'I never told you that.' Delara's eyes twinkled maliciously. 'Though perhaps I was not honest with your son.'

'You're one of the Lutums,' said Pherri, her mouth half-hanging open. She felt a fool for not seeing it before: Delara's poor clothes; her peculiar reading of Erland's history; her hatred for the Adrari and Eryi. None of it had made any sense.

'My great-grandmother could see droughts and famines years before they happened,' Delara continued. 'She was married into the lord's family in the hope that she would give him children with the gift. After she died, people watched her descendants, looking for any sign of the gift in them.

'When I was twelve, I showed. I was married that same week, to a man whose mother had been a famed seer. Didn't matter that I was royal by birth, a daughter of the line of the old kings on the Mountain. All my father wanted was grandchildren who could serve him with predictions and prophecies. Preferably boys, so he could name one his heir. My husband was four times my age, with a face like a sack of turnips and about as clever.

'Once we were wed he set to sticking me every chance he got. But every child either died inside me or during my labour. After my eighth pregnancy failed, he finally died, and I was left alone. I was not twenty summers old and already an old maid, used up and ill-fated. Eager young wives would come and see for a telling of their child, and would-be warriors looking for a vision of their first foray into the White. Such was my life for half a century, a curiosity for the bored and vain and foolish, until Gelick Whitedoe and his foolish prophecies.

'Magic is a curse, and when Pherri told me of her dreams I recognised the signs. I did it to save her from a life of loneliness and regret. That is all you offer her, wizard.'

Theodric had kept his eyes trained on Delara all the while, though her own eyes never left Eryispek. The room was deathly still.

'And since coming to Piperskeep, you have kept to your rooms, for fear of being discovered by me,' said Theodric. 'Are we to believe then, that you escaped the Lutums and disguised yourself to prevent Pherri becoming a magus? How could you have known?'

'I didn't. I did it to escape Gelick Whitedoe. I went to Basseton with the rest of them, and while they were looting and killing, I hid myself. I knew Merivale would respond, so I disguised myself in servants' clothes. It was pure chance that led me to you and Pherri, but when I learnt of her dreams I knew I had to act.' She looked to Pherri. 'I did it for your sake, child.'

Viratia turned on Delara, her eyes cold and furious. 'You are not to speak to my children. Ever. I welcomed you into my home, and you repaid me by lying and poisoning my child. I ought to gut you, witch.' She looked at Theodric. 'Will Pherri live?'

Pherri's heart lurched. Surely Delara would not have put her life in danger?

Theodric's smile reassured her. 'Her life was never in danger, and if she stops taking it immediately, she will suffer no long-term effects. It has temporarily dulled Pherri's connection to other worlds, but that will return. Even at this dose, it would have been months before the poison was sufficiently concentrated to deaden it completely.'

Viratia nodded, apparently satisfied. 'Delara, you are banished from my service. You have until sunset to leave Merivale. Be thankful you did no lasting harm to Pherri. If Lord Theodric is wrong, I will hunt you down and kill you myself.'

Her mother's tone left Pherri in no doubt that she meant it, but Delara showed no fear. 'As you wish, Lady,' she said, her proud chin raised stubbornly. 'Let the wizard have her.' She hobbled towards the door.

'Delara,' Theodric called just as she reached the handle. 'Where did the Lutums go? Why did you leave?'

The mountain-woman turned. 'I told you: to escape Gelick Whitedoe. He may think himself a prophet, but he does not understand the forces he is meddling with. They have gone up the Mountain. Where else could they go?' She looked to Pherri, and Pherri could not tell whether the look in her eye was sad or triumphant. 'I tried to stop it, Pherri. Remember that.' She left, without a backward glance.

Viratia looked down at the pungent jar. 'Orsian, get that foul potion out of my sight. Pour it away into the snow. I have misjudged you, Lord Theodric,' she said, gesturing for him to sit. 'And I apologise. How can I repay you?'

'You can allow me to tutor Pherri.'

Viratia looked at him quizzically, and Pherri waited with bated breath. If she did not agree now, after Theodric had uncovered Delara's treachery, she would never agree. Half of her still expected to be sent back to Merivale.

After what felt like an age, Viratia knelt by Pherri's chair, and reached out a hand to push Pherri's haystack-yellow hair back from her eyes. 'Pherri, my hopes for you were always much of a muchness, marriage and grandchildren, like every mother. Then when you were born there was something extraordinary about you. So quiet and slow to cry. You spoke later than either

Errian or Orsian, but you devoured books, though nobody ever taught you to read, and then one day the words just came pouring out of you, like you had prepared a list of questions and decided that was the day you must have answers. It was too much for me, so I took on tutors who could sate your curiosity.

'I wondered if I was dooming you to a life of disappointment. Your father... it would never cross his mind to deny me my freedom, but as we have just heard, not all women are so lucky. For you, a small life might have been the most acute cruelty, but for most women that is all there is.

'And yet, despite Delara's crime, there is some truth in what she said. The magi of the Imperium came to a sad end, and stories of magic in Erland are little better. Men and women will fear you, lords and kings desire you.

'I leave this choice to you, Pherri. You do not need to decide now, and you can always change your mind. Neither answer will disappoint me.' Tenderly, she wiped a tear that fell from Pherri's eye.

Pherri sniffed. She had already known what she wanted, and Delara's warning had not swayed her. For all her lies, perhaps the old woman really had sought to help, but Pherri had seen too much to go back. She thought of Da'ri. If he had been in her place she had no doubt what his decision would have been. Da'ri had lived for knowledge, knowledge for its own sake.

She wrapped her arms around her mother's neck, burying her face in her chest and breathing in the smell of her perfume. 'I want to learn,' she said. 'Thank you.'

CHAPTER 33

'Good morning, cousin.'

Errian waved to her as he approached. He did not look much the worse for his imprisonment, Helana thought. Though he would not be joining them today, he was still dressed for the hunt, the illusion destroyed only by the six guards dogging his steps, keeping their eyes alertly upon him, and their hands close to their swords.

'I'm sorry you won't be able to join us,' said Helana. 'Next time, perhaps?'

Errian scoffed. 'I doubt it. These Westerners are too afraid of me to let me near a horse or a hunting bow. See how these six follow me, like goslings and a mother goose.' The guards behind him shifted uncomfortably.

Helana laughed. Captivity had not robbed Errian of his spirit. 'I'll bring some venison back for you.'

The last few days had seen the snow around Irith begin to thaw, and for the bored nobles of Irith that meant it was time to hunt. Their woods were not as wild nor as thick as Merivale's, but Rymond assured her that there was good hunting to be had.

Helana hoped for a boar; she still smarted from when Creya had killed the last one.

Rymond would lead their party, and with him would come the master-at-arms Adfric, his friends Will and Dom, some minor local lordlings, and to Helana's surprise the taciturn Chieftain Ba'an, draped in a wolf pelt and with a horn the size of a man's forearm hanging from his neck. Helana kept her distance from him. It was he who had killed Jarhick. She glared at the back of his head, wondering what it would look like with a hunting spear buried in it.

She felt a flash of anger towards Rymond. He had ensured that Strovac Sigac was not present. He might have done the same with Count Ba'an for her sake.

There was plenty to like about her would-be husband – he was clever and courteous; he read books, unlike most Erland lords, usually accounts of ancient kings of the Old Line; there were moments when he seemed to care for the people he ruled, at least compared to Hessian; she enjoyed his company in small doses – but he was just so bloodless and *vain*. For all his faults, Orsian was more of a man; he knew what it was to work hard, to make sacrifices. Rymond just moved through the world without a care, like it owed him something. Even going to war he did not seem to take entirely seriously, as if the violence could not touch him. What would he have done if Jarhick had not died? Probably just spent the rest of his life drinking and whoring his way around Irith. Then there was how he had spoken about the burning of the East Erland harvest, as if it had been unavoidable, and not an awful crime that could condemn hundreds to starvation.

She had wracked her mind for some other way to bring peace. If only Rymond had a sister they might have married Errian to. Rymond seemed to like her at least, but if he actually asked her to marry him, could she find the courage to say yes?

A low cough alerted her to a presence at her shoulder.

Helana turned, and recoiled as the weathered face of Chieftain Ba'an stared back at her. She could have sworn he was in front of her.

'Princess.' He inclined his head respectfully. 'I am sorry, about your brother.'

For a moment, Helana was too appalled to reply. Her mouth opened, yet no sound came out, as a white-hot anger thundered in her ears. Her finger itched for the knife at her belt.

'His death was not my doing, I swear.'

'You mean you did not wield the blade yourself?' she replied scornfully. 'Spare me. If my cousin Errian were still here he would gut you like the swine you are.'

Ba'an barely reacted, his broad, windburnt face as implacable as old oak. 'You misunderstand me. But we will speak again.' He turned his horse away.

Helana watched him leave, more confused now than she was angry. He had seemed sincere enough, but for him to deny involvement in Jarhick's death was absurd. The Thrumb had started the war with their raiding, and Jarhick had died at their hands.

'Shall we?' said Rymond, pulling his horse up next to hers, making Helana jump.

The Lord of Irith did cut a fine figure on a horse, she had to admit. His mount was as slim and golden as its rider, the cold had brought some colour to his pale cheeks, and his blue eyes shimmered in the snow like frozen pools. 'I've been ready for half an hour,' she said. 'It's your entourage that's keeping us. Do you usually bring half the castle with you when you hunt?' She nodded behind them, where in addition to the hunters was an extensive escort of young men, with spare mounts, food, and hunting spears. Rymond's friends were already passing a wine-skin between themselves.

Rymond chuckled. 'Sorry to have kept you waiting, Lady. Nobody wants to miss this.'

They rode out of the city, where the walls gave way to farms and countryside. Helana touched the bow and spear that hung from her back. It was a reassuring feeling; she had not held a weapon since that day with Creya. Mitra brayed restlessly, so Helana let her have her head, and she galloped away from their party towards the woodland on the horizon, ignoring the shouts of her companions, and savouring the breeze in her hair.

She was surprised to hear hoofbeats gaining on her, and turned around to see Rymond closing the distance between them. He guided his horse next to her, breathing hard.

'I did not take you for a horseman,' she called over the beating hooves.

'It's a good horse,' he replied, grinning. 'Shall we slow down though?'

Helana flashed him a wicked smile. 'If you can catch me.' She dug her heels into Mitra's flanks and urged her onward, daring Rymond to follow.

They were almost at the woods now, but Helana did not stop. She coaxed Mitra on into the trees, keeping herself flat against the mare's neck to avoid low-hanging branches.

Where the trees grew thicker, she pulled hard at the reins, bringing Mitra to a skidding halt. She turned back the way she had come, enjoying the warmth of her sweat down her back, looking for Rymond.

She gave a satisfied smile to see he had followed her, but had been unable to keep up. He brought his mount to her at a more sedate pace.

'You ride like a demon, Lady.'

'It is in my blood,' she said. 'The ancient Meridivals lived almost their whole lives in the saddle.'

'I wouldn't mention that in these parts. There are old men in the taverns who still speak of it like they fought the Meridivals themselves.'

'If they want to boast of being on the losing side, let them. The old men of East Erland fought real battles.'

'Perhaps I should try and tempt them into my army. I could use the experience.' He looked behind him, where the rest of their party were still a long way back. 'We should wait for them before we go further.'

'And let them scare everything away with that racket? You can wait if you want; I'm going hunting.' Helana urged Mitra forward. Rymond frowned, but nevertheless followed, to her slight irritation. She would have been happy enough hunting alone.

The woods were cold and quiet, and the trees bare, their branches reaching for the sky like grasping fingers. A lonely bird sang, and from somewhere came the pattering of tiny feet as an animal fled up a tree away from them.

'We should leave the horses,' said Helana, as Mitra snorted. 'They'll make too much noise for us to catch anything.'

Rymond looked at her, perplexed. 'What if we have to chase a stag?'

'Do you see any stags? We'll be lucky to find a rabbit. Some wood you've got here.'

'I promise you, if you're patient—'

'I never learnt patience.' Helana threw her spear to the ground and dismounted, then led Mitra and hitched her to an oak tree.

Rymond did the same, shaking his head. 'They'll ride right past us.' They could hear the rest of their party shouting and stomping somewhere behind them.

Helana ignored the sound, and looked for where the under-growth was thickest. 'That way,' she said, seizing her spear and heading in that direction.

She crept like Creya had taught her, checking her way for any dead wood or detritus before moving her feet, and watching her clothes and spear did not snag on anything. Rymond moved lightly behind her, breathing shallowly and following her footsteps.

As they went deeper, the forest seemed to liven around them. The birdsong faded, but the bushes and thickets that still held their leaves seemed to thrum with life. More than once, Helana heard rustling around her feet. The slate-grey sky shrank to small windows between the branches. Helana knew she was no tracker, but she had picked up bits of the art from Creya. She smelt at the air, and checked for droppings and loose fur.

When they were some way in, a patch of wiry, muddy-brown hair caught her eye, snagged on the limb of a shrub at around waist height. She examined it, and lowered her head for a sniff. It was wet. A pungent odour of damp and foul dung filled her nostrils.

Helana's heart quickened. She touched her sheathed knife, and tightened her grip on the spear. 'A boar came this way,' she whispered to Rymond behind her.

He looked alarmed. 'A boar? We should find the others.'

Helana shook her head. 'What for? They'll only frighten it away. We should go quietly.'

'We can't hunt a boar with two people. What if there's more than one?'

'Maybe you can't. I can. Stay here if you want.' Helana turned away, and after a moment heard Rymond sigh and follow her. She rolled her eyes. There was naught so predictable as a man's pride.

As they went deeper, the way sloped downwards and grew muddier. Helana moved more cautiously, wary that her feet did not slip from beneath her. The air smelt like the fur had. Their way led them down, towards a gloomy dell.

Helana saw it just as Rymond did. 'There,' he said, unnecessarily, pointing between the trees to a patch of churned-up mud. A large dark shape shifted, and Helana glimpsed the unmistakable features of a boar. If she was any judge, it was even bigger than the one she had hunted with Creya. The animal was rubbing itself against a tree, shaking the whole thing with its vast weight, snorting.

Helana reached carefully for her bow, trying not to make a sound, and drew an arrow. Only Rymond's hand on her arm stopped her.

'We should get closer,' he whispered. 'You won't kill it at this range.'

'You don't know that,' hissed Helana, irritated with him for interrupting her shot. 'Fine, we'll get closer, but if it sees us, it's your fault.'

They crept down slowly, while the boar continued rubbing against the tree, oblivious. Where the ground dropped sharply into the dell, they stopped, barely twenty yards from their quarry. The smell was like a privy somebody had forgotten to clean for a week.

'Close enough for you?' whispered Helana. She had a clear shot from here. She was going to put an arrow right through the boar's eye.

Rymond was already drawing his bow.

'What are you doing?' she hissed. 'My tracking, my shot.'

'I just want to be ready if you miss.'

'I won't miss.' He would never have even suggested it if she were a man. 'Get your horn ready; we'll need the others to carry that thing out of here.' She squared her feet side-on, awkwardly on the muddy, sloping ground, fitted an arrow to her bow, and drew it back. She breathed out, as Creya had taught her, ready to release.

Then the whole forest seemed to give way beneath her.

Her front foot slipped in the mud, and suddenly she was falling. Her bow jumped upwards, and the arrow shot harmlessly off into the trees. Panicked, she tried to get her feet underneath her, but the ground just kept moving. She reached for Rymond, anything to grab onto, and clutched only at air.

Helana slid down the slope on her back, covering her clothes in mud, all the way to the boar's swampy wallowing ground. She fell over a sharp edge and landed with a thud.

As little as ten yards away, the boar stopped rubbing against the tree. It fixed her with a stare, eyeing her curiously with its beady yellow eyes.

Helana stared back, open-mouthed. She had lost her bow during the fall, and had somehow dropped her spear as well. To her relief, her knife still hung from her belt, so she reached for it, slowly.

Something moved over to her right.

A second shape, smaller than the first, and Helana's breath caught in her throat. There was another boar. A female, but still twice her weight. It came sleepily to its feet, grunting gutturally, deep in its throat, and its mate joined in.

Helana's blood ran cold. She wanted to turn and run, but couldn't take her eyes off them. The female grunted angrily, staring and stomping a hoof on the ground. As Helana unsheathed her knife, it charged.

Helana flashed back to the forest outside Merivale, half-expecting Creya to burst from the trees and save her, but nobody was coming this time. She froze, terror pulsing through her veins.

An arrow burred through the air and caught the boar in the shoulder.

It squealed in pain, slowing its charge and veering in agony away from Helana. A second arrow flew, and missed, sticking in the ground a few feet away.

On instinct, Helana leapt out to the side, as from nowhere the male gored at where her abdomen would have been a moment before. It turned clumsily, snorting hot breath from its nostrils, ready for a second charge.

Rymond leapt between her and the boar, waving his spear wildly in front of him. 'Back, back!'

The boar paid him no heed. It lowered its head and charged, faster than Helana would have believed possible.

The point of Rymond's spear caught its neck, drawing a spurt of black blood. The boar squealed, but the momentum of its charge drove it forward, and its head smashed into Rymond's thigh, with a sickening crash that echoed around the forest. He fell back with a scream, spinning, knocking Helana to the ground with him. He landed on top of her, driving the breath from her body.

From the ground, Helana looked around frantically for the boars. The one Rymond had speared had collapsed, breathing shallowly, its lifeblood gushing out from the wound in its neck. The female was nowhere to be seen. Relief flooded through her.

She looked up, ready to tell Rymond to get the fuck off her, and found his piercing blue eyes staring straight back.

'I thought you were dead,' he gasped, his eyes wild, his breath hot against her nose. She stared up at him. He smelt of sweat and smokesticks. 'Are you all right?'

'Yes, fine.' There was something wet on her hip. She looked down. Blood was seeping through her trousers. But she hadn't been hit, had she? She looked again. Rymond's blood, coursing from where the boar had gored him in the leg. 'You're bleeding,' she said, stupidly.

Fear flashed in his eyes, and he rolled off her. Blood was soaking into his clothes and furs at alarming speed.

'Shit, sit down.' Helana helped him to a tree, and he slumped against it. With her knife she cut away his clothes, and found the wound. The boar's tusk had torn a long, deep gash in his thigh.

'I told you there might be two,' he said, with a weak smile.

Helana shushed him. 'You need to stay still, don't talk.' Her head and heart were pounding. She needed to do something, fast. Rymond let out a moan of pain as she pressed his hand to the wound. 'Keep the pressure on.' The clothes she had torn away were soaked in blood, so she cut a strip from her sleeve to form a tourniquet, and bound it tightly about his thigh, trying not to look.

Rymond winced. 'If you wanted to get me naked—'

'Shut up, idiot.' She slapped him on the arm. 'By the Norhai, you could have been killed. Why didn't you just stick to the bow?'

'Some thanks I get for saving your life. I thought I was doing pretty well until it gored me.'

'Some thanks I'll get if you die. Think you can blow that horn? I can't carry you back myself.'

'Probably not; my head is spinning.'

Even when his life was at stake he could not help being lazy. With a sigh, Helana reached up to take the horn from his neck, and before she knew what was happening, Rymond seized her face and kissed her.

She felt a moment of outrage, ready to slap him across the cheek, wounded or not, but his lips were like velvet, and her body responded against her will, kissing him back forcefully. Time seemed to stop. The earth and the trees spun, as if she were drunk.

Coming to her senses, Helana pushed him away, and sat up, wiping her mouth. 'What the fuck are you doing?'

He grinned, or grimaced. His skin was translucently pale, and there was a sheen of sweat on his skin. 'I didn't want to die without kissing you.'

CHAPTER 34

'Fight me, you shitspawn!'

Orsian raised his shield just in time to block the wild over-hand swing aimed for his head. The weight behind it shook his arm all the way to the shoulder and forced him back a step. A second opponent stabbed at him from the side, but Orsian checked the blow on his sword and on his backstroke rang the man's helmet like a bell. He spun away, narrowly dodging a thrust that with sharpened steel would have split his abdomen open.

He stepped back quickly, putting some distance between him and his opponents. They were young men from the quarries, ox-strong and built like boulders, compelled to sign up by the promise of three meals a day. It had been two of them at first, and now he could beat two consistently it was three. Naeem insisted that a man of the *Hymeriker* was a match for five ordinary men.

Orsian wiped the sweat from his brow and reset his stance. This trio had probably barely held a sword until this winter, but they were the three best of the boys who had answered the king's summons for new warriors, and by their faces were eager to prove themselves.

The one whose helmet he had struck was the smallest, of a height with Orsian and just as broad. There was blood trickling down the side of his face. Not waiting for his fellows, he rushed towards Orsian with a roar.

Orsian did not even bother with his sword. He feinted with it, then at the last moment switched his stance and smashed his shield into his opponent's head, putting every drop of his anger into it. Helana had left, Pherri would barely speak to him, and the king was a madman, and nothing better quelled the disgust he felt for himself than smashing somebody in the face.

He heard the boy's nose break with a crack and a cry, and then the other two were on him, swinging their swords together. He spun between their blades and swept one's feet from beneath him, sending him sprawling into the snow, and followed with a kick to his hand that sent his sword flying across the yard.

As the third turned with a hurried thrust, Orsian dodged, setting him off-balance, and then Orsian was on him. He let his sword and shield drop, and leapt at him, driving him to the ground in a barrage of punches to his chest and head.

It took both Burik and Derik to drag him off, by which time the older boy was curled up in a ball whimpering, his sword lying useless in the snow.

'By Eryi, Orsian!' His father was there almost immediately, anger and confusion written across his face. 'He's just a boy. We're supposed to be training them, not killing them.'

'Errian used to beat me three times as bad as that,' he spat, 'and you never did a damn thing.' The words were out of his mouth before he could stop himself. He had never spoken back to his father before. Half the yard was staring.

If his father was shocked he gave no sign of it. He looked

down at him, judging silently. 'You're done for today,' he said finally. 'Get out of my sight. Come back when you learn some Norhai-cursed self-control.'

Orsian stalked away, snow crunching under his boots and fresh fall melting on his face, mingling with his sweat. He threw down his helmet and stalked back to the keep.

He returned to his room and tore off his armour, flinging it recklessly to the floor piece by piece. This wasn't how it was supposed to be. He had returned a hero, and Helana had run away. He had tried to protect his sister, and she had scorned him. Since the battle it felt like everything had gone wrong.

He stood there, letting the anger drain out of him, leaving behind only a feeling of stupidity. The boy had not deserved that. Nor had Orsian's father.

He needed to talk to someone, and the only person who might be able to help him was Pherri, if he could get her to speak with him. By Eryi, he would just have to make her. He changed quickly, and set out in the direction of her chamber.

He knocked forcefully, and heard Pherri hurrying to open the door.

'Oh, it's you,' she said as she opened it, obviously disappointed. 'I thought you might be Theodric.'

'No, just me. I'm here to apologise again, if you're ready to accept it.'

Reluctantly, she held the door open for him. 'Theodric says I should forgive you. He said you were only doing what you thought was best for me.'

'I really was! And at least we found out Delara was poisoning you... Anyway, I'm sorry, really sorry.'

'Apology accepted.' She smiled at him, and reached up for a hug. Orsian embraced her.

'Why aren't you out practising in the yard?' she asked, taking a seat at the window while Orsian slumped onto the edge of her bed.

'I may have attacked somebody.'

Pherri sniffed. 'I thought that was the whole point.'

'Father didn't think so on this occasion. I got angry. It was stupid.'

'Because of Helana?'

Orsian sat bolt upright. 'What about Helana?'

Pherri smirked at him. 'A servant told me they heard you arguing with her before she escaped. They thought you had a bit of a thing for each other.'

He felt a blush rising on his cheeks. 'You're too young to think about such things. And you can't trust everything servants tell you.'

'Theodric said you can learn a lot from speaking to servants. They see far more of Piperskeep than the rest of us.'

That was hard to deny. How far in the castle had the gossip spread? 'Well, yes, it might be a bit about her. I thought...' He sighed. 'Never mind what I thought. She's gone, and I don't know where she is. I still don't understand why she left.'

'Theodric says she was unhappy.'

'Is there anything Theodric doesn't have an opinion on?'

'Probably not,' said Pherri happily. 'He's impossibly clever. He hates that he can't find Helana. He could have before. The king's been upset with him.'

'It doesn't take much to upset the king.'

'Or to make you angry, apparently.'

Orsian sighed, downcast. 'I shouldn't have let her leave,' he bemoaned. 'I thought... I don't know what I thought. I suppose I thought things would be different now I've been in a battle, but all I keep asking myself is what the point of it was. The king is...' He hesitated. 'Hessian is Hessian, and half the city is starving. But all I can do is keep fighting. What else is there?'

'A whole world.' She threw a book onto the bed next to him. He read the title: *Sea Stories*, by Captain Shurgill. 'Try this. He was the captain of a trading vessel out of Cliffark half a century ago. He went all over the world, from the Imperium to the edge of the Silent Sea. It might expand your horizons.'

Orsian picked it up and examined it. 'I won't be going to sea any time soon,' he said, turning the pages. 'Father says going to sea was some of the most miserable weeks of his life. Nothing to eat, and if you fall in your armour will drag you under, so in battle you've got the choice between drowning and getting stabbed. Land battles are treacherous enough.' He rose to pour them each a cup of heavily watered wine, and spared a glance out of the window. The snow was coming down in sheets now, and he could feel the wind's icy breath through the thin gaps at the edge of the glass. 'How are lessons with Theodric going?'

'Better since he stopped Delara poisoning me, but not very well in truth.' Pherri sighed. 'I've got *phisika*, but I can't do *shadika* or *inflika* to save my life. Theodric says I'm still too young to focus properly.'

'I don't even know what any of that means,' said Orsian with a shrug. 'I hope it's nothing dangerous.'

From the highest tower of Piperskeep, the noon bells began to chime, twelve notes from highest to lowest. 'Fiddlesticks,' said Pherri, rising in a hurry and rushing to gather her cloak. 'I'm supposed to have a lesson with Theodric. I'll see you later; I'm glad we're friends again.' She kissed Orsian quickly on the cheek and ran out, leaving him to bemusedly traipse after her, faced with the prospect of finding something to do with himself for the afternoon.

He was barely halfway back to his room when a harassed-looking servant approached him in a hurry. 'I've been looking for you everywhere, Lord,' he said breathlessly. 'King Hessian desires your presence in his solar. Immediately.' He gave Orsian no chance to reply before he hurried off again.

Orsian stared after him, slightly horrified. Was his father sending him to the king for punishment? Or what if Hessian was going to ask him about Helana? He cursed under his breath. A few months ago he would have given everything for Hessian to notice him; now he just wanted to stay as far away from him as possible. Hopefully he was still in a good mood about the prospect of an heir.

He climbed the king's tower, with a sinking feeling in his stomach, and nodded to the two guards before proceeding inside. His father was sitting with Hessian, leaning over the Erland-shaped table with their heads together in discussion.

'...the man bargains like a hag with a herring,' Hessian was grumbling. 'An Imperial enclave in Merivale! He asks too much. I will not feed Merivale by selling the kingdom to the Imperium.' He looked up at the intrusion. 'Orsian!' The king beckoned him forward enthusiastically. 'We were about to discuss the plan for spring.'

Orsian blinked in surprise. This was the last thing he had expected.

'I want you more involved,' said his father gruffly. 'You proved yourself last time, don't think I didn't notice. But if you ever do something like you did today again, you can stay at Merivale. I can't have a *hymerika* who attacks his own side.'

'What?' Orsian exclaimed. His father had said '*hymerika*'. A huge grin broke out across his face. 'Do you mean it?'

Hessian laughed. 'You've made the boy's day, Andrick.'

'It's long overdue. He saved us.'

Orsian flexed his hand, feeling the fresh skin stretch where his palm had been burnt. It had been worth it. *Hymerika*. Finally. 'Am I the youngest ever?' He was younger than Errian had been.

Hessian laughed again. 'I doubt it. Maybe in the last century. I'll have the librarian check. I assume you accept then?'

Orsian nodded mutely, all his misgivings about Hessian forgotten. *Hymerika*.

'Good. The formalities then, no sense in waiting. Andrick, your sword.'

With a hiss of metal on leather Andrick unsheathed and passed his sword to Hessian. Orsian fell to a knee before him, and Hessian rested the flat side of the blade against the crown of his head. 'Orsian, son of Andrick. I charge you to defend your king, to obey all those of the Blood, and to give your life for theirs if necessary.'

It was all happening so fast. The doubts he had expressed to Pherri were a distant memory. 'I accept this burden, my King,' said Orsian, repeating the words he had known since he was a child.

'Rise, then, as one of the *Hymeriker*.'

Orsian stood, feeling ten times taller. His father took back the sword and clapped Orsian on the shoulder, while Hessian poured them ruby-red wine from a flagon.

'To Orsian,' said the king. '*Hymerika*.'

Orsian drank, grapes bursting like fire on his tongue.

'You earnt this, Orsian,' said his father. 'And you know what you can't do, as one of the *Hymeriker*?'

Orsian nodded. 'Fight in the yard with common soldiers.'

'You can fight them if I command you to. Just remember whose side they're on, and who the true enemy is. Now, come and look at this map.'

Orsian joined him at the table, feeling giddy. Pherri could keep her sea stories, and Helana could hide in Cliffark for as long as she pleased. He was a *hymerika* now, a true warrior.

'Have you been to Whitewater?' asked his father, pointing to the north, where the Pale River flowed into the sea.

Orsian shook his head.

'It's built across two sides of the river, joined by a bridge.' He pointed to the western side, where a fortress was marked. 'Whitewater Motte is built in the old style, just a wooden wall

with a simple stone bailey inside. Lord Darlton has declared for
Rymond Prindian, which is no surprise given they're cousins.'

'He's my cousin too, the treacherous weasel,' added
Hessian.

'We will strike on the first day of spring,' said Andrick.
'We'll capture the castle and take the family captive. At the
same time, we'll send a small force to hold Halord's Bridge. If
Prindian rides to meet us at Whitewater we'll fight him, on our
choice of ground. If not, we'll press into the west and fall upon
Irith.'

'You mean to trade the Darltons for Errian,' Orsian
observed.

Andrick nodded. 'Once we have your brother back, we are
free to win this war. The Darltons are kin to half of West
Erland; if Prindian refuses us, those lords will revolt.'

'How many men do we have?'

'Eighteen thousand, by spring. Three thousand should hold
Halord's Bridge.'

Orsian nodded. He was not thrilled by the prospect of Errian's return, but perhaps now Orsian was a *hymerika* and Errian
had got himself captured he would show more humility. 'And
the Prindians have less than us?'

'Around the same. Slightly fewer, perhaps.'

'Traitors all,' spat Hessian, spraying wine from his lips
across the table. 'I want Prindian and Sigac dragged before me
in chains, Andrick. I'll put Prindian in the same cell his brother
died in. You can kill the rest.'

Orsian kept his eyes upon the map. Hessian's bloodlust
troubled him; the West Erlanders were their brothers, they
would need to make peace with them once this war was over.
That was meant to be the whole aim; holding the country
together to resist the Imperium. He remembered Helana's
words: '*My father wants to rule all of Erland because it suits*

him.' He had never been surer of that than right now. His head itched where Hessian had placed his sword. Should he have refused? He could never have refused.

Andrick gave a tight nod. 'The Prindian defeat will be absolute, my King. I give you my word.'

CHAPTER 35

Tansa pulled her thin blanket around her shoulders again, trying to stop her teeth chattering, and edged as close to their small fire as she dared. She had relented in the end, about a fire. The risk of freezing to death this winter had been a far greater concern than the risk of being discovered.

They still shared the same room on the top floor of the empty house. It was comfortable, but it had begun to smell, and all three of them were losing patience with their confinement. Tansa went out occasionally to buy food, keeping her hood low over her face and watching for Imperials. In a city that was slowly freezing, she looked no different to any other Merivalian, shuffling through the snowy streets in search of bread or any other food she could get her hands on.

Nearly three months had passed since her flight from the Witch's Abyss and the Imperials. Cag had grudgingly accepted their necessary imprisonment, but the same could not be said of Tam. On countless occasions now, he had tried to sneak out at night, and on Tansa's command Cag had bodily restrained him to prevent him doing so. Tam had grown so wild last time he had caught Cag in the nose with his fist, and Tansa had had to set the broken bone. That at least had shamed Tam into accepting his fate.

Their fortune was down to a few coins now. The city was not just freezing, but starving; the price of bread had increased fivefold, and there were armed guards at the door of anywhere selling food. Some days they could get none at all, and would spend the evening cold and hungry, snapping at one another. From what she had seen, it was no better for most of the city. In the streets, some men sold cooked rats from filthy braziers, their tails as hard and stiff as fire pokers, and in the alleys, others sold a brown stew which only a fool would have asked the contents of. Tansa had not sunk so low, fortunately.

She had spent what little funds remained booking a return journey to Cliffark, leaving tomorrow. The country was no longer shin-deep in snow, and she and Cag were adamant that it was time to go home. They had had their fill of winter in the shadow of Eryispek, and even if the Imperials were still after them, they would be safer in Cliffark, where they knew every alley and cut-through like it was written on their palm. Tam too had finally accepted that this was their only choice.

For their meal this evening, Tansa had cooked a broth from chicken offcuts and bones, purchased from the first vendor she had come to at eight times its usual price. She would not risk being caught by the Imperials on their final night in the city by searching further afield. It was at least hot, but thin and taste-less, though Tansa was too hungry to worry about that.

Tam pushed his bowl away. 'This is disgusting. Cag, you can have mine.' The larger boy gratefully accepted, having already downed his portion straight from the bowl.

'You'll regret that on the journey back,' warned Tansa. 'If there's no food here, think what it's like between here and Cliffark.'

Her brother shrugged. 'I'm just glad to be going back. I can manage a few days of hunger for the chance to see Cliffark again.'

Tansa eyed him suspiciously. 'If you're thinking—'

'I swear I'm not!' he objected, raising his hands in protest. 'Just tired of being hungry and cold, that's all. Even sleeping outside in Cliffark we were never this cold.'

Tansa nodded, satisfied for the most part. Even if Tam was thinking of trying to escape again, the three of them slept so close he would not be able to move without waking her or Cag. She returned to her stew.

When they were finished, she piled the bowls in a corner, never to be used again. They would leave Merivale with the clothes on their backs and barely enough coins to clink together.

'The caravan leaves an hour after first light,' she told them. She felt strangely lethargic, which she could only put down to the cold. Truly the sooner they were back in Cliffark the better. 'We best get some sleep.'

Ciera slept poorly, tossing and turning inside her sheets, somehow at once both too hot and too cold. She had always found sleep easily before, but her pregnancy seemed to have unbalanced her. She was a few months along, with only a hint of swelling, but in bed she found she could not get comfortable. When she tried to sleep the baby seemed to grow in size, beating and kicking at her insides. The midwife had told her such things were not possible so early, but the Sangreals were known for their uncommon height, and when she was abed Ciera swore it was a monster growing inside her.

At least Hessian left her alone now. Since he had learnt of her pregnancy he had been almost deferential to her, arranging the affairs of the keep to please her. All day the smell of Ciera's favourite bread wafted from the kitchens, and each morning there were fresh winter flowers on her dresser. When she had mentioned in passing that she enjoyed the fiddle player at their marriage celebration, the king had even sought out the finest fiddler in the city to play for her, and give her lessons if she desired.

This was how she had got him to listen to her about the city's entrance levy. 'A five-man band might have a four-wheeled cart and a horse,' she had told him. 'That's a big outlay for them to enter the city where they don't even know if their act will be well-received. Even worse for a company of troupers that could have a dozen members. I would love to see a play again, and it might take the mind of the citizens from the hard winter they have endured.' Hessian had grumbled, but relented. From spring, Merivale's entry levy would be paid only per horse and per cart. It was not much, but it was a beginning, and if the change proved successful, she could make further proposals.

Ciera enjoyed the fiddler, and the flowers, and Hessian's willingness to listen to her, but no gesture could erase how he had treated her before she carried a child. If she birthed a girl the presents and the willingness to heed her ideas would stop and the pain would begin again. And not all the changes were good. Ciera's guard of two had been raised to six, and at least four of them accompanied her always, including standing outside her chambers while she slept.

Occasionally, she still thought of Tam. She had resisted at first, or tried to, but three times now she had lit a candle in her window, yet Tam had not come. Occasionally she would look over Merivale from her window, wondering. Maybe he was dead; there was word the city had been a dangerous place this winter.

If Tam was the father, would Hessian believe the babe was his? Or would one look at its face reveal the truth? Lords and kings were supposed to be different from common men.

Too anxious to sleep, Ciera rose with a groan, and walked to her chamber pot in the corner. Dawn was still hours away. If she could get comfortable she could still steal a few hours of rest. She could even lock her door to ensure she was not disturbed by the servant who brought the flowers each morning.

She had just returned to bed when she heard a gentle tapping at her window.

Ciera jumped, and had to cover her mouth to suppress a shocked scream. She turned to the window, and though she had little doubt who it would be, was delighted to see Tam, smiling broadly, curled in the alcove with his index finger raised to the glass. She raced across the room to release the latch.

'You have to be quiet,' she whispered as Tam climbed through.

Tam was shivering with cold, his teeth chattering so loudly she was sure the guards would hear. Ciera tiptoed to her trunk and pulled out a collection of blankets. 'Take your clothes off,' she whispered.

Tam grinned. 'Y-you don't n-n-need to ask t-twice,' he managed to say, already bending down to remove his trousers.

Ciera slapped him playfully, smiling. 'Your clothes must be freezing; you'll warm quicker if you just wrap yourself in the blanket.'

Tam obeyed and sat down on the edge of the bed, keeping the blankets pulled tight around him. Ciera sat with him patiently, rubbing her hands up and down his arms in an effort to warm him.

He had come back. Finally. A frisson of excitement ran through her.

Soon, Tam's shivering slowed, and he managed to speak. 'Thank you. If I had been out there any longer I might never have warmed up again.'

'It's only a few hours from dawn. How long were you out there?'

'I've been stuck on the wall half the night waiting for the men in the yard to disperse. Are they riding for war?'

Ciera nodded. 'Now spring is here Lord Andrick is taking to the field again.'

'I've been inside all winter losing my mind,' said Tam. 'After Tansa caught me coming back last time she forbade me from leaving. Cag threatened to break my arm to stop me.' He reached inside his jerkin for something. 'I got this for you,' he said, holding up a silk purse stitched with small jewels.

'When you didn't come back, I thought you were dead.'

'I had to come back. We're going back to Cliffark tomorrow. Tansa says we came to Merivale to be safe, and instead we've spent all winter stuck inside, terrified that the Imperials might find us, and all our money is gone. I can't stay here and abandon them, but I knew I couldn't leave without seeing you, so I dosed their food with drowshroom and sneaked out the window.'

Ciera did not reply. *I thought he was dead, and now he's leaving again.* She immediately felt foolish. What had she thought would happen? That he would sneak in through the window indefinitely, even as her belly swelled and she birthed a prince?

'Come with me,' he said suddenly. 'Come back to Cliffark with me. It's a big city; they would never find you.'

'Tam, I'm pregnant.'

Tam looked as though he had been struck by lightning. He gaped, blinking. 'Is it...?'

'Yours? I don't know. I'm so scared, Tam. What if it comes out and looks nothing like the king? He'd kill me, I'm sure of it.'

'Babies always look the same,' replied Tam uncertainly. 'But you can come with me. It won't matter if it looks like the king, I'll be a father.'

'I can't.' Ciera pressed her nails into her palms. 'They would hunt me to the ends of the earth. He wants an heir, and if I run away he can't have one. We would never be safe.'

'Please,' he said, taking her hand. His fingers were freezing, but his touch sent a hot shiver through her. 'I can't leave without you. What if the child is mine?'

Ciera felt tears springing to her eyes. He was the only person she could be honest with. 'Just stay,' she whispered. 'Just stay until morning. Please. In the morning, I'll give you an answer.' Perhaps Hessian could tell the world she was dead, and marry again. She could return to Cliffark with Tam, and years from now, once Hessian was gone, reveal to her father that she still lived.

She kissed him, long and deep, and he wrapped his arms around her as if he had been waiting for this moment, with one hand at the small of her back and one in her hair. Warmth spread through her body like an inferno. She pushed him down onto the bed, and pulled her nightdress over her head.

Afterwards, they fell asleep in each other's arms, their limbs tangled together like tree roots.

They were still locked together the next morning, when Ciera heard her door creak, and her eyes sprang open.

A servant girl was in her room, holding the flowers she brought every morning. Ciera's heart raced. As long as she stayed still, the girl should not look at the bed. She willed her to quickly place the flowers and leave.

Tam stirred slightly, and yawned, raising an arm above the covers. The girl reflexively looked in their direction to see a slender, youthful body with tawny hair, which was obviously not the king.

She screamed, and Tam sat up with a start. He saw the girl and leapt from the bed, dashing for the window like someone used to narrow escapes.

For a moment, Ciera thought he might make it. She did not worry that he was still naked, nor that he would have to navigate his way down the wall and out of the keep in the light of day. But the girl was still screaming, and the four guards posted outside her door barged their way in and went straight for Tam.

Tam dodged the blow of the first guard, and leapt over the dive of the second, but the third was quicker, and his wild punch caught Tam's jaw and splattered blood across the floor. The guard followed up with a vicious blow to the gut that dropped Tam to his knees. He curled into a ball, while the guards peppered his back and groin with brutal stamps and kicks.

Ciera cried out in horror for them to stop, but it made no difference. They did not even seem to hear her. She could not look away, even as Tam whimpered and squirmed uselessly to avoid their blows. She felt every strike as if they were doing it to her.

When they had finished, Tam's body was a mess of blood and bruises, and several of his teeth lay scattered across the floor. As the others carried Tam's broken body from the room, one of the guards addressed her, his eyes fixed on the wall, ignoring her nakedness. 'Stay here. The king will need to speak with you.' He turned to the terrified servant girl, cowering by the flowers. She had finally stopped screaming. 'You, help her dress. Then leave and lock the door from the outside.' He turned on his heel, and followed the others from the room.

CHAPTER 36

Rymond laid down his cards, unable to keep the grin off his face. 'The pot is mine, Lady.' He stretched forward to gather the coins, for the purpose of their game each worth twenty times their weight.

Helana raised an eyebrow. 'That's a good hand, Lord.' She showed her cards. 'But not good enough.'

Rymond stared for a moment, blew out his cheeks, and sat back in his chair. 'How did you get so good at this?'

'The guards at Piperskeep are always playing triumph,' she replied, reaching out to gather the coins. 'I started playing them for pennies when I was eight.'

'That's reassuring. If I am ever captured I will at least not be short of entertainment.'

They were in Rymond's rooms, which were significantly cleaner now than after his drinking jag with Will and Dom. The injury to his leg was healing nicely, but Rymond was self-medicating with whisky in any case. He took another sip, still trying to work out how Helana had beaten him, again.

'You'll never improve your game if you drink whisky while you play,' said Helana, taking a sip of her own watered wine.

She gathered up the cards and began shuffling. 'And you should pray you are never captured. My father is less merciful than a boar.'

'I know that,' said Rymond, running a hand anxiously through his hair. He thought he knew what he wanted now, but why was it so hard to admit? The idea of returning to war filled him with dread. Every day men continued to gather, and in the yard Adfric drilled youths he did not recognise, but for weeks Rymond's mind had been anywhere but war.

He looked up at Helana, studiously shuffling the cards. Every day she seemed to grow more beautiful. He smiled to himself. What was war or a crown next to her? He adjusted his weight to reach for a smokestick, wincing at the pain in his thigh. The healers said it was only her tourniquet that had stopped him bleeding to death. And he had saved her life too, even if she was loath to admit it. She was brave, and sharp, and spoke to him with an honesty that bordered on disdain. Even when he had jumped in front of a boar for her, she had told him he was a fool.

And she had kissed him back that day. Even giddy with the blood coursing from his thigh, he had felt that. He was still yet to find the courage to try it again though. If he caught her at the wrong moment he could expect a swift punch in the mouth.

But still, *marriage*. Was that what he wanted? What if Hessian still would not accept peace? And Helana was the sort of woman who would demand he be faithful. There would be no late-night jaunts in the Smoking Sow with Dom and Will. And he did not want just a marriage of peace; he wanted to impress Helana, to prove he was worthy of her, even if he could not quite figure out why.

'Will we eat together again tonight?' asked Helana, dealing them five cards each. They had dined in his chambers almost every night since the hunt, on slices of the boar that Rymond had killed.

Rymond shook his head. 'Not tonight. Will and Dom are joining me for dinner. You are free to eat something other than boar.'

He caught the smirk on Helana's lips. 'A liquid dinner for you, then?'

There was a knock at the door, and without waiting Breta burst into the room in a cloud of sweet perfume.

Rymond set his cards down with a sigh. 'What is it, Mother?' She had a real knack for picking her moments.

'Would you care to join us for a game, Lady Prindian?' asked Helana. 'You might be able to win back some of Rymond's money.'

She smiled thinly. 'Another time, perhaps. I need to speak with my son, alone.'

Rymond tried not to let his frustration show. Another whisky and he might have been ready to try kissing Helana again. This was not like courting girls in taverns, even if she had already proposed marriage. 'Of course.' He looked to Helana. 'Would you give us a few minutes?'

'It will take longer than that, I'm afraid,' said Breta, taking a seat on the third chair. 'Best you leave us for a time, child.'

'Of course.' Rymond knew Helana was not the sort to take offence. She kissed his mother on the cheek and withdrew, leaving him regrettably alone with her.

Her news burst out of her as soon as Helana had left. 'The girl is pregnant.'

Rymond sighed. This was obviously not going to be a quick conversation. 'Which girl?'

'Which girl do you think, you fool? Ciera Istlewick, who I told you to marry!' Her eyes flicked down to the smokestick and the whisky. 'Unless you have stopped caring about the war?' she added with a sneer.

Rymond's heart leapt. If Hessian's child were a boy, that would change everything. He would no longer be heir. The war would be pointless; he was not going to kill a newborn child to claim the crown. Nor would Hessian need to fight him. And he would be free to marry Helana, he realised, with a burst of elation. It could bring peace, as she hoped.

He nodded. 'In that case, I will marry Helana, and sue for peace.'

His mother reacted as he had thought she would, with an icy stare that sought to pin him to his chair. 'No. That is no longer an option. I meant for you to marry her to shore up your claim, not for peace. If Hessian's child is a boy, you will not be the heir.'

'I know. This has always been your war, Mother. I was willing because Hessian tried to kidnap me, but if I marry Helana I should be safe.' He took a deep breath. 'I love her, Mother.' He had scarcely been surer of anything in his life.

His mother stared at him mutely, and Rymond reflected that he had finally found a way to shut her up. Then, after a moment, she threw back her head and laughed, long and maniacally, as if she meant to die of it. Rymond looked down at the books piled on his table. They had never appealed when he was younger – too many endless Halords to keep track of – but this winter he had found an unexpected appreciation for the tales of the ancient Prindian kings. He had known, of course, of Halord the First who had first conquered Erland, but less of Halord the Third, who had defeated an invasion from the Sorrowlands and slain the Sorrowmen's leader Twelve-Finger Tarl in single combat, and less still of Hamond Honey-tongue, who had outlawed thraldom in Erland. His own achievement of silencing his mother did not fare well in comparison.

When she finally finished, she wiped a tear from her eye. 'All those years you spent bringing women back here, most of whom I never saw again, and now you say you've fallen in love with Helana Sangreal.' She laughed again. 'Fine. Marry her. Bed her.

Put a child in her. By Eryi, I spent long enough trying to get you to marry Ciera Istlewick, and you've fallen for the first pretty, nobly born girl to look twice at you. But this war is not over. Topple the bridges into the river, and declare yourself king of West Erland.'

Rymond shook his head. 'If I will not have peace, she will not marry me.'

'And do you suppose Hessian will let you have peace after you burnt his harvest?'

'Helana believes it is possible, and I trust her.'

'Then you are a fool, and an even greater fool than I thought.' She stood abruptly, and swept out of the room without another word.

Rymond stared after her, confused as to why his mother had given up so quickly. He had expected to argue with her for hours. But at least he had made a decision. Tonight, drink with Dom and Will. Tomorrow, propose to Helana that he was ready to marry her.

Helana was woken by the loud cries of a servant coming from the corridor outside her chamber. 'To the hall! Lord Prindian summons you all to the hall!'

Wiping sleep from her eyes and resisting her urge to castigate the man, Helana dressed quickly, throwing the previous day's clothes on and wrapping a long coat about herself. By the cold and the dim light, it was still hours from dawn. She had not expected Rymond to emerge after an evening with his friends until past noon; what reason could he have to wake the whole castle?

Helana joined a throng of servants and attendants moving towards the hall, all looking no less confused than she was, and followed them through the double doors into the hall. The long room was already aglow with high candlelight, and both walls lined with guards.

At the far end, Rymond sat uneasily upon the throne of West Erland. It was an ugly chair, carved from ash and oak that twisted between each other like clasped fingers. He had told her it was something of an embarrassment, a monument to West Erland's defeat by the Imperium and their surrender to the Sangreals centuries ago.

Helana kept to the back of the hall, but Rymond's gaze found her all the same. Even so early in the morning he looked handsome, if weary, and perhaps slightly anxious. What had he summoned them here for? She smiled slightly at him, touching her finger instinctively to her lips.

It had been shock, she told herself, kissing him. They had both almost been killed; of course she had kissed him back.

She had grown fond of him though, she would admit. He was no warrior, but brave enough to leap in front of a boar for her. Lazy, but clever, and sure of himself in a way that Orsian would never be.

From behind her, Adfric appeared at her shoulder. 'What's happened?' she asked him. There were deep bags under his eyes and a fresh bruise rising over his cheek. A smear of blood stained his surcoat.

'He killed five men to escape the keep,' he said, his voice hoarse and tired, barely seeming to realise who she was. 'We caught him at the gate, but he'd already killed the two guards and somehow got the portcullis up. Someone managed to grab his reins, but he killed four more before we could get the sword off him. The horse is dead too.'

'What?' she demanded. Who was he talking about?

Adfric had already stepped away, stalking up the hall towards Rymond. He whispered something in his ear. Rymond raised a hand, and the hall fell silent.

'Bring him in,' he croaked, his voice thick with tiredness.

Too late, Helana realised who Adfric had been speaking of. Errian's hands and feet were chained to an iron belt at his waist, tied with weights that dragged screeching against the slate floor. Six guards escorted him, each with a spear pointing at his throat. Despite his chains and the blood dripping from his temple, he walked the hall as proud as a king, his eyes defiantly holding Rymond's gaze, and stopped before the throne. He wore an oversized guard's uniform that must have belonged to one of the dead, and Helana could feel the tightly coiled fury in the room. She gave thanks to Eryi that he had been taken alive.

Rymond ran his hand anxiously through his golden hair. 'Lord Errian,' he began, his voice tight, 'few prisoners have ever been treated so well as you. I gave you all you asked for. And you repaid me by killing eleven of my guards, and an unarmed man.'

Errian spat blood on the floor in front of him. 'You have no authority, Lord. You are in rebellion against the one rightful king of Erland, and regardless of whatever trinkets you offer me I am within my rights to escape. Next time I mean to succeed.'

A guard stepped forward and jabbed Errian in the stomach with the butt of his spear, and Helana had to cover her mouth to stop herself from shouting out in protest. Errian grunted and doubled forward, but swiftly rose, the same unquenchable fire burning in his eyes.

Eleven guards. No wonder she could sense bloodlust in the room.

'Take him to the dungeons and lock him in irons.' Rymond rose and stalked towards his private antechamber, limping slightly from his hunting injury.

A buzz of angry murmurs washed over the hall. The guards escorted Errian from the room, and by the set of their faces each of them given the chance would have killed him himself.

Without hesitation, Helana followed after Rymond, ignoring the hall's pointed stares. She opened the door to find him at the table, his head in his hands. He looked up as she entered, his eyes tired and distant. 'I gave your cousin all the luxury he desired,' he said morosely, 'and as thanks he has killed a dozen men.'

'All luxury except his freedom,' Helana retorted. 'You cannot imprison a man and expect him not to try and escape.' It had been inevitable Errian would try; one only had to spend a few minutes with him to see that.

'It was not just the guards.' Rymond buried his head in his hands again. 'They found Will, bleeding out in the snow. He had gone to fetch something from his horse, and on the way he encountered Errian. My friend, since I was a boy.' He clenched his fist. 'Errian must be punished. One hundred and twenty lashes, ten for every man killed, to be administered by Strovac Sigac.'

Helana gaped at him. 'You can't! Strovac will kill him!'

'I can and I will!' There were tears on Rymond's cheeks as he rose angrily from his chair and stepped towards her. For a fearful second, Helana thought he was going to strike her.

Instead he kissed her, as forcefully and desperately as he had in the forest, and despite her surprise Helana felt herself permitting him, letting herself be carried away in the heat of his lips on hers. His hands were in the small of her back, holding her, pulling her to him. Helana felt her face growing hot.

With a gasp she found the will to push him away. 'What are you doing?' She hated how flustered she sounded. 'Have you wounded yourself again? Don't expect me to save your life this time.'

'Marry me,' he said wildly. 'I want peace, and I want you.'

It was about the last thing Helana had expected him to say. Suddenly she was conscious of how close he was, and took a step back. 'I'm not going to marry you if you give my cousin to that animal.'

'Helana, he killed a dozen men, including my friend, who

was unarmed!' roared Rymond, his face flushed with rage. 'It won't kill him – the lashes will be given twenty a day, for six days. Anything less and I will have a revolt on my hands. Nobody would ever respect me again. Just marry me, please. Then I can return Errian to his father.'

The door suddenly opened. Helana breathed a sigh of relief. It was Adfric, looking alarmed, with a young messenger wearing stained riding gear at his side.

'What is it?' snapped Rymond. He slumped into a chair. 'Errian will be punished, Adfric, have no fear on that front.'

'It is not that, Lord.' Adfric looked to the messenger and gestured for him to speak. 'Tell Lord Rymond what you told me.'

'The Barrelbreaker, Lord.' The young man swallowed. 'Fifteen thousand East Erlanders, marching west.'

The walls of Whitewater Motte were built in the old style: in wood, with sharpened logs forming the palisade, and a simple stone bailey inside. The only natural defence was the slight mound upon which the fort stood.

Watching from the east, Andrick shook his head, and stretched his aching shoulder. *Yet another joy of old age.* The wound he had taken to his shield arm at Imberwych had troubled him all through winter. If he moved too quickly it would twinge painfully, and if he stayed still too long it was liable to stiffen.

It was, though, unlikely to present an issue today. The Motte was too lightly guarded. It baffled him that the Darltons could have paid such scant attention to their defence, but Lord Prindian's third cousins were not known for their cunning. They had not even bothered to set men watching the bridge that linked the two halves of Whitewater.

The Motte had been designed with an invasion by sea in mind, near to the cliffs and with its stronger defences facing north. It was barely adequate to defend against a land attack, and even with the two sides of Erland on a war footing, the current Lord Darlton had clearly not seen the threat from the east.

It had been easy enough to get the most influential residents of Whitewater on their side. Most were loyal to Hessian, and Andrick Barrelbreaker arriving as night fell with fifteen thousand men at his back had persuaded any whose loyalties might have been divided. The bridge had been closed off, and a curfew instituted to prevent any Darlton loyalists attempting to cross. There had been only three attempted defectors during the night, all now safely chained up in the jail.

As dawn broke, Andrick led a third of his men across the bridge, while a low sun at their back cloaked them in shadow and raised a mist from the ice-dappled ground. Either it blinded the watchman on the eastern wall, or he had been half-asleep, because there was no sign that their approach had been seen until they were within sixty yards, when a single desperate bell began to toll, waking the fort from its slumber.

'Should I send men to watch the western gate, Lord?' asked Naeem.

'Yes, but let the first two men go. Anyone after that try to keep alive if possible.'

Naeem scrunched his face, misshaping the hole where his nose had been. 'Let them go, Lord?' Andrick nodded, and a slow smile spread across Naeem's face. 'Because you want Prindian to come running. Think he will?'

It was likely, Andrick thought. Prindian had been close to victory last time, and that disappointment would have blunted any caution he might have had. And after a winter of waiting Strovac Sigac would be as impatient as a dog in heat. 'I do. Once we have Lord Darlton's family we'll send our own messenger offering to exchange them for Errian.'

Naeem frowned. 'Begging your pardon, Lord, but if I were Rymond Prindian that's not an exchange I'd be making. Your son for a couple of distant cousins?'

Andrick had his own doubts, but did not give voice to them. 'It's the plan I have. We'll have our own hostages at least.'

The fort's eastern palisade was now lined with archers. It was hard to tell at this distance, but they were likely to be older soldiers, and their various states of attire suggested some had been roused from their beds. 'That's close enough, Lord!' called one of them.

Andrick pressed Valour forward a step, and the speaker loosed an arrow from his shaking fingers. It landed weakly a few yards in front of Andrick. Laughter rose from the men behind him, and Andrick let the disdain show on his face. 'Orsian, put two arrows either side of his head.'

Quick as smoke, Orsian loosed two arrows one after the other. The first whistled within inches of the man's head. The second flew the other side, and there was a scream as it grazed his ear, drawing a whisper of blood.

'Any of you who shoots at me again will get one in the eye!' Andrick called, advancing Valour within the range of their bows. 'Now one of you go and tell Lord Darlton that Andrick Barrelbreaker is here in the name of King Hessian, and he's got fifteen thousand men with him!'

Within the hour, Andrick was inside the fort. As he had expected, it was manned by greybeards, and there were no more than fifty of them. All the others had gone west to join up with Rymond Prindian, including the lord's son.

Lord Darlton walked out to meet him. He was older even than his guards, but with the powerful shoulders of a man who had not left his sword on the wall to rust, even if he had lost the wits to set a proper guard around his home and watch the bridge.

If I age so well as Lord Darlton, perhaps I can fight on, Andrick reflected. He had not yet told Hessian of his intention; that was a conversation for once the war was won. He would not stand down as *balhymeri* – at least not until Errian or Orsian was ready to take over – but he did not intend to lead men into battle again. Young as he was, if Orsian continued to show the same swiftness of thought he had in the Battle of Imberwych it would go some way to proving he was ready to lead.

'The fabled Andrick Barrelbreaker,' began Lord Darlton. 'I have to admit, I am disappointed. The man they tell stories of was not one to sneak up on his enemies in the dark like a thief in the night.'

Andrick let the insult roll over him. 'It is morning, Lord. This man would have set a proper watch. This man would also have answered the summons of his king, not of some up-jumped pup who does not know one end of a sword from the other. I had hoped to give my men a proper fight – it has been a long winter – so you are not the only one who is disappointed.'

Lord Darlton spat on the ground. 'My son took all the young men to Irith, to protect Lord Rymond's birthright as the heir before Hessian can drop him in a cell to rot.' His face twisted in the rictus of a smile. 'Besides, the way I hear it told, that up-jumped pup almost pulled your trousers down a few months ago.'

Andrick dismissed Darlton to his chambers with his grand-children, wife, and daughter-in-law, under guard. They would remain here for three days, and then they would be on the march again. An army staying in one place too long would eat the town and countryside bare. Whether or not the Prindians would accept the exchange of hostages, they would press on into West Erland. Once they did, battle would not be far away.

CHAPTER 37

Pherri looked into the cat's luminous yellow eyes, keeping the image of a slice of ham at the forefront of her mind. At least the cat seemed to trust Pherri now, happy to sit opposite her in the chair with minimal encouragement. That had taken several patient hours, and more than a little assistance from Theodric. He said her name was Tinks, and that the tetchy, old tortoise-shell was mother to half the cats in Piperskeep.

'Come on,' Pherri whispered, edging the dish of carrots nearer to her.

Tinks swished her tail, and with her paw swiped one of the carrots off the dish onto the floor. She flashed Pherri a look of contempt, leapt down from the chair, and strutted away.

'Eryi curse it,' muttered Pherri, putting the dish down and wiping the sweat from her forehead. 'I swear I almost had it.'

From across the room, Theodric chuckled. 'I believe you did. She's a stubborn old girl.'

Their lessons were a daily occurrence now. Pherri had perfected *phisika*; Theodric said he had never seen anyone take so well to it: she could move books, candles, and sheets of parchment from one room to another as easy as breathing. But the acts of *shadika* – summoning shadows from another world – and *inflika* – influencing somebody's perception to recall something differently or see something other than what was there – continued to elude her. And every time she failed, Theodric seemed encouraged, as if the mere fact she had tried was cause enough for praise. Rather than trying to improve her abilities, many of his lessons dealt with matters of theory, such as the energy required to move a pea from one side of Erland to the other, if such a thing were possible, and how to eat inhuman quantities of food, which he insisted was essential to any would-be magus.

Pherri exhaled heavily. Why was he so sanguine about her failures? 'Would it not be easier with a dog?' she asked. Pherri preferred dogs. She had played with every one of her father's wolfhound litters.

'Yes, but it would be pointless. Dogs will eat anything, especially if they think it will please you.' He took a slice of ham from his own plate.

'I'm not hungry,' said Pherri quickly. The upside to practising *inflika* was that it did not leave her physically exhausted the way *phisika* and her attempts at *shadika* did.

'It's not for you; it's for her.' Theodric beckoned Tinks towards him, and held the ham out. She stood up on her back legs and snatched it with her paws, then ate it off the floor, purring contentedly. 'It will take time, you know,' he said. 'The focus will come with age, and you are still young enough to learn. Fortunately, you have will in abundance.'

'What's the fourth discipline again?'

'*Spectika*: to narrow all possibilities to a single certain and known position. Energy, will, and focus, in equal measure. It is the hardest of the four, and the most powerful, and I believe it may have deserted me forever. Once I could have told you whether it is raining in Thrumbalto, and now I rely upon spies and informers to tell me simply what is going on inside Piperskeep.' He sat down with a sigh. 'Helana missing, the Lutums have still not returned, and the Adrari report further strangeness on Eryispek... And it all reaches me too slowly, third or fourth hand, so I have no way of sifting the true from the false.'

Pherri chewed her lip. Theodric was an endlessly encouraging teacher, but when he had to think on anything outside his rooms he always seemed to become morose. 'I could help?' she offered. 'You said my dreams were magic. Perhaps I'd be better at *spectika* than *inflika*?'

'It doesn't work like that, sadly. Your dreams were *prophika*, the fifth and most elusive of the disciplines. *Spectika* requires training; your *prophika* is an inherent ability perhaps only one in twenty magi is born with.'

'Like Delara. They've stopped now, my dreams.' Pherri had expected her peculiar visions to return since she had stopped taking Delara's brew, but she had not had a single one. Theodric had searched for the Lutum woman, after her departure, sure there was more she could tell him, yet she had somehow escaped Piperskeep and Merivale without a single gate guard seeing her.

Theodric's usually bright eyes were ringed with weariness. 'It is said the magi of old who were blessed with *prophika* dreamt only of matters of great importance, and only those they might be able to change. That your dreams have stopped suggests that whatever they were warning you of has now come to pass. I only wish I understood what they meant.' He sighed. 'You told me you saw men starving in the snow, a doe, and a shadowy face with cold, pale eyes?'

Pherri felt a cold shiver run up her spine. She nodded. 'The doe spoke to me. Do you think my dreams are connected to the Lutums?'

'It certainly seems likely. The letter you showed me that

your tutor planned to send troubles me also – the Thrumb and the Adrari are old tribes, with long memories, and it may be they know something we do not – but Hessian cannot spare the men we would need to go searching Eryispek for a rogue tribe of fanatics.' He suddenly stood, in a moment his mood changing from despairing to invigorated. 'And it is all the more reason we must continue with your lessons. Try again with Tinks for me.'

'There's no point; she doesn't like me.'

Theodric smirked. 'Some cats don't like anybody. If she liked you it would be easy. People do not want you altering their thoughts. That's why we practise with cats, not dogs.'

'Fine.' Pherri stood up, preparing to coax Tinks towards her. She had leapt onto the windowsill, and was staring northwards towards Eryispek, flicking her tail rhythmically back and forth. With the coming of spring, snow had stopped falling, and the little that was left on the ground had begun to melt, but the Mountain was still draped in mist, hanging from it like a vast cloak. Pherri still liked to try and trace it upwards through the clouds, but in the dense haze that had coated it for months there was no hope of that.

Approaching Tinks carefully, Pherri looked out of the window for a moment. The thick mists around Eryispek twisted and spun in the high winds, and like a faltering mirage its silhouette seemed to thrum before her eyes. A sudden gust roared, rattling the window frame, and Pherri felt an icy chill spreading through her body, making her gasp and shiver. Then, just as quickly as it had arrived, the sensation ceased.

She shook herself to her senses. Delara had been right about one thing: there was more to Eryispek than just rocks and snow. But it was so far, she shouldn't have been able to feel that in Piperskeep. She must have imagined it; perhaps *inflika* had taken more from her than she thought.

To Pherri's surprise, when she tried to project to Tinks the image of her leaping into her arms, the cat did just that. Pherri held her, and the cat purred, clawing happily at her shoulders. The first few tries she usually just ran away.

It would not last, she was sure. Pherri returned her to the chair, and assumed her place opposite, picking up the carrots and looking into the cat's eyes.

Lifting her nostrils, Pherri smelt, searching for the salty-sweet waft of the ham on Theodric's table. She imbibed it, filling the illusion she wanted to create in the cat's mind with the scent. She focused on the cat's eyes, letting the image of the ham expand until her vision swam with it.

It's ham. Eat it. The words filled her head with the force of a hammer, and she projected the strength of that feeling towards the cat.

Tinks blinked slowly, and licked one of the carrots. Her ears fell flat, and she lowered her head to nibble at it uncertainly.

Pherri was too shocked to contain herself. 'I did it, I did it!' She leapt up in celebration, and Tinks bolted, zooming frantically around the room in a cloud of black and orange fur. 'I did it!'

Theodric beamed at her, clapping enthusiastically. 'Progress! That was so much better; well done. You did something different; what was it?'

Pherri blinked at him. 'Nothing. You saw. She jumped into my arms, and when I pictured the ham she accepted it.' She glanced briefly again towards the window, where the shadow of Eryispek glistened in the mist. Strangely, she did feel more focused. 'Am I ready to try *spectika* now?' Orsian was riding to war; with *spectika* she might be able to keep an eye on him.

'In time. Fetch the cat and try again. There is still a whole dish of carrots for her to eat.'

With a sigh, Pherri went in search of Tinks.

For the first time since Delara had left, Pherri dreamt that night. She was sitting on a snowdrift, staring up at the frost-dusted firs of towering pine trees. Not even the merest shoot of green poked above the heavy snowfall. Mist covered the trees like a shroud. All the world was white.

The snow reminded her of the dreams that had troubled her before, though there was no sign of the shambling figures, nor the doe, nor the pale-eyed shadow. She stood, and turned on the spot. Nobody was there. It was just her and the pines.

It was a strange sort of dream, she thought. Dreams were chaos, like her previous ones, full of unexplained images, and never still for a moment. This was peaceful.

A whispering wind tickled the evergreen firs, rattling their branches. Pherri turned, following the sound, and this time something moved.

The snow shifted, and across the clearing a dark shape rose. Pherri's stomach dropped as the snow fell from its shoulders. It was the same man she had seen with his back to her in her last dream, though she had not realised then how young he was, perhaps only slightly older than Orsian. The heavy white fur was still draped over his torso, but where he had once been broad with muscle he was now emaciated. Ribs stuck out like tree knots; his cheeks were sunken and scabbed, his legs pale and bare.

Gelick Whitedoe. He was shivering, she realised. The white pelt was all he wore.

Then he saw her.

'Help me,' he gasped. His mouth pleaded, but his eyes were grim and black.

Pherri took a step backward, and something grasped at her ankle. She screamed, and leapt away, stumbling and barely keeping her balance.

The snow was moving. The ground shook, and hands broke

from the cold earth, dozens of them, corpse-grey yet writhing vigorously. Pherri stared, her heart pounding. There were more than the ground could possibly have contained, dead fingers reaching for her like flowers towards the sun. They were all around her, with more rising every moment. Pherri twisted and turned on the spot, searching for an escape.

Panicked, she ran, and stepped straight into one. It grasped at her, with bony fingers cold as death. She struggled, but its grip was firm, and before she knew what was happening other hands were reaching for her too, tearing at her clothes, pulling at her hair, dragging her to the icy ground.

It's only a dream, she insisted to herself. But what if *prophika* dreams were different? Desperately, she reached for the will required for *phisika*.

The wave of power that burst forth shook the mountainside like an earthquake. Across the snow, the dead face of Gelick Whitedoe froze, his mouth open in a silent howl of anguish. The hands that grasped Pherri began to crumble like sand before the tide, and Pherri wriggled away from them. All around, the dream was dissolving, the black night fading to purple and to blue, the snow melting to reveal the sheets of Pherri's own bed.

'No!' she heard a voice on the wind, a voice she knew on instinct as the pale-eyed man's, screaming at some unseen foe. '*You're trapped, you're trapped!*'

Pherri woke in bed, with morning streaming through the window, so soaked in sweat that her sheets clung to her like a second skin. She shook them off, and leapt out of bed, putting as much distance as she could between herself and the nightmare.

'Not a dream,' she whispered, breathing hard. She could almost feel the malevolent presence of the pale-eyed man in the room with her. It had been his voice she heard, and it had been his voice the doe spoke with in her first dream. The other man, the dead one, that had been Gelick Whitedoe, she was sure of it.

But there had been something else in the dream too. Something older. It had not been Pherri who had fought off the rising dead. And whatever it was, it had terrified the pale-eyed man almost as much as he terrified Pherri.

CHAPTER 38

Rymond woke with a start to the harrumphing of horns. It took him several seconds to realise they were the horns of his own men, and not a sign they were about to be butchered in the night by Lord Andrick. He breathed a sigh of relief. His body ached from sleeping on the cold ground, and there were drops of condensation forming on his bare skin. In their haste to leave Irith he had not had time to arrange for the packing of his usual grand tent and its ornate furnishings, and so was suffering in Adfric's considerably smaller one. It did not agree with him.

'Gerant,' he called, seeking his attendant, a grandson of Lord Storaut, who had insisted that Rymond take the boy on. 'Gerant!' Rymond had been happy enough to do so to secure the lord's loyalty, but he was beginning to believe the boy was a simpleton.

'Yes, Lord?' The boy was there in a moment, poking his moonish face in through the tent flap like a servant checking on the cook.

'What is that noise for?' asked Rymond. 'Hand me my clothes.'

The boy blinked. 'Noise, Lord?'

'The horns, Gerant! The bloody horns!'

'Oh that noise. I'll go check, Lord.' Gerant pulled his head back outside the tent before Rymond could reply.

'No, my clothes! Gerant!' But the boy had raced off. Muttering irritably to himself, Rymond threw off his covers and traipsed to his trunk, shivering. Light was rising outside. It was almost dawn. He could already hear the clamour of soldiers and the striking of flint for the fires that would cook their breakfast.

The tent flap was thrown open while Rymond was balanced on one foot putting his second leg into his trousers, and he toppled backwards with a surprised yelp. It was Adfric, looking harassed and sleepless but wearing his armour.

Adfric ignored Rymond's fall and the indignant look on his face. 'Lord Andrick, Lord! He's set camp barely a mile away; they must have come in the night.'

'What?' Rymond thrust his leg into his trousers and stood up quickly. 'You were meant to send scouts out ahead of our advance. How could they have sneaked up on us again?'

'We *have* been sending scouts out ahead of us. Some of their bodies were left outside our camp this morning. The sentries just discovered them.'

Rymond felt slightly ill. They could have crept in here and killed him if they wished. 'Double the sentries,' he said, 'and give them more braziers. If they can do that without us seeing them they may be bolder next time.'

'Begging your pardon, Lord, but that won't be necessary. I've already got the men readying for battle. The Sangreal army is forming up to attack.'

Rymond looked at Adfric, dumbfounded. 'No, no no no.' Fear rose in his stomach. 'Raise a flag of truce.'

Adfric raised a quizzical eyebrow. 'You still mean to seek peace, Lord?'

'Yes. In any case, we need time.' He did want peace, but Helana was still in Irith, too angry with him over Errian to give him an answer. 'If I have to I'll tell them Helana is in Irith, and I mean to marry her.'

'That might sound like she's your hostage, Lord.'

'Never mind that, just send that stupid boy of Storaut's in. I'll need my armour.'

With Gerant's assistance, he donned his armour, feeling sour. Errian had buggered everything up trying to escape. Why had he had to do it the night before Rymond meant to ask Helana to marry him? If he had just waited a day they could have freed him.

He met Adfric again at the rear of their camp, on a raised mound that gave them a wide view over what by the afternoon might be a battlefield, though through the dense early morning fog they could see little of it. Strovac arrived soon after, in the company of some of his Wild Brigade, as ugly as they were intimidating. Rymond felt a pang of sadness as he saw Dom, standing forlornly apart from everyone, with a skin of wine to himself. It had been the carefree Will who held their trio together. He felt a surge of anger; if not for Will's death he might have been prepared just to let Errian fester in the dungeons.

He beckoned Strovac over. 'How is our prisoner?'

Strovac flashed a rictus grin, as cold and empty as the smile of a skull. 'Not so well, Lord. His back's a bit sore.'

Rymond felt a moment of nausea, recalling the torn, bloody mess that had been left of Errian's back. He had not appreciated quite how much damage a man of Strovac's strength and ferocity could do with a whip. His punishment had now concluded, but Errian Andrickson might be a very different man for it. 'If it comes to battle, you will lead the centre. If we win today the kingdom will shake.'

'Lord, look,' said Adfric. He pointed across the field. A single rider rode through the fog, bearing the white flag of parley.

'They've accepted your parley offer, Lord,' said Adfric, surprise evident on his face.

'Why?' muttered Strovac, his small eyes narrowing in suspicion. 'They have the numbers, and they've caught us by surprise. What are they waiting for?'

'Hostage exchange,' replied Rymond with certainty. 'They're hoping a bushelful of my distant cousins will be of an equal weight to Lord Errian.'

'Lord,' said Adfric, indicating over Rymond's shoulder to where some of the lesser lords had congregated. His cousin Rudge Darlton, Lord Darlton's heir, was stomping towards them. The look on his face suggested he had heard Rymond, his jowls and absurd moustache wobbling indignantly. A good warrior supposedly, but a lifetime of gluttony had given him the stature and bearing of a portly innkeeper.

'Cousin!' hailed the man. 'Do not price the lives of my kin so cheaply. They are captured only because my lord father sent so many men to join you at Irith.'

'What do you care about your father, Darlton?' said Strovac. 'If he dies you're Lord of Whitewater. Sounds a fair trade to me, a father for a lordship.'

Rudge Darlton bristled, drawing himself up to his full height as if preparing to challenge Strovac. The idea was comical, like a sleepy housecat provoking a bear. 'I am not so debased as you, that I would trade my honour for a lordship. Not that you had any to begin with.'

'Save your jibes for after the battle, both of you,' growled Adfric. 'Lord Rymond, we should meet this emissary.'

They met at the edge of the camp, where Adfric had already set men to preparing for battle, sharpening swords and digging pits along their flank. The emissary was not a lord, as Rymond had thought, but an older common man who would have been otherwise unremarkable if not for the great hole where his nose should have been. Naeem, Rymond recalled.

His eyes caught Rymond staring at it as he approached, and he seemed to enjoy his discomfort, scratching openly at his scar. 'I've a message from Lord Andrick. He sent me to ensure it was taken seriously.' The man's face betrayed nothing, save a look of unbridled contempt when his eyes fell upon Strovac. 'Lord Andrick offers your cousin Lord Darlton and his family in exchange for Lord Errian.' He looked again at Strovac, murder in his eyes. 'I did counsel that you might consider exchanging them for the head of the traitor Strovac Sigac, but he says he will take that anyway.'

'*Lord* Strovac Sigac, to you, Naeem,' said Strovac, sneering.

Naeem ignored him and looked back to Rymond. 'If you agree, bring Errian to the middle of the field in an hour. We'll make the exchange, and meet on the field of battle at noon.'

Naeem gave Strovac one last look of loathing, then turned and rode away.

'I'll come with you, Lord,' said Strovac, placing a meaty hand on Rymond's shoulder. 'I beg the honour of carrying your banner.'

Rymond blinked at him. It was not like Strovac to willingly offer to do anything. *He must really want that lordship.* There was no chance of him getting it if peace could be made; that was not the deal they had struck. 'Thank you, Strovac. Be sure to have Lord Errian ready.'

Rymond gazed over the field. By the fires in the East Erland camp beyond the mist their numbers were evenly matched, but even with over thrice the men West Erland had lost. If he could not win peace, they would need both Eryi and the Norhai on their side.

CHAPTER 39

Tansa woke groggily, her eyelids stuck together like two slabs of meat. Her head was heavy, and when she tried to move the room swam before her eyes. Beside her, Cag snored like a bull, radiating heat, with what felt like half his weight on top of her. She tried to move him, but her muscles would not obey her, and despite the cold her body was clammy with sweat.

'Cahh,' she said, trying to form his name. 'Cahh!' He did not stir. The breath of his snoring in her ear was hot and sour, a wave of muggy air that nearly made her retch. Struggling against her nausea and leaden limbs, she wiggled away from Cag and lay on her back, groaning.

With a great effort she stood, and stumbled to the window. The shadows were short, and the air was bright. It was nearer to noon than dawn, when they usually woke. Horrified, she realised the merchant caravan for their journey back to Cliffark would have left ages ago, an hour after first light. She tried to make sense of it. Her mouth ached for water and her limbs were weak, but they had not had liquor in weeks. Had something in the broth gone bad?

Looking back at the room, her eyes focused on the

haphazard arrangement of blankets they had made their sleeping area. To her shock, she realised Tam was not there, just Cag, still snoring away like a furnace.

His absence was like cold water poured over her, shaking off her fatigue in a way the departure of the merchant caravan had not. 'Cag!' she shouted, kicking him on the shoulder with her bare foot. He stopped snoring, mumbled something, rolled the other way, and began snoring again. She kicked him again, hard in the small of his back. 'Cag!'

'Wha'?' He moved like a bear rising from hibernation, sitting up with a slack-jawed expression on his broad face. 'Stop kicking me, I feel like my head's been pickled.'

'Tam's gone, and we've missed our caravan.' She remembered suddenly that Tam had not had a single spoonful of the broth the night before, he had given his to Cag. *The drowshroom.* It seemed like forever ago she had stolen it from the inn before she fled. She had almost forgotten about it. Her hand flew to her forehead. 'He drugged the broth; that's why we can barely speak.'

She was furious with her brother, but more furious with herself for not seeing this coming. Half-a-dozen times she had had to get Cag to stop Tam leaving. She should have known he might do something like this, though she would never have imagined that he might go so far as to drug them.

'I'm going to strangle him,' she said once they had roused themselves, pulling on her boots and wrapping layers around her for the cold spring air. 'He's gone too far this time.'

'Better pray we find him first.' Cag had already dressed and was itching to leave. 'He wouldn't have planned for us to wake up before he got back. If the Imperials have caught him...'

Tansa tried not to think about it. 'Let's start by walking up the keep. He'll have gone that way.'

But Tam was not near the keep. Nor was he anywhere else they tried.

For three days they traipsed the city, trying every inn, pawnshop, and jail asking after someone of Tam's description. If he had been in any of them Tansa was sure they would remember him, given his brown hair among the straw-heads of Merivale, but none admitted to seeing him.

On the fourth day, Tansa and Cag sat together in the Witch's Abyss, still the cheapest, most rundown inn they could find, nursing their sorrow with mugs of thick ale with visible bits floating in it. Fortunately the barman did not appear to recognise Tansa as the girl who had briefly worked there. It was early, barely after noon, and the inn was deserted aside from a young boy sweeping the floor and a few regulars propped up at the bar, smelling of stale beer and rotten sweat. Such was Tansa and Cag's hunger they had even taken the risk of ordering food from the kitchen.

Tansa sat in silence, miserable. The only explanation left was that Tam was inside Piperskeep, which could surely only mean he had been caught and was in the dungeons. She had no intention of leaving him, but they had no way of getting inside. They were stuck.

'I could become a guard?' ventured Cag. 'Or knock a guard out and take his uniform.'

Tansa shook her head. 'That could take months, and you getting yourself thrown in jail for impersonating a guard wouldn't help.' She thought for a moment. 'We could try to reach the queen, but I'm told she never leaves the keep, so we're back to the same problem.' She slammed her mug down in frustration.

'You headed up to the keep?' Tansa and Cag both looked up at the voice. It was the young boy who had been sweeping, barefoot and skinny in oversized clothes.

Tansa blinked at him. 'What's it to you?'

The boy shrugged. 'Thought you said you were going to the keep. It's sixthday, when they let folk inside the walls to see the hangings. Busy one too, I heard.'

Minutes later, Tansa and Cag were walking swiftly up the Castle Road, having thrown their money on the table and left without finishing their drinks or touching the food that had just emerged from the kitchen. Tansa wanted to hurry, but to break into a run would draw unwanted attention. They were part of a steady stream of people moving uphill towards Piperskeep, more pouring out from every side street.

Tansa did not give voice to the fear eating away at her empty stomach. She tried not to even think about it. The tight concentration on Cag's face as he weaved a path for them between the knots of people suggested he shared her distress.

What will I do if it's Tam on the gallows? Inside the walls would be crawling with guards. They had no hope of breaking him out. Would they give family and friends the chance to beg for the lives of the condemned, as they did at hangings in Cliffark? To reveal themselves might also earn her and Cag the hangman's noose. Tansa imagined Tam's face, turning purple as the rope bit into his neck. She gasped and almost stumbled to her knees, but Cag reached out a meaty hand to hold her steady. They walked on, trying to move ahead of the swelling crowd towards the gate.

They passed under the arch as the guards hurried the crowd on. The interior was the same monolithic grey-black stone as the outer wall, and gurning gargoyles stared down at them from the high walls either side, slick with the night's rain that seemed to animate their twisted features. Their bulging eyes and loose hanging mouths made Tansa feel sick, and she kept her eyes focused on the backs of those ahead of them, clutching Cag's hand white-knuckle tight.

The castle's yard was huge, as large as the main square in Cliffark. Though the high and heavy shadow of the keep loomed over them, it was the wooden gallows that drew Tansa's eyes. It stood at the centre, lacquered dark wood, each beam thick and flawless. The noose hung ominously, swaying in the steady wind.

The square was not even a quarter full, but the crowd were spreading out quickly. 'Come on,' said Cag. He led her towards the gallows, where a horse-drawn cart held a crowd of prisoners, hands bound behind their backs and their mouths gagged. Tansa felt dizzy, as if her legs might collapse underneath her, but her eyes flicked from prisoner to prisoner, looking for Tam. Her heart lifted when she realised none of them was her brother.

'He's not there,' she whispered to Cag.

Cag had been looking at them as well. 'I think they're from the jail in the city. There could be more held inside the keep. We should get closer.'

They found a spot only a few rows back from the gallows. People were pressed closely together by the growing crowd, and the atmosphere was hot with nervous excitement. Over the noise she picked out a few shouts aimed for the cart, family members of the condemned hoping for some final words with their loved ones. One man had somehow removed his gag, and called back to somebody, 'Trisha! Trisha!' Three guards responded immediately, stepping into the cart and beating the defenceless man into silence.

Tansa's eyes were drawn to the keep's balcony overlooking the square. She squinted, making out the straight postures and fine robes of the arriving nobility. At the middle of them was a tall, sallow-skinned figure draped in blood-red, a gold circlet resting over his brow. Tansa had never seen King Hessian before, but she had heard enough to recognise him. The crowd clearly saw him too: a ripple of excitement passed through them, neighbour turning to neighbour and pointing towards him. Her eyes darted along the line looking for the queen who had so beguiled her brother, but the balcony was all men. A shorter figure next to the king wore the bright merchant clothing so often worn in Cliffark by visiting foreigners. There was something familiar about him, but before Tansa could place him, there was a cheer from the crowd, and she saw a large man in a black leather tunic climbing the gallows' steps. The man gave several strong tugs on the rope, drawing cheers from the crowd as the beam did not bend an inch.

She looked back to the balcony. *If these people were not such fools they would hang the lords instead, for stealing their land and hoarding their food.* She clutched Cag's hand more tightly.

A smaller man in the robes of an upper servant standing next to the gallows produced a scroll. 'Uren Smithy,' he called, 'charged with the theft of the king's ham from the kitchen. You shall be hanged from the neck until dead.'

The crowd jeered as the man was dragged from the cart to the gallows, and some threw rotten vegetables. Tansa's could feel her heartbeat in her ears, so hard and hot she thought her head might burst.

'We should never have left Cliffark,' she whispered to Cag.

Cag swallowed. 'Reckon you're right.' His voice was dry as dust.

The man did not struggle as he was hauled to the rope and placed over the trapdoor with the noose around his neck. 'Is there any here who will pay for the life of this man?' cried the herald.

'That man is my husband,' a woman called from near the front, 'and father to my four children. He's a good man; he stole because we were starving! Please spare him!' Her voice grew in its desperation as she spoke, and when she tried to speak further she broke down in wild sobs.

The herald spoke slowly, as if addressing a child. 'Do you have the fee?'

'N-no, Lord. I swear we will work to pay off the debt. All of us.'

The herald snorted. 'And will you also pay to feed and clothe him while he sits in jail awaiting your payment? Payment must be today.' A few cries for mercy came from the crowd, but most were silent, their eyes fixed on the tableau at the gallows. He turned to the noosed man. 'Do you have any last words?'

The man spoke so thinly he could barely be heard over the crowd. 'I love you, Eisther. Tell the chil'en I love them an' all.'

'Drop!' The herald made a chopping motion towards the hangman, and he pulled the lever. The trapdoor fell. The rope went taut. Tansa screamed with the man's wife as his neck broke, the crack echoing around the square.

Cag's face was white. 'If they've got Tam,' he said, 'we'll pay everything we have left.' He looked at Tansa, eyes unfocused. 'Won't we?'

The man's widow was still screaming, and a pair of guards dragged her away as the trapdoor was reset and the man's corpse removed from the noose. 'Five silvers for the body!' called the herald as it was placed on the back of a cart.

Eight more hangings followed. Each time, the herald called for any who would pay the fee to spare the condemned, but only one man was saved from the noose, a local merchant who had been charged with giving change in clipped coins. A weeping daughter paid the toll in jewellery taken straight from her wrist. Tansa watched every single death, her despair giving way to outrage as each corpse was carried from the gallows.

I do not know who is worse, the man who kills them or the fools who cheer it.

After each drop, Cag asked if she wanted to leave, but she clung to his hand and insisted they stay. The king remained impassive throughout. As the last man's neck broke, he bent down to whisper something in the ear of the colourful merchant next to him, making both of them laugh.

As they dragged the last body away, the crowd began to disperse, and the knot in Tansa's stomach dissolved, replaced with the fierce hunger she had felt hours earlier. It felt as if she had held her breath throughout the whole ordeal. Somewhere her brother lived.

'Hold on, gentlefolk!' The herald's voice broke over the dissipating crowd. 'There is one more criminal to be dealt with today. A scoundrel of such villainy that the king has ordered that he be given... *the short drop!*'

The crowd cheered and surged back towards the gallows, while some were still trying to leave the square, creating a maelstrom of flesh that dragged Tansa and Cag along with it. Tansa's feet were lifted from the ground for a moment in the swirl of bodies, but she held onto Cag, and when the mob stilled the two of them found their feet together. The crowd reeked with the stench of sweat, infesting her mouth and nostrils. The press of bodies in front of them was so thick Tansa could no longer see the gallows, but she knew from the baying response of the crowd that another prisoner had been brought out. She stood up on her toes to try and see.

In the days that followed, she would convince herself that she had always known that it would end this way. She would even convince herself that she could have done more. That she should have immediately stormed the gallows, or started a riot while she had the chance.

But Tansa had not known. Not until she saw him. Her brother Tam, chained at the ankle, wrist, and neck, being dragged by four guards towards the gallows, his face wracked with pain.

Tansa beat and pushed against the wall of bodies ahead of her, screaming at them to move, but they ignored her, or perhaps did not notice her at all. The crowd had already used up their rotten vegetables, and compensated by doubling the volume of their jeers. Tansa tried to scream at Tam over the top of them, but could barely hear herself.

'Get on my shoulders,' said Cag firmly. 'Don't waste your voice shouting now. When the herald asks for money tell him we have it.' He picked her up easily. People behind Cag were already struggling to see past him, and one tapped him on the shoulder indignantly. Cag ignored them, but when the man grew more insistent he turned around with a snarl, sending the man a step back.

Tam was at the gallows now, taking small, shuffling steps towards the noose with his chained feet, urged on by the guards. One kicked him forcefully in the back, sending him sprawling, unable to raise his hands in time. The crowd laughed and jeered as Tam's face bounced off the wood.

The hangman ushered the guards away and placed the noose around Tam's neck. He did not move to the lever, but to the vertical beam where the end of the rope was secured, which he unhooked and tied up in his huge arms, pulling down to take the strain just enough to put Tam on his tiptoes as the noose bit into his neck.

Tansa called his name, but the noise of the crowd was deafening. 'We can pay!' she shouted desperately as the herald mounted the stage. 'We can pay!'

The herald either did not hear, or chose to ignore her. 'Gentlefolk!' he began, 'the crimes of the man who stands here are beyond imagination. Four nights ago, he crept into the keep under cover of darkness, where he not only stole from your king, but also took an item of great value from a guest of Erland, a noble friend and emissary. His ill-gotten gains were found on him when he was caught *raping a servant girl, of only nine years old!*'

The herald's voice cracked dramatically as he finished, drawing angry gasps from the crowd. Small pieces of stone and metal flew towards Tam, and with his arms bound he could not protect himself. Something struck him on the forehead, and blood began to flow down his face.

'*We will pay!*' screamed Tansa, though she knew they could not, '*we will pay!*' She could barely hear herself over the crowd and the pounding of blood in her ears.

The herald gave no sign he had heard her. 'The price for his crimes is death.' He nodded to the hangman, who pulled hard on the rope, lifting Tam from the floor.

Tansa screamed, but it was as if the sound came from someone else, and she was watching from overhead. 'Put me down!' she shouted to Cag, 'we've got to help him.'

Cag tried to push his way through the crowd and Tansa followed in his wake, but the press of bodies formed a thick wall of flesh before them, and they had made it only yards forward when the crowd became impassable. Bellowing his frustration, Cag began throwing men aside in a frenzy, clearing a path through which Tansa could see Tam dancing at the end of the rope, feet searching for ground that was not there, slowly turning purple. She felt faint, her legs numb.

Cag did not see the punch coming. Tansa's scream of warning caught in her throat as one of the men he had pushed aside swung at Cag's head with a windmilling fist. The man was huge, a fleshy gut the size of a boulder protruding from under his butcher's apron, and the blow was enough to send an unprepared Cag sprawling, taking half-a-dozen others with him. They dominoed into those next to them, drawing indignant cries, and the already bloodthirsty crowd became a swirl of fists and flesh. Tansa was thrown from her feet as those who had been unbalanced came roaring back in the direction of the disturbance, and her forearms collided painfully with the hard ground.

I have to save him. Tansa tried to rise, but the wind was forced from her lungs as a heavy body fell on top of her. Cag's parting of the crowd had drawn them into the early exchanges of a full-blown riot. Above her, punches and kicks flew, no man troubling to see if his opponent was friend or foe. She tried to rise again, and a pair of huge hands pulled her to her feet. It was Cag, dripping blood from his temple, his knuckles grazed.

'He's still alive!' he shouted into her face. 'I'll have to throw you.' Before she could argue, Cag lifted her over his head and threw her forward.

Tansa landed straight on the head of a woman in the front row, knocking her to the ground, cushioning Tansa's landing. She pushed herself to her feet, weaved around the grasping hand of the woman's angry husband and raced towards the gallows.

Only a single guard stood ahead of her, but she skidded to a halt just in front of him, still yards from the gallows. Tam's legs had stopped moving, and his face was purple-grey, his mouth hanging open, guileless black marbles staring at her from gaping sockets. Dead.

Too late. Tansa collapsed to her knees and retched up a tide of yellow bile from her empty stomach.

Through the crowd, Cag appeared next to her, moving towards the gallows as if he could still save Tam. Then he saw him, and the hope drained from his face.

'We're too late,' he said, his voice quavering.

'We're taking his body.' Tansa looked around the crowd, at the guards who had run from the gallows to quell the scuffling, back to the black shadow of the hangman approaching Tam. 'I'm going to cause a distraction; you grab Tam and run for the gate.'

Cag swallowed, wiping the tears from his eyes, and nodded.

Tansa eyed the square, pupils darting around for her target. The crowd was still heaving. Some were trying to push through towards the exit, but towards the back of the crowd, people were obviously still pressing forward. Others had stopped to yell abuse at the guards for injuries caused to their fellows. Tansa struggled to get her eyes to centre on individuals, all the crowd blurring into one mass. She had to focus. As long as she focused she would not have to think about Tam.

She picked her mark, a skinny man and his wide-backed wife, trying to walk back towards the gate to escape the crush. Tansa squeezed herself into a gap next to the man, and turned back to look at Cag before she let out a high indignant scream. She swung a wild, open-palmed slap into the man's face, mustering as much force as she could. 'Get your hands out of my skirt!' she yelled, and pushed him into his wife.

Both of them kept their feet, but their stumble set the crowd shifting and colliding again, causing a new round of angry disagreements. The man turned on Tansa, but before he could say anything, his wife pushed him. Tansa barely got out of the way as he stumbled again, and within seconds the violence had started again, as mistaken accusations escalated into pushing and then punches.

The guards moved back towards the crowd, and Tansa managed to make her way back towards the gallows, where Cag leapt onto the platform and with his knife sawed through the noose. The hangman moved to intervene, but seeing the size of Cag seemed to think better of it. Cradling Tam like a child, Cag plunged back into the crowd, Tansa following close behind as he ploughed towards the gate.

They ran from Piperskeep as fast as they could.

It was only when they had escaped the city and laid Tam's body down in woodland that Tansa let the tears overcome her. She buried her face in Cag's chest, soaking his shirt, while his own tears fell like raindrops on her head. When they first had fled the castle and found a quiet corner, Cag had pounded on Tam's chest until his fists were bruised and the breastbone cracked, but he would not stir. When that did not work, Tansa had opened his mouth in the hope she could breathe life into her brother. It was then that they discovered the swelling and blood where Tam's tongue had been cut from his mouth. They had peeled back his thin shirt, and found the bruises and weeping burn marks that had been left on his chest.

When they ran out of tears, Tansa attended again to Tam's body, while Cag busied himself building a pyre. Tansa frowned as she noticed the patch of dried blood that had blossomed in the rags at Tam's crotch. With a sense of dread, she pulled back the rags. Tam's groin was a mess of exposed blood vessels and filth.

They gelded him. Tortured him. She ran clumsily to vomit against a tree, again coughing up nothing but yellow bile.

Cag left his pile of wet wood and came over to look. He visibly paled as he took in the bloody mess where Tam's genitals had been, his knees almost buckling. 'Why, Tansa? How could they do this to him?'

'Because he bedded Hessian's queen,' she said, certain of it for the first time. 'They took his tongue to stop him challenging their lies, but the rest was the king's vengeance.' She clenched her fists and looked to the sky. *And one day, I shall have my vengeance. I swear it by my brother's soul.*

CHAPTER 40

'I don't like it, Lord,' said Naeem. 'The way Strovac looked at me... Who knows what goes on behind those beady eyes of his.'

Orsian was in his father's command tent, watching their exchange. Naeem's words elicited a rare chuckle from his father. It was clear he felt far more confident about this battle than the last. And why not? They had many more experienced soldiers than the Prindians. Orsian could not help his fingers reaching to his belt occasionally to feel the reassuring weight of his sword. He itched for battle, his stomach churning rhythmically with nervous excitement.

'We will take every precaution,' said Andrick, moving model troops about the table. 'I had always intended to exchange the prisoners myself; why change the plan now? Because you suspect that Strovac Sigac is a treasonous dog? We *know* he is a treasonous dog: all the more reason to free Errian. You and Orsian will ride with me, with ten others, your choice who. Once Errian is safe, we attack. I'll take the centre, Lady Gough the right, and you the left.'

Surprise flashed across Naeem's face. 'But I am not a lord,

Lord. You should give it to one of the new generation; there are many younger men who are eager to test themselves.'

Orsian suspected the greater objection would be to Lady Gough leading their right. For a woman to lead soldiers in the field was almost unheard of. She dressed in armour with the Tallowton crest etched into the chest, and her blonde hair tied up in a knot. She was no more than thirty years old, already widowed twice, and in the absence of a male heir had taken on all the duties of a lord on her father's death. He wondered if Helana had met her.

Andrick grunted. 'The most able of the new generation is Lady Gough.' He placed his hand solemnly on Naeem's shoulder. 'I trust none of them more than you. You have more than earnt a lordship. Once we return to Merivale I shall request it of the king.'

Naeem dropped to one knee. 'I am not worthy, Lord.' Orsian thought he saw the sliver of a tear on his cheek.

'You are if I say you are. Now, go and find those men, and bring Lady Gough. Orsian, help me with my armour.'

'You've done well befriending Burik and Derik,' said Andrick, as Orsian prepared his father's mail. 'You'll need loyal men like them when you're older.'

'Errian knows them better,' said Orsian quietly. 'They're nearer his age.'

'Errian got himself captured. While he's been held at the pleasure of the Prindians you've been making a name for yourself. Show yourself to them, and men will follow you.'

'They'll be with Errian again, when he returns.' Perhaps when Errian learnt of Orsian's exploits he might show him more respect. Orsian smiled wryly at the unlikeliness of it. Captivity would probably have made him even more disagreeable.

'The prospect thrills you, I am sure,' said Andrick dryly. 'I'm glad I never had a brother. My brother was more of a father to me in truth.' He looked at Orsian. 'For all Errian's faults, he is your brother, and when he returns you'll make your peace with him.'

'Yes, Father.'

They rode out together. Lord Andrick on Valour at the tip of a diamond, Naeem and Orsian behind him to either side carrying their banners, the wolfhounds Numa and Gyrwulf bounding along behind. Arrayed behind them were the rest, among them Naeem's twins and Lady Gough. Their Darlton hostages rode at the centre, having been spared the ignominy of being chained up in a cart.

The morning's mist parted before them as they crossed the field, and closed behind them again. After a quarter-mile, they could no longer see their army behind them. Orsian wondered if they would ever find the Prindians in the fog, but the mist thinned as they trotted on, and they soon spied a row of a dozen torches riding to meet them. With apprehension, he noticed the Prindians had come in force, two men to every one of theirs.

Rymond Prindian himself rode at the centre, looking every inch a young king, resplendent in armour decorated with green and gold and a cape hemmed with emeralds hanging from his shoulders. He was flanked by his grizzled master-at-arms, and the hulking Strovac Sigac, riding a monstrous black stallion that looked as bad-tempered as its master. Next to him rode several of the Wild Brigade, surly and bearded, each looking more dangerous than the last.

They were dragging something behind them. Squinting through the fog, Orsian glimpsed a cage fallen on its side. A ragged figure lay inside, caked with blood and bruises, wearing once fine clothes pulled to ribbons. Orsian caught a shock of golden hair encrusted with filth and with a start realised it was Errian.

His father saw him too. 'Is this your idea of fair treatment?' he called to Rymond in dismay. 'Your own blood have been allowed to ride here, in return for no more than a promise.'

Rymond shrugged unhappily. 'He was treated as well as any other guest under my roof, until he tried to escape. My obligation to fair treatment ended there. He is fortunate that I was merciful.'

'How *fortunate* for him,' sneered Andrick. 'That does not appear to have stopped you beating him senseless, nor dragging him here in a cage like a common cur.'

'You are in no position to lecture me,' snapped Rymond, surprising them all with his anger. 'Hessian left my brother to die in an oubliette, and tried to have me kidnapped and killed for the crime of being the next in line and my name being Prindian. Look to your own house before you patronise me.'

Andrick gave a mirthless chuckle. 'The boy finally shows his claws. I was beginning to wonder if such a bloodless fop could truly be the son of the fearsome Breta Prindian.' He beckoned Burik forward, leading a spare horse. 'I'll send over the oldest and youngest hostages first. Put my son on this horse and then we'll release the others.'

Lord Darlton rode forward, his youngest grandson riding with him, and Andrick encouraged the riderless horse towards Rymond Prindian with them. The mount was collected by a serving-man, who opened the cage for Errian.

'You're awfully quiet, Strovac,' Andrick called, as Errian was helped onto his horse, struggling to pull himself up and place his feet in the stirrups. 'Thinking about what awaits you after the battle? I've never been one for gods, but if there's a life after this one, the darkest depths belong to those who betray their king.'

'Whereas no doubt Eryi's great feast above the clouds awaits you,' replied Strovac with a mocking twist of his lip. 'I've always thought it sounded slightly boring; all these righteous folks sat around reminiscing of their past glories. Though you may not enjoy it too much. You'll be missing your eyes and tongue once I cut them from your head.'

'If you want them, come and take them.'

In that moment, their eyes locked, each ready to go for their blade if the other should dare. Time froze, each man poised and ready to meet steel with steel.

And then Errian mounted, and the spell was broken. He slumped in the saddle, but succeeded in steering the horse towards his father. Andrick patted him on the shoulder as he passed, and with an escort at each side to catch him if he fell, his horse carried him into the fog. Once he was clear, Andrick ushered the remaining Darlton hostages forward, and they gratefully crossed the short distance to safety.

The exchange complete, Andrick nodded goodbye to Lord Rymond. 'Until we meet in battle, Lord Prindian.' He turned his horse to leave, Orsian and the rest following.

'Lord Andrick, wait,' said Rymond, a hint of desperation in his voice. 'I have a proposal.'

Andrick turned his head back towards him. 'And what proposal is that?'

'Peace.'

The turn of Andrick's head saved his life. Just as Rymond spoke, a throwing axe flew past his nose, released from the hand of one of Strovac's brutes, while two more of them bore down on him with their blades up.

'To me!' cried Andrick, drawing his sword immediately into a parry against a wild thrust from one of his attackers.

Orsian drew his sword, his blood racing, and drove his horse towards his father, already ably fighting his two assailants. The guards who had escorted Errian were pouring out of the mist, surrounding their smaller party, and the air was soon filled with the song of steel as his companions were forced to defend themselves.

The Prindians had played them false.

Orsian had almost reached his father when he instinctively wheeled right to block a powerful overhand swing. His shoulder spasmed, but his block held. It was Adfric, the master-at-arms. He had hung back at first, seemingly as surprised as the East Erlanders, but was now wading into the chaos with murder in his eyes. He wielded his sword expertly, flashing it towards Orsian's unguarded face in a series of strikes that Orsian barely caught on his own blade. He gave ground, letting Adfric put more distance between him and his father, who had fought off the first two attackers but was now hard pressed by two more.

To his right, he caught a glimpse of Derik locked in combat with Strovac Sigac, which ended when Strovac drove a knife into his neck and pushed him from his horse. The body had hardly hit the ground when Naeem went at him, snarling in fury. Strovac barely raised his sword in time to block. Just beyond them, Lady Gough had been knocked from her horse, but leapt lithely up behind one of their foes and slit his wind-pipe. A man on foot ran at her with a spear, only for Andrick's enormous hound Gyrwulf to leap onto his back and tear his throat out. Away from it all was Rymond Prindian, still ahorse, his mouth hanging open as if he did not know what to do with himself.

And still Adfric kept coming. Orsian had trained with the sword ever since he was old enough to walk, but none of it had prepared him for the old master-at-arms' strength and skill. He was fit and fast enough to keep blocking and parrying, but eventually he would miss, and die with that heavy sword buried in his skull. Anyone who might have helped was occupied with their own battles.

He would have to save himself. After blocking the next blow, Orsian cried with false pain and let his guard drop slightly. For all Adfric's experience, he took the bait, swinging his sword in a blur of strength that would have taken Orsian's head from his shoulders, had he not been ready to duck underneath it. Adfric's sword passed harmlessly over him, and with a wild cry Orsian threw himself from his saddle and straight at the older man, the point of his blade finding a joint in the shoulder of his armour. Their mounts shifted, and together they fell in a mess of limbs. Adfric's horse broke their fall, landing heavily underneath them.

Orsian hit the ground hard but came up unhurt. He had lost his sword, but Adfric was struggling to rise, red blood running thick from his shoulder. Behind him, his horse lay screaming, its leg broken. Orsian looked around for his sword, and his eyes met those of a Prindian horseman, riding hard upon him, a blade pointed directly at Orsian's head. With no time to think, Orsian readied himself to leap from the man's path.

That was when his father saw him.

Andrick Barrelbreaker was surrounded by fallen enemies, all dead or dying, his blade locked in a test of strength with one of the Wild Brigade. But by some sixth sense he turned towards Orsian.

'Orsian!' Andrick let his opponent's strength overmatch him, then spun his sword around to bury it in his enemy's face in a spray of bone and blood. He turned and dug his heels into Valour's flanks, driving him towards the man who would dare raise a blade against his son.

It was clear from the outset of his charge who would prevail. The man tried to veer away, and Andrick's blade took him at the elbow. The attacker screamed as blood gushed and his forearm fell to the ground.

As the man's sword arm hit the floor, Orsian spotted his own blade, barely five feet from him. He stepped towards it, but his eye was caught by a flash of movement to his father's left. Strovac Sigac held an axe high over his head, riding at a canter towards Andrick's blind side.

Later, when Orsian played it back in his mind, he was not sure if he called out a warning, or if the words caught in his throat. At the last moment, his father seemed to sense the danger. He looked left, his shield came up, too slowly, and too late. The axe struck the back of Andrick's head, with a sickening crack of iron on bone.

Incredibly, it looked for a moment as if his father had survived. He turned his horse to face Strovac, his sword ready, his dark features set in disbelief. His arm twitched to swing his sword and came up short, seemingly taking the last of whatever strength was left to him. The blade slipped from his fingers, and he fell from his horse, blood pouring from his split skull. He was dead before he hit the ground.

And then Orsian screamed. A wild, bestial scream that seemed to echo off the sky and cover the whole battlefield in its sorrow, and drew the eyes of every man left alive to where the corpse of Andrick Barrelbreaker lay. His father was dead. Orsian screamed again, as tears fell in rivers down his cheeks.

Hours seemed to pass, but when Orsian came to his senses, the battle still raged, and Strovac Sigac was staring at him from his horse. The giant warrior discarded the axe, and felt at his waist for the hilt of his sword, then seemed to remember that he did not have it. He snarled in annoyance, and dismounted to steal Andrick's weapon from his dead fingers.

Orsian ran to his own sword, and willed his hand not to shake as Strovac advanced on him. He looked around for help, but all his allies were dead or hard-pressed. A guard of Lady Gough had reached her, and the two of them were making a fighting retreat. Naeem was locked in combat with one of the Wild Brigade, while another lay howling on the ground, trying to stop the flow of guts spilling from the gaping wound in his belly. Rymond Prindian still stood apart from everything, staring in wonder at the violence he had unleashed. It looked as if he had not moved since the fight began.

'I'm going to kill you, boy.' Strovac advanced slowly, wiping a thick sheen of blood from the stolen blade on his surcoat. 'But slowly. You'll be begging me for death by the end.'

Somewhere beyond the fog, Orsian heard horses galloping

towards them. He gripped his sword, ready, when from nowhere two dark shapes slammed into Strovac. One of the wolfhounds leapt for Strovac's neck, while the other pincered his ankle between its jaws. Strovac screamed in panic as Gyrwulf worried his throat, snapping at the tender flesh. He whirled clumsily, trying to shake the dogs off him, then screamed in pain as Numa's sharp teeth penetrated the leather protecting his ankle.

It was over almost as suddenly as it began. With a roar of rage, Strovac swung his sword in a wild downward arc, nearly cutting Numa in half. With his other hand he found a grip on the back of Gyrwulf's neck, and though the dog was the weight of a small man lifted and held the frenzied hound at arm's length. He sliced Gyrwulf from neck to groin, then tossed him to the ground like meat. The hound whined in agony as the life left his eyes.

Orsian felt powerful hands grab him from behind. He realised with relief that it was Naeem, the old warrior limping but alive, and before Orsian could protest he was being pushed towards a horse. His father's horse, Valour.

'Ride, lad.' Naeem shoved Orsian up onto Valour's back, barely giving him time to get his feet in the stirrups. 'Warn them. Get the men ready.' The hoofbeats were growing louder, and somewhere a horn was blowing. Orsian opened his mouth to protest, but Naeem led the horse around, and before Orsian could stop him slapped its rump with the broad side of his sword. Valour leapt away at a gallop, carrying Orsian into the dissipating mist.

Orsian looked back, expecting to see Naeem engaged in combat with Strovac, but the monstrous warrior had instead seized the green Prindian banner, waving it back and forth in the air and beckoning their forces onward. Orsian saw Naeem throw himself back into the fray, but Valour soon outdistanced the chaos, and the mist reduced Orsian's view of the scene to no more than wraiths cavorting in some murderous drama.

He turned away and bent himself low over Valour, digging his heels into the beast's flanks to draw a burst of speed from him. Valour tossed his head in protest, unused to anyone other than his father in the saddle, but Orsian clung on.

Don't think about it, he urged himself. He had seen what he had seen, but even so, he must have imagined it, or it was some trick of his father's. He could not be dead. Naeem would save him, or his father would save Naeem. He looked back, half-expecting to see him riding out of the mist, demanding that Orsian return his horse.

The East Erland force soon came into view, and he was relieved to see that they were in some sort of order, with men arranged across the field by the hundred in ten-by-ten squares, with the *Hymeriker* and other regular soldiers spread among the new recruits to bolster them.

'Orsian!' A *Hymeriker* captain on horseback whose name he could not recall greeted him. 'Where's your father? Where's Naeem?'

Orsian tried to speak, but his tongue felt like it was made of sawdust. He reached for his skin and took a long drink. 'They're coming!' he gasped. 'Shield wall!' A properly formed shield wall could withstand a horse charge, and the slope of the ground favoured them. Despite the Prindian ambush, they could still prevail.

The man frowned at him. 'Does that command come from your father? He said he would issue orders on his return.'

'No, he's—' What was he? 'He's... still there. We need to form a shield wall!'

'Look!' cried a soldier from a nearby square, pointing into the mist.

Orsian turned, and fifty yards away his father's face stared down at him from atop a long pole. They had spiked it upon the

Prindian banner, now stained with the gore that was seeping from his father's head. Below rode Strovac Sigac, a black grin as wide as the Pale River stretched across his mouth.

'The Barrelbreaker is dead!' he cried, waving the head to and fro. He turned his horse, and rode laughing back and forth across the field several times, giving the whole East Erland line a view of his grisly trophy.

Orsian felt the shock and dismay that spread across their host like a wave. Behind Strovac, the mist had diminished to little more than a thin curtain, and a vast force of West Erland horsemen was riding out of it, waving swords and spears and drowning out Strovac's laughter with their war cries.

'Shield wall!' cried the *hymerika* Orsian had spoken with. Others were taking up the cry, and on the ground, other *hymerikai* were pushing and pulling their charges into order, shouting for them to get their spears up. Orsian looked back at Strovac, wishing he had his bow to hand, and then rode to join them, guiding Valour through a gap in the line and calling for the men to tighten up, to move forward, to lift their spears. The Prindians were holding back behind Strovac – there was still time.

But he could see fear and reluctance on the faces of the less experienced soldiers, those who had never seen battle before, either forced here by the lord they were sworn to or who had answered the king's summons over winter.

'If the Barrelbreaker's dead, what's the point?' cried one man as he tried to resist the press of his fellows towards the front of the line. Several more threw down their weapons and ran, and Orsian saw another grasp for a *hymerika*'s reins and receive a sword point through the throat for his disrespect.

'Hold the line!' Orsian screamed, turning to face their foe.

With a roar, Strovac Sigac thrust the banner into the ground, raised his sword high in the air, and the West Erlanders charged.

They broke upon the barely formed Sangreal shield wall like a storm, and the line splintered like driftwood. Men fled, stumbling over their fellows in their haste to escape, as the Prindian swords rose and fell and the air thickened with the screams of the maimed. Someone tried to pull Orsian from the saddle, and as he thrust his sword down in defence he realised it was one of their own men. Another reached for the reins and went down shrieking as Valour bit off a chunk of his face. From nowhere, a man on horseback swung a sword towards Orsian. He blocked it on instinct and in desperation ran his blade across the side of the horse's neck, cutting a deep gash and sending it galloping away in terror.

'Retreat! Retreat!' someone was yelling further along the line, with a voice as loud as a horn. 'Back towards Whitewater! *Hymeriker* to me!' Orsian looked, and was shocked to see it was Naeem, ahorse but unarmed, cradling his shoulder and with blood seeping from a cut at his temple. The *Hymeriker* were rallying to him, locking their shields and beating back the West Erlanders around them.

Orsian looked around him again. The shield wall had disintegrated; even the *Hymeriker* were falling back. He kicked away another of their own men who attempted to pull him from the saddle, and spurred Valour towards Naeem.

He was thirty yards away when something heavy struck him on the back of the head. His vision wavered, his awareness tumbled, and black unconsciousness rose up to meet him.

CHAPTER 41

Ciera woke to raised voices outside her bedroom. Her hair was a tangle of neglect, matted to the pillow by a stain of saliva, and her eyes were bleary and bloodshot from a week of flitting between sleep and tears. By the glow from the window it was past midday. The room was hot, smelling of sweat and unwashed sheets. She groaned, and grabbed her pillow to roll to the other side of the bed. Sleep was the only sanctuary left to her now.

She had been confined to her room for over a week, ever since the guards had taken Tam. A maid brought her food twice a day, and when Ciera tried to question her about what was happening the woman insolently ignored her. Not even asking who she was and what had happened to her old maid had drawn a response. On the first day, Ciera had tried to run past her to the door, and the woman had caught her shoulder and pinched so tightly that Ciera had cried out in pain and been unable to resist being dragged back to the bed, as she thrashed uselessly and yelled for the woman to release her. She had tried twice more to escape since, with the same result.

Sometimes, the maid would place a hand on Ciera's

growing stomach, grunt, and shake her head slightly. Could she tell simply by placing a hand whether the child was the king's? What if he would rather kill her than let her bring a bastard into the world? Ciera bit down on her thumb, her eyes filling with tears. It was only for the baby's sake that she forced down the food she was brought each day.

When she was not occupied by endless, exhausted sleep, Ciera thought of Tam, turning the stolen bracelet she had retrieved from his clothes over and over between her fingers. Someone had come and taken his gifts to her; the elegant box and the silk purse. She had begged the mute maid to tell her what had happened to him, and written half-a-dozen letters to the king pleading for mercy. The maid had refused to deliver them with a shake of her head, and burnt every single one over a candle. Not knowing was more than Ciera could bear.

She tried to get back to sleep, but the voices outside the door were growing louder. She folded a second pillow over her head to drown them out. Would they tell her father? Perhaps that was him at the door now, demanding entry to see her. But her father was too mild and meek for that. Maybe it was her mother, perhaps the only person who could make Ciera's situation any worse.

What was clearly now an argument reached a crescendo. Ciera sat up in bed, just as her door was thrown open and crashed loudly against the wall.

An angry female voice followed. 'Eryi's blood, just get out of my way!'

'The king will hear of this!' a guard cried.

'Tell him then! If he orders me harmed, who do you think I'll blame when Lord Andrick returns? By Eryi, have some mercy for the poor girl.'

The new woman spoke with certainty, and swept confidently into the room. 'Close the door, Drayen.'

The guard retreated, muttering darkly, and Ciera's heart

leapt as she recognised Lord Andrick's wife, Lady Viratia. They had exchanged pleasantries on a few occasions, but mostly Ciera knew her by her fierce reputation. She might be brave enough to plead with Hessian for her, or find out what had happened to Tam. Ciera sat up in bed, feeling self-conscious of her dishevelled appearance next to Viratia's composed beauty.

Viratia sat down on the bed, and held a cool palm to Ciera's cheek. 'What have they done to you?' She gently ran her fingers through Ciera's hair, wincing at the knots she found. She returned to the door, and opened it to whisper hurried orders to somebody.

'I brought Yuliea, my maid, with me,' she said, returning. 'She'll fetch everything we need.' Viratia took Ciera's hand. 'Tell me everything. What happened?'

Ciera stared at her, but after a moment began to recount the tale which she had told nobody else, that until now had belonged only to her and Tam. She told Viratia of Cliffark, of the playhouse and the stolen bracelet, the arrival of Lord Andrick and the sudden marriage and journey to Merivale, and the foiled kidnapping she could barely remember. When she told her of the king's late-night visits to her chamber, Ciera broke down in tears, and could not continue for several minutes. Viratia held her, letting Ciera's tears soak her neck and dress. It was as safe as she had felt in months. Then she told her of Tam's reappearance, her pregnancy, and finally Tam being caught and beaten to a pulp.

'And they've held me in here ever since,' she finished tearfully. 'You're the first person who's spoken to me in a week.'

'By the Norhai...' While Ciera told her story, the maid had returned with a brush and warm water to wash Ciera's face, and Viratia was now teasing the knots from Ciera's birds'-nest hair. She stopped to embrace her, and Ciera felt so pathetically grateful she almost burst into tears again. 'My dear... I'm so sorry. You have been treated horribly, and nobody has lifted a finger. I should have come to see you months ago.'

'It's fine,' sniffed Ciera, wiping her nose on her sleeve. 'Just help me save Tam, please. I'll do anything.'

'Oh my dear girl...' Viratia took her hand and looked at her softly, her eyes glistening with tears. 'There was a boy... They hanged him four days ago, in the yard. I'm so sorry. He died bravely.'

Tam is dead. Ciera had known it, deep down, but that made it no easier to bear. Her abdomen convulsed, and her whole body stiffened as she fought to hold back her sobs. 'Dead?' she whispered. 'But he never hurt anyone. They should have punished me; I'm the one who...' She gulped uselessly, struggling for breath. How could she live with herself?

'Hush, child.' Viratia wrapped her arms around her, stroking her hair as her small body spasmed with sobs.

'It's my fault,' sobbed Ciera. After a week, she had thought she would have no more tears to cry, but they flowed down her cheeks as freely as the Pale River. 'I should never—'

'No.' Viratia broke their embrace, and looked at Ciera sternly. 'Look at me. This is not your fault. You were placed in an impossible position, treated like a broodmare by a wicked old man, and expected to bear the weight of continuing a dynasty. A boy is dead, but it is not your fault. The king's, my husband's maybe, and the boy... I must bear my share as well. I knew what you were likely enduring, and I did nothing. You have been treated horribly. I never, *never*, want to hear you say again that this is your fault. Do you understand me?'

Ciera nodded tearfully.

'Good. Now, tell me, truthfully: do you know whose the child is?'

Ciera shook her head, willing herself not to cry again. 'I don't know,' she whispered. 'It could be either of them.'

Viratia squeezed Ciera's hand. 'You will have to lie. You

must tell Hessian that he only came to you after you were with child.'

'Lie to the king?' The thought filled Ciera with dread. 'He will never believe me.'

'That depends how well you lie. He will want to believe you, for he desires an heir above all else. Swear to him the child must be his, and he may forgive you. Tell him the boy forced you, and you are glad that your honour has been avenged.'

Ciera gaped at her. How could she taint what she and Tam had shared with such a lie? She could never. She owed Tam better than that.

'I know, Ciera. It is a horrible thing, but it is necessary.' She gripped Ciera's hand insistently. 'I was almost in your position, once. My father intended for me to marry a man older even than Hessian. He had rubbery lips that were always dripping with wine, and a mole on his cheek with a hair growing out of it as long as my finger. His eyes would follow me all around the room, peeling back my clothes. When I complained to my mother, she told me, "You may not love him, but you will love your children."

'Andrick saved me from that, but I never forgot what my mother told me. I can only imagine how Hessian has treated you, but you should do what is right for your child, and for yourself. Tam would not want you to die for his sake.'

'I loved him,' Ciera whispered. 'And he loved me.' She saw a flicker of disbelief mar Viratia's sympathy. 'He did! He came here all the way from Cliffark. He climbed the castle walls, just for me. We were going to escape together. He was so brave, and they killed him for it.' She held back a sob. 'How long do I have to decide?'

'Until the king comes to see you,' said Viratia, pushing back loose strands of hairs from Ciera's forehead with her fingers. 'He is too proud to come to you now, too proud and cruel for a great many things. But eventually he will be curious about the child, and he will come. If you lie, and the child is a boy with his look, he will want to claim it, but he will not believe the word of a wife who took another man willingly into her bed. You must convince him the child is his, and that you were true to him.'

Ciera wiped the tears from her cheeks. She could do it. Her life and the life of the babe within her depended on it. Stiffening her resolve, she rose and went to the looking glass at her dressing table. Her face was pale as bleached bone, and her eyes were red from crying. This was not how a queen behaved, nor a daughter of Cliffark. *I will be stronger than this*, she swore to herself.

She would never be so helpless again. All she had achieved – the reduction in taxes, the opening of hunting in the king's wood – she had done through Hessian, and it was not enough. She would make him believe her, and after that she would be a queen in more than just name. She had relied upon her marriage to Hessian, when she should have been wielding power in her own right. Her mother would never have let herself be reduced as Ciera had, locked away and relying upon the goodwill of her husband. That which was given could also be taken away.

Hessian would never love her, and she had been foolish to put herself at his mercy. She needed her own power. Hessian would not live forever, and when he was gone, she would be the one to take his place, in the name of her son. And if the child that grew within her was a girl, she and Hessian would try again. There could be no victory without sacrifice.

Ciera placed a hand to her belly. 'I will do it for you,' she whispered. She would do it for Tam, too. But most of all she would do it for herself.

CHAPTER 42

The castle was pitched in darkness, the sconces and fires having burnt down hours ago. Somewhere, a guard snored softly. A faint hum of activity drifted upward from the kitchen, where the work never stopped.

Helana kept a hand to the wall, creeping blindly through the corridors with a dagger clutched in her fist. Word of the West Erlanders' victory had reached Irith earlier that day. She could only assume nobody had come for her, whether to lock her up or drag her to the celebrations, because they had forgotten she was there.

At every corner, she imagined coming face to face with a guard, and kept low to the wall, her breath soft and steady. This was how Errian should have escaped, if only he had the sense. If anyone discovered her she would say she was taking a walk to calm her nerves.

Finally, she reached the back door she had known was there. She opened it and winced as the hinge gave a loud squeak. Holding her breath, she waited for the sound of somebody coming to investigate. When she was sure it was safe, she stepped outside, closing the door carefully behind her.

The next part would be the hardest. Helana had watched Breta Prindian attentively. The woman was dangerously clever, but she was not immune to being spied upon. Helana followed the route she had seen Breta take, keeping close to the walls and hiding in their shadows.

It was not this she feared, but what came next.

In the darkness, the guard's brazier burnt like a beacon, marking her exit through a postern gate. Heart pounding, she approached him, readying a coin in one hand and her blade in the other.

He must have been half-asleep, because he did not see her until she was right next to him. She dropped a coin into his palm, and he stared up at her slackly.

'Who—?'

Before she knew what she was doing, Helana drove the dagger into his windpipe, clamped a hand over his mouth, and lowered him from his chair to the floor. He struggled feebly, but she let him fight, until she felt his body shudder its last.

She exhaled with her hands on her knees, fighting a wave of nausea. She had not meant to kill him, but waiting to see if he would let her out would have been too much risk. He could have overpowered her if she had not acted quickly. She fumbled at his belt for a brass ring of keys, and with shaking hands tried several in the sally port lock before it clunked open. 'Sorry,' she whispered to the man's corpse.

She had to put as much distance as she could between her and Irith by daybreak, and dawn was only hours away.

This was where her foolhardiness had led her. She had come searching for peace and safety, and it had ended with her driving a dagger into a man's throat. She could not understand it; Rymond had wanted peace. Had Errian killing his friend enraged him enough to sacrifice everything? And how had he defeated Andrick?

She found Mitra outside the walls, where she had left her

earlier that day. The patient horse whinnied at her approach, and Helana soothed her with an apple, taking a moment to stroke her head and neck. Mitra nuzzled at her affectionately.

'Hope you've got some strength left for a journey home,' Helana murmured. The horse might be her only friend left in the world.

She set out eastward, the horizon already melting from black to indigo with the promise of dawn. Helana's mind whirred as she rode, calculating the days and hours it would take her to reach Halord's Bridge, and how brief her rests would have to be to keep ahead of any pursuit. She was a better rider than any who might pursue her, but if they came they would come in force.

At mid-morning, she stopped by a stream, letting Mitra drink while she splashed cold water on her face and refilled her waterskin. The day was cool, with a blustery wind that rose and fell like the clamour of city bells. Helana watched the horizon, and for the first time in months, she felt alive.

She had made a mistake. A marriage to Rymond – to anybody – would have been a disaster. Her home was the woods and the open fields, not the lord's chambers and the birthing bed. She had forgotten how good it felt to ride under the open sky, with possibility over every horizon.

In that sense, she supposed she was blessed that the two sides had battled at Whitewater. She hoped Orsian was alive.

Helana whirled around at the sound of hooves to see three riders coming straight for her. Quickly, she ran to Mitra, vaulting into the saddle. She watched their approach, ready to turn and ride for her life at the first sign of a bow being drawn. She was sure she could outrun them, but how had they caught her so quickly?

A flash of red-gold hair gave her an answer. Breta Prindian must have known the moment she left Irith. Helana cursed under her breath.

The pursuers pulled up twenty yards away. Neither of Breta's escorts drew a weapon.

'What do you want?' Helana called to her.

Breta smiled. 'Did you think I would not notice that you had not brought your horse inside to the stables?'

'Are you here to take me back?'

'No. You were my guest, free to leave as you pleased. Shame a guard had to die for it.'

Helana did not believe her. 'Why are you here, then?'

'I seek Rymond returning, to hear of the battle. The information I have received has been... inconsistent. And I came to invite you to speak with him before you leave. It may be the last time you see each other.'

'And why would I want to see the man who is at war with my family?'

'Because you care for him, incredible as it seems. It was a rare moment of good judgement, him falling for you. Not something I had foreseen. Come, ride with me. I promise you safe conduct.'

Helana looked at her. If Breta spoke truly, she could ride away right now. What good would seeing Rymond do, now it was too late?

An explanation though. He owed her that.

Helana nodded. 'Let's go.'

They rode in silence, Helana ever casting suspicious glances at Breta Prindian and her escorts. She did not seem the least bit surprised that the two sides had fought. Had she not wanted peace? Why else would she have invited Helana into her home?

'Why did you allow me to meet Rymond?' she asked, when the silence became unbearable.

'Your claim,' said Breta, without hesitation. 'A marriage would have strengthened Rymond's claim if your father died. Worthless now, if the queen births a boy. It will be by force of arms he takes the crown, or not at all.'

Her words sent a shock of understanding through Helana. Of course. Breta had ensured the two sides came to blows. She had been a fool to trust her, for a second time. She cursed herself, trying to hide her surprise. 'And now I am free to go?'

Breta chuckled. 'We have no further use for you. Rymond need not marry you, and you would make a poor hostage.

'I have enjoyed our time together. I am sorry to have manipulated you with your foolish desire for peace. You are a rarely capable woman, and I can respect that. But there can be no peace.'

Helana replied only with silence. She needed to speak to Rymond.

It was mid-afternoon when they saw the banners above the horizon: Prindian emerald green silhouetted black against the sky, and behind it the pale blue and white of Lord Storaut, and half-a-dozen others Helana did not recognise. There was laughter and merrymaking on the wind, the unmistakable sound of victory. Rymond was at the column's head, with thousands of soldiers snaking behind him in a column like a hideous black reptile.

Next to Rymond's banner, somebody carried a second, flagless pole. It was only when they got closer that Helana saw it was topped by a man's head, with a dark beard unmistakable beneath the tar that preserved it. Dried black blood caked its face and neck like a foul birthmark, obscuring the victim's features. Helana's mouth went dry, and she urged Mitra on.

When they were close enough for Rymond to hail them in greeting, Helana realised with horror to whom the head belonged. Her uncle's grim visage stared down at her, bloodsoaked and twisted in horror, his dark hair slick with gore. They had driven a spike through his neck and all the way through the top of his head. His tongue lolled from his mouth like a swollen worm, and yellowing skin hung from his skull like wax.

Helana turned and vomited, then grasped for her waterskin

to wash the burning taste from her mouth. She looked up again at her uncle's head, and, unable to stop herself, vomited again.

The men close to Rymond laughed, and the man carrying the pole waved it back and forth in the air, then forward, towards Helana. He swayed in the saddle, obviously drunk. They were Strovac Sigac's men, and Helana's face flushed with anger as she saw the big warrior in the middle of them, smirking.

Breta Prindian looked approvingly up towards the head. 'I see the signs of victory. But why are there so few of you?'

Strovac chuckled darkly. 'Have no fear, Lady Prindian. We left some men behind to chase down the Sangreal dogs. We return with prisoners, and to celebrate.' The men around him cheered, tossing wineskins to one another and drinking deeply, the deep red dregs running down their chins.

Rymond was at the front, looking pale and embarrassed, unable to meet Helana's eye. He turned around and said something. The men behind him stopped their revelry, and rode on around Helana and Breta, still bearing the head.

Helana averted her eyes, unable to look at it any more, her heart sick with grief. What if there was another pole along the column, bearing Orsian's head? Behind Rymond, the whole column split, riding around her. He rode closer to her, accompanied only by Adfric, whose left arm was bound in a splint.

'I'm sorry,' Rymond said, as the last of the men passed, finally meeting her gaze. He seemed dazed, as if this were a dream he expected to wake from.

Helana was in no mood to hear his apologies. She wanted to reach out and strike him. Her hand itched for the dagger she had sheathed at her thigh, and her anger must have shown, because Adfric brought his mount closer to Rymond, his hand ready on his sword.

'Could we speak privately?' asked Rymond, his eyes pleading with her. 'It's not what you—'

'Not what I think?' Helana stared at him, incredulous. 'You mean that wasn't my uncle's head I just saw?'

'I didn't mean—'

'Didn't mean for what?' Helana's eyes bored into him. 'When you proposed to marry me, were you already planning to murder my uncle?'

'I didn't murder him! I offered peace, and then Strovac threw an axe at him! After that—'

'It was murder!' declared Adfric. He was near as drunk as the rest of them, but morose with it rather than jubilant. 'It shamed us all.'

Rymond's eyes were low, his face downcast. 'I couldn't stop it. I'm sorry.'

Helana looked towards Breta, wishing she were close enough for her blade to reach the older woman's neck. She knew by her subtle smile for whom Strovac Sigac had killed her uncle. It had not been just for his own vengeance and bloodlust, she was sure of that. Half the country seemed to dance to Breta Prindian's bloody tune.

'What of Orsian, my cousin? Did you kill him too?'

Rymond shook his head. 'He escaped.'

'And then you routed them.' With Andrick dead, the West Erlanders would have cut through them like flame through parchment.

'I had no choice! If—'

'You told me you wanted peace.' Helana's grip on her reins tightened, making Mitra twitch restlessly. 'My uncle was a good man. You could never have defeated him without treachery.'

'I didn't want this. If—'

Helana raised a hand to stop him. 'Spare me.' Next to her, she felt Breta Prindian's smug triumph rolling off her in waves. A winter wasted in Irith, hoping this man – this boy – would be different to what her father had claimed the Prindians were. They had made a fool of her, all of them.

By Eryi, Orsian. What had she done? He worshipped his father. She had to get back to him, if he lived.

She wiped her eyes, willing her voice to hold steady. Beneath her, Mitra whickered, sensing her rider's distress. 'Anything I might have said to you, about marriage, or anything else, forget it. If it takes the rest of my life, I will see justice for what you have done.'

Rymond opened his mouth to argue, and seemed to think better of it. He shook his head sadly. 'As you will. Just believe me when I say that I'm sorry.'

'Does Errian live?'

'Yes. We freed him before... before it happened.'

Helana touched the dagger at her thigh. She would make a fight of it; she would make them kill her before she let them take her. 'I'm going home, Rymond. If you have a shred of honour left to you, you will grant me safe passage.'

He nodded, giving his consent. Helana tried not to feel pity for how pathetic he looked. Even with his army and his victory, he was still just a boy. 'Go then. Nobody will stop you.'

'Won't they?' Breta's voice behind her was sharp as a blade. 'Lord Strovac, take the Lady Helana into custody.'

Helana had been ready. It had taken her far too long, but finally she was wise to Breta Prindian's treachery. She dug her heels into Mitra's side, lashed her reins, and galloped past an open-mouthed Rymond, as the cries of pursuit began.

Grass and trees rushed past her, the wind deafening in her ears. She would need to lose her pursuers before she rode for Halord's Bridge. Sighting a distant wood, she rode for it, driving Mitra forward in a mud-churning gallop. A stream appeared from nowhere, and the horse leapt it easily.

Helana looked back. There were eight of them, Strovac and some of his men, and Chieftain Ba'an with a few Thrumb. They were some eighty yards back, riding hard. She gritted her teeth and urged Mitra on. The mare was fast, but there were so many of them, and if she lamed or broke a leg then Helana was done for. Her best hope was to lose them in the woods.

She looked back again as the wood rose up before her. Most of Strovac's men had fallen back now, but Chieftain Ba'an and his Thrumb were keeping pace, with Strovac not far behind them on his monstrous stallion. Helana dropped low to Mitra's neck and plummeted into the wood, as thick tree trunks flew past and low-hanging branches whipped at her. Still she did not slow. More than once, only Mitra's swift reactions saved them both from going headlong into a tree. She dared not look back, but there was no sound of pursuit behind her, and she allowed herself to think she had lost them.

At the edge of the wood, she slowed. Mitra's breath was coming hard and heavy, the mare's flanks were drenched in sweat, and there was white foam at the edge of her mouth. Helana looked back, and saw no one. If she veered back into the wood and went carefully, she could emerge on a different side, and they would have no way of knowing which way she had gone.

But as she emerged into the faint sunlight, a rider came across her path. Chieftain Ba'an sat before her, broad-jawed and powerful, and when Helana tried to turn away another Thrumb blocked her path. A third man seized her reins from the other side. She went for her dagger, and the second man seized her wrist and bent it back.

'Do not hurt her,' rumbled Ba'an. 'Princess Helana is to be our honoured guest.'

CHAPTER 43

The cliffs over the stone beach near Whitewater were pocked with caves, wide inlets worn into the stone by time and the fierce waves blown across the Shrouded Sea. Once they had given sanctuary to smugglers who sought to avoid the lords' taxes by landing on the beach in the dead of night under black sails and muffled oars, but those men were long gone, either drawn into the town's whaling trade or driven away by it.

The caves now gave sanctuary to deserters, refugees of the battle where Andrick the Barrelbreaker had been struck down by the coward Strovac Sigac, and his army driven from the field by the rampaging force of Rymond Prindian. In the days that followed, the West Erlanders had scoured the countryside, cutting down any man who had fought for the Sangreals.

It was Orsian's fourth day hiding in the cave. He had discarded his armour, but kept his sword. His father's horse Valour had tried to follow him down to the beach. It had taken a mighty slap on the horse's rump with his blade to send him south-east towards Merivale. Hopefully the brave beast would find his way home. Orsian could not risk going with him. Every day more broken men poured into the caves with tales of narrow escapes from Prindian soldiers intent on killing any East Erlander this side of the bridge.

He did not know what had struck him in the chaos, but the tender lump left on Orsian's head was the size of a child's fist. That errant blow might have saved his life. Somehow, his unconscious body had stayed in the saddle, and Valour had carried him from the battlefield. He had woken with the scent of the sea in his nostrils, under a grey drizzle that had soaked him down to his undershirt, with the horse peaceably pecking at the grass and his head ringing with pain.

There were five others in the cave, sworn to a number of different lords, but each fiercely loyal to his father, and every day swearing vengeance against the whoreson Strovac Sigac who had killed the finest son of Erland ever to wield a sword. These men might have broken and ran before the Prindian assault, but they were proud men, proud and dangerous.

Orsian closed his eyes, remembering it again, like a scab he could not resist scratching at. It was his fault. He had lost his sword, he had seen Strovac riding towards his father, and he had not shouted loudly enough to warn him. The crack of the axe against his father's skull reverberated between his ears.

I am not solely to blame for this, he swore to himself furiously. He had been sold a lie, where righteousness and the strength of the *Hymeriker* were immutable truths, as certain as the rising of the sun. He had done everything he was supposed to do – train hard, listen to his father, become a *hymerika* – and it had all been for nothing, all beaten and betrayed in a few moments of stark treachery. How could they have been so foolish? How had his father been so wrong?

He was wary of the others, minding his words carefully to avoid giving any clue of who he was. Who knew what they might do to the foolish boy who had let Strovac Sigac cave his father's head in with an axe?

He was the youngest by some years, and the others seemed

content to accept that as the reason for his stoic silence, perhaps thinking him a shy young squire to a minor lord. And if they knew that Orsian cried himself to sleep each night, they never mentioned it.

Food was scarce, but the oldest of them, named Sedrik, had that morning shared with him a fish he had skewered with his sword, which for now kept Orsian's stomach from rumbling. It was cold and meagre, but after two days starving it tasted as fine as anything ever made in the Violet Hall kitchens.

Others were not so lucky. They huddled morosely against the cave wall, growing hungrier and more frustrated with each passing hour. Cadwell, a black-bearded bear of a man, had just returned from the beach, and threw his spear down in a fit of frustration.

'It's no bloody good,' he announced. 'Can't catch a damn thing with this shit.' He glared at Sedrik. 'Catch us some fish, old man. It's not fair that you eat while we starve.'

'Not my problem,' replied Sedrik. 'I'm not risking that beach any more than I have to. You can see them damn Prindians up on the cliff, eyeing me with their bows.'

Cadwell snorted. 'Coward. I reckon skewering that fish is more use than your sword ever saw in the battle.'

Sedrik was on his feet in an instant. 'I killed three Prindians with this sword before they broke through. Never saw you standing there with me. Prove me wrong.'

Orsian could feel the atmosphere changing, despondence giving way to the threat of violence. The three others were eyeing Sedrik and Cadwell with cold-eyed interest. Each of them was sour with hunger, and spoiling for a fight.

Cadwell shifted his gaze to Orsian. 'Boy, give me your sword. Steel that sharp is wasted on a mewling pup like you.' Orsian said nothing, but gripped his sword hilt tightly, as if Cadwell might tear it from his scabbard. 'You give it to me,' Cadwell said again, moving threateningly towards him. 'Or I'll give you something to really cry about, snivelling little coward.'

'You leave him be,' said Sedrik, stepping between Cadwell and Orsian.

'I'll leave him be if you catch us some fish.'

'I'll be damned—'

Sedrik never got to finish his sentence. Cadwell swung a meaty uppercut into the older man's jaw, snapping his head back and sending a spray of gore and teeth arcing over the cave wall. Two other men were on their feet in moments, moving to defend Sedrik from Cadwell's assault, until one was grabbed by a third, and they fell to the ground in a flurry of punches.

Cadwell had Sedrik on the defensive, the older man covering his jaw under a barrage of punches. Another man grabbed Cadwell's arm from behind, but Cadwell seized the man by the hair and threw him over his shoulder and onto the cold floor of the cave with a sickening crack. The man did not rise.

Orsian dodged around them and ran, out of the cave and onto the beach. The heavy steps of Cadwell followed him. Orsian kept going. The stone beach was unsteady under his feet, slowing him. Cadwell's powerful legs and longer stride fared better, and Orsian could hear him gaining. He stumbled, and his leg buckled. Rocks tore through the worn cloth at his knee, drawing blood, and grazed the hand he flung out to break his fall.

He whipped his sword from its scabbard and turned on the spot, swinging it in a wide arc behind him. If Cadwell ever saw the blade coming, he was too slow to stop it. It caught him in the abdomen, right above his pelvis. He looked down in shock at the blade embedded in his gut, and grasped at it weakly with both hands. Orsian stood, and pushed Cadwell in the chest as he withdrew the blade. Cadwell fell to the ground, clutching his wound, dying.

Orsian wiped the blood from his sword, disgusted. *I never meant to kill him. I never meant to kill an East Erlander.* Perhaps this was what happened when men lost a battle, turning on each other over a fish barely big enough to feed one of them. They should have just caught more fish.

He could not go back to the cave now. At least two of the men he had shared it with were dead, perhaps more. He took one last look back to see he was not followed, and set off eastwards.

He moved slowly, watching his feet. His knee and hand stung where they had taken the weight of his fall, so he walked down to the sea to bathe them in saltwater. The tide was low, but it would not remain so for long. When it rose, it would rise fast, and he would need to find shelter.

I can't go home. Going home would mean retelling his father's death to his mother and the king. And to Errian. *Errian.* The shame of letting his father die was far greater than Errian's shame at being captured.

He replayed it in his mind, over and over again. The rider bearing down on him. His father's desperate charge that split the man's arm at the elbow. Strovac Sigac, with his axe. The warning cry that may have never left his throat. The back of his father's head, smashed open in a sickening thud of iron on bone. Better to die than tell his mother how his failure had killed his father. Better to be forgotten.

All his life he had dreamt of being one of the *Hymeriker*, of fighting for Erland. What had he been thinking? Helana was right: the king was a madman, no more interested in the lives of Erlanders than in the lives of insects. Orsian had been so sure of the righteousness of their cause, and all he had succeeded in doing was getting his father killed.

He did not know how far he walked. Evening fell, and the water began to rise. The sky was grey and purple, and the horizon flashed silver and gold and blue with the lightning of a distant storm.

It was then that the Prindians found him. Two of them, bearing the deep green Prindian colours on their cloaks and shields.

'Halt, boy!' called one of them, shaking Orsian from his gloom. They were walking down towards him from the cliffs, swords drawn. 'We can already tell you're another East Erland runaway, so don't bother denying it.'

'Just out for a walk, I reckon,' sniggered his fellow.

'We're here to take you in,' continued the first, tapping his sword against the rocks. 'Show us where your friends are, and we'll go easy on you.'

'Got no friends,' said Orsian, trying to disguise his nobility with muddied vowels. 'Leave me be.' He drew his sword.

The two men laughed. 'Reckon we'll enjoy this,' said one, as they moved down towards Orsian, their swords raised.

The men were competent swordsmen, but Orsian had trained at the knee of his father, and having shed his armour could move even more swiftly than usual. They rushed him, one high and right as the other went left and low. Orsian ducked under one and leapt over the other in a single motion, and their blades crashed clumsily together, breaking the silence of the beach like a pealing bell. Before the men could adjust, Orsian was on them, putting all his anger behind his sword as he swung it wildly across each of their necks. The two men fell, hands clutching at their opened windpipes.

Orsian sheathed his sword, warm tears rolling down his cheeks. It had been so easy to save himself. Why could he not save his father? He stared at the waves lapping up the beach. If he stood here for another hour, they would swallow him, pull him out to sea or dash him against the rocks. His soul may never find Eryi above the clouds, but that was where his father was,

probably cursing him. If he stayed here, Orsian Andrickson
could be washed away with the waves.

'Ho, lad!'

Orsian looked up in alarm, reaching for his sword. But it
was just one man, waving to him and walking swiftly up the
beach rather than down it, thickset and white-bearded in dark,
drenched leathers, his face craggy with windburn. Along the
shore, Orsian could see two men carrying a wooden rowing boat
up the beach, out of the reach of the waves. 'Reckon you could
put that strong sword arm to an oar? The wind has blown us off
our course from Whitewater. We'll need four of us if we're to
get back to the ship without the water dragging us under or
smashing us against the rocks.'

Orsian looked at the man doubtfully. 'You've just seen me
slice open two men's necks with this sword. What makes you
think I won't do the same to you?'

The man shrugged. 'Looked the sort of men that needed
killing, and as it happens I'm out of options.' He pointed up at
the cliffs. 'Looks like you are too.'

Orsian turned, his gaze following the man's finger. For a
moment he did not see them, but silhouetted against the rock
face were a half-dozen West Erlanders, picking their way
towards the beach down a sheer winding path. He cursed. It
was a slow and treacherous route, but they were already
halfway down.

'Looks like you might need off this beach worse than I do.'
The man stepped forward and thrust his hand out. 'Abner, first
mate on the *Jackdaw*.'

Orsian looked for a moment at the man's hand, and then
took it gratefully. He did need to escape the beach, the swifter
the better. Besides, there was something about this man, with
his bright gaze and wild white eyebrows threatening to take over
his forehead and his indifference at the two dead soldiers at

Orsian's feet. In that instant, he decided he liked Abner, first mate on the *Jackdaw*.

Abner grinned a row of teeth stained yellow with smokestick residue. 'Follow me, lad.'

Orsian followed him to the rowboat, which was already being lapped by the rising waves. 'You don't need the names of these,' said Abner, indicating the others. 'But the idiot in the boat is Phinn.' Orsian peered into the boat, where a young man lay prone under a covering of sacks and leathers, sound asleep. 'Damn fool got drunk in town while we were getting some last-minute supplies.' Abner reached down to slap the man on the back of the head. 'It'll be a dozen lashes when we get back, Phinn, you see if it's not!'

Abner addressed all of them. 'We'll push off, and then row our bollocks off to get away from this beach. Once we're far enough from the cliffs we can think about aiming towards the *Jackdaw*, if we live that long.'

It was backbreaking, muscle-burning work. Orsian had trained to fight encumbered by armour from dawn till dusk, but within five minutes of putting his arm to the oar his back was soaked in sweat, even in the cold of the open water, and behind him all the while was Abner, yelling for him to pull. Even with the tide against them, eventually they were able to make clear water, and turned the boat towards the silhouette of a long, high-sailed ship barely visible against the darkening sky.

When they pulled alongside the *Jackdaw*, Abner threw a rope up to the deck, and a ladder was dropped for them. Orsian leant back on his bench, exhausted.

Abner slapped him hard twice on the back. 'Well, you row like a girl, but there's strength in those arms.' The old man was breathing hard but looked like he was ready to row to shore and back again that minute. 'Never caught your name, lad.'

Orsian stared at him. 'Ranulf,' he replied, after a moment's panic, taking for some reason the name of Rymond Prindian's dead brother.

'Fancy name, that,' said Abner with a smirk. 'The captain will like it.'

'Will you drop me back in Whitewater tomorrow?' asked Orsian.

Abner grinned apologetically through his filthy teeth. 'Afraid not, lad. We're shipping out tomorrow, heading up north where there are whales so big they could sink us with a splash of their tail, and plenty more besides. Good honest pay for those with muscles and the wits to use them, and I'm afraid by helping me out you've signed up as crew for a half-year contract.'

Orsian opened his mouth to protest, and barely got a word out before suddenly he was seized from behind by two men, pinning his arms to his sides. He struggled against them, but he was weak from rowing, and they gripped him as if they meant to squeeze the breath from his lungs.

Abner's face had hardened, the twinkle in his eye replaced by cold avarice. 'You can come aboard with us, or you can swim back to shore by yourself. Reckon the water would kill you first, but them on the beach would do for you otherwise. Now, what do you say?'

CHAPTER 44

The sky over Piperskeep was cloudless, a bright blue that promised a warm summer. Without a single gust of wind in the air, the guards had cast off their furs and let their braziers burn low.

Viratia walked the battlements in silence, her head hooded, and her eyes rimmed with red. Andrick had promised her it would be his last war, and so it had come to pass. Her wild and beautiful boy. Dead.

Naeem had brought the news. He had returned to Merivale at the head of an army, with barely half the men they had left with. She had gone to her balcony to watch them, and when she could not see her husband on his great black warhorse nor his brown-on-green standard, she had known. She kept her composure long enough for Naeem to ignore the king's summons and come to her. Lord Andrick Barrelbreaker was dead.

Naeem had told her of the Prindians' treachery, how they had ambushed them under a pretence of parley, and how Strovac Sigac had buried an axe in Andrick's skull. He had spared her a retelling of the desecration of his corpse, but that tale had reached her soon enough. Andrick's body had been emasculated, and his head stuck atop a pole alongside the Prindian standard, so that no man would doubt his death.

I will have his body returned. And Orsian, whether he lives or not. Naeem had told her how he had thrown Orsian onto Andrick's horse and sent them from the field. They had waited in hope that Orsian would return, but yesterday Valour had appeared, without a rider. She had gone to Theodric for help, and asked him three times a day if he had word of her son. So far the wizard had heard nothing.

Errian though. Errian she had. He was a shell of the boastful youth he had been when she had last seen him, but he was safe. Andrick's death, though, seemed to have drained the last of his spirit. He slept a lot, and when awake he was usually drunk. It broke Viratia's heart to see him brought so low.

At least she had Pherri still, alive and unharmed. But Pherri had never truly been a child, certainly not a child who needed a mother. She was lost to her as well now, in a way. Viratia knew next to nothing of what Pherri might be learning, but wondered if in time she would be able to know things she had no business knowing, as Theodric used to. She was just glad to see her daughter happy.

Hessian had not been seen. When Naeem had brought him the news he had retired to his solar and stayed there, as was his wont during his black moods. He had only just emerged from the one which had followed his queen's betrayal. Viratia could not blame him. To lose a brother and learn that the babe growing inside his wife may not be his was more than most men would bear.

But the realm cried out for leadership. So many men were still pouring into the city with wounds and ailments that the Brides of Eryi were overwhelmed with treating them. There were tales that some men had turned brigand, hiding in the countryside to harass and rob those they had once fought alongside. The king did nothing to protect his people, just wallowed in his grief and bitter recriminations.

For now, the West Erlanders were drunk on their victory, but in time their gaze would turn to the lands over the river. Who would lead Erland in the battles to come? Andrick was dead. Errian broken. Orsian missing. The men would follow Naeem, but he had always been Andrick's firm hand, not a firm head. Theodric worked in the shadows, and most were terrified of him. Helana had been missing for months, and Hessian did not seem to care to look for her. Lady Gough was whip-smart and tough as old leather. She led men into battle, but would other men follow a woman who wore mail and was said to bed with female paramours? None of the lords who had stayed loyal to Hessian filled Viratia with confidence. All were either past their prime or young and untested.

She needed to speak with Hessian. Viratia turned and marched towards the king's tower.

She knew where his rooms were, but had never climbed the stairs herself. Only Andrick and Theodric dared trouble Hessian in his solar without a summons.

The guards at the top were familiar to her, men Andrick had trained himself. He would have known their names, and the names of their wives and families, but Viratia had never troubled to learn. It had never seemed important until now.

'Forgive me,' she said, 'you are both of the *Hymeriker*, but I am afraid I do not know your names.'

'Gawen,' said one, sketching a brief bow.

'Jarad,' said the other, following suit.

'I am here to speak with the king. Will you allow me entry?'

The two guards looked uncomfortably at one another. 'My apologies, Lady,' said Gawen, 'but we cannot allow you entry without word from the king.'

Viratia had expected this, but had not considered what she would do next. To her good fortune though, the door opened.

Hessian's long frame stood in the doorway, a cup of wine grasped in his hand. His eyes were glassy and unfocused. 'Who is it?' he demanded. He looked worse than ever, every line in his face like a ravine, his long, grey hair limp and knotted.

Viratia dropped into a curtsy. She had always found Hessian distasteful, ever since she was young when his eyes would casually wander over her body as if it was his to own, but she could not fear the pitiful figure that stood before her, half-drunk before noon. 'I apologise for troubling you, Majesty. I was hoping to speak with you.'

The king blinked, and seemed to recall who she was. 'Viratia... forgive me. I am not well. Join me.' He stood aside to allow her entry.

He closed the door, dropped into a large armchair, and buried his head in his hands. Viratia was surprised to realise he was crying, heavy teardrops echoing on the floor. 'Andrick... I am so sorry, Viratia. When the war is over we will build a statue of him, twenty-foot high, all in bronze.' He lifted his wine in a lonely toast. 'To Andrick, the finest son of Erland, and the brother I loved above all others. May Eryi take him from the Earth and to Eryispek above the clouds.'

He drank deeply, draining his cup, before flinging it across the room to crash against the door, making Viratia jump. 'Forgive me,' he whimpered, burying his head in his hands again. 'Forgive me for everything. I have drunk too much. There is a jug of water on the table; would you pour me some?'

Bugger your statue. You can get his body back first. Viratia's dislike and anger wrestled with the pity and kinship she felt for the man before her, who for all his faults had loved Andrick as much as she. 'I doubt he could have imagined any greater honour. Is there any word of his body?'

'None,' the king replied thickly, as she poured him water into a fresh cup. 'Theodric has sought his corpse, but he cannot even find the living at the moment, as you know. His powers wane by the day.'

'And who will lead the *Hymeriker* now?'

'I do not know. Errian perhaps, when he recovers himself.'

'Errian?' retorted Viratia, more aggressively than she intended. 'He's not been sober an hour since he returned.' Had Hessian spoken to him, even laid eyes on him? 'You'd do better to name Naeem. Let my son rest, for his father's sake.' She would not lose another son in service to Hessian while he sat in his high tower playing with men's lives.

'Errian will recover.' Hessian pushed himself up in his chair, regaining some of his old steel. 'And I will not be lectured by a woman about how I rule *my kingdom*. Naeem is a fine soldier, but common. I will have Errian, and you will live with it. If you loved your husband, show me the same respect he gave to me. And do not question me again, or I'll have you dragged back to Violet Hall.' Conviction dripped from his lips like wine.

Old, infirm, and drunk as he was, Viratia was in no doubt that he meant it. She could still remember the stomach-shredding dread she had felt around him when she was younger, the sunken eyes that followed her steps and the honey-laced voice that whispered of the cruelty behind them. The years had not changed him, save to perhaps make him even more unpredictable.

But the years had changed Viratia. Andrick and Orsian may be lost to her, but she would save Errian.

Hessian seemed to take her silence for agreement. 'Good.' He waved his tankard carelessly in the direction of the door, sloshing water over the sides. 'Now leave me. You can see yourself out.'

Viratia curtsied, keeping her eyes down. 'Thank you, Majesty.' She turned on her heel and walked to the door.

The guards nodded to her as she left, and halfway down the stairs Viratia stopped for a moment to compose herself. Even

Andrick's death had not mellowed the man. He was as cruel and capricious as ever.

She had wasted half her life waiting at Violet Hall while Andrick fought for Hessian, and it had killed him and lost her both her sons. She would stand for it no more. If he would not protect Errian, she would.

The barracks adjoined the kitchens, across the yard in the lesser part of the keep. Viratia had never had reason to enter, but she knew the way well enough. Andrick had loved the barracks as much as he had the men who lived in them. It was where men drank and told their war stories, where stories became tales, and where some of them passed into legend. Andrick had lived for duty, to realm and family, but after that he had lived for his men, and the bond that could be forged only between those who fought alongside one another.

The room was stark, grey brick and black mortar, adorned only by burning wall-torches, dark wood tables and benches, and a few tapped barrels in the corner. The air was heavy with the fumes of ale, and the benches so alive with laughter that no man noticed Viratia as she entered.

She paused in the doorway, hesitant for a moment to disturb them. A man was standing at the end of the tables, one arm bound in a sling and a foaming mug of ale in the other, cavorting along the benches to gales of laughter. Viratia smiled to realise it was Naeem, the man who Andrick had said he trusted more than any man alive, regaling the men with the story of when he and Andrick had first met, some thirty years ago.

'...so there I am, twenty-two years old, full of spunk and with the eye of every lady in my village.'

This drew laughter from the benches, but he grinned and continued. 'I still had my nose back then – as handsome a nose as you'll ever see. Anyhow, we're all reckoning we're probably going to die in the morning. We're all down in the dumps trying to get our fires lit, and there's hardly any food, and then word comes down the line that old Lord Ingleside has croaked his last, and that there's a commotion in the command tent and someone's been stabbed.

'Now, when the lords start killing each other, you know it's bad. At this point – I won't lie to you – some of us were talking about maybe deserting.'

There were jeers from the crowd.

'I know, me, deserting! As I said, twenty-two years old, barely a thought in my head that didn't involve my pecker, so all I'm really looking to do is to get out alive.

'Anyway, we're settling in to get good and drunk on what might be our last night on this earth. Maybe some of us are thinking about getting the courage up to run off when it gets dark. And then, word comes down that the new commander, some by-blow of the king, is out for a walk, and telling every man to pour his ale away!' Naeem splashed a drop of ale on the floor, before downing the rest of his tankard and picking up another from the table, to cheers from the crowd.

'Now we've already had a few at this point, so we're on our feet and storming up the line, where there's already a bit of a ruckus. Our new commander is a streak of beardless piss, green as grass, and his guards are looking awful nervous, because he's about to have a full-blown mutiny on his hands.

'So we're all shouting, and he's just standing there leaning on his sword looking at us like he's a kennel-master waiting for his dogs to calm down. Which is appropriate, because at his feet are these two massive hounds.'

Cheers from the crowd, as if they had only just realised who this young commander was. Viratia smiled.

'We're all a bit baffled. Lords are usually shouting at us to get to this and get to that, and here's this foreign-looking boy who seems content to wait for us to shout ourselves out. And eventually we do, and he raises his sword in the air and finally speaks.

'Now, I can't recall exactly what he says, but the gist of it is that he can put our beer to use better than we can, and that if we want to live, we'll let him. And if any man has a problem with that, we can choose our best five swords, and fight him for the beer.

'As you know, I'm a fine swordsman.'

Laughter and jeers from the crowd.

'Got the children to prove it, don't it? Any one of you against me and I'll put you on your bony young arse. So I'm straight up there, and the lads have seen me fight, and they're pushing me forward too, and I'm there with four others, all mean as a Sorrowlands goat-rider and ugly as a Whitewater whaler's wife.

'He tells his guard not to intervene, no matter what. Same with his dogs, and I'll swear to this day they understood every word. And then, we fought, the five of us against him.

'Now I was quick as piss down your leg, but I'll never see anything as fast as he was. Two ran straight at him, and he just feints each way before cutting their throats while their eyes are still trying to follow where he's gone.

'The other three of us take it slow, trying to get in behind him. None of us could get near him. Every move we made, his sword or shield were there in the way. It was like fighting a man with six arms. He was strong too, stronger than a skinny lad had any right to be. When our blades clashed it was like my whole arm went numb up to the shoulder; nearly dropped my sword he hit me so hard.

'So after a few minutes of this, all three of us are panting and sweating buckets, and he's still there in the middle of us looking like he's out for a stroll. And then he attacked, fast and deadly as fire. One second he was in front of you and the next his sword was almost up your arse and you'd be on the turn, praying that one of your mates got to him first. This worked for a while, but then the two other lads went down, and I was on my own.

'He came in slow, and now I'm praying for a miracle. He feints right, left, right, and I just back away from that sword of his, because I know as soon as I move he'll be in behind me again and I'm done for. It felt like an age, but eventually he strikes, and I barely get my sword up before he slams into my shield and puts me on my back.

'Then he stands over me, with his blade resting on my neck.' Naeem tapped a spot in the middle of his throat. 'I think it's all over for me, so I'm just trying not to piss myself and hoping he makes it clean. And then he puts his hand out, and when I take it he pulls me to my feet.

'I'm so pathetically grateful I almost fall to my knees, but he holds me steady. "You're good," he says to me, "but you're better than you think you are and you're still not half as good as me." I was hardly in a position to argue with that. "Will you swear to serve me, and tell true to any man what happened here?"

'"Aye," I says to him. "Till my dying day. But you'll have to give me your name first, Lord."'

The room had gone peculiarly quiet and, through the gloom, Viratia saw that some men's cheeks were wet with tears.

'"Andrick," he says. "Lord Andrick. The man who's going to keep every bastard here alive, if you'll listen to me." I dropped to my knees and swore my oath to him.

'We did as he told us after that. Every barrel of ale we had was rolled down the hill and split open with axes to sodden the ground. When they attacked the next morning, they got bogged down in it, and our horses took them in the rear. Lord Andrick killed Lord Storaut in single combat.

'And that's how he got his name,' he said hoarsely. 'Andrick Barrelbreaker, the finest man I ever knew.' He raised his tankard. 'May Eryi take him.'

'May Eryi take him,' came the men's reply, and Viratia joined them.

As he raised his cup and drank, Naeem's eyes met Viratia's, still standing in the doorway, causing him to almost choke on his beer.

'Lady Viratia,' he said, spluttering, and leading every man's eye to where she stood in the doorway. 'Forgive me, I did not know you were there.'

The men all turned to stare. Viratia expected she was the first noblewoman to ever stand in this room. 'That was less than a year after I first met him,' she said. 'I still have the letter he sent me from the Battle of the Hill. Two years later he stole me from my father's castle and forced a travelling priest to marry us. Another good tale, but now is not the time to tell it.'

On the other side of the room was a low dais, where Viratia imagined Andrick had stood to address his men perhaps half a thousand times. She walked towards it in pin-drop silence, every eye following her, stopping only to take a spare tankard of ale from a table. She did not know what she would say, only that she needed these men to follow her. It was time to learn what being the widow of Lord Andrick Barrelbreaker counted for in this new world forged by his death.

She wet her lips with the ale, hoping the thick, sour liquid might settle her nerves.

'I loved my husband ever since I first saw him. It was in this very keep, at a banquet to celebrate thirty years since the old king's succession. My father had brought me here in the hope of securing a good match, and paraded me like a prized horse before a dozen lords. I was miserable, and though many of them asked me to dance I refused every one of them, pleading a headache. My father was furious.

'And then across the room, a boy's gaze met mine. He was at the king's table, sat at an end. He had dark skin, like oak, and wore a doublet quartered in Sangreal red and midnight-blue.

He had these wild eyes, like the banquet was a cage he longed to be free of. Almost how I felt.

'When he saw me, his eyes never left mine, and when he came to my table he never said anything, just offered me his hand and motioned to the floor where people danced. Needless to say, I took it, and he never let go.

'I expect you're wondering why I'm telling you this. No doubt the Andrick I knew and the one each of you knew were different people. But we all loved him.

'I have not slept a wink since I learnt of his death. It is not that I have a woman's weak and feeble heart, and stay up sobbing into my sheets and pounding my pillow in despair. It is because I am consumed. Consumed by thoughts of *vengeance*.'

There were murmurs of agreement from the assembled men.

'Strovac Sigac and Rymond Prindian *murdered* my husband, and *mutilated* his body. I want my husband burnt at Violet Hall, not thrown in a pit, or torn into quarters, or whatever foul indignity the Prindians have planned. I *will* have his body returned to me. I will have my son Orsian, whether he be living or dead. More than that, I will have Strovac Sigac brought before me in chains, so I can feast upon his fear when I tear the heart from his chest.' She paused a moment, watching them, letting their anger rise. 'Is there any man here who feels otherwise?'

Fists crashed into tables, and tankards flew, as every man came to his feet in a wild cacophony of oaths and curses, every one of them baying for the blood of Rymond Prindian and Strovac Sigac.

'What will you do then?' shouted Viratia over the din. 'Will you sit here and drink, or will you follow me, for Erland, and for vengeance?'

'Vengeance!' cried back Naeem. 'Vengeance for Andrick!' Amidst the confusion, he climbed onto a table, and began stomping out a war cry. Within moments every man was with him.

'VENGEANCE! VENGEANCE! VENGEANCE! VENGEANCE! VENGEANCE! VENGEANCE!' they cried, until slowly it became 'VIRATIA! VIRATIA! VIRATIA!'

She smiled down on them, savouring the moment, wondering if Andrick was watching her from above the clouds, and whether he would be proud or horrified. *I will lead them, not Errian. I will lead them, and I will have vengeance.*

CHAPTER 45

Kvarm reclined lazily in his chair, his grey chest hair blossoming like a thornbush from the red sable cloak gifted to him by King Hessian, Merivale visible through the high window behind him. The gilded box sat in front of him, the wood as gleaming and marbled as the day it had been stolen. 'You have done well, Hrogo. The recovery of this box would not have been possible without you. And the purse. Even if it did take longer to locate them in Merivale than I would have liked.' He held in his right hand a glass of oily, dark whisky, and paused to take a sip of it. 'Hessian is lying to me about where he found them, though. If the boy was just a thief caught escaping from Piperskeep, why did Hessian take his tongue before giving him to me? He is hiding something, not that it matters.'

Hrogo kept his eyes downcast. The boy's lack of tongue had not stopped Kvarm torturing him, and Hrogo had been present for every one of the nameless boy's screams. The Erland king had a reputation for cruelty, but even he had seemed disquieted by Kvarm's taste for pain. Hessian had given Kvarm the boy for only a few hours, and then demanded he be returned to his custody.

'How will you celebrate?' asked Kvarm. 'Perhaps with a pile of nubile young girls to ride your cock till it's raw?' He laughed, a high, cruel sound thick with mockery.

Hrogo ignored Kvarm's jibe, staying quiet and suppressing a grimace. He would indeed be spending the night in the company of women, all of them slaves. His infertility had never stopped Kvarm persevering with forced mating in the hope that by some miracle a child might be formed. Once, Hrogo had resisted the pouring of fortifying pills and potions down his throat that only seemed to make him retch and lose control of his bowels, but those days were long past. He had learnt the futility of it the hard way. Rebellion tasted sweeter when you had a chance of winning.

The women never knew why they were made to lie with him. To them this was just some cruel game of the master's, making them bed down with a fat cripple. Hrogo supposed this might be some men's idea of paradise, but it had long lost any pleasure for him. He never forgot the look of confused disgust when a new bed partner was introduced to him.

'Suppose I gave you the night off,' continued Kvarm, 'to do whatever you please. What would you do?'

Sneak into your bedchamber and kill you. He could have done it, if he were braver. 'I don't know, Master. Sleep, I expect.'

'Sleep, he says! Truly freedom would be wasted on slaves.' Kvarm gestured vaguely out of the window. They were staying in a vast manse in the innermost circle of Merivale, with a high view over the city below, all the way to the walls. The homes furthest from them were more like hutches than houses, pressed up against the walls like birds' nests.

Kvarm stood, and on unsteady legs walked to the window. 'Look at the squalor they live in. My slaves eat better than they do. The meat my slaves eat eats better than they do. You would think Hessian would welcome my offer of an Imperial enclave to feed his people, but instead he spits in my face. This city is a sewer. When you see this place and think of Ulvatia, who can doubt Imperial superiority? We should have brought this country under our boot long ago.' He brought his foot down hard on the floor.

'We would, if I were kzar,' he finished, mumbling into his glass as he downed the dregs of the whisky. He stood a moment, surveying the city, but with his mind evidently firmly on Ulvatia.

Hrogo's eyes were drawn to Kvarm's knife, lying upon a pile of unsealed parchments, its curved hilt pointing towards him. *I could do it*, he thought. His fingers itched to reach for it, to sneak up behind his master and bury the blade in his back. Then he took a step forward, and the scrape of his chains against the floor was enough to halt him. He could no more sneak up on somebody than he could sire a child. Thwarted, he dropped his hand to his side. Twenty years ago, he might have tried, when he was braver, before Kvarm had imprisoned him in this twisted body.

'We'll be returning to Ulvatia as soon as we are ready,' said Kvarm with finality. 'I had hoped to leave sooner, but the chaos of the last few days requires that I stay and give my condolences to the king.' He lifted his glass to take a sip, only then noticing that it was empty. 'By summer this country will have torn itself apart. I do not intend to get stuck here in the middle of a civil war.' He looked at Hrogo, sea-green eyes boring into him. 'I will need your help in the coming months. Fat, infertile sack of shit that you are, I need you.'

Bent as his back already was, Hrogo bowed as low as his aching joints and heavy chains would allow. 'I live to serve, Master.' At least there were slaves in Ulvatia even lowlier and more crippled than him. Blind weavers, eunuch guards for senators' mistresses, sewer cleaners with their sense of smell burnt away... There was no solace to be found in Merivale. It was as brutal as he had heard, and even in winter the smell was putrid, but his vague hope that Kvarm might somehow meet his demise here had proved fruitless.

Kvarm smiled. 'Do you know what this box does, Hrogo?'

'N-no, Master.'

'Allow me to show you.'

Kvarm produced a scrap of parchment, flattened it against his desk, and began to write. Hrogo watched the quill move across the page as Kvarm laid down his will in tiny scratches of ink.

To my most exalted servant.

I apologise for the delay in responding. Matters here have taken longer than I would have liked.

There is civil war in Erland. Andrick Barrelbreaker is dead. The country is tearing itself apart. The land is ripe for invasion.

The kzar though will not countenance it. He must be removed. I leave that in your hands. I will return to Ulvatia within the next month.

Smiling to himself, Kvarm opened the box. The inside was lined with purple velvet, but Kvarm reached under the lid and with a sharp fingernail twisted a small screw. The bottom of the lid popped open to reveal a hidden compartment.

'A relic of when the magi ruled the Imperium, Hrogo. Just as you are, I suppose.' Kvarm placed the parchment within, replaced the false bottom, and twisted the screw the other way. 'Now you see why I was so desperate to retrieve this. That note will arrive with my agent in Ulvatia immediately.' Kvarm smiled again, his thin lips pressing together until they disappeared. For once, his smile even reached as far as his eyes.

'Under my brother's rule, the Imperium has become the image of him: bloated, lazy, complacent... Content to stand on the shoulders of the better men who forged it. It is time we returned to our roots; the Imperium's greatest days were when we went out into the world and took what was ours. There is land here ripe for plunder, wasted upon these barbarians who scrape the soil and fight over whatever loose dirt they turn over. I mean to be kzar, Hrogo, and when I am, I will do what our ancestors could not. I will conquer Erland.'

CHAPTER 46

'Pherri,' said Theodric, apparently noticing he did not have her full attention. 'If you don't want to have lessons today, we don't have to.'

'No, it's fine,' she said quickly, snapping her eyes away from the window. 'I want to learn.' She needed the lessons. Despite her success with Tinks, *inflika* and *shadika* still did not come easily. All efforts since to get the bad-tempered cat to eat carrots had ended in failure.

Some days had passed since the first men of her father's broken host had returned, and more seemed to arrive every hour. The plains outside the city walls were coming to resemble a new city, with a chaotic hodgepodge of tents and hastily erected shelters, connected by streets of grass and mud. It was a constant hive of activity, as healers moved from camp to camp, and more and more corpses were removed. Those from the garrison had been allowed to return to Piperskeep, and those with the coin to pay for shelter had done so, but food was already scarce, and Merivale could not support every returning soldier.

With those first arrivals had come the tidings of her father's death. Pherri's mother had summoned her and broken the news, along with that of Orsian's disappearance. Viratia had wept, and held Pherri so tightly she had thought one of her ribs might crack.

Pherri had not cried, and she felt guilty for it. She loved her father – had loved him – but he had been a stranger for most of her life, always away from Violet Hall or preoccupied with Errian and Orsian. She knew he had loved her too, in his own way, offering her crumbs of clumsy conversation, addressing her as he might a much younger child, or a particularly beloved dog.

The dogs. That was the one thing she and her father had in common. She had seen twelve litters born to Andrick's prized wolfhounds, and played with every single pup. Gyrwulf had been one of her favourites. By the time he was a year old he had been big enough to carry Pherri on his back, with her tiny fingers wound up in his thick, wiry fur and her feet skimming along the ground. Her mother had winced to see her daughter's trust placed in a beast strong enough to rip her in two, but Pherri knew Gyr would never hurt her. Now he was dead too. Him and Numa, the patient old bitch her father had doted on. Pherri felt the tears welling in her eyes. Was she a bad daughter, to find tears for her father's dogs but not her father?

'If you're sure,' said Theodric, with a heavy sigh. 'Though in truth I am not certain I want to teach you today. Would you not prefer to visit your brother?'

Pherri was about to remind him that Orsian was still missing, and then remembered that Errian had returned. Pherri had greeted him briefly, at her mother's behest, but he had looked straight past her. It was the first time she had seen him since Da'ri's murder, but one look at him told her that no good would come from berating him for that now. He was a shell of the man he had been then. It was possible he did not even remember.

Pherri was not worried about Orsian. As she had reassured her mother, Orsian was too brave and resourceful to be dead.

He would return, soon or in his own time. He could not be dead. Theodric might claim that *spectika* was still beyond her, but if Orsian were dead, she would have felt it, wouldn't she?

He could not be dead.

'Can you sense Orsian?' she asked Theodric. 'I'm not worried, but if you could it would give some comfort to my mother. I tried to tell her, but I think she thought I was being foolish. I know you said you can't use *spectika* any more, but if you could just try...'

Theodric's eyes took on a faraway look. For the merest moment, Pherri thought she could feel him reaching out for something. Then it was gone, and with a heavy sigh, he shook his head. 'Your mother asks me every day. If I could still do it, do you think I would have let your father die? Let Jarhick die? Let one of your brothers be captured and the other go missing? A year ago, I could have told you where Orsian was, and half a year ago if he was alive, but now... I am sorry.'

'But why?' In a moment of dread, Pherri wondered if she was imagining that she knew Orsian was alive. 'Why can't you use *shadika*? Are you sick?'

'I don't know.' Theodric collapsed into a chair. 'I'm sorry, Pherri.'

Pherri's eyes flicked again to the window. The weather was fine, and she could see Eryispek clearly, up to where it became obscured by cloud. It had been after she looked at Eryispek that she had used *inflika*, hadn't it? There had been a sudden gust of wind, that had prickled her skin and for a moment left her shivering. Unless she had imagined it? She had been so focused on the cat that she barely registered it.

She had not told Theodric. What if he thought she was mad and refused to teach her? He had said nothing about Eryispek as a source of magic.

Pherri stood and hesitantly approached the window. Her hands gripped the sill, waiting. Straining her eyes, she tried to bring the distant Mountain into sharper focus, willing something to happen.

Nothing did. Eryispek was as silent and obdurate as a guardsman. Pherri sighed, and dipped her head, disconsolate. She had just been lucky before. Eryispek had nothing to do with it. She might never find Orsian, or succeed at *inflika* again. Her vision swam with tears.

She looked up once more at Eryispek, and a blast of icy wind struck her in the face. She gasped in shock, as cold spread through her, all the way to her fingers and to the depths of her bones.

It stayed, filling her whole body, rising through her like a flash flood. Tears sprang to her eyes, and her breath caught in her throat. She felt like an overfilled kettle, except instead of boiling water she was filled with the purest ice, as hard and unyielding as a glacier. She was going to freeze.

Magic would save her. *Energy, will, focus.* Behind her Theodric shouted a warning, but Pherri ignored him. She reached out, letting the cold out of her in a wave, spreading her perception wide. With a great breath of relief, she welcomed the warm air of Theodric's room back into her lungs, and the sensation of life back to her limbs.

And then it felt like she was everywhere at once.

All of East Erland opened up before her. Atop the tallest tower, ravens cawed to one another, and on the battlements bored guards threw dice, and...

'Pherri, no!' Theodric grabbed her from behind and shook her, spun her, and Pherri tumbled back into her own skin.

He wouldn't stop shaking her. 'I'm fine!' Pherri pushed him away, and Theodric stumbled back, surprising Pherri with her own strength. She turned on him angrily. 'Why did you do that? I was doing *spectika!*'

'I know!' Theodric's eyes were bright with wonder. 'How?'

Pherri blinked at him, momentarily dizzy from being back

inside her body. 'I don't know... Eryispek. There was... a cold-
ness, a power... it let me...' She stopped, unable to explain it.
'Why did you stop me?' she demanded.

'Forgive me, I did not understand; I was worried. Here.'
Theodric handed her a crust of bread, and Pherri ate it in two
bites, suddenly ravenous. 'Eryispek helped you do magic?'

Pherri nodded. 'I was so cold; it was like I was there. I didn't
even have to think about it after that. The focus and will just
happened, and I could see everything.' She closed her eyes,
trying to resummon the sensation.

'Stop that.' Theodric shook her again, and Pherri's eyes
snapped open. 'Let me try something.'

Theodric edged her out of the way, and gazed out towards
Eryispek. He placed his hands against the sill, took a long, deep
breath, and half-closed his eyes.

Nothing happened. Pherri was close enough to sense the
tension in Theodric's stance and his steady, shallow breaths, but
she caught no sensation of any magic flowing from him, *spectika*
or otherwise.

His eyes flashed open. 'Nothing,' he said.

Pherri looked up at him sympathetically. 'Maybe it only
works for me. Maybe because I'm so new at it—'

Theodric shook his head, and Pherri was surprised to see a
soft, almost satisfied smile creep across his face. 'Come with me.
Bring your furs.'

Without bothering to explain, Theodric walked to a bookshelf, pressed his ear to the wall, and gripped hold of an unlit
sconce, which he twisted until he heard a clicking sound. He
gave a satisfied nod, then stretched his arms to pull out two
books from either end of the shelf.

To Pherri's astonishment, a section of wall began to rotate,
revealing a dark annexe and a set of cobwebbed wooden stairs
leading upwards.

'Follow me.' Theodric barely waited long enough for her to

put her furs on, and then he was walking through the hole in the wall and up the stairs, with Pherri running to keep up, still trying to wrap her furs around herself.

'What is this place? Where are we going?' she asked breathlessly as they climbed. Theodric was taking the stairs two at a time, setting a punishing pace. Pherri shrieked and almost fell backwards as she walked straight into a thick cobweb housing a spider.

'This leads to the parapet,' said Theodric without stopping. 'It doesn't hurt to use these old passages once in a while, though if you value my life you won't tell anyone I showed you, particularly the king. I hope none of the stairs have woodworm. Mind your step please.'

The steps ended below a tarnished metal grate, through which Pherri could see the open sky. Theodric pushed upwards and shook, dislodging chunks of rust, and the grate squeaked open. Theodric lifted Pherri up and climbed after her, and then he was off again, hurrying while Pherri struggled to keep up.

They stopped at the north-eastern corner of the battlements, Eryispek looming over the horizon, splitting the sky in two. It was pure white under the clouds that encircled it, coated in a thick blanket of snow, and even this far away there were windblown flakes of it visible in the air. Pherri could feel them melting against her hood, dripping into her hair. She had not realised how cold the battlements were, and drew her furs tightly around herself.

All Pherri's life, Eryispek had been there, as reliably as night follows day. Was there any place in Erland it could not be seen from? Any place in the world? She had long given up trying to work out how it could truly be endless. It would send a person mad, like trying to count the stars or asking why there were stars in the sky at all. Who could know what lurked above the clouds, except the few who had braved its icy wilderness?

Theodric surveyed it, his hands knotted behind his back. 'It puts everything in perspective sometimes. You can just be going about your day, and then you see that and remember you're living in the shadow of something beyond your comprehension. No wonder it has inspired two religions.' He reached into his robe and pulled out a smokestick. Pherri had never seen him with one before. 'What you did before, could you try again? But this time, try to focus on Eryispek.'

'Why?'

'Something on Eryispek is hindering my magic, while helping yours. It all begins and ends with Eryispek... The Lutums, Jarhick's death, the war...' He paused, looking up at the Mountain. 'And your pale-eyed man is connected too, I am sure of it. Your dreams must mean something.'

Pherri had told Theodric of her last dream, with the dead hands and the fearful, hidden presence of the pale-eyed man, but there had been no dreams since. She had been relieved; the pale-eyed man scared her. And whatever had so terrified him scared her even more.

Nevertheless, she took a deep breath. She stared towards the Mountain, letting her gaze become soft and unfocused. She tried to lose her awareness of the distance between herself and Eryispek, until she could imagine it directly in front of her. Her skull thrummed as she pulled it closer. She acted on instinct, knowing if she pulled too hard her connection would shatter, so steadied herself and reached out, letting the power of the Mountain cast its shadow over the entire kingdom. Cold filled her, but this time she embraced it, drawing and releasing it in a steady stream. She breathed out, closed her eyes, and leapt into the ether.

It started in the keep. Below them, Errian drank long from his whisky bottle, and Georald tensed as he felt Pherri's strange sight upon him, as soft as a feather on the breeze. Pherri swept over them both, and out into Erland. In the plains, shepherds tended their flocks, and wild horses drank from a stream that rushed on into the relentless flow of the Pale River.

Find the pale-eyed man, her mind whispered as the land rushed past her, but Pherri felt her own instinct pulling at her. *Find Orsian.* She followed it, letting herself be drawn along the Pale River to where it opened into the Shrouded Sea.

She felt something. *Orsian.* He had been here, recently. He was alive, but gone. She reached for Eryispek again, drawing it closer to her and embracing it, letting the cold in to sharpen her senses of Erland. She thrust her gaze out further, searching for Orsian as a fisherman trawls for fish.

With a rush like wind through an open door, Eryispek dragged her towards it. Pherri tried to pull back, but found herself travelling upwards, frost and fog shooting past her in a tumult of white, and soft blue sky unfurling above her like a spreading ink stain across a page.

Out of nowhere, the Mountain tapered to a peak, of jutting ice shards and snow so fresh and bright that it hurt to look at. Pherri could not help but gaze upon it in wonder. *There is a summit.*

And then she saw him, the pale-eyed man, trapped in the middle of it on a lake of ice, at the centre of everything, visions swimming around him in a confused maelstrom of colour. A boy, dragging his knife across the neck of a doe, and then events falling one by one like dominoes. Errian riding to Basseton; Prince Jarhick dying in a pool of blood; armies clashing on the green plains of Erland; Pherri in the library with Theodric...

The pale-eyed man's pupils flashed open and found her. They rose before Pherri like two ancient moons, cold and deep with all the knowledge of the world. She should have felt afraid. But in that moment, Pherri understood everything. He opened his mouth to speak.

Something pushed Pherri hard, and then she was falling,

the vast behemoth of Eryispek revolving in her eye like a spinning blade.

Yet she landed softly, on a green cushion of Erlish grass, and
something new stirred in her vision. Delara, levering herself
towards Eryispek with her staff, linked to it by an imperceptible
thread thinner than silk. On instinct, Pherri grasped for the
thread, somehow caught it, and pulled.

The Mountain rose up before her again, filling the sky,
filling the world. But this time, Pherri found herself being
pulled *into* it, not up it, through snow and stone, deep into the
heart of Eryispek, where a well of power blazed so intensely
that Pherri could feel the skin sloughing off her fingers, her eyes
collapsing in on themselves like burnt-out stars. She tried to
scream, but her mouth was locked in place by the weight of
power pressing against her. She felt her head expanding, and a
single voice filled it, with a name, and a message.

VULGATYPHA.

STAY AWAY.

It was as if a heavy door had been slammed in Pherri's face.
She fell backwards, and would have landed painfully on her
backside had Theodric not reacted quickly to place a
supporting hand on her back. She let him steady her, gulping
down air. Her skin was drenched in sweat under her furs.

'What did you see?' he asked before she could recover her
breath. 'And are you well? I should never have let you... If I'd
known you would—'

'I'm fine,' she gasped. 'Orsian's alive, I can find him.' Whatever else it all meant, she had to find him. Before Theodric
could stop her, Pherri reached for Eryispek again, heedless of
the exhaustion from her last effort. She felt it once more, the
cold vibration through her body, slowly rising in its intensity as
the Mountain reared up ahead of her...

And then the door slammed on her again, hard enough that

Theodric had to react quickly with both hands on her shoulders.

'For Eryi's sake, Pherri! Warn me before you do something like that!' Theodric was visibly shaken. 'Stop. I'm sorry, I should never have... Tell me what happened. Everything.'

Pherri told him, starting with how Erland had opened to her *spectika*, and her sense of Orsian by the Shrouded Sea, and then the pale-eyed man atop Eryispek, Delara, the power that had threatened to overwhelm her, and her sudden severance from the Mountain.

'You were right,' she gasped. 'It was the pale-eyed man, at the summit. I think he's...' *Eryi?* But that made no sense at all. 'He did it, he killed Jarhick! He arranged all of it. But there's someone else. Do you know who Vulgatypha is?' She reached for it again, but whatever had allowed her to connect to Eryispek had run dry.

'They're both trapped, or at least they were.' Her words were falling out of her in a torrent, faster than she could understand them herself. 'She's stronger' – somehow, she knew Vulgatypha was a *she* – 'and Delara is linked to her somehow, but she can't influence things like he can, not yet.' She remembered her dream; the pale-eyed man screaming at an unseen foe. 'I think he's scared of her.'

'Slow down, Pherri.' Theodric was gripping her tightly, as if to stop her reaching for Eryispek again. He looked grave, as though all his worst fears had been proved true. 'If you are right, that settles it. One of them, or perhaps both, has blocked me from drawing on Eryispek. I never even realised I was doing it. Perhaps all the magi did, without ever knowing. Do you think they are working against Erland?'

Pherri nodded her head vigorously. 'I told you, he killed Jarhick.' She recalled suddenly the words in Da'ri's letter. *They are waking.* What else could he have meant except the two powers on Eryispek? But if the pale-eyed man was Eryi, who or what was Vulgatypha?

Theodric's eyes were hard as two shards of flint. 'Then we will have to stop them. There is something strange happening on Eryispek, and you and I are going to find out what.'

EPILOGUE

The wind howled like a lost child, and cold sleet tore at his skin like a wolf. Their tiny fire flickered, and died, their pitiable pit of rocks providing the flames scant protection from the cold.

A trail of their corpses littered the Mountain now. Every morning, more of them failed to wake. They buried them as best they could, under ice and snow, with blue limbs protruding like tree roots. Some had left to make their own way, and they had found them the next day, their bodies frozen in the earth. Others had turned on each other, and died by the axe.

No matter which way they went, they stumbled upon their dead. So many times they had tried to descend, not caring which side of the Mountain they were on, and within an hour they would find the marks of their passage: corpses, dead fires, and footprints being swiftly erased by the never-ending snow. They were travelling in circles. There was no way off this Mountain. Death waited for them, its icy touch so close that Gelick could almost see its hand on his companions' shoulders.

Yet somehow, he endured. He hungered like the rest of them, traipsing from one camp to the next, searching in vain for some sign of a route down, yet his body endured. His stomach was firm, his arms lean and muscled. He could have run back to Redfort, if only he knew the way.

Gelick looked despairingly across the fire at his remaining companion. Errek had been a priest back in Redfort, famed for his fiery sermons, and one of the first to take up Gelick's cause when he had returned demanding the Lutums fight to restore the Mountain and the tribe to glory. For days now, Errek had spoken only four words. 'The Norhai test us.'

'Should we try going down again?' asked Gelick, though he knew it was hopeless.

He had hoped Errek might show some sign he had heard, but his head was slumped into his chest. Knowing what he would find, Gelick rose, and crossed the fire to prod Errek in the shoulder with his toe. The man did not stir. Errek, the last of the Lutums, had breathed his last.

Gelick sank to his knees in the snow, letting the tears flow freely, warming his frozen cheeks. He had wanted to free them, not kill them. And now he was alone. Would he die as they had? Or had the voice doomed him to stumble for eternity across the Mountain, never weakening and never dying?

The voice cackled inside his head. '*It is done then. Good. They served a purpose, nothing more. Death was their destiny, as it is for all.*'

'I never wanted any of them to die,' sniffed Gelick. The snow was falling heavily, thick enough that the fresh corpses were already being covered.

Gelick gasped as an invisible hand suddenly clutched his windpipe with icy fingers that squeezed the breath from him. '*There is reason in death,*' came the cold whisper of the voice. It was louder now, as if it were no longer inside his head, but thundering in his ear. '*You should be thanking me for sparing you.*' The hand on his throat tightened, and Gelick clawed at his neck helplessly. A vice-like grip enveloped him, crushing his torso and driving the air from his lungs. He opened his mouth to scream, and nothing came out.

Under his feet, the whole Mountain was shaking. Gelick felt power being drawn from him, flowing through his bones into the snow. Flesh and muscle seemed to melt from his body like candlewax.

Horrified, he realised Errek's body was moving. It shambled to its feet with jerky, puppet-like motions. The corpse raised its face to look at him, and Gelick's own eyes looked back at him, icy-blue and terrifying. Gelick was staring into the face of his own corpse.

Terror flooded him, but still his screams would not come. He could not move. The voice's laughter echoed around his head, so loud he thought his skull might burst.

'*They come.*'

As suddenly as it had begun, the Mountain stopped its rumbling. The voice released him, and Gelick fell to his knees, gulping down desperate lungfuls of cold air. He felt exhausted, and he realised with a stab of horror that his body was no longer his own. Where once had been taut muscles were shrunken blue limbs, and his ribs protruded like those of his dead friends.

All around him, corpses were rising from the snow, and every one of them wore his face, with sunken grey cheeks and dead, sightless eyes. Some bore the marks of frostbite, with missing fingers and blackened cheeks, and others lacked eyes or had open wounds that exposed the sinew and bone underneath. They stumbled towards him, with slack, guileless expressions on their faces.

'What is this?' he managed to say.

'*What your friends died for. I value loyalty above all else, and who would be more loyal to me than you? These are you as you might have been, in other lives, where I was not there to save you.*'

Gelick swallowed. 'This is unnatural. I would rather have
died.'

'*That is no longer your choice to make.*'

A sharp, splitting pain struck inside Gelick's head, like a
dagger to the back of his skull. He fell, writhing in the snow,
screaming wordlessly, as two dozen copies of his own corpse
stared down at him. They wore his friends' clothing and held
his friends' weapons, but their faces were unmistakably his.

The pain doubled, and Gelick's body twisted in protest. He
clutched his skull, praying for the voice to kill him.

'*I can drive you mad, Gelick.*' As the voice spoke his name,
his head pulsed and Gelick keened with agony, fire flashing
behind his eyes like lightning.

'Stop!' he begged. 'Please!'

The voice laughed, and as suddenly as it had gripped him
the pain receded to a dull ache through his whole body. Gelick
pushed himself to his feet, gasping, grateful to be alive. No man
could have withstood such unnatural torment.

'*Do as I ask, or I swear you will never be free of me.*'

Gelick nodded, defeated. His body felt as formless as water,
ready to collapse on him at any moment. 'Whatever you ask.
Anything.'

The dead copies of himself had surrounded him now. They
stood in a circle, gazing blindly at him, as if waiting for something. Gelick screwed his eyes shut and covered his face with
his hands. *This is a nightmare. I will wake up, still at the fire
with Errek.*

'If it is a dream, wake up,' said the voice, dripping with
mockery. '*I have seen every grain of you, Gelick Whitedoe. There
are no secrets now.*'

'What do you want?' he pleaded.

The voice laughed, and a pair of pale eyes flashed suddenly
in Gelick's head. '*Revenge. Victory. Everything. There is a girl, a*

skinny girl with straw-coloured hair. She will come, because I have arranged it so. You must bring her to me. Her name is Pherri.'

A LETTER FROM R.S. MOULE

Dear Reader,

Thank you sincerely for reading, and hopefully finishing, *The Fury of Kings*. There have never been more fantasy novels available to read, so it is deeply gratifying that somebody would take the time to read mine over all the other things you could have been doing. I would be even more grateful if you could write and share a review.

If you enjoyed *The Fury of Kings* and would like stay informed about the next book in the Erland Saga, just sign up at the following link. Your email address will never be shared, and you can unsubscribe at any time.

www.secondskybooks.com/rs-moule

If you have any thoughts you would like to share with me, I would love to hear from you. Please get in touch through any of the links to social media below. These are also a good way to stay notified of my new releases.

Book 2 is well under way. I can't wait to share it with the world, and I very much hope you will read that one as well.

Thank you so much for your support.

Roger Moule, February 2023

 twitter.com/RS_Moule

ACKNOWLEDGMENTS

Writing this book would not have been possible without a team of people. My thanks to the following.

Jack Renninson, my editor, for believing the version of *Fury* he first saw was worth his talent and time, and for his tireless and meticulous work to improve it. It is an immeasurably better book for Jack's involvement.

Aaron Munday for his incredible cover. I stare at it at least twelve times a day.

Philip Womack, whose comments on the opening few chapters of an early draft encouraged me to keep going; Clem Flanagan, who read *Fury* before it was *Fury* and provided much-needed insight on areas for improvement; and Anne C Perry, for her generous suggestions on unagented routes to publication.

All my friends who have read and commented upon various drafts. Alex Chatburn, Susan Chatburn, Alex Henderson, Tim Heasman, Eamon Brennan, Stuart O'Hara, David Walton, Harriet Leighton-Porter, Charlie Greig, Bryan and Jean Kirk, and all my other friends and family who asked after my progress and were too polite to tell me to stop talking about my book.

My mum and dad, who instilled in me a love of reading from a young age and have supported me in everything I have ever sought to achieve.

My sister Georgie, who always buys me books and encouraged my love of the fantasy genre.

Though they are unlikely to ever read this, Emmylou

s, Explosions in the Sky, and the late Ennio Morricone, nose music soundtracked and inspired some of the most difficult chapters.

Tinks. The only real-life creature I love enough to immortalise in print.

Above all others, my eternal, endless gratitude, admiration, and love to my wife, Eloise Konieczko. Much as I could not live with anyone else, I doubt anyone else could live with me. No one else has expressed more opinions on *Fury* than you, and there is no one whose opinions I value more (even the ones I disagree with). I am sorry your favourite characters had to die.